RADICALS

RADICALS

AUDACIOUS WRITINGS BY
AMERICAN WOMEN,
1830–1930

VOLUME ONE

Fiction, Poetry, and Drama

EDITED BY

Meredith Stabel and Zachary Turpin

UNIVERSITY OF IOWA PRESS, IOWA CITY

University of Iowa Press, Iowa City 52242

ISBN 978-1-60938-766-2 (pbk)
ISBN 978-1-60938-767-9 (ebk)

www.uipress.uiowa.edu
Printed in the United States of America

Cover design by Kathleen Lynch / Black Kat Design
Text design by April Leidig

Printed on acid-free paper

Cataloging-in-Publication data is
on file with the Library of Congress.

For my parents, who made everything possible—MS

For my wife, who wins the bet—ZT

Contents

List of Illustrations

"A lifted world lifts women up,"
  The Socialist explained.
    "You cannot lift the world at all
    While half of it is kept so small,"
  The Suffragist maintained.

—Charlotte Perkins Gilman,
  "The Socialist and the Suffragist" (1910)

Foreword

Writing as a woman, as a black woman, as a queer woman, is a radical act. I have always believed this, that wielding the power of writing, to any end, is a way of making a mark on the world, making myself heard. In part, writing is a radical act because literacy has always been a privilege rather than an inalienable right for marginalized people. During the antebellum era, several states enacted antiliteracy laws for the singular purpose of continuing to subjugate enslaved people. If black people could read and write, they could agitate for liberation and upend the American economy. Following Nat Turner's rebellion in 1831, nearly all of the Southern states passed laws denying black people the right to literacy. It was not until after the Civil War that these laws were repealed and even then, black people had to fight for the right to be literate.

Though not codified by law, there have been, throughout American history, many efforts to deny women literacy, for many of the same reasons black people were denied literacy. When people have access to knowledge, they are better equipped to challenge their oppression and the status quo.

This anthology offers up writing from women at a time when women's literacy was largely the privilege of wealthy and upper-middle-class white women, and women were expected to write demure, well-mannered things. These writings are not that. They represent a hundred years of women writing their way into public discourse, giving voice to the complexities of their inner lives, their desires, their sentiments about the constraints of womanhood, the political climate, the strictures of class, and their places in their families, communities, and the world beyond.

In Alice Moore Dunbar-Nelson's poem, "I Sit and Sew," she writes of the tedium and futility of a woman's domestic tasks when so much more is happening in the world that women want to be a part of. Each of the poem's three stanzas are filled with yearning, the sharp edge of anger. The poem ends with a question. "God, must I sit and sew?" Must women limit themselves, she asks, to passivity and bearing witness rather than having an active role in the shaping and reshaping of the world?

Fanny Fern's autobiographical novel *Ruth Hall* also functioned as a means for interrogating womanhood. It is the story of a woman who writes her way into independence and success despite the bigotry of men's low expectations of women and the rampant misogyny she encounters time and again. Considering her brother, Ruth Hall observes, "That she should have succeeded in any degree without his assistance, was a puzzle, and the premonitory symptoms of her popularity, which his weekly exchanges furnished, in the shape of commendatory notices, were gall and wormwood to him." The novel is imbued with sly wit, and Fern elegantly skewers condescending men whenever she can. In the portrayal of one Mr. Lescom, she presents a man who cannot help but diminish women in the most subtle but insidious ways. But the most striking thing about *Ruth Hall* is that we see a woman who is confident in herself and knows what she deserves more often than not. She advocates for herself and pursues her ambitions on her own terms. As a writer, the character of Ruth Hall achieves a great deal of success, so much so that some of her readers assume "her to be a man, because she had the courage to call things by their right names, and the independence to express herself boldly on subjects which to the timid and clique-serving, were tabooed." To do these things was radical. To write that independence and bold expression was possible for a woman was radical, and still is, today.

Writing as a black queer woman is a radical act, but often, I find that the bar for what we consider radical is quite low. It has become radical to believe that everyone deserves universal healthcare, including mental healthcare, that women are people and have a right to reproductive freedom and bodily autonomy and safety, that people have the right to the gender expression that best represents who they really are, that everyone deserves equal pay for equal work, that everyone has the right to live and love without limitations or authoritarian impositions. These are not radical ideas and yet they are. These ideas challenge the status quo. They challenge the power structures unduly influencing the trajectories of our lives. They challenge the people who benefit from those power structures and will do anything to preserve their dominion.

When women writers challenge these power structures, implicitly or explicitly, they are being radical even if it doesn't feel that way in those moments of writing. I do not know whether the women whose words comprise this anthology thought themselves radical, but they were. They dared to believe their voices mattered at a time when men rarely acknowledged that women even had voices. They dared to believe they had a right to publicly articulate their understanding of the world. Whether through prose, poetry, or drama, they challenged societal expectations. They challenged, perhaps, what they expected of themselves. They made their mark on their world. They created work that endures. And that is the most radical thing of all.

Roxane Gay
Los Angeles, August 13, 2020

Introduction

American literature is often read, studied, and taught as if it makes the same basic demands of each reader. Before beginning this anthology, it is important to set aside such an assumption as not only incorrect and useless but dangerous.

Here is what the American literary tradition has always, or anyway up until quite recently, asked of its readers: *Do you have the strength to be an individualist? (Even as I deny the very fullness of your personhood?)*

The first question is all-embracing. It is the inquiry that makes Americans Americans, and as such it is the seed of Americanism in its many forms: Puritanism, republicanism, Unitarianism, transcendentalism, pragmatism, American modernism, intersectional feminism, and more. The second question, on the other hand, is heard only by some. Americans in power, Americans of privilege, Americans unaware of their overrepresentation in culture and politics, do not hear it, nor are they commonly forced to consider it. But many more are. It reverberates, soundlessly inquiring year after year: Can you live a life of fullness, self-determination, love and common bonds—can you be an individualist—when society denies your individuality?

The women of these volumes answer in thunder. What their answers are, you will have to read on to hear and understand. One commonality you may notice is that many of them deny the very premise that individualism precludes collectivism as the foundation of American society. It is a premise that, in the nineteenth and early twentieth centuries—the time span of this anthology—yielded immeasurable suffering. As summed up by Emma Goldman, anarchist and radical par excellence, it is a presupposition that preserves power for the few. "The oft repeated slogan of our time," she writes,

[is] that ours is an era of individualism, of the minority. Only those who do not probe beneath the surface might be led to entertain this view. Have not the few accumulated the wealth of the world? Are they not the masters, the absolute kings of the situation? Their success, however, is due not to individualism, but to the inertia, the cravenness, the utter submission of the mass. The latter wants but to be dominated, to be led, to be coerced. As to individualism, at no time in human history did it have less chance of expression, less opportunity to assert itself in a normal, healthy manner.[1]

In other words, if America is pulsed forward by regular and radical redefinition, it is not the inward-looking but the outward-embracing person who has the deepest soul, is the fullest patriot, and joins what Goldman calls the "non-compromising pioneers of social changes." For that, it takes thinkers who are willing to smash the contradictions that hide beneath social norms, and the women in these volumes are just such iconoclasts.

Today, perhaps more than at any time in living memory, social and cultural upheaval has come to define the American way of life. Even as we write this introduction, in the summer of 2020, the United States is undergoing radical changes of an extremity that hasn't been seen in generations. Though born of tragedy, many of these shifts promise to be uplifting. The murders by police of George Floyd and Breonna Taylor, as well as hundreds of other innocent African Americans just this year alone, have led to worldwide displays of solidarity for the Black Lives Matter movement and widespread activism toward police reform. Likewise, after decades of legal struggle, the U.S. Supreme Court's Obergefell v. Hodges ruling has cemented protections for LGBTQ Americans under the Fourteenth Amendment, protections that have long been suppressed by American employers and legislators alike. At a more local level, communities and regional governments across the country (as well as protest groups, when localities refuse) have been removing Confederate flags and pulling down Confederate monuments, disposing of a longstanding Jim Crow iconography designed to discount the terrors of slavery and enshrine racism in the American public sphere. Finally, as of this writing, the United States is poised to elect its first woman vice-president, having narrowly missed electing its first woman president in 2016. These events—and many others similarly monumental—suggest that the twenty-first century may be one in which radical American voices move the world further toward the good: toward equality, enfranchisement, and essential freedoms protected by law.

As in the twentieth century—when such voices impelled the passages of the Nineteenth Amendment and the Civil Rights Act, the enactment of the New Deal, the near passage of the Equal Rights Amendment, and Supreme Court decisions such as Loving v. Virginia and Roe v. Wade— radicalism is a force for good, not merely an example of fringe individualism or eccentricity. The same is not so often assumed of nineteenth-century radicals. Despite its seismic struggles over slavery, suffrage, and legal enfranchisement, the nineteenth century is an era rarely represented as a time of widespread radicalism in the United States. In particular, the extent to which radicalism surged through the daily lives, thoughts, and writings of American women in the nineteenth and early twentieth centuries is hardly well represented in textbooks or trade volumes today.

Even the word itself, "radical," is all too rarely used to describe early American women's voices, especially the voices of women of color. Worse yet, if early American women's words are represented in collections of history or literature as radical, it is too often in the etymological sense of acting as a root and thus being root-*like*: staid and unmoving, inflexible. Where in the word—or in the anthologies built around it—is the movement, the energy, the color of early radicalism? Where are the works by all those women who, as Zora Neale Hurston says, were busy sharpening their oyster knives?

In this anthology, you will find them. These volumes are perhaps the first of their kind: a full-length collection of radical writings by early American women, with little-known rarities included, voices of color prioritized, and all major genres represented (fiction, poetry, drama, memoir, essays, and oratory). Our selections span from early radical works such as Sarah Louise Forten's antislavery poem, "The Grave of the Slave" (1831), and Sojourner Truth's *Narrative of Sojourner Truth*, a memoir of bondage and liberation (1850), to Angelina Weld Grimké's antilynching sonnet, "Trees" (1928), and Charlotte Perkins Gilman's essay in favor of euthanasia, "The Right to Die" (1935). In between, the reader will discover many lesser-known and unknown texts, most of which, while vibrant and challenging, often go uncollected, crowded out by more commonly anthologized major texts.

In this anthology, we intend to represent the underrepresented. Thus, we include a number of texts that are rarely, or in some cases have never been, anthologized. For example, we include Emily Dickinson's more overtly erotic poems, those usually passed over in favor of other verses that, when taken alone, misleadingly suggest celibacy or a disinterest in sex on Dickinson's part. We include a pair of Kate Chopin's later tales, "An Egyptian Cigarette," her first-person fictional account of smoking pot or hashish—originally published in *Vogue*, of all places—and "The Storm," a story so sexually explicit that it did not see publication in her lifetime.

This is also true of Emma Lazarus's "Assurance," an erotic sonnet that her sisters (in their role as literary executors) left out of her posthumous, still standard *Poems*. We have included it alongside three longer, overtly queer poems that have also somehow missed collection, even though they appeared in the widely circulated *Lippincott's Monthly Magazine*. Until only a few years ago, these poems were almost entirely unknown. New to readers, as well, will be Rebecca Harding Davis's "At Noon," a story that until recently lay dormant in the pages of an 1887 issue of *Harper's Bazaar*. Its complex critique of upper-class womanhood almost certainly raised the eyebrows of readers of the *Bazaar*, who were used to the magazine's lighter fare on fashion and ice creams. Today, Davis's tale still has the power to shock.

Indeed, many of the pieces in these volumes are included at the expense of more well-known texts. In these pages, for instance, readers will not find such foundational works as Chopin's *The Awakening*, Lazarus's "The New Colossus" (famously inscribed in the Statue of Liberty), nor Davis's *Life in the Iron-Mills*. In our view, such writings have been so thoroughly anthologized—and rightfully so—that it is time to present more from these women and their peers, especially those texts that typically miss collection for being too uncompromising, idiosyncratic, or hard to categorize.

The poet and scholar Tillie Olsen, herself an important anthologist (and the rediscoverer of *Life in the Iron-Mills*), defines the absence of such readings in modern anthologies as *silences*—"some silences hidden; some the ceasing to publish after one work appears; some the never coming to book form at all." This anthology thus exists to continue the work of Olsen and many other scholars before and since in undoing such silences by amplifying many important works of literature that often go unread and undiscussed.

In these pages, then, you will not find the standard version of Sojourner Truth's "Ain't I a Woman?" with the refrain that yielded its now famous title. Instead, we include Truth's speech as it was first recorded and published, a month after its delivery to the Women's Rights Convention in Akron, Ohio, in May 1851. Truth's original language has a power that its later editing and rewriting by white abolitionists cannot hide. Likewise, you will not find Julia Ward Howe's "The Battle Hymn of the Republic," the unofficial song of the Union during the U.S. Civil War, and perhaps the most famous American lyrics of their day. Instead, we include excerpts from *The Hermaphrodite*, her unpublished novel that is one of the earliest, and certainly the most sensitive of, nineteenth-century treatments of intersex life in America.

Rather than reproduce Gilman's immortal short story "The Yellow Wallpaper," we have collected a number of her lesser-known works, to display her incredible range of style and subject. These include the tale "When I Was a Witch," her political poem, "The Socialist and the Suffragist," excerpts from her feminist utopian novel, *Herland*, and essays such as "What Is Feminism?," "Maternity Benefits and Reformers," and "The Right to Die," which is Gilman's final essay, drafted while she was suffering from inoperable breast cancer and completed shortly before she took her own life with chloroform. Likewise, we have not included Harriet Jacobs's *Incidents in the Life of a Slave Girl*, if only because such a foundational slave narrative is today widely available. Harder to find is Jacobs's "Letter from a Fugitive Slave," her first published work (included in volume 2) and a powerful response to "The Women of England vs. the Women of America," that infamous defense of slavery penned by former First Lady Julia Gardiner Tyler.

All that said, this anthology is not constructed exclusively from lesser-known writings. Indeed, many of the works will be immediately recognizable to the average reader. From Frances E. W. Harper's "Learning to Read" to Adah Isaacs Menken's "Judith," from Pauline Hopkins's "Talma Gordon" to Emma Goldman's "A New Declaration of Independence," from Margaret Fuller's *Woman in the Nineteenth Century* to Elizabeth Cady Stanton, Susan B. Anthony, and Matilda Joslyn Gage's introduction to their *History of Woman Suffrage*, these texts help form a continually expanding canon of American women's literature, some of whose elements are so unique that they are essentially one of a kind.

Indeed, in some instances we reproduce the only known writings of an author. In such cases, we aim to further popularize what are still under-read texts, many of them written by authors of color and some of which were rediscovered only recently. For example, we include long excerpts from Harriet E. Wilson's *Our Nig* (1859), possibly the earliest novel published by a Black woman in the United States, uncovered by scholar Henry Louis Gates Jr. in 1981; *Gifts of Power*, the long-unpublished autobiography and revelations-record of African American Shaker eldress Rebecca Cox Jackson; *Louisa Picquet, the Octoroon*, the memoir of a mixed-race freedwoman and her experiences of sexual and psychological mistreatment as a slave; and Ida B. Wells-Barnett's *Southern Horrors*, a record of lynchings and lynch laws in the Jim Crow South, for which Wells-Barnett received death threats—and, just this year, a posthumous Pulitzer Prize for Journalism.

While many of the women represented in these volumes were professional writers, just as many were not. Cox Jackson was a preacher, Julia A. J. Foote a deacon, Dickinson a gardener and baker, Buffalo Bird Woman a traditional Hidatsa agriculturalist and promoter of matriarchal culture. Others were orators, abolitionists, suffragists, and women's rights advocates, whose active public-speaking schedules precluded their writing as prolifically as they might have liked. And more than a few were political trailblazers: Victoria Woodhull and Belva Lockwood, for example, were the first American women to run for president, Woodhull in 1872 (illegally) and Lockwood in 1884, shortly before she became the first woman lawyer to practice before the U.S. Supreme Court. (Lockwood's life would inspire generations of women lawyers, including the late Supreme Court justice Ruth Bader Ginsburg.) Woodhull's letter "To the Women of the South" and Lockwood's speech on "The Growth of Peace Principles" both appear in volume 2, for the first time anywhere since their initial publication. Overall, this anthology exists to re-present—or in some cases, present for the first time—the many beautiful, lesser-known examples of early radical womanhood in America.

It should be noted that some of these words are disputed, and justifiably so. *Womanhood*, for example, may seem obvious enough to need no explanation. But as Margaret Fuller writes at the early date of 1843, maleness and femaleness, which one might expect to "represent the two sides of the great radical dualism," are in fact "perpetually passing into one another." She adds, with a resounding full stop, that "there is no wholly masculine man, no purely feminine woman." It is the Tao-like crux of Fuller's manifesto on empowered womanhood: any gender line, once drawn, will prove porous. Womanhood is no more monolithic than manhood. Because gender is embodied, enacted, constructed, discovered, to be a woman is in some ways a perpetual exercising of individualism—a finding of the self, a learning to "live *first* for God's sake," as Fuller says, and an asking of an ancient question yet again: What *is* womanhood, and what can it be? That so many writers in this volume ask this very question, and not merely for the individual but for the collective, is why we call them *radicals*.

As a term of politics, "radical" is often taken to mean "progressive" when used to describe an attitude of or toward American womanhood— and in that regard, many of the writers included are radical, even by today's standards. Their works, however, are also radical in the second, etymological sense mentioned earlier, of rooting the foundations of their era. All this, added to their vibrancy and unorthodoxy and self-determination, is what makes them implicitly—and often explicitly—*feminist*.

Indeed, all the writings in this anthology may be described as examples of First-Wave feminist thought—to the point that we strongly considered foregrounding the First Wave as this anthology's uniting theme. It will become clearer as you read through these volumes, however, that the First Wave is not the only one represented by these writings. The longer we linger in the writings of the early waves of feminism, the easier it is to see the hallmarks of later waves presaged within them. Chopin's fictions, for example, are pivotal First-Wave texts, depicting the difficulties of living as a white woman without legal enfranchisement, within the straits of traditional gender ideology. Many of her concerns, though—desire, sexuality, work, and autonomy—look ahead to the Second Wave of the 1960s. Perkins Gilman, likewise, continually looks forward to the Second Wave while also forecasting Third-Wave concerns, including reproductive rights, the reclamation of derogatory terms, and sex positivity. Further still, Fuller's *Woman in the Nineteenth Century*, perhaps *the* core First-Wave text in America, posits ideas about gender roles, race, and equal opportunity that resoundingly preecho today's Fourth Wave. Thus, while we might have framed these volumes as a collection of First-Wave feminist thought and life—and they certainly are that—they are more broadly a celebration of the timeless expressions of radical womanhood, whose continuity has no obvious interval.

Doubtless, to represent advances as "waves" is, in the symbolism of history, to sacrifice complexity for intelligibility. History *is* sequential, of course. Event succeeds event like swells in the ocean, and this is true enough of the waves of woman's advancement. But on what shore do they break? Where do they end? Consider the First Wave, whose crest, arguably, is 1920, the year of the ratification of the Nineteenth Amendment enfranchising white women voters. Its "conclusion," however, does not arrive until at least 1965 (the year the Voting Rights Act finally ensured the vote for Black women voters in the South), if not much later—or even at all, considering current and very real erosions of voting rights in many states. Similarly, while the Second Wave women's liberation movement may appear to be consigned to the 1960s and 1970s, in reality it is hardly concluded, thanks to twenty-first-century legislative and judicial assaults on reproductive rights. The Third Wave is subject to similar attacks. All this is to say that the waves of feminism, represented (or presaged) throughout this anthology, are not only a historical sequence of steps made toward equality, equity, and justice but also a chaotically beautiful, back-and-forth system, a roiling confluence of waves passing, crashing, and receding through the others, reinfusing, eddying, and surging forward again.

To further complicate things, the texts in these volumes will occasionally present readers with contradictions of philosophy or intent between and among avowed suffragists, women's rights activists, and abolitionists, many of whom were comrades, to say nothing of the contradictions to be found within the writings of any single author. For scholars of the writings of early radical women in the United States, this may come as no surprise, but for students it will almost certainly be startling. It is the shock of what lawyer and critical race theorist Kimberlé Crenshaw has termed "intersectionality," the combination of overlapping and interrelated elements of identity—such as race, class, gender, sexuality, and physical ability—whose interaction yields unique injustices for some, unique blind spots to (and benefits from) injustice for others.

Thus, among the authors collected in these volumes, cross-purposes inevitably arose, many of them traceable to the political and social leveraging exerted by nineteenth-century and early twentieth-century white feminists. While their contributions to literature and law are unquestionable, we endeavor in these volumes to counterbalance their voices with a greater proportion of writings by underanthologized Black feminists, Native feminists, and Asian American feminists, many of whom were writing for their lives and the lives of their families and communities, often at the risk of being harassed, slandered, dispossessed, disenfranchised, or killed.

At that, not every text may seem all that radical or even feminist by contemporary standards. Julia A. J. Foote and Rebecca Cox Jackson, for example, chiefly recount their conversions to Christianity and calls to preach. Buffalo Bird Woman counsels the reader in the clearing and planting of land. These women, however, document working their way toward access to power, speech, and an audience. They promote morality, independence, and matriarchy. And they out-think, out-pray, and out-philosophize their male gatekeepers all along the way.

Their writings are also deeply human. The works included in *Radicals* are records of the vanguard of a new era, but they are also, regardless of time period, the original efforts of powerful artistic minds. Hence, we include excerpts from Pauline Hopkins's *Of One Blood*, a novel of alchemy and the undead, and Amelia E. Johnson's *Clarence and Corinne*, a traditional romance novel. In an era when many of the writers represented were legally considered property, had few or no voting rights, and led lives in which reading and writing were seen as privileges of the free and wealthy, simply publishing one's words was an assertion of autonomy and selfhood. Thus, to write for pleasure and enjoyment, beyond any effort to prove one's humanity to disbelieving others, was a radical act all its own.

One and all, these were women of genius and audacity, and as Adah Isaacs Menken writes, "this very audacity is divine."

NOTE

1. See Goldman's "Minorities versus Majorities," *Anarchism and Other Essays* (New York: Mother Earth Publishing Association, 1910), 75–84.

A Note on the Text

Generally, we maintain all variant spellings, vernacular English, typos, and errors as they appear in the original versions of texts. For readerly ease, we do not use [*sic*]. In a few cases, when the meaning of a passage is altered or unclear because of an original typo, we have silently amended it.

While we standardize a few minor typographical elements—such as converting single quotation marks to full quotation marks and removing spaces before colons and semicolons—we largely maintain those elements of nineteenth-century typography that, while nonstandard today, were common for the period. These include spaced contractions (e.g., *do n't* for *don't*, *must n't* for *mustn't*) and midsentence exclamation and question marks (e.g., *American Mothers! can you doubt that the slave feels as tenderly for her offspring as you do for yours?*).

RADICALS

Kate Chopin

1850–1904

KATE CHOPIN was well known by the 1890s for her short fiction, which appeared in such prestigious outlets as *Vogue*, the *Atlantic Monthly*, *Harper's Young People*, and *Century Magazine*. She also published two novels, *At Fault* (1890) and *The Awakening* (1899), the latter of which was condemned at the time but is her most read work today. Her fiction often focuses on the Louisiana Creole community that she was a part of and features sensitive, intelligent female protagonists and proto-feminist themes. Within a few years of her death, she was widely recognized as one of the foremost writers of her time.

The Storm (1898)
A Sequel to the Cadian Ball

I

The leaves were so still that even Bibi thought it was going to rain. Bobinot, who was accustomed to converse on terms of perfect equality with his little son, called the child's attention to certain sombre clouds that were rolling with sinister intention from the west, accompanied by a sullen, threatening roar. They were at Friedheimer's store and decided to remain there till the storm had passed. They sat within the door on two empty kegs. Bibi was four years old and looked very wise.

"Mama'll be 'fraid, yes," he suggested with blinking eyes.

"She'll shut the house. Maybe she got Sylvie helpin' her this evenin'," Bobinot responded reassuringly.

"No; she ent got Sylvie. Sylvie was helpin her yistiday," piped Bibi.

Bobinot arose and going across to the counter purchased a can of shrimps, of which Calixta was very fond. Then he returned to his perch on the keg and sat stolidly holding the can of shrimps while the storm burst. It shook the wooden store and seemed to be ripping great furrows in the distant field. Bibi laid his little hand on his father's knee and was not afraid.

II

Calixta, at home, felt no uneasiness for their safety. She sat at a side window sewing furiously on a sewing machine. She was greatly occupied and did not notice the approaching storm. But she felt very warm and often stopped to mop her face on which the perspiration gathered in beads. She unfastened her white sacque at the throat. It began to grow dark, and suddenly realizing the situation she got up hurriedly and went about closing windows and doors.

Out on the small front gallery she had hung Bobinot's Sunday clothes to air and she hastened out to gather them before the rain fell. As she stepped outside, Alcée Laballière rode in at the gate. She had not seen him very often since her marriage, and never alone. She stood there with Bobinot's coat in her hands, and the big rain drops began to fall. Alcée rode his horse under the shelter of a side projection where the chickens had huddled and there were plows and a harrow piled up in the corner.

"May I come and wait on your gallery till the storm is over, Calixta?" he asked.

"Come 'long in, M'sieur Alcée."

His voice and her own startled her as if from a trance, and she seized Bobinot's vest. Alcée, mounting to the porch, grabbed the trousers and snatched Bibi's braided jacket that was about to be carried away by a sudden gust of wind. He expressed an intention to remain outside, but it was soon apparent that he might as well have been out in the open: the water beat in upon the boards in driving sheets, and he went inside, closing the door after him. It was even necessary to put something beneath the door to keep the water out.

"My! what a rain! It's good two years since it rain' like that" exclaimed Calixta as she rolled up a piece of bagging and Alcée helped her to thrust it beneath the crack.

She was a little fuller of figure than five years before when she married;

but she had lost nothing of her vivacity. Her blue eyes still retained their melting quality; and her yellow hair, dishevelled by the wind and rain, kinked more stubbornly than ever about her ears and temples.

The rain beat upon the low, shingled roof with a force and clatter that threatened to break an entrance and deluge them there. They were in the dining room—the sitting room—the general utility room. Adjoining was her bed room, with Bibi's couch alongside her own. The door stood open, and the room with its white, monumental bed, its closed shutters, looked dim and mysterious.

Alcée flung himself into a rocker and Calixta nervously began to gather up from the floor the lengths of a cotton sheet which she had been sewing.

"If this keeps up, *Dieu sait*[1] if the levees goin' to stan' it!" she exclaimed.

"What have you got to do with the levees?"

"I got enough to do! An' there's Bobinot with Bibi out in that storm—if he only didn' left Friedheimers!"

"Let us hope, Calixta, that Bobinot's got sense enough to come in out of a cyclone."

She went and stood at the window with a greatly disturbed look on her face. She wiped the frame that was clouded with moisture. It was stiflingly hot. Alcée got up and joined her at the window, looking over her shoulder. The rain was coming down in sheets obscuring the view of far-off cabins and enveloping the distant wood in a gray mist. The playing of the lightning was incessant. A bolt struck a tall chinaberry tree at the edge of the field. It filled all visible space with a blinding glare and the crash seemed to invade the very boards they stood upon.

Calixta put her hands to her eyes, and with a cry, staggered backward. Alcée's arm encircled her, and for an instant he drew her close and spasmodically to him.

"*Bonté!*"[2] she cried, releasing herself from his encircling arm and retreating from the window, "the house'll go next! If I only knew w'ere Bibi was!" She would not compose herself; she would not be seated. Alcée clasped her shoulders and looked into her face. The contact of her warm, palpitating body when he had unthinkingly drawn her into his arms, had aroused all the old-time infatuation and desire for her flesh.

"Calixta," he said, "don't be frightened. Nothing can happen. The house is too low to be struck, with so many tall trees standing about. There! aren't you going to be quiet? say, aren't you?" He pushed her hair back from her face that was warm and steaming. Her lips were as red and moist as pomegranate seed. Her white neck and a glimpse of her full, firm bosom disturbed him powerfully. As she glanced up at him the fear in her liquid blue eyes had given place to a drowsy gleam that unconsciously betrayed a sensuous desire. He looked down into her eyes and there was nothing for him to do but to gather her lips in a kiss. It reminded him of Assumption.

"Do you remember—in Assumption, Calixta?" he asked in a low voice broken by passion. Oh! she remembered; for in Assumption he had kissed her and kissed and kissed her; until his senses would well nigh fail, and to save her he would resort to a desperate flight. If she was not an immaculate dove in those days, she was still inviolate; a passionate creature whose very defenselessness had made her defense, against which his honor forbade him to prevail. Now—well, now—her lips seemed in a manner free to be tasted, as well as her round, white throat and her whiter breasts.[3]

They did not heed the crashing torrents, and the roar of the elements made her laugh as she lay in his arms. She was a revelation in that dim, mysterious chamber; as white as the couch she lay upon. Her firm, elastic flesh that was knowing for the first time its birthright, was like a creamy lily that the sun invites to contribute its breath and perfume to the undying life of the world.

The generous abundance of her passion, without guile or trickery, was like a white flame which penetrated and found response in depths of his own sensuous nature that had never yet been reached.

When he touched her breasts they gave themselves up in quivering ecstasy, inviting his lips. Her mouth was a fountain of delight. And when he possessed her, they seemed to swoon together at the very borderland of life's mystery.

He stayed cushioned upon her, breathless, dazed, enervated, with his heart beating like a hammer upon her. With one hand she clasped his head, her lips lightly touching his forehead. The other hand stroked with a soothing rhythm his muscular shoulders.

The growl of the thunder was distant and passing away. The rain beat softly upon the shingles, inviting them to drowsiness and sleep. But they dared not yield.

The rain was over; and the sun was turning the glistening green world into a palace of gems. Calixta, on the gallery, watched Alcée ride away. He turned and smiled at her with a beaming face; and she lifted her pretty chin in the air and laughed aloud.

III

Bobinot and Bibi, trudging home, stopped without at the cistern to make themselves presentable.

"My! Bibi, w'at will yo' mama say! You ought to be ashame'. You oughtn' put on those good pants. Look at 'em! An' that mud on yo' collar! How you got that mud on yo' collar, Bibi? I never saw such a boy!" Bibi was the picture of pathetic resignation. Bobinot was the embodiment of serious solicitude as he strove to remove from his own person and his son's the signs of their tramp over heavy roads and through wet fields. He scraped the mud off Bibi's bare legs and feet with a stick and carefully removed all traces from his heavy brogans. Then, prepared for the worst—the meeting with an over-scrupulous housewife, they entered cautiously at the back door.

Calixta was preparing supper. She had set the table and was dripping coffee at the hearth. She sprang up as they came in.

"Oh, Bobinot! You back! My! but I was uneasy. W'ere you been during the rain? An' Bibi? he aint wet? he aint hurt?" She had clasped Bibi and was kissing him effusively. Bobinot's explanations and apologies which he had been composing all along the way, died on his lips as Calixta felt him to see if he were dry, and seemed to express nothing but satisfaction at their safe return.

"I brought you some shrimps, Calixta," offered Bobinot, hauling the can from his ample side pocket and laying it on the table.

"Shrimps! Oh, Bobinot! you too good fo' anything!" and she gave him a smacking kiss on the cheek that resounded, *"J'vous reponds,"*[4] we'll have a feas' to night! umph-umph!"

Bobinot and Bibi began to relax and enjoy themselves, and when the three seated themselves at table they laughed much and so loud that anyone might have heard them as far away as Laballière's.

IV

Alcée Laballière wrote to his wife, Clarisse, that night. It was a loving letter, full of tender solicitude. He told her not to hurry back, but if she and the babies liked it at Biloxi, to stay a month longer. He was getting on nicely; and though he missed them, he was willing to bear the separation a while longer—realizing that their health and pleasure were the first things to be considered.

V

As for Clarisse, she was charmed upon receiving her husband's letter. She and the babies were doing well. The society was agreeable; many of her old friends and acquaintances were at the bay. And this first free breath since her marriage seemed to restore the pleasant liberty of her maiden days. Devoted as she was to her husband, their intimate conjugal life was something which she was more than willing to forego for a while.

So the storm passed and every one was happy.   K. C.

<u>July 19—1898.</u>

An Egyptian Cigarette (1900)

My friend, the Architect, who is something of a traveler, was showing us various curios which he had gathered during a visit to the Orient.

"Here is something for you," he said, picking up a small box and turning it over in his hand. "You are a cigarette-smoker; take this home with you. It was given to me in Cairo by a species of fakir, who fancied I had done him a good turn."

The box was covered with glazed, yellow paper, so skillfully gummed as to appear to be all one piece. It bore no label, no stamp—nothing to indicate its contents.

"How do you know they are cigarettes?" I asked, taking the box and turning it stupidly around as one turns a sealed letter and speculates before opening it.

"I only know what he told me," replied the Architect, "but it is easy enough to determine the question of his integrity." He handed me a sharp, pointed paper-cutter, and with it I opened the lid as carefully as possible.

The box contained six cigarettes, evidently hand-made. The wrappers were of pale-yellow paper, and the tobacco was almost the same color. It was of finer cut than the Turkish or ordinary Egyptian, and threads of it stuck out at either end.

"Will you try one now, Madam?" asked the Architect, offering to strike a match.

"Not now and not here," I replied, "after the coffee, if you will permit me to slip into your smoking-den. Some of the women here detest the odor of cigarettes."

The smoking-room lay at the end of a short, curved passage. Its appointments were exclusively Oriental. A broad, low window opened out upon a balcony that overhung the garden. From the divan upon which I reclined, only the swaying tree-tops could be seen. The maple leaves glistened in the afternoon sun. Beside the divan was a low stand which contained the complete paraphernalia of a smoker. I was feeling quite comfortable, and congratulated myself upon having escaped for a while the incessant chatter of the women that reached me faintly.

I took a cigarette and lit it, placing the box upon the stand just as the tiny clock, which was there, chimed in silvery strokes the hour of five.

I took one long inspiration of the Egyptian cigarette. The gray-green smoke arose in a small puffy column that spread and broadened, that seemed to fill the room. I could see the maple leaves dimly, as if they were veiled in a shimmer of moonlight. A subtle, disturbing current passed through my whole body and went to my head like the fumes of disturbing wine. I took another deep inhalation of the cigarette.

"Ah! the sand has blistered my cheek! I have lain here all day with my face in the sand. To-night, when the everlasting stars are burning, I shall drag myself to the river."

He will never come back.

Thus far I followed him; with flying feet; with stumbling feet; with hands and knees, crawling; and outstretched arms, and here I have fallen in the sand.

The sand has blistered my cheek; it has blistered all my body, and the sun is crushing me with hot torture. There is shade beneath yonder cluster of palms.

I shall stay here in the sand till the hour and the night comes.

I laughed at the oracles and scoffed at the stars when they told that after the rapture of life I would open my arms inviting death, and the waters would envelop me.

Oh! how the sand blisters my cheek! and I have no tears to quench the fire. The river is cool and the night is not far distant.

I turned from the gods and said: "There is but one; Bardja[5] is my god." That was when I decked myself with lilies and wove flowers into a garland and held him close in the frail, sweet fetters.

He will never come back. He turned upon his camel as he rode away. He turned and looked at me crouching here and laughed, showing his gleaming white teeth.

Whenever he kissed me and went away he always came back again. Whenever he flamed with fierce anger and left me with stinging words, he always came back. But to-day he neither kissed me nor was he angry. He only said:

"Oh! I am tired of fetters, and kisses, and you. I am going away. You will never see me again. I am going to the great city where men swarm like bees. I am going beyond, where the monster stones are rising heavenward in a monument for the unborn ages. Oh! I am tired. You will see me no more."

And he rode away on his camel. He smiled and showed his cruel white teeth as he turned to look at me crouching here.

How slow the hours drag! It seems to me that I have lain here for days in the sand, feeding upon despair. Despair is bitter and it nourishes resolve.

I hear the wings of a bird flapping above my head, flying low, in circles. The sun is gone.

The sand has crept between my lips and teeth and under my parched tongue.

If I raise my head, perhaps I shall see the evening star.

Oh! the pain in my arms and legs! My body is sore and bruised as if broken. Why can I not rise and run as I did this morning? Why must I drag myself thus like a wounded serpent, twisting and writhing?

The river is near at hand. I hear it—— I see it—— Oh! the sand! Oh! the shine! How cool! how cold!

The water! the water! In my eyes, my ears, my throat! It strangles me! Help! will the gods not help me?

Oh! the sweet rapture of rest! There is music in the Temple. And here is fruit to taste. Bardja came with the music—— The moon shines and the breeze is soft—— A garland of flowers——let us go into the King's garden and look at the blue lily, Bardja.

———————

The maple leaves looked as if a silvery shimmer enveloped them. The gray-green smoke no longer filled the room. I could hardly lift the lids of my eyes. The weight of centuries seemed to suffocate my soul that struggled to escape, to free itself and breathe.

I had tasted the depths of human despair.

The little clock upon the stand pointed to a quarter past five. The cigarettes still reposed in the yellow box. Only the stub of the one I had smoked remained. I had laid it in the ash tray.

As I looked at the cigarettes in their pale wrappers, I wondered what other visions they might hold for me; what might I not find in their mystic fumes? Perhaps a vision of celestial peace; a dream of hopes fulfilled; a taste of rapture, such as had not entered into my mind to conceive.

I took the cigarettes and crumpled them between my hands. I walked to the window and spread my palms wide. The light breeze caught up the golden threads and bore them writhing and dancing far out among the maple leaves.

My friend, the Architect, lifted the curtain and entered, bringing me a second cup of coffee.

"How pale you are!" he exclaimed, solicitously. "Are you not feeling well?"

"A little the worse for a dream," I told him.

SOURCES

Chopin, Kate. "The Storm: A Sequel to the Cadian Ball," 1898. Transcribed from original manuscript, Missouri Historical Society. https://mohistory.org /collections/item/resource/176302.

———. "An Egyptian Cigarette." *Vogue Magazine*, April 19, 1900, 252, 254. Transcribed from digital page images provided by the Missouri Historical Society. https://mohistory.org/collections/item/resource/174887.

NOTES

1. God knows (French).
2. Goodness! (French).
3. In the manuscript, Chopin appears to overwrite the word "bosom" with the more explicit "breasts."
4. I answer you (French).
5. "Bardja" does not correspond to any widely known theological figure. In Albanian folklore, a *Bardha* is an elf-like creature that lives underground and can be appeased through food offerings—but it is unlikely that Chopin refers to this. For Emily Toth's and Marilyn Bonnell's opinion that "Bardja" is an invention of Chopin's, see Kate Chopin's *A Vocation and a Voice: Stories*, ed. Emily Toth (New York: Penguin, 1991), 194n69.18.

Rebecca Harding Davis

1831–1910

REBECCA HARDING DAVIS grew up in a small industrial town in what would become West Virginia. *Life in the Iron-Mills* (1861), the novella she wrote about the experiences of workers in the mills and factories of the nation, quickly established her as an acclaimed writer and a pioneer of literary realism in American literature. She was extremely prolific and, as a white woman, sought to use her writing to effect social change for immigrants, women, African Americans, Native Americans, and the working class. She was all but forgotten by the time of her death but was rediscovered in the 1970s by feminist author Tillie Olsen, who reintroduced her work and biography to the public.

At Noon (1887)

The tiny Swiss clock, hid in a gold chalet on the table beside her, struck twelve. At the same instant a dozen clocks—Dutch, Russian, colonial—throughout the house struck twelve. Mrs. Fitch yawned impatiently. If one of them would only go wrong, it would not be so intolerable. Presently they would strike one together, and then two, and so on, day in and day out, measuring off the deadly dulness of the time.

A year ago she had a fancy for clocks, and her collection was unrivalled in the city. Before that her hobby was fans; last year, Italian majolica. The year before that she built this house. Strangers from the West came every day to look at it as a marvellous reproduction of one of Inigo Jones's designs. She had seen an architect on the other side of the street to-day explaining to his companion its fine lines, just as the artists swarmed into her gallery of Dutch engravings every Tuesday.

For herself, she knew nothing of lines or engravings—no more than of the machinery of the clocks. Their enthusiasm was so paltry! When she had a fancy for a thing, she paid the money for it, and looked at it until it grew tiresome.

What a wretched blank in the day this hour of noon was! The sun blazed down on the dusty street outside, and on two laughing shop-girls scurrying along. Could it be that she too had once worn gilt bracelets and cotton gloves?

She dropped the curtain and sat down. A jewelry box was open on the table near her, and the chain of sapphires which she had worn last night lay on top. When was it that she had a fad for collecting sapphires? She pulled them toward her. Why had she liked them? Really they were no bluer nor clearer than the big glass beads she used to string when she was a child.

Only five minutes past noon! She had been used to stay in bed until two o'clock; but of late, since this queer worry of not sleeping had come to her, she rose in the morning, to the dismay of the servants. For four days she had not slept as many hours. Bromides and chlorals had apparently lost all effect.

This morning, while she tossed, aching and hot from head to foot, she suddenly bethought herself of a certain *plat* which Alphonse the *chef* had made once, and had ordered it for breakfast. She rose at once with a feeble sense of expectation, for Mrs. Fitch was a gourmande. She retained enough of her old country prejudices to dislike to breakfast in bed. But the dish when it came was tasteless. Her palate had lost its power. Water and champagne alike were flat to it.

Breakfast was over—what should she do? For months past that question recurred to her day and night with unaccountable persistency—what should she do now?

She took out her book of engagements. It was in the middle of the tea season. Four that afternoon, and as many receptions; to-night the Van Cleves' opera party and her own masked ball.

Adèle could send cards, as far as the teas were concerned. Why should she tire herself to conciliate cheap, stupid people? She had half a mind to take the afternoon train for New Orleans, and cut the opera and her own ball. She would be in time for the Mardi-Gras. But the Mardi-Gras was a bore last year.

Suppose she sent for Colonel Ford to take her incognita to that Bowery variety show? They had gone once, and it was no end of fun. But even while she thought of it she yawned and clasped her hands behind her neck. It was all so heavy to carry! She tried to prick herself into life by thinking how jolly her mythological masked balls were two winters ago. They were her own device. Not that she knew much about mythology, but those old gods and goddesses were so deliciously vicious! Only the young married women—the Roses—were invited; no Buds. Mrs. Fitch was Queen of the Roses then. She was Venus. Colonel Ford had designed her costume. When it came home, and she tried it on (what there was of it), she remembered that her very fingers seemed to blush. What a fool she was! The papers described the dress as classic, and gave a half-page of glowing eulogy to the lovely wife of the great Silver King. She had kept possession of the Society columns ever since. Her gowns, her receptions, her bull-terrier, her Chinese footmen in the costume of mandarins, had been chronicled day by day with "display" headings. She could not go into a shop nor toss a coin to a beggar without furnishing an item for some correspondent. They had even published ugly accounts of quarrels between herself and her husband, with hints of scandals leading to a divorce court. She laughed aloud as she thought of this. She and Samuel Fitch were not such senti-mental fools. He took his way, and she hers. It did not trouble her that he spent ten months of the year in San Francisco, where report said he had another wife and family. It did not trouble her either that Colonel Ford was going to marry that little Mapes girl. She would no doubt support him comfortably. Mapes was king of the tobacco men.

But—

What should she do now? She yawned again. Her costume tonight had been designed by Tadema when she was in England last month. It was an airy gauze. She was to be Cleopatra. She jumped up as if she had been stung, and found yesterday's newspaper. Some truthful reporter had de-scribed her as "fat and red-faced," "a milkmaid beauty who had grown gross and vulgar."

Was it true? She had fancied that the young men who crowded about her for invitations to her dinners and balls watched her waltz lately with sly smiles.

Was it true? If she was not the Queen Rose, what was she?

Jane Fitch leaned back on the white satin cushions of her lounge and crushed the dirty paper in her hands with a sudden sense of utter vacancy in the world. It had been dull and torpid before, but now it was empty.

If she was to be jostled from her place in her set! If Mrs. Ames's theatre for amateurs would draw everybody away from her masked balls! It had done so last week. The Society columns were filled now with the "Great Rancher's Bride, Celia Ames," her diamonds, her gowns, and her pet cat, while in yesterday's *Fact* there was a full account of her own marriage. "The pretty waitress at an inn where Samuel Fitch, then a successful miner, had stopped overnight."

That was not true!

Mrs. Fitch sat upright. She felt as much indignation as could penetrate through her fleshy body and a brain muddled by long overfeeding. She had never been a servant at an inn. Her father was a country doctor. She had sewed and cooked and ironed with her sisters. What fun they used to have! She remembered how she used to waken at dawn that she might surprise her mother with the breakfast all ready when she came down. And when the baby was born, how proud they were of it! A tender smile flickered over her coarse face. That dear little baby! They all nursed it, but it loved her best of all. "Janey" was the first word it spoke. It used to cry for her when it was ill, and it was in her arms when it died.

Her own child? She shuffled uneasily in her chair. It was different, of course, with that child. It was put into the arms of a wet-nurse at its birth. Mrs. Fitch had a suite of rooms ready for its use, and a matron and trained nurse to superintend its dressing and baths and watch its every motion. Once she had complained that she had nothing to do with her own baby; but she speedily saw that it would not do. She could not be expected to give up Society to be the servant of that little bald, toothless creature. Besides, it was more than her child; it was the heir of many millions, and must be guarded officially like a moneyed institution.

She had met the boy with his *bonne* yesterday on the stairs. But she could not talk to him. She did not speak French, and he was not allowed to learn English until his accent should be formed. Her mind now wandered from the boy. She had no interest nor part in his future.

What could she do? The question irritated her persistently as never before. The utter flatness of her life had grown intolerable. How could she find any change in it?

Some women read and were musicians. It had been her plan when she was a child to study to fit herself to be a teacher. But she was pretty. She became the village belle. The gilt bracelets, the sleazy silk gowns, the flowers for her hat—these soon were the things which made life worth living to her. When Mr. Fitch, who could buy for her diamond bracelets and lace flounces which queens had worn, asked her to marry him, she did not take an hour to consider her answer.

Hence, while other women find help and strength in books and music, a blank wall stretched across that way in her life. A blank wall shut in every way. She had no friends. Not one human being in the world knew that her name was Janey, or called her by it. Even to her husband she was Jeanne.

The sun glared into the room. How dazzling and hateful it was! The air was heavy with rank stagnant perfumes. She might ring for Adèle to close the curtains, but she was tired of the sight of Adèle. She would not be forced to listen to her babble.

She pulled a book toward her. It was a Bible. Seeing the name, she tossed it aside. It was another book, also in a green binding, that she wanted— a volume of choice French recipes of Francalette's which somebody had sent her. She read of some *entrées*, and tried to fancy how they would taste; but even her palate's memory failed, and she laid down the book. It did not once occur to her, on this lowest dreary flat marsh of her life, to open the Bible or to turn to God. These thoughts belonged away back to the days when she had the measles, and played with dolls, or "tripped up" in the spelling class.

She was tired even of recipes for Alphonse to try. She was tired of it all. The dishes were tasteless and the balls a bore, and even Colonel Ford's coarse flatteries were poured into another woman's ears. There was nothing to keep in the past, nothing to strive for in the future. As she lay back in her chair she opened and closed her hand slowly. It was empty. If she could only sleep, and forget how it all bored her!

She put out her hand mechanically for the bottle of laudanum and the spoon. A goblet stood near them. What if she should fill the goblet instead of the spoon! It was such a little thing to do. But it would end all. These empty days—

She lay looking at the muddy liquid and the goblet. When she was the child Janey she would have faced Death with some pang, some thought not unbefitting his mighty presence. A frightened cry, perhaps, to the God of whom she heard in church would have escaped her. But now her brain was full of darting, trifling thoughts, like newts in a stagnant pool.

She glanced at the mirror. If, after all, she was growing gross and fat!

Pretty soon the wood-cuts of her in the papers would make her look like a fish-wife; the last had given her the figure of an oil keg. How Mrs. Ames had laughed at it!

Suppose she did fill the goblet, how many people would care? "A good many, for they would miss their ball," she said, with a grim smile.

She lifted the bottle and uncorked it. Just then she heard her boy's step on the stairs. He stopped and tapped softly at her door. She did not open it.

The next day the newspapers contained full accounts of Mrs. Samuel Fitch's death from disease of the heart. "Mrs. Fitch's masked ball," it was stated in the Society column, "which was to have been the most brilliant of the season, will of course not take place. Mrs. Ames's private theatricals are now occupying the attention of our first circles. It is whispered that she will give an out-door representation of *The Tempest*, in the park surrounding her mansion on the Hudson, in the early future. Some of the most noted beauties in New York, Baltimore, and Philadelphia are to take part."

Nothing was said of the empty bottle or goblet, which, in obedience to a nod from Mr. Fitch, had been removed by the prudent Adèle.

The curtains shut out the glaring noon light from Mrs. Fitch's room, where she lay, her hands empty, and a strange vacuous look on her face. Down in the sunny street below, the two shop-girls were hurrying again home to lunch, chattering and laughing as they went.

The Bible lay unopened on the table beside her. In the chamber overhead her little boy sat on the lap of his *bonne*, who suddenly, without any reason, as he thought, hugged him close to her breast and kissed him, with tears in her eyes.

SOURCE

Davis, Rebecca Harding. "At Noon." *Harper's Bazaar* 20, no. 51 (December 17, 1887): 874.

Emily Dickinson

1830–1886

EMILY DICKINSON was a member of a prominent white family from Amherst, Massachusetts. Largely unknown in her lifetime, she is now considered one of the greatest American poets of all time. Although she is often characterized as "reclusive" and narrow in experience because the majority of her life was spent on the grounds of her family's property, her poetry and letters reveal a complex and passionate inner life. She exploded poetic conventions with her elliptical, experimental style, and wrote about major historical events, such as the U.S. Civil War, as well as the vicissitudes of everyday life. Because she never married and had few overtly romantic relationships, Dickinson is often assumed to have been a functionally sexless adult, but the poems collected in this section, as well as her late-life letters to love interest Judge Otis Lord (see volume 2) suggest otherwise.

For each extatic instant (ca. 1859)

For each extatic instant –
We must an anguish pay
In keen and quivering ratio
To the extasy –

For each beloved hour
Sharp pittances of Years –
Bitter contested farthings –
And Coffers heaped with Tears!

Come slowly – Eden! (ca. 1860–61)

Come slowly – Eden!
Lips unused to Thee.
Bashful – sip thy Jessamines –
As the fainting Bee –

Reaching late his flower,
Round her chamber hums –
Counts his nectars –
Enters – and is lost in Balms.

He fumbles at your Soul (ca. 1862)

He fumbles at your Soul
As Players at the Keys –
Before they drop full Music on –
He stuns you by degrees –

Prepares your brittle ⁺ substance _{+ nature}¹
For the Ethereal Blow
By fainter Hammers – further heard –
Then nearer – Then so – slow –

Your Breath has ⁺chance _{+ time} to straighten –
Your Brain – to bubble Cool –
Deals One – imperial Thunderbolt –
That ⁺peels _{+ scalps} your naked Soul –

When Winds hold Forests in the Paws –
⁺ The firmaments – are still –
⁺ The Universe – is still ⁺

He touched me, so I live to know (ca. 1862)

He touched me, so I live to know
That such a day, ⁺ permitted so –
I groped opon his breast –

It was a boundless place to me
And silenced, as the awful Sea
Puts minor streams to rest.

And now, I'm different from before,
As if I breathed superior air –
Or brushed a Royal Gown –
My feet, too, that had wandered so –
My Gipsy face – transfigured now –
To tenderer Renown –

Into this Port, if I might come,
Rebecca, to Jerusalem,
Would not so ravished turn –
Nor Persian, baffled at her shrine
Lift such a Crucifixal sign
To her imperial Sun.

⁺ persuaded so – I perished –
⁺ Accepted so – I dwelt –

SOURCES

Dickinson, Emily. "Come slowly – Eden!" Manuscript packet XXXVII, fascicle 10,
  Houghton Library, Harvard University. https://www.edickinson.org/editions/2
  /image_sets/74855. This poem text is in the public domain, and is reproduced
  with all due thanks to Harvard University Press and the Houghton Library.
———. "For each extatic instant –," derived from the "So from the mould" manu-
  script #fascicle 83 (asc:8068 - p. 9). The Emily Dickinson Collection, Amherst
  College, Archives & Special Collections. https://www.edickinson.org/editions
  /4/image_sets/80195.
———. "He fumbles at your Soul." Manuscript packet XIX, fascicle 22, Houghton
  Library, Harvard University. https://www.edickinson.org/editions/34/image
  _sets/9932. Reprinted with permission from Harvard University Press, from *The
  Poems of Emily Dickinson: Variorum Edition*, edited by Ralph W. Franklin, Cam-
  bridge, Mass.: The Belknap Press of Harvard University Press. Copyright © 1998
  by the President and Fellows of Harvard College. Copyright © 1951, 1955 by the
  President and Fellows of Harvard College. Copyright © renewed 1979, 1983 by
  the President and Fellows of Harvard College. Copyright © 1914, 1918, 1919, 1924,

————. "He touched me, so I live to know." Manuscript #fascicle 85 (asc:17626 - p. 3). The Emily Dickinson Collection, Amherst College, Archives & Special Collections. https://www.edickinson.org/editions/1/image_sets/235617. Reprinted with permission from Harvard University Press, from *The Poems of Emily Dickinson: Variorum Edition*, edited by Ralph W. Franklin, Cambridge, Mass.: The Belknap Press of Harvard University Press. Copyright © 1998 by the President and Fellows of Harvard College. Copyright © 1951, 1955 by the President and Fellows of Harvard College. Copyright © renewed 1979, 1983 by the President and Fellows of Harvard College. Copyright © 1914, 1918, 1919, 1924, 1929, 1930, 1932, 1935, 1937, 1942 by Martha Dickinson Bianchi. Copyright © 1952, 1957, 1958, 1963, 1965 by Mary L. Hampson.

NOTE

1. We transcribe the "+" symbols that Dickinson uses in the original manuscript, as well as the word "nature," which she writes in smaller lettering, to insert it between the word "substances" and the next line. We continue to transcribe these elements throughout the poems in this section.

Alice Dunbar-Nelson

1875–1935

ALICE DUNBAR-NELSON was a mixed-race poet, playwright, journalist, editor, activist, and teacher from New Orleans. She was a prominent figure of the Harlem Renaissance. Much of her work focused on the color line and the realities of racism in America, including lynching; some gestured toward her intimate relationships with women. Because of its subject matter, she struggled to get her work published in the male- and white-dominated fields of journalism and literature. She took on significant roles as coeditor of the *A.M.E. Church Review* and the Wilmington *Advocate*, and compiled anthologies of African American writings. She was heavily involved in organizing for women's suffrage and for antilynching legislation.

If I Had Known (1895)

If I had known
Two years ago how drear this life should be,
And crowd upon itself allstrangely sad,
Mayhap another song would burst from out my lips,
Overflowing with the happiness of future hopes;
Mayhap another throb than that of joy.
Have stirred my soul into its inmost depths,
                 If I had known.

If I had known,
Two years ago the impotence of love,
The vainness of a kiss, how barren a caress,
Mayhap my soul to higher things have soarn,
Nor clung to earthly loves and tender dreams,
But ever up aloft into the blue empyrean,
And there to master all the world of mind,
                 If I had known.

The Praline Woman (1899)

The praline woman sits by the side of the Archbishop's quaint little old chapel on Royal Street, and slowly waves her latanier fan over the pink and brown wares.

"Pralines, pralines.[1] Ah, ma'amzelle, you buy? S'il vous plaît, ma'amzelle,[2] ces pralines, dey be fine, ver' fresh.

"Mais non, maman, you are not sure?

"Sho', chile, ma bébé, ma petite,[3] she put dese up hissef. He's hans' so small, ma'amzelle, lak you's, mais brune.[4] She put dese up dis morn'. You tak' none? No husban' fo' you den!

"Ah, ma petite, you tak'? Cinq sous, bébé,[5] may le bon Dieu[6] keep you good!

"Mais oui, madame,[7] I know you étangér. [8] You don' look lak dese New Orleans peop'. You lak' dose Yankee dat come down 'fo' de war."

Ding-dong, ding-dong, ding-dong, chimes the Cathedral bell across Jackson Square, and the praline woman crosses herself.

"Hail, Mary, full of grace—

"Pralines, madame? You buy lak' dat? Dix sous,[9] madame, an' one lil' piece fo' lagniappe[10] fo' madame's lil' bébé. Ah, c'est bon!

"Pralines, pralines, so fresh, so fine! M'sieu would lak' some fo' he's lil' gal' at home? Mais non, what's dat you say? She's daid! Ah, m'sieu, 't is my lil' gal what died long year ago. Misère, misère![11]

"Here come dat lazy Indien squaw. What she good fo', anyhow? She jes' sit lak dat in de French Market an' sell her filé,[12] an' sleep, sleep, sleep, lak' so in he's blanket. Hey, dere, you, Tonita, how goes you' beezness?

"Pralines, pralines! Holy Father, you give me dat blessin' sho'? Tak' one, I know you lak dat w'ite one. It tas' good, I know, bien.

"Pralines, madame? I lak' you' face. What fo' you wear black? You' lil' boy daid? You tak' one, jes' see how it tas'. I had one lil' boy once, he jes' grow 'twell he's big lak' dis, den one day he tak' sick an' die. Oh, madame, it mos' brek my po' heart. I burn candle in St. Rocque, I say my beads, I sprinkle holy water roun' he's bed; he jes' lay so, he's eyes turn up, he say 'Maman, maman,'[13] den he die! Madame, you tak' one. Non, non, no l'argent,[14] you tak' one fo' my lil' boy's sake.

"Pralines, pralines, m'sieu? Who mak' dese? My lil' gal, Didele, of co'se. Non, non, I don't mak' no mo'. Po' Tante Marie get too ol'. Didele? She's one lil' gal I 'dopt. I see her one day in de strit. He walk so; hit col' she shiver, an' I say, 'Where you gone, lil' gal?' and he can' tell. He jes' crip close to me, an' cry so! Den I tak' her home wid me, and she say he's name Didele. You see dey wa'nt nobody dere. My lil' gal, she's daid of de yellow fever; my lil' boy, he's daid, po' Tante Marie all alone. Didele, she grow fine, she keep house an' mek' pralines. Den, when night come, she sit wid he's guitar an' sing,

"'Tu l'aime ces trois jours,
Tu l'aime ces trois jours,
    Ma coeur à toi,
    Ma coeur à toi,
Tu l'aime ces trois jours!'[15]

"Ah, he's fine gal, is Didele!

"Pralines, pralines! Dat lil' cloud, h'it look lak' rain, I hope no.

"Here come dat lazy I'ishman down de strit. I don't lak' I'ishman, me,

non, dey so funny. One day one I'ishman, he say to me, 'Auntie, what fo'
you talk so?' and I jes' say back, 'What fo' you say "Faith an' be jabers"[16]?'
Non, I don' lak I'ishman, me!

   "Here come de rain! Now I got fo' to go. Didele, she be wait fo' me. Down
h'it come! H'it fall in de Meesseesip, an' fill up—up—so, clean to de levee,
den we have big crivasse,[17] an' po' Tante Marie float away. Bon jour, ma-
dame,[18] you come again? Pralines! Pralines!"

I Sit and Sew (1918)

I sit and sew—a useless task it seems,
My hands grown tired, my head weighed down with dreams—
The panoply of war, the martial tred of men,
Grim-faced, stern-eyed, gazing beyond the ken
Of lesser souls, whose eyes have not seen Death,
Nor learned to hold their lives but as a breath—
But—I must sit and sew.

I sit and sew—my heart aches with desire—
That pageant terrible, that fiercely pouring fire
On wasted fields, and writhing grotesque things
Once men. My soul in pity flings
Appealing cries, yearning only to go
There in that holocaust of hell, those fields of woe—
But—I must sit and sew.

The little useless seam, the idle patch;
Why dream I here beneath my homely thatch,
When there they lie in sodden mud and rain,
Pitifully calling me, the quick ones and the slain?
You need me, Christ! It is no roseate dream
That beckons me—this pretty futile seam,
It stifles me—God, must I sit and sew?

SOURCES

Dunbar, Alice. "The Praline Woman." In *The Goodness of St. Rocque and Other Stories*, 175–79. New York: Dodd, Mead and Company, 1899.
Dunbar-Nelson, Alice Moore. "I Sit and Sew." *A.M.E. Church Review* (1918).
Moore, Alice Ruth. "If I Had Known." In *Violets and Other Tales*, 154–55. Boston: Monthly Review, 1895. https://www.loc.gov/resource/lcrbmrp.t8114/?sp=158.

NOTES

Chapter opening photo: Alice Dunbar-Nelson in 1902. From the New York Public Library, https://digitalcollections.nypl.org/items/510d47da-768b-a3d9-e040 -e00a18064a99.

1. A confection made of nuts (usually pecans) and melted, browned sugar.
2. If you please, miss (French).
3. My baby, my little one (French).
4. But brown (French).
5. Five cents, baby (French).
6. The good God (French).
7. But yes, madame (French).
8. Foreign (French).
9. Ten cents (French).
10. A small gift given to customers after purchase.
11. Misery, misery! (French).
12. Gumbo filé, a spicy herb powder made from sassafras.
13. Mama, mama (French).
14. No, no, no money (French).
15. "You love him these three days, / You love him these three days, / My heart to yours, / My heart to yours, / You love him these three days!" (French).
16. A mild Irish oath, for "by Jesus."
17. Crack (from the French *crevasse*).
18. Good day, madam (French).

Sui Sin Far

1865–1914

SUI SIN FAR is the pen name of Edith Maude Eaton, a Canadian-American journalist and author who was of English and Chinese descent. She began her career by writing anonymous journalistic accounts of the local Chinese community for Montreal's English-language newspapers. By 1896 she was publishing short fiction about Chinese Americans under her pen name. They served as appeals for an end to discrimination against working-class Chinese Americans during a time when the Chinese Exclusion Act was in effect, banning Chinese immigration to the United States.

A Chinese Ishmael (1899)

In the light of night, on the detached rocks near the Cliff House, the sea-lions are clambering and growling; the waters of the Pacific are foaming around them, and their young, in the clefts of the rookeries, are drifting into dreamland on lullabies sung by the waves.

Mark that great fellow ensconced on a rocky pedestal. Why does he roar so restlessly and complainingly? I wonder, if he could speak, if he would tell where Leih Tseih and Ku Yum lie. I almost fancy that he sees the lovers quiet and still under the waters.

Ku Yum leant over the balcony of the big lodging-house on Dupont Street. She was very tired, for she was a delicate little thing and her tiny hands and feet were kept moving all day; her mistress had a heart like a razor and a tongue to match. Underneath the balcony there passed a young man, and as he went by, some spirit whispered in Ku Yum's ear, "Let fall a Chinese lily."

Ku Yum obeyed the spirit, and the young man, whose name was Leih Tseih, raised his eyes, and seeing Ku Yum, loved her. The Chinese lily he lifted from the ground and carried it away in his sleeve. Thereafter every day, going backward and forward to his work, Leih Tseih passed under the balcony where he had first seen Ku Yum, but the maiden no longer leaned over the railing. She had grown shy, and contented herself with peeping out of the door of the upper room. At last Leih Tseih, who was beside himself with love, threw her a note wrapped around a stone. Ku Yum caught and demurely retired with it; but just as she was placing it in the sole of her shoe her mistress came behind her and twisted it out of her fingers.

"You wicked, wicked thing!" cried the woman. "How dare you keep company with a bad man!"

Poor little Ku Yum's transparent face flushed.

"If I am a wicked thing, a bad man is fit company for me," she cried. "But he who wrote me that is a superior man."

At that her mistress fell to beating her with a little switch. Ku Yum screamed; but instead of receiving help, her mistress's husband appeared and relieved his wife as switcher, having a stronger arm.

There lived on the floor just below the Lee Chus, the owners of Ku Yum, a woman who had compassion on the slave-girl. She too had seen Leih

Tseih pass and the tossing up of the note, and had said to herself, "Now, there are a fine-looking young man and a pearl of a girl becoming acquainted. May they be happy!"

So when Ku Yum's screams rent the air, her heart swelled big with pity, and though she dared not interfere between mistress and maid, she resolved to watch for Leih Tseih and tell him what she knew concerning Ku Yum.

When Leih Tseih learned what had befallen the girl of his heart for his sake, the blood rushed to his head, and he would have leapt up the stairs and carried Ku Yum away by force, but A-Chuen, the woman, restrained him, saying: "Be discreet, and I will assist you; be rash, and you will lose all."

"But," demurred Leih Tseih, "if a man will not enter a tiger's lair, how can he obtain her whelps?"

"By coaxing them out," replied A-Chuen.

Then the woman and the young man conferred together, and it came to pass that when the stars were in the sky, Ku Yum, in a peach-colored blouse, a present from a cousin in China, stood with downcast eyes in A-Chuen's sitting-room and listened to words from her lover. She could not be induced to look at Leih Tseih, but he caught the shine of her eyes underneath the lids, and thought her as sweet as a li-chee.

"Dear child," said A-Chuen, "do not tremble so; you are with friends."

Then Leih Tseih told how he had planned to remove her from the people who had treated her so cruelly. A-Chuen, who had an old husband who loved her well enough to do all that she wished, would leave the house on Dupont Street and take a small house for herself. There Ku Yum should safely abide. Meanwhile, A-Chuen with amiable and flattering words would induce the Lee Chus to allow Ku Yum to come to A-Chuen's room to work some embroidery on garments for her husband's store, thereby preventing Ku Yum from being abused.

"You are very good and very kind," responded Ku Yum. "But unless I am bought from the Lee Chus, I cannot leave them. I have heard them talking of an offer that Lum Choy has made for me. It is dollars and dollars, and before many moons go by I fear I shall be obliged to be his."

"Who is Lum Choy?" asked Leih Tseih, his face white with anger and surprise.

"He is a very ugly man," said Ku Yum, "and there is a scar right across his forehead. But he has made money, they say, in more ways than the way of labor."

"And you wish to be sold to him?" queried Leih Tseih jealously.

"That I did not say," replied Ku Yum, "but this I do say: I am only a slave, but still a Chinese maiden. He is a man who, wishing to curry favor with the white people, wears American clothes, and when it suits his convenience passes for a Japanese."

"Shame on him!" cried A-Chuen.

"Kind friend," said Leih Tseih to A-Chuen, "if you so please, I would speak to Ku Yum alone."

A-Chuen left the room, and Leih Tseih, seating himself beside Ku Yum said, "I would like to tell you of myself."

"What you like to tell, I like to hear," replied Ku Yum.

"Then, listen," said Leih Tseih. "I am the son of a high mandarin, but being possessed of a turbulent and unruly spirit I ran away from home in my eighteenth year and through the agency of the Six Companies came to San Francisco. Here I obtained work, but the Gambling Cash Tiger had all of my thoughts, and it came to pass in the heat of a game, when I saw my adversary, the very Lum Choy you speak of, playing me false, that I struck at him with a knife and left him lying wounded. I escaped punishment and followed a seafaring-man's life for several years. Then came shipwreck and drifting for days alone upon the mighty waters, and my soul at last was humbled; and one solemn night, when naught could be heard save the washing of the waves against the side of my small boat, I acknowledged with sorrow to the Parent of All that I had indeed wandered far from the path of virtue, and vowed, if my life were spared, to follow my conscience,—for I had indeed been the bad man your mistress called me."

"Good or bad," cried little Ku Yum, "you are you and I am I." And she patted his hand shyly to show that what she had heard had not changed her feelings. Then she added, "And now I vow I will never be Lum Choy's, but ever yours, who have the grace of the well-born."

Leih Tseih smiled and exclaimed, "What a woman!" and declared that he loved every inch of her skin and the spirit that dwelt behind her eyes.

"I was picked up by a sailing-vessel bound for San Francisco," continued Leih Tseih, "and since returning to this city, I have conformed to virtue in every respect. I sought work and I obtained it. I have saved money—almost sufficient to pay to the Six Companies the amount of my indebtedness. It was with the object of relieving myself of that obligation that I saved. But now, my Ku Yum, that sum will take you and me together far away from here to another city on the other side of this world. What do you say?"

Little Ku Yum shook her head.

"I told my mistress," said she, "that you were a superior man."

"So be it," returned Leih Tseih, rebuked, "I will take the punishment I deserve, and after my debt has been paid will wait for you until I have made money enough to buy you."

"No; when you have paid your debt and are able to take me away, I will fly with you wherever and whenever you wish."

"Even though I steal you."

"That I will consider a righteous theft. Besides, the sooner you are out of this city the better. Are you not afraid that you may be recognized and thrown into prison?"

"I am not afraid. Life on the ocean transformed me both inwardly and outwardly."

"That may be, but I fear for you now. Be careful, I pray you. If you meet Lum Choy there will be trouble; and should he become aware that you and I have met, he would be a bloodhound on your track."

"Well, for your sake I will watch and be cautious."

When A-Chuen reappeared, Leih Tseih said, "Kind woman, we have agreed when the proper time comes to seek another city where we can be united. Here there are laws to separate us, but none to bind."

Which was true; for how could Leih Tseih and Ku Yum ask either Chinese priest or American in San Francisco to make them man and wife?

"One might as well look for a pin at the bottom of the ocean," growled Lum Choy.

He spoke to the Lee Chus, who had been vainly searching for weeks for Ku Yum.

"Well, it may be that she has given herself to the sea," answered Lee Chu, who was not very bright.

"Imbeciles!" was his wife's quick rejoinder as she snapped her eyes at the men. "A girl with a new lover can always be found—by him."

"What do you mean?" asked Lum Choy.

"Why, this: Ku Yum had a lover who passed here every day. It is to his embraces, not to those of cold water that Ku Yum has given herself. The shameful thing! If I had her here I would tear her eyes out."

Lum Choy's face had become livid.

"Do you know this man?" said he. "If so, I will trace her through him."

"I should know him were I to see him," said Lee Chu's wife, "but he has not passed for three or four weeks. I had the letter which he wrote to Ku Yum, but the girl stole it from me before she left."

"He will pass again," replied Lum Choy. "Ku Yum is not here now, so he does not make this his way. But he must pass some time. Tell me the hour when he was wont to go by and I will watch day after day and never weary until I have run him down."

The presidents of the Six Companies had met together in the council hall.

The chief of the Sam Yups, an imposing man with thought-refined features, was urging the advisability of expending a sum of money for the relief of some sick laborers, when a rapping was heard, followed by the entrance of the Six Companies' secretary, who approached the aged chief of the Hop Wos and whispered a few words in his ear.

"You can admit him," responded the old man.

The secretary left the room, and in a few minutes returned with a repulsive-looking fellow whose forehead bore a huge scar.

"This is Lum Choy," announced the secretary.

"Well, Lum Choy, what is your complaint?" inquired the Hop Wo chief.

"My complaint," said Lum Choy, in a high, rasping voice, "is that living in this city is a man named Leih Tseih, who owes this honorable body the cost of his transportation from China to America, and as well sundry other taxes. His debt is of many years' standing, yet he works as a free man and himself receives the good of every cent he earns. More than this, Leih Tseih is a fugitive criminal, having some five years ago assaulted a man with murderous intent and escaped the consequences of his crime. I, Lum Choy, am the man he assaulted, and bear on my forehead the mark of his knife. I also complain that this Leih Tseih has abducted a slave girl named Ku Yum, or rather, stolen her from one Lee Chu, and that he has secreted her in a house on Stockton Street, to which I can lead you. And I petition that you engage officers of the law to capture this lawless man, and that you prosecute him, as it is in order for the Six Companies so to do."

There were a few seconds of silence after Lum Choy had finished speaking; then the Sam Yup chief arose. He regarded gravely the mean figure of Lum Choy, and said: "Presidents of the Yeong Wo, Kong Chow, Yan Wo, Hop Wo and Ning Yeong Societies, you may remember that less than one month ago I delivered over to the Six Companies' Fund a sum of money, which, as I then stated, had been paid to me by one of our delinquent emigrants, whose name I had been requested by him to withhold. You did not press me to reveal that name, but the time has come to do so. The man who paid me that money was Leih Tseih, and the amount, as shown in our books, covers the whole of his indebtedness. We, therefore, have no legal claim against Leih Tseih, and are not authorized to punish him for the deeds which Lum Choy has charged him with."

Lum Choy could not restrain himself. "What!" he cried, "the powerful Six Companies have no jurisdiction over the men they have brought to this country?"

"In some cases we have," replied the Hop Wo chief suavely; "but this case lies with the American courts. Although so many years have elapsed since Leih Tseih assaulted you, I believe you still have recourse against him, and as you are one of our men, we will certainly do what we can to assist you in avenging yourself according to law."

"But the slave girl, Ku Yum?"

"Are you interested in her?" queried the Sam Yup.

"I am," returned Lum Choy. "I have paid a large sum for her, which Lee Chu will not refund, and it was on the day that she was to have come to me that she fled with Leih Tseih. In my search for her I discovered the man, and I have made no mistake, for day after day, night after night, I have dogged his footsteps."

The chief of the Ning Yeongs then said: "Lum Choy has suffered grievous wrongs, and we must do all in our power to assist him in bringing his wronger to justice; but the purchase of slave-girls, which is just and right in our own country, is not lawful in America. Therefore, the task of recovering Ku Yum cannot be undertaken by the Six Companies. It must be intrusted to the hands of private parties and conducted secretly. Otherwise Lum Choy and Lee Chu will have as much to answer for, according to the law of this country, as had Leih Tseih."

"And," rejoined the Sam Yup president, "that being so, I would advise Lum Choy to let matters rest. He who strives for a woman makes much trouble for himself. Besides, is it not better to forgive an injury than to avenge one?"

"Great and noble are your sentiments, benevolent Sam Yup chief," broke in Lum Choy, with a scarcely concealed sneer; "but they are not the sentiments of a man who has been injured as I have been, and I will have vengeance if it costs me my life."

With these words he left the council-room. Desire for a woman, hate for a man, had changed the nature of the once shrewd and clear-headed Lum Choy, and his mind was fired with one idea—vengeance.

"If," meditated he in the darkness of midnight, "I imprison Leih Tseih for a few months, perhaps a year, Ku Yum will be his at the end of that time and love him more than ever. If I use secret means to obtain Ku Yum, and do obtain her, the sweetness of the fruit will not be for me, for her mind and heart will be with my rival. If I kill Leih Tseih, Ku Yum's spirit will follow his, for that is the way with women who dare what she has dared. What, then, can I do to satisfy myself and draw Ku Yum's heart from Leih Tseih? This only—kill Lum Choy and make Leih Tseih his murderer. Oho! devils, I shall soon be one of you! And now I must arrange so that he shall be the last person with me. I know where I can obtain a knife of his, and I know how I can lure him here. He will be overjoyed with my offer to relinquish my claim on Ku Yum for a small tax on his weekly wages, and while he is pouring out his gratitude to me for abandoning my vengeance, I will dabble him well with blood from a cut arm. He must come here in the dusk of the evening and immediately after his departure, the deed will be done. Ha, ha! what a revenge!"

"Your eyes are strange; there is blood on your garments!" cried Ku Yum to Leih Tseih, who without warning had appeared before her.

Leih Tseih's set face relaxed.

"Be not afraid, my bird," said he; "but to-night you and I must part."

"Part! O, no, no!" She sprang to his side and caught his hand.

"It is true. I am hunted again. Lum Choy has been found dead with a knife in his heart. I was the last person seen to enter his room. And as you see, my garments are blood-stained."

For a second the girl shrank back; then, alas for the lost soul of Lum Choy, pressed closer to her lover and whispered in his ear, "If all men save Leih Tseih were killed by Leih Tseih, still would Ku Yum remain with Leih Tseih."

"I am unworthy," murmured Leih Tseih, brokenly. "Though I am guiltless of the deed for which I know they will condemn me, yet my past has been such that it justifies the condemnation. But you, O sweetest heart! you must forget me!"

Ku Yum shook her head. "I can die, but I cannot do what you have asked of me."

Some silent seconds, then Leih Tseih said in a clear voice, "We will die together—you and I."

"Ah! that will be happiness—to enter the spirit-land, hand in hand. When my cousins in China hear of it, they will say, 'How fine! Our cousin, Ku Yum, who was a slave-girl on earth, walks the Halls of Death with the son of a high mandarin.'"

To the Cliff they sped. Arrived where from a parapet they could leap into the Pacific, they embraced tenderly and were gone. None can point to the spot where life with all its troubles ended, for their bodies were never found; but in that part of San Francisco called the City of the Chinese it is whispered from lip to ear that the spirits of Leih Tseih and Ku Yum have passed into a pair of beautiful sea-lions who wander in the moonlight over the rocks, meditating on life and love and sorrow.

A Chinese Boy-Girl (1904)

The warmth was deep and all-pervading. The dust lay on the leaves of the palms and the other tropical plants that tried to flourish in the plaza. The persons of mixed nationalities lounging on the benches within and without the square appeared to be even more listless and unambitious than usual. The Italians who ran the peanut-and-fruit stands at the corners were doing no business to speak of. The Chinese merchants' stores in front of the plaza looked as quiet and respectable and drowsy as such stores always do. Even the bowling-alleys, billiard-halls, and saloons seemed under the influence of the heat, and only a subdued clinking of glasses and roll of balls could be heard from behind the half-open doors. It was almost as hot as an August day in New York city, and that is unusually sultry for southern California.

A little Chinese girl with bright eyes and round cheeks, attired in blue cotton garments, and wearing her long shining hair in a braid interwoven with silks of many colors, paused beside a woman tourist who was making a sketch of the old Spanish church. The tourist and the little Chinese girl were the only persons visible who did not seem to be affected by the heat. They might have been friends; but the lady, fearing for her sketch, bade the child run off. Whereupon the little thing shuffled across the plaza, and in less than five minutes was at the door of the Los Angeles Chinatown school for children.

"Come in, little girl, and tell me what they call you," said the young American teacher, who was new to the place.

"Ku Yum be my name," was the unhesitating reply, and said Ku Yum walked into the room, seated herself complacently on an empty bench in the first row, and informed the teacher that she lived on Apablaza street, that her parents were well, but her mother was dead, and her father, whose name was Ten Suie, had a wicked and tormenting spirit in his foot.

The teacher gave her a slate and pencil, and resumed the interrupted lesson by indicating with her rule ten lichis (called "Chinese nuts" by people in America) and counting them aloud.

"One, two, three, four, five, six, seven, eight, nine, ten," the baby class repeated.

After having satisfied herself by dividing the lichis unequally among the babies, that they might understand the difference between a singular and a plural number, Miss Mason began a catechism on the features of the face. Nose, eyes, lips, and cheeks were properly named, but the class was mute when it came to the forehead.

"What is this?" Miss Mason repeated, posing her finger on the fore part of her head.

"Me say, me say," piped a shrill voice, and the new pupil stepped to the front, and touching the forehead of the nearest child with the tips of her fingers, christened it "one," named the next in like fashion "two," a third "three," then solemnly pronounced the fourth a "four head."

Thus Ku Yum made her début in school, and thus began the trials and tribulations of her teacher.

Ku Yum was bright and learned easily, but she seemed to be possessed with the very spirit of mischief; to obey orders was to her an impossibility, and though she entered the school a voluntary pupil, one day at least out of every week found her a truant.

"Where is Ku Yum?" Miss Mason would ask on some particularly alluring morning, and a little girl, with the air of one testifying to having seen

a murder committed, would reply: "She is running around with the boys."
Then the rest of the class would settle themselves back in their seats like a
jury that has found a prisoner guilty of some heinous offense, and, judging
by the expression on their faces, were repeating a silent prayer somewhat
in the strain of "O Lord, I thank thee that I am not as Ku Yum is!" For the
other pupils were demure little maidens who, after once being gathered
into the fold, were very willing to remain.

But if ever the teacher broke her heart over any one it was over Ku Yum.
When she first came she took an almost unchildlike interest in the rules
and regulations, even at times asking to have them repeated to her; but
her study of such rules seemed only for the purpose of finding a means to
break them, and that means she never failed to discover and put into effect.

After a disappearance of a day or so she would reappear bearing a gor-
geous bunch of flowers. These she would deposit on Miss Mason's desk
with a little bow; and though one would have thought that the sweet-
ness of the gift and the apparent sweetness of the giver needed but a gra-
cious acknowledgment, something like the following conversation would
ensue:

"Teacher, I plucked these flowers for you from the Garden of Heaven."
(They were stolen from some park.)

"Oh, Ku Yum, whatever shall I do with you?"

"Maybe you better see my father."

"You are a naughty girl. You shall be punished. Take those flowers
away."

"Teacher, the eyebrow over your little eye is very pretty."

But the child was most exasperating when visitors were present. As
she was one of the brightest scholars, Miss Mason naturally expected her
to reflect credit on the school at the examinations. On one occasion she
requested her to say some verses which the little Chinese girl could re-
peat as well as any young American, and with more expression than most.
Great was the teacher's chagrin when Ku Yum hung her head and said
only: "Me 'shamed, me 'shamed!"

"Poor little thing," murmured the bishop's wife. "She is too shy to recite
in public."

But Miss Mason, knowing that of all children Ku Yum was the least
troubled with shyness, was exceedingly annoyed.

Ku Yum had been with Miss Mason about a year when she became convinced that some steps would have to be taken to discipline the child, for after school hours she simply ran wild on the streets of Chinatown, with boys for companions. She felt that she had a duty to perform toward the motherless little girl; and as the father, when apprised of the fact that his daughter was growing up in ignorance of all home duties, and, worse than that, shared the sports of boy children on the street, only shrugged his shoulders and drawled, "Too bad, too bad!" she determined to act.

She interested in Ku Yum's case the president of the Society for the Prevention of Cruelty to Children, the matron of the Rescue Home, and the most influential ministers, and the result, after a month's work, was that an order went forth from the Superior Court of the State decreeing that Ku Yum, the child of Ten Suie, should be removed from the custody of her father, and, under the auspices of the Society for the Prevention of Cruelty to Children, be put into a home for Chinese girls in San Francisco.

Her object being accomplished, strange to say, Miss Mason did not experience that peaceful content which usually follows a benevolent action. Instead, the question as to whether, after all, it was right, under the circumstances, to deprive a father of the society of his child, and a child of the love and care of a parent, disturbed her mind morning, noon, and night. What had previously seemed her distinct duty no longer appeared so, and she began to wish with all her heart that she had not interfered in the matter.

Ku Yum had not been seen for weeks, and those who were deputed to bring her into the sheltering home were unable to find her. It was suspected that the little thing purposely kept out of the way—no difficult matter, all Chinatown being in sympathy with her and arrayed against Miss Mason. Where formerly the teacher had met with smiles and pleased greetings, she now beheld averted faces and downcast eyes, and her school had within a week dwindled from twenty-four scholars to four. Verily, though acting with the best of intentions, she had shown a lack of diplomacy.

It was about nine o'clock in the evening. She had been visiting little Lae Choo, who was lying low with typhoid fever. As she wended her way home through Chinatown, she did not feel at all easy in mind; indeed, as she passed one of the most unsavory corners and observed some men frown and mutter among themselves as they recognized her, she lost her dignity in a little run. As she stopped to take breath, she felt her skirt pulled from behind and heard a familiar little voice say:

"Teacher, be you afraid?"

"Oh, Ku Yum," she exclaimed, "is that you?" Then she added reprovingly: "Do you think it is right for a little Chinese girl to be out alone at this time of the night?"

"I be not alone," replied the little creature, and in the gloom Miss Mason could distinguish behind her two boyish figures. She shook her head.

"Ku Yum, will you promise me that you will try to be a good little girl?" she asked.

Ku Yum answered solemnly:

"Ku Yum *never* be a good girl."

Her heart hardened. After all, it was best that the child should be placed where she would be compelled to behave herself.

"Come see my father," said Ku Yum, pleadingly.

Her voice was soft, and her expression was so subdued that the teacher could hardly believe that the moment before she had defiantly stated that she would never be a good girl. She paused irresolutely. Should she make one more appeal to the parent to make her a promise which would be a good excuse for restraining the order of the court? Ah, if he only would, and she only could prevent the carrying out of that order!

They found Ten Suie among his curiosities, smoking a very long pipe with a very small ivory bowl. He calmly surveyed the teacher through a pair of gold-rimmed goggles, and when under such scrutiny it was hard indeed for her to broach the subject that was on her mind. However, after admiring the little carved animals, jars, vases, bronzes, dishes, pendants, charms, and snuff-boxes displayed in his handsome show-case, she took courage.

"Mr. Ten Suie," she began, "I have come to speak to you about Ku Yum."

Ten Suie laid down his pipe and leaned over the counter. Under his calm exterior some strong excitement was working, for his eyes glittered exceedingly.

"Perhaps you speak too much about Ku Yum alleady," he said. "Ku Yum be my child. I bling him up as I please. Now, teacher, I tell you something. One, two, three, four, five, six, seven, eight, nine years go by, I have five boy. One, two, three, four, five, six, seven years go by, I have four boy. One, two, three, four, five, six years go by, I have one boy. Every year for three year evil spirit come, look at my boy, and take him. Well, one, two, three, four, five, six years go by, I see but one boy, he four year old. I say to me, Ten Suie, evil spirit be jealous. I be 'flaid he want my one boy. So I take my one boy. I dless him like one girl. Evil spirit think him one girl, and go away; no want girl."

Ten Suie ceased speaking, and settled back into his seat.

For some minutes Miss Mason stood uncomprehending. Then the full meaning of Ten Suie's words dawned upon her, and she turned to Ku Yum, and taking the child's little hand in hers, said:

"Good-by, Ku Yum. Your father, by passing you off as a girl, thought to keep an evil spirit away from you; but just by that means he brought another, and one which nearly took you from him, too."

"Good-by, teacher," said Ku Yum, smiling wistfully. "I never be good girl, but perhaps I be good boy."

SOURCES

Sui Sin Far. "A Chinese Boy-Girl." *Century Magazine* 67, no. 6 (April 1904): 828–31.
———. "A Chinese Ishmael." *Overland Monthly* 34, no. 199 (July 1899): 43–49.

NOTE

Chapter opening photo: Sui Sin Far, ca. 1895–1914. From the private collection of Diana Birchall, granddaughter of Winnifred Eaton.

Fanny Fern

1811–1872

FANNY FERN, born Sara Payson Willis, was the highest-paid newspaper columnist in the United States by 1855. Known for her conversational style and ability to connect with her primarily middle-aged, female readers, she also wrote children's books and two novels, including *Ruth Hall*, which is based on her own life and her struggle to support herself and her family through journalism after her husband's death. Fern championed literature that was considered ahead of its time throughout her career, and cofounded Sorosis, the first major club for women writers and artists in New York City.

From *Ruth Hall: A Domestic Tale of the Present Time* (1855)

CHAPTER LXIV.

"I have good news for you," said Mr. Lescom to Ruth, at her next weekly visit; "your very first articles are copied, I see, into many of my exchanges, even into the ——, which seldom contains anything but politics. A good sign for you, Mrs. Hall; a good test of your popularity."

Ruth's eyes sparkled, and her whole face glowed.

"Ladies *like* to be praised," said Mr. Lescom, good-humoredly, with a mischievous smile.

"Oh, it is not that—not that, sir," said Ruth, with a sudden moistening of the eye, "it is because it will be bread for my children."

Mr. Lescom checked his mirthful mood, and said, "Well, here is something good for me, too; a letter from Missouri, in which the writer says, that if "Floy" (a pretty *nom-de-plume* that of yours, Mrs. Hall) is to be a contributor for the coming year, I may put him down as a subscriber, as well as S. Jones, E. May, and J. Noyes, all of the same place. That's good news for *me*, you see," said Mr. Lescom, with one of his pleasant, beaming smiles.

"Yes," replied Ruth, abstractedly. She was wondering if her articles were to be the means of swelling Mr. Lescom's subscription list, whether *she* ought not to profit by it as well as himself, and whether she should not ask him to increase her pay. She pulled her gloves off and on, and finally mustered courage to clothe her thought in words.

"Now that's *just* like a woman," replied Mr. Lescom, turning it off with a joke; "give them the least foot-hold, and they will want the whole territory. Had I not shown you that letter, you would have been quite contented with your present pay. Ah! I see it won't do to talk so unprofessionally to you; and you needn't expect," said he, smiling, "that I shall ever speak of letters containing new subscribers on your account. I could easily get you the offer of a handsome salary by publishing such things. No—no, I have been foolish enough to lose two or three valuable contributors in that way; I have learned better than that, 'Floy';" and taking out his purse, he paid Ruth the usual sum for her articles.

Ruth bowed courteously, and put the money in her purse; but she sighed as she went down the office stairs. Mr. Lescom's view of the case was a business one, undoubtedly; and the same view that almost any other business man would have taken, viz.: to retain her at her present low rate of compensation, till he was necessitated to raise it by a higher bid from a rival quarter. And so she must plod wearily on till that time came, and poor Katy must still be an exile; for she had not enough to feed her, her landlady having raised the rent of her room two shillings, and Ruth being unable to find cheaper accommodations. It was hard, but what could be done? Ruth believed she had exhausted all the offices she knew of. Oh! there was one, *The Pilgrim*; she had not tried there. She would call at the office on her way home.

The editor of *The Pilgrim* talked largely. He had, now, plenty of contributors; he didn't know about employing a new one. Had she ever written? and what had she written? Ruth showed him her article in the last number of *The Standard*.

"Oh—hum—hum!" said Mr. Tibbetts, changing his tone; "so you are 'Floy,' are you?" (casting his eyes on her.) "What pay do they give you over there?"

Ruth was a novice in business-matters, but she had strong common sense, and that common sense said, he has no right to ask you that question; don't you tell him; so she replied with dignity, "My bargain, sir, with Mr. Lescom was a private one, I believe."

"Hum," said the foiled Mr. Tibbetts; adding in an under-tone to his partner, "sharp that!"

"Well, if I conclude to engage you," said Mr. Tibbetts, "I should prefer you would write for me over a different signature than the one by which your pieces are indicated at *The Standard* office, or you can write exclusively for my paper."

"With regard to your first proposal," said Ruth, "if I have gained any reputation by my first efforts, it appears to me that I should be foolish to throw it away by the adoption of another signature; and with regard to the last, I have no objection to writing exclusively for you, if you will make it worth my while."

"Sharp again," whispered Tibbetts to his partner.

The two editors then withdrawing into a further corner of the office, a whispered consultation followed, during which Ruth heard the words, "Can't afford it, Tom; hang it! we are head over ears in debt now to that paper man; good articles though—deuced good—must have her if we dispense with some of our other contributors. We had better begin low though, as to terms, for she'll go up now like a rocket, and when she finds out her value we shall have to increase her pay, you know."

(Thank you, gentlemen, thought Ruth, when the cards change hands, I'll take care to return the compliment.)

In pursuance of Mr. Tibbetts' shrewd resolution, he made known his "exclusive" terms to Ruth, which were no advance upon her present rate of pay at *The Standard*. This offer being declined, they made her another, in which, since she would not consent to do otherwise, they agreed she should write over her old signature, "Floy," furnishing them with two articles a week.

Ruth accepted the terms, poor as they were, because she could at present do no better, and because every pebble serves to swell the current.

Months passed away, while Ruth hoped and toiled, "Floy's" fame as a writer increasing much faster than her remuneration. There was rent-room to pay, little shoes and stockings to buy, oil, paper, pens, and ink to find; and now autumn had come, she could not write with stiffened fingers, and wood and coal were ruinously high, so that even with this new addition to her labor, Ruth seemed to retrograde pecuniarily, instead of advancing; and Katy still away! She must work harder—harder. Good, brave little Katy; she, too, was bearing and hoping on—mamma had promised, if she would stay there, patiently, she would certainly take her away just as soon as she had earned money enough; and mamma *never* broke her promise—*never*; and Katy prayed to God every night, with childish trust, to help her mother to earn money, that she might soon go home again.

And so, while Ruth scribbled away in her garret, the public were busying themselves in conjecturing who "Floy" might be. Letters poured in upon Mr. Lescom, with their inquiries, even bribing him with the offer to procure a certain number of subscribers, if he would divulge her real name; to all of which the old man, true to his promise to Ruth, to keep her secret inviolate, turned a deaf ear. All sorts of rumors became rife about "Floy," some maintaining her to be a man, because she had the courage to call things by their right names, and the independence to express herself boldly on subjects which to the timid and clique-serving, were tabooed. Some said she was a disappointed old maid; some said she was a designing widow; some said she was a moon-struck girl; and all said she was a nondescript. Some tried to imitate her, and failing in this, abused and maligned her; the outwardly strait-laced and inwardly corrupt, puckered up their mouths and "blushed for her;" the hypocritical denounced the sacrilegious fingers which had dared to touch the Ark; the fashionist voted her a vulgar, plebeian thing; and the earnest and sorrowing, to whose burdened hearts she had given voice, cried God speed her. And still "Floy" scribbled on, thinking only of bread for her children, laughing and crying behind her mask,—laughing all the more when her heart was heaviest; but of this her readers knew little and would have cared less. Still her little bark breasted the billows, now rising high on the topmost wave, now merged in the shadows, but still steering with straining sides, and a heart of oak, for the nearing port of Independence.

Ruth's brother, Hyacinth, saw "Floy's" articles floating through his exchanges with marked dissatisfaction and uneasiness. That she should have succeeded in any degree without his assistance, was a puzzle, and the premonitory symptoms of her popularity, which his weekly exchanges furnished, in the shape of commendatory notices, were gall and wormwood to him. *Something* must be done, and that immediately. Seizing his pen, he despatched a letter to Mrs. Millet, which he requested her to read to Ruth, alluding very contemptuously to Ruth's articles, and begging her to use her influence with Ruth to desist from scribbling, and seek some other employment. What employment, he did not condescend to state; in fact, it was a matter of entire indifference to him, provided she did not cross his track. Ruth listened to the contents of the letter, with the old bitter smile, and went on writing.

[. . .]

CHAPTER LXXVII.

And now our heroine had become a regular business woman. She did not even hear the whir—whir of the odd lodger in the attic. The little room was littered with newspapers, envelopes, letters opened and unopened, answered and waiting to be answered. One minute she might be seen sitting, pen in hand, trying, with knit brows, to decipher some horrible cabalistic printer's mark on the margin of her proof; then writing an article for Mr. Walter, then scribbling a business letter to her publishers, stopping occasionally to administer a sedative to Nettie, in the shape of a timely quotation from Mother Goose, or to heal a fracture in a doll's leg or arm. Now she was washing a little soiled face, or smoothing little rumpled ringlets, replacing a missing shoe-string or pinafore button, then wading through the streets while Boreas contested stoutly for her umbrella, with parcels and letters to the post-office, (for Ruth must be her own servant,) regardless of gutters or thermometers, regardless of jostling or crowding. What cared she for all these, when Katy would soon be back—poor little patient, suffering Katy? Ruth felt as if wings were growing from her shoulders. She never was weary, or sleepy, or hungry. She had not the slightest idea, till long after, what an incredible amount of labor she accomplished, or how her *mother's heart* was goading her on.

"Pressing business that Mis. Hall must have," said her landlady, with a sneer, as Ruth stood her dripping umbrella in the kitchen sink. "Pressing business, running round to offices and the like of that, in such a storm as this. You wouldn't catch me doing it if I was a widder. I hope I'd have more regard for appearances. I don't understand all this flying in and out, one minute up in her room, the next in the street, forty times a day, and letters by the wholesale. It will take me to inquire into it. It may be all right, hope it is; but of course I like to know what is going on in my house. This Mis. Hall is so terrible close-mouthed, I don't like it. I've thought a dozen times I'd like to ask her right straight out who and what she is, and done with it; but I have not forgotten that little matter about the pills, and when I see her, there's something about her, she's civil enough too, that seems to say, 'don't you cross that chalk-mark, Sally Waters.' I never had lodgers afore like her and that old Bond, up in the garret. They are as much alike as two peas. *She* goes scratch—scratch—scratch; *he* goes whir—whir—whir. They haint spoke a word to one another since that child was sick. It's enough to drive anybody mad, to have such a mystery in the house. I can't make head nor tail on't. John, now, he don't care a rush-light about it; no more he wouldn't, if the top of the house was to blow off; but there's nothing plagues me like it, and yet I aint a bit curous nuther. Well, neither she nor Bond make me any trouble, there's that in it;

if they did I wouldn't stand it. And as long as they both pay their bills so reg'lar, I shan't make a fuss; I *should* like to know though what Mis. Hall is about all the time."

Publication day came at last. There was *the* book. Ruth's book! Oh, how few of its readers, if it were fortunate enough to find readers, would know how much of her own heart's history was there laid bare. Yes, there was the book. She could recall the circumstances under which each separate article was written. Little shoeless feet were covered with the proceeds of this; a little medicine, or a warmer shawl was bought with that. This was written, faint and fasting, late into the long night; that composed while walking wearily to or from the offices where she was employed. One was written with little Nettie sleeping in her lap; another still, a mirthful, merry piece, as an escape-valve for a wretched heartache. Each had its own little history. Each would serve, in after-days, for a land-mark to some thorny path of by-gone trouble. Oh, if the sun of prosperity, after all, should gild these rugged paths! Some virtues—many faults—the book had—but God speed it, for little Katy's sake!

"Let me see, please," said little Nettie, attracted by the gilt covers, as she reached out her hand for the book.

"Did you make those pretty pictures, mamma?"

"No, my dear—a gentleman, an artist, made those for me—*I* make pictures with a-b-c's."

"Show me one of your pictures, mamma," said Nettie.

Ruth took the child upon her lap, and read her the story of Gertrude. Nettie listened with her clear eyes fixed upon her mother's face.

"Don't make her die—oh, please don't make her die, mamma," exclaimed the sensitive child, laying her little hand over her mother's mouth.

Ruth smiled, and improvised a favorable termination to her story, more suitable to her tender-hearted audience.

"That is nice," said Nettie, kissing her mother; "when I get to be a woman shall I write books, mamma?"

"God forbid," murmured Ruth, kissing the child's changeful cheek; "God forbid," murmured she, musingly, as she turned over the leaves of her book; "no happy woman ever writes. From Harry's grave sprang 'Floy.'"

SOURCE

Fern, Fanny. *Ruth Hall: A Domestic Tale of the Present Time*, 250–56, 330–33. New York: Mason Brothers, 1855.

NOTE

Chapter opening photo: Fanny Fern, ca. 1866. Library of Congress, Prints & Photographs Division, LC-USZ62-113065.

Charlotte Perkins Gilman

1860–1935

CHARLOTTE PERKINS GILMAN—a feminist, political theorist, and social activist who called for women to gain economic independence—is probably best known today for her story "The Yellow Wall-paper" (1892), inspired by her own experience with postpartum depression. The author of a great deal of poetry, fiction, and essays, Gilman published much of her work in *The Forerunner*, a magazine focused on women's issues and social reform, which she established, edited, and for seven years wrote single-handedly. Though radically progressive, some of Gilman's views, particularly her eugenical ideas, are problematic by contemporary standards. She was, however, widely considered one of the leading minds of the early twentieth-century women's movement. After being diagnosed with inoperable breast cancer, she died by suicide in 1935. Her essay "The Right to Die" (see volume 2) was published posthumously, at her request.

When I Was a Witch (1910)

If I had understood the terms of that one-sided contract with Satan, the Time of Witching would have lasted longer—you may be sure of that. But how was I to tell? It just happened, and has never happened again, though I've tried the same preliminaries as far as I could control them.

The thing began all of a sudden, one October midnight—the 30th, to be exact. It had been hot, really hot, all day, and was sultry and thunderous in the evening; no air stirring, and the whole house stewing with that ill-advised activity which always seems to move the steam radiator when it isn't wanted.

I was in a state of simmering rage—hot enough, even without the weather and the furnace—and I went up on the roof to cool off. A top-floor apartment has that advantage, among others—you can take a walk without the mediation of an elevator boy!

There are things enough in New York to lose one's temper over at the best of times, and on this particular day they seemed to all happen at once, and some fresh ones. The night before, cats and dogs had broken my rest, of course. My morning paper was more than usually mendacious; and my neighbor's morning paper—more visible than my own as I went down town—was more than usually salacious. My cream wasn't cream—my egg was a relic of the past. My "new" napkins were giving out.

Being a woman, I'm supposed not to swear; but when the motorman disregarded my plain signal, and grinned as he rushed by; when the sub-way guard waited till I was just about to step on board and then slammed the door in my face—standing behind it calmly for some minutes before the bell rang to warrant his closing—I desired to swear like a mule-driver.

At night it was worse. The way people paw one's back in the crowd! The cow-puncher who packs the people in or jerks them out—the men who smoke and spit, law or no law—the women whose saw-edged cart-wheel hats, swashing feathers and deadly pins, add so to one's comfort inside.

Well, as I said, I was in a particularly bad temper, and went up on the roof to cool off. Heavy black clouds hung low overhead, and lightning flickered threateningly here and there.

A starved, black cat stole from behind a chimney and mewed dolefully. Poor thing! She had been scalded.

The street was quiet for New York. I leaned over a little and looked up and down the long parallels of twinkling lights. A belated cab drew near, the horse so tired he could hardly hold his head up.

Then the driver, with a skill born of plenteous practice, flung out his long-lashed whip and curled it under the poor beast's belly with a stinging cut that made me shudder. The horse shuddered too, poor wretch, and jingled his harness with an effort at a trot.

I leaned over the parapet and watched that man with a spirit of unmitigated ill-will.

"I wish," said I, slowly—and I did wish it with all my heart—"that every person who strikes or otherwise hurts a horse unnecessarily, shall feel the pain intended—and the horse not feel it!"

It did me good to say it, anyhow, but I never expected any result. I saw the man swing his great whip again, and—lay on heartily. I saw him throw up his hands—heard him scream—but I never thought what the matter was, even then.

The lean, black cat, timid but trustful, rubbed against my skirt and mewed.

"Poor Kitty" I said; "poor Kitty! It is a shame!" And I thought tenderly of all the thousands of hungry, hunted cats who stink and suffer in a great city.

Later, when I tried to sleep, and up across the stillness rose the raucous shrieks of some of these same sufferers, my pity turned cold. "Any fool that will try to keep a cat in a city!" I muttered, angrily.

Another yell—a pause—an ear-torturing, continuous cry. "I wish," I burst forth, "that every cat in the city was comfortably dead!"

A sudden silence fell, and in course of time I got to sleep.

Things went fairly well next morning, till I tried another egg. They were expensive eggs, too.

"I can't help it!" said my sister, who keeps house.

"I know you can't," I admitted. "But somebody could help it. I wish the people who are responsible had to eat their old eggs, and never get a good one till they sold good ones!"

"They'd stop eating eggs, that's all," said my sister, "and eat meat."

"Let 'em eat meat!" I said, recklessly. "The meat is as bad as the eggs! It's so long since we've had a clean, fresh chicken that I've forgotten how they taste!"

"It's cold storage," said my sister. She is a peaceable sort; I'm not.

"Yes, cold storage!" I snapped. "It ought to be a blessing—to tide over shortages, equalize supplies, and lower prices. What does it do? Corner the market, raise prices the year round, and make all the food bad!"

My anger rose. "If there was any way of getting at them!" I cried. "The law don't touch 'em. They need to be cursed somehow! I'd like to do it! I wish the whole crowd that profit by this vicious business might taste their bad meat, their old fish, their stale milk—whatever they ate. Yes, and feel the prices as we do!"

"They couldn't you know; they're rich," said my sister.

"I know that," I admitted, sulkily. "There's no way of getting at 'em. But I wish they could. And I wish they knew how people hated 'em, and felt that, too—till they mended their ways!"

When I left for my office I saw a funny thing. A man who drove a garbage cart took his horse by the bits and jerked and wrenched brutally. I was amazed to see him clap his hands to his own jaws with a moan, while the horse philosophically licked his chops and looked at him.

The man seemed to resent his expression, and struck him on the head, only to rub his own poll and swear amazedly, looking around to see who had hit him. The horse advanced a step, stretching a hungry nose toward a garbage pail crowned with cabbage leaves, and the man, recovering his sense of proprietorship, swore at him and kicked him in the ribs. That time he had to sit down, turning pale and weak. I watched with growing wonder and delight.

A market wagon came clattering down the street; the hard-faced young ruffian fresh for his morning task. He gathered the ends of the reins and brought them down on the horse's back with a resounding thwack. The horse did not notice this at all, but the boy did. He yelled!

I came to a place where many teamsters were at work hauling dirt and crushed stone. A strange silence and peace hung over the scene where usually the sound of the lash and sight of brutal blows made me hurry by. The men were talking together a little, and seemed to be exchanging notes. It was too good to be true. I gazed and marvelled, waiting for my car.

It came, merrily running along. It was not full. There was one not far ahead, which I had missed in watching the horses; there was no other near it in the rear.

Yet the coarse-faced person in authority who ran it, went gaily by without stopping, though I stood on the track almost, and waved my umbrella.

A hot flush of rage surged to my face. "I wish you felt the blow you deserve," said I, viciously, looking after the car. "I wish you'd have to stop, and back to here, and open the door and apologize. I wish that would happen to all of you, every time you play that trick."

To my infinite amazement, that car stopped and backed till the front door was before me. The motorman opened it, holding his hand to his cheek. "Beg your pardon, madam!" he said.

I passed in, dazed, overwhelmed. Could it be? Could it possibly be that—that what I wished came true. The idea sobered me, but I dismissed it with a scornful smile. "No such luck!" said I.

Opposite me sat a person in petticoats. She was of a sort I particularly detest. No real body of bones and muscles, but the contours of grouped sausages. Complacent, gaudily dressed, heavily wigged and ratted, with powder and perfume and flowers and jewels—and a dog.

A poor, wretched, little, artificial dog—alive, but only so by virtue of man's insolence; not a real creature that God made. And the dog had clothes on—and a bracelet! His fitted jacket had a pocket—and a pocket-handkerchief! He looked sick and unhappy.

I meditated on his pitiful position, and that of all the other poor chained prisoners, leading unnatural lives of enforced celibacy, cut off from sunlight, fresh air, the use of their limbs; led forth at stated intervals by unwilling servants, to defile our streets; over-fed, under-exercised, nervous and unhealthy.

"And we say we love them!" said I, bitterly to myself. "No wonder they bark and howl and go mad. No wonder they have almost as many diseases as we do! I wish—" Here the thought I had dismissed struck me again. "I wish that all the unhappy dogs in cities would die at once!"

I watched the sad-eyed little invalid across the car. He dropped his head and died. She never noticed it till she got off; then she made fuss enough.

The evening papers were full of it. Some sudden pestilence had struck both dogs and cats, it would appear. Red headlines struck the eye, big letters, and columns were filled out of the complaints of those who had lost their "pets," of the sudden labors of the board of health, and interviews with doctors.

All day, as I went through the office routine, the strange sense of this new power struggled with reason and common knowledge. I even tried a few furtive test "wishes"—wished that the waste basket would fall over, that the inkstand would fill itself; but they didn't.

I dismissed the idea as pure foolishness, till I saw those newspapers, and heard people telling worse stories.

One thing I decided at once—not to tell a soul. "Nobody'd believe me if I did," said I to myself. "And I won't give 'em the chance. I've scored on cats and dogs, anyhow—and horses."

As I watched the horses at work that afternoon, and thought of all their unknown sufferings from crowded city stables, bad air and insufficient food, and from the wearing strain of asphalt pavements in wet and icy weather, I decided to have another try on horses.

"I wish," said I, slowly and carefully, but with a fixed intensity of purposes, "that every horse owner, keeper, hirer and driver or rider, might feel what the horse feels, when he suffers at our hands. Feel it keenly and constantly till the case is mended."

I wasn't able to verify this attempt for some time; but the effect was so general that it got widely talked about soon; and this "new wave of humane feeling" soon raised the status of horses in our city. Also it diminished their numbers. People began to prefer motor drays—which was a mighty good thing.

Now I felt pretty well assured in my own mind, and kept my assurance to my self. Also I began to make a list of my cherished grudges, with a fine sense of power and pleasure.

"I must be careful," I said to myself; "very careful; and, above all things, make the punishment fit the crime."

The subway crowding came to my mind next; both the people who crowd because they have to, and the people who make them. "I mustn't punish anybody, for what they can't help," I mused. "But when it's pure meanness!" Then I bethought me of the remote stockholders, of the more immediate directors, of the painfully prominent officials and insolent employees—and got to work.

"I might as well make a good job of it while this lasts," said I to myself. "It's quite a responsibility, but lots of fun." And I wished that every person responsible for the condition of our subways might be mysteriously compelled to ride up and down in them continuously during rush hours.

This experiment I watched with keen interest, but for the life of me I could see little difference. There were a few more well-dressed persons in the crowds, that was all. So I came to the conclusion that the general public was mostly to blame, and carried their daily punishment without knowing it.

For the insolent guards and cheating ticket-sellers who give you short change, very slowly, when you are dancing on one foot and your train is there, I merely wished that they might feel the pain their victims would like to give them, short of real injury. They did, I guess.

Then I wished similar things for all manner of corporations and officials. It worked. It worked amazingly. There was a sudden conscientious revival all over the country. The dry bones rattled and sat up. Boards of directors, having troubles enough of their own, were aggravated by innumerable communications from suddenly sensitive stockholders.

In mills and mints and railroads, things began to mend. The country buzzed. The papers fattened. The churches sat up and took credit to themselves. I was incensed at this; and, after brief consideration, wished that every minister would preach to his congregation exactly what he believed and what he thought of them.

I went to six services the next Sunday—about ten minutes each, for two sessions. It was most amusing. A thousand pulpits were emptied forthwith, refilled, re-emptied, and so on, from week to week. People began to go to church; men largely—women didn't like it as well. They had always supposed the ministers thought more highly of them than now appeared to be the case.

One of my oldest grudges was against the sleeping-car people; and now I began to consider them. How often I had grinned and borne it—with other thousands—submitting helplessly.

Here is a railroad—a common carrier—and you have to use it. You pay for your transportation, a good round sum.

Then if you wish to stay in the sleeping car during the day, they charge you another two dollars and a half for the privilege of sitting there, whereas you have paid for a seat when you bought your ticket. That seat is now sold to another person—twice sold! Five dollars for twenty-four hours in a space six feet by three by three at night, and one seat by day; twenty-four of these privileges to a car—$120 a day for the rent of the car—and the passengers to pay the porter besides. That makes $44,800 a year.

Sleeping cars are expensive to build, they say. So are hotels; but they do not charge at such a rate. Now, what could I do to get even? Nothing could ever put back the dollars into the millions of pockets; but it might be stopped now, this beautiful process.

So I wished that all persons who profited by this performance might feel a shame so keen that they would make public avowal and apology, and, as partial restitution, offer their wealth to promote the cause of free railroads!

Then I remembered parrots. This was lucky, for my wrath flamed again. It was really cooling, as I tried to work out responsibility and adjust penalties. But parrots! Any person who wants to keep a parrot should go and live on an island alone with their preferred conversationalist!

There was a huge, squawky parrot right across the street from me, adding its senseless, rasping cries to the more necessary evils of other noises.

I had also an aunt with a parrot. She was a wealthy, ostentatious person, who had been an only child and inherited her money.

Uncle Joseph hated the yelling bird, but that didn't make any difference to Aunt Matilda.

I didn't like this aunt, and wouldn't visit her, lest she think I was truckling for the sake of her money; but after I had wished this time, I called at the time set for my curse to work; and it did work with a vengeance. There sat poor Uncle Joe, looking thinner and meeker than ever; and my aunt, like an overripe plum, complacent enough.

"Let me out!" said Polly, suddenly. "Let me out to take a walk!"

"The clever thing!" said Aunt Matilda. "He never said that before."

She let him out. Then he flapped up on the chandelier and sat among the prisms, quite safe.

"What an old pig you are, Matilda!" said the parrot.

She started to her feet—naturally.

"Born a Pig—trained a Pig—a Pig by nature and education!" said the parrot. "Nobody'd put up with you, except for your money; unless it's this long-suffering husband of yours. He wouldn't, if he hadn't the patience of Job!"

"Hold your tongue!" screamed Aunt Matilda. "Come down from there! Come here!"

Polly cocked his head and jingled the prisms. "Sit down, Matilda!" he said, cheerfully. "You've got to listen. You are fat and homely and selfish.

You are a nuisance to everybody about you. You have got to feed me and take care of me better than ever—and you've got to listen to me when I talk. Pig!"

I visited another person with a parrot the next day. She put a cloth over his cage when I came in.

"Take it off!" said Polly. She took it off.

"Won't you come into the other room?" she asked me, nervously.

"Better stay here!" said her pet. "Sit still—sit still!"

She sat still.

"Your hair is mostly false," said pretty Poll. "And your teeth—and your outlines. You eat too much. You are lazy. You ought to exercise, and don't know enough. Better apologize to this lady for backbiting! You've got to listen."

The trade in parrots fell off from that day; they say there is no call for them. But the people who kept parrots, keep them yet—parrots live a long time.

Bores were a class of offenders against whom I had long borne undying enmity. Now I rubbed my hands and began on them, with this simple wish: That every person whom they bored should tell them the plain truth.

There is one man whom I have specially in mind. He was blackballed at a pleasant club, but continues to go there. He isn't a member—he just goes; and no one does anything to him.

It was very funny after this. He appeared that very night at a meeting, and almost every person present asked him how he came there. "You're not a member, you know," they said. "Why do you butt in? Nobody likes you."

Some were more lenient with him. "Why don't you learn to be more considerate of others, and make some real friends?" they said. "To have a few friends who do enjoy your visits ought to be pleasanter than being a public nuisance."

He disappeared from that club, anyway.

I began to feel very cocky indeed.

In the food business there was already a marked improvement; and in transportation. The hubbub of reformation waxed louder daily, urged on by the unknown sufferings of all the profiters by iniquity.

The papers thrived on all this; and as I watched the loud-voiced protestations of my pet abomination in journalism, I had a brilliant idea, literally.

Next morning I was down town early, watching the men open their papers. My abomination was shamefully popular, and never more so than this morning. Across the top was printing in gold letters:

All intentional lies, in adv., editorial, news, or any other
    column......Scarlet
All malicious matter......Crimson
All careless or ignorant mistakes......Pink
All for direct self-interest of owner......Dark green
All mere bait—to sell the paper......Bright green
All advertising, primary or secondary......Brown
All sensational and salacious matter......Yellow
All hired hypocrisy......Purple
Good fun, instruction and entertainment......Blue
True and necessary news and honest editorials......
    Ordinary print

You never saw such a crazy quilt of a paper. They were bought like hot cakes for some days; but the real business fell off very soon. They'd have stopped it all if they could; but the papers looked all right when they came off the press. The color scheme flamed out only to the bona-fide reader.

I let this work for about a week, to the immense joy of all the other papers; and then turned it on to them, all at once. Newspaper reading became very exciting for a little, but the trade fell off. Even newspaper editors could not keep on feeding a market like that. The blue printed and ordinary printed matter grew from column to column and page to page. Some papers—small, to be sure, but refreshing—began to appear in blue and black alone.

This kept me interested and happy for quite a while; so much so that I quite forgot to be angry at other things. There was *such* a change in all kinds of business, following the mere printing of truth in the newspapers. It began to appear as if we had lived in a sort of delirium—not really knowing the facts about anything. As soon as we really knew the facts, we began to behave very differently, of course.

What really brought all my enjoyment to an end was women. Being a woman, I was naturally interested in them, and could see some things more clearly than men could. I saw their real power, their real dignity, their real responsibility in the world; and then the way they dress and be-have used to make me fairly frantic. 'Twas like seeing archangels playing jackstraws—or real horses only used as rocking-horses. So I determined to get after them.

How to manage it! What to hit first! Their hats, their ugly, inane, out-rageous hats—that is what one thinks of first. Their silly, expensive clothes—their diddling beads and jewelry—their greedy childishness—mostly of the women provided for by rich men.

Then I thought of all the other women, the real ones, the vast majority, patiently doing the work of servants without even a servant's pay—and neglecting the noblest duties of motherhood in favor of house-service; the greatest power on earth, blind, chained, untaught, in a treadmill. I thought of what they might do, compared to what they did do, and my heart swelled with something that was far from anger.

Then I wished—with all my strength—that women, all women, might realize Womanhood at last; its power and pride and place in life; that they might see their duty as mothers of the world—to love and care for every-one alive; that they might see their duty to men—to choose only the best, and then to bear and rear better ones; that they might see their duty as human beings, and come right out into full life and work and happiness!

I stopped, breathless, with shining eyes. I waited, trembling, for things to happen.

Nothing happened.

You see, this magic which had fallen on me was black magic—and I had wished white.

It didn't work at all, and, what was worse, it stopped all the other things that were working so nicely.

Oh, if I had only thought to wish permanence for those lovely punish-ments! If only I had done more while I could do it, had half appreciated my privileges when I was a Witch!

The Socialist and the Suffragist (1910)

Said the Socialist to the Suffragist:
   "My cause is greater than yours!
     You only work for a Special Class,

We for the gain of the General Mass,
   Which every good ensures!"

Said the Suffragist to the Socialist:
   "You underrate my Cause!
      While women remain a Subject Class,
      You never can move the General Mass,
   With your Economic Laws!"

Said the Socialist to the Suffragist:
   "You misinterpret facts!
      There is no room for doubt or schism
      In Economic Determinism—
   It governs all our acts!"

Said the Suffragist to the Socialist:
   "You men will always find
      That this old world will never move
      More swiftly in its ancient groove
   While women stay behind!"

"A lifted world lifts women up,"
   The Socialist explained.
      "You cannot lift the world at all
      While half of it is kept so small,"
   The Suffragist maintained.

The world awoke, and tartly spoke:
   "Your work is all the same:
      Work together or work apart,
      Work, each of you, with all your heart—
   Just get into the game!"

From *Herland* (1915)

CHAPTER V. *A Unique History.*

It is no use for me to try to piece out this account with adventures. If the people who read it are not interested in these amazing women and their history, they will not be interested at all.

As for us—three young men to a whole landful of women—what could we do? We did get away, as described, and were peacefully brought back again without, as Terry complained, even the satisfaction of hitting anybody.

There were no adventures because there was nothing to fight. There were no wild beasts in the country and very few tame ones. Of these I might as well stop to describe the one common pet of the country. Cats, of course. But such cats!

What do you suppose these Lady Burbanks had done with their cats? By the most prolonged and careful selection and exclusion they had developed a race of cats that did not sing! That's a fact. The most those poor dumb brutes could do was to make a kind of squeak when they were hungry or wanted the door open, and, of course, to purr, and make the various mother-noises to their kittens.

Moreover, they had ceased to kill birds. They were rigorously bred to destroy mice and moles and all such enemies of the food supply; but the birds were numerous and safe.

While we were discussing birds, Terry asked them if they used feathers for their hats, and they seemed amused at the idea. He made a few sketches of our women's hats, with plumes and quills and those various tickling things that stick out so far; and they were eagerly interested, as at everything about our women.

As for them, they said they only wore hats for shade when working in the sun; and those were big light straw hats, something like those used in China and Japan. In cold weather they wore caps or hoods.

"But for decorative purposes—don't you think they would be becoming?" pursued Terry, making as pretty a picture as he could of a lady with a plumed hat.

They by no means agreed to that, asking quite simply if the men wore the same kind. We hastened to assure her that they did not—drew for them our kind of headgear.

"And do no men wear feathers in their hats?"

"Only Indians," Jeff explained. "Savages, you know." And he sketched a war bonnet to show them.

"And soldiers," I added, drawing a military hat with plumes.

They never expressed horror or disapproval, nor indeed much surprise—just a keen interest. And the notes they made!—miles of them!

But to return to our pussycats. We were a good deal impressed by this achievement in breeding, and when they questioned us—I can tell you we were well pumped for information—we told of what had been done for dogs and horses and cattle, but that there was no effort applied to cats, except for show purposes.

I wish I could represent the kind, quiet, steady, ingenious way they questioned us. It was not just curiosity—they weren't a bit more curious about us than we were about them, if as much. But they were bent on understanding our kind of civilization, and their lines of interrogation would gradually surround us and drive us in till we found ourselves up against some admissions we did not want to make.

"Are all these breeds of dogs you have made useful?" they asked.

"Oh—useful! Why, the hunting dogs and watchdogs and sheepdogs are useful—and sleddogs of course!—and ratters, I suppose, but we don't keep dogs for their *usefulness*. The dog is 'the friend of man,' we say—we love them."

That they understood. "We love our cats that way. They surely are our friends, and helpers, too. You can see how intelligent and affectionate they are."

It was a fact. I'd never seen such cats, except in a few rare instances. Big, handsome silky things, friendly with everyone and devotedly attached to their special owners.

"You must have a heartbreaking time drowning kittens," we suggested. But they said, "Oh, no! You see we care for them as you do for your valuable cattle. The fathers are few compared to the mothers, just a few very fine ones in each town; they live quite happily in walled gardens and the houses of their friends. But they only have a mating season once a year."

"Rather hard on Thomas, isn't it?" suggested Terry.

"Oh, no—truly! You see, it is many centuries that we have been breeding the kind of cats we wanted. They are healthy and happy and friendly, as you see. How do you manage with your dogs? Do you keep them in pairs, or segregate the fathers, or what?"

Then we explained that—well, that it wasn't a question of fathers exactly; that nobody wanted a—a mother dog; that, well, that practically all our dogs were males—there was only a very small percentage of females allowed to live.

Then Zava, observing Terry with her grave sweet smile, quoted back at him: "Rather hard on Thomas, isn't it? Do they enjoy it—living without mates? Are your dogs as uniformly healthy and sweet-tempered as our cats?"

Jeff laughed, eyeing Terry mischievously. As a matter of fact we began to feel Jeff something of a traitor—he so often flopped over and took their side of things; also his medical knowledge gave him a different point of view somehow.

"I'm sorry to admit," he told them, "that the dog, with us, is the most diseased of any animal—next to man. And as to temper—there are always some dogs who bite people—especially children."

That was pure malice. You see, children were the—the *raison d'etre* in this country. All our interlocutors sat up straight at once. They were still gentle, still restrained, but there was a note of deep amazement in their voices.

"Do we understand that you keep an animal—an unmated male animal—that bites children? About how many are there of them, please?"

"Thousands—in a large city," said Jeff, "and nearly every family has one in the country."

Terry broke in at this. "You must not imagine they are all dangerous— it's not one in a hundred that ever bites anybody. Why, they are the best friends of the children—a boy doesn't have half a chance that hasn't a dog to play with!"

"And the girls?" asked Somel.

"Oh—girls—why they like them too," he said, but his voice flatted a little. They always noticed little things like that, we found later.

Little by little they wrung from us the fact that the friend of man, in the city, was a prisoner; was taken out for his meager exercise on a leash; was liable not only to many diseases but to the one destroying horror of rabies; and, in many cases, for the safety of the citizens, had to go muzzled. Jeff maliciously added vivid instances he had known or read of injury and death from mad dogs.

They did not scold or fuss about it. Calm as judges, those women were. But they made notes; Moadine read them to us.

"Please tell me if I have the facts correct," she said. "In your country— and in others too?"

"Yes," we admitted, "in most civilized countries."

"In most civilized countries a kind of animal is kept which is no longer useful—"

"They are a protection," Terry insisted. "They bark if burglars try to get in."

Then she made notes of "burglars" and went on: "because of the love which people bear to this animal."

Zava interrupted here. "Is it the men or the women who love this animal so much?"

"Both!" insisted Terry.

"Equally?" she inquired.

And Jeff said, "Nonsense, Terry—you know men like dogs better than women do—as a whole."

"Because they love it so much—especially men. This animal is kept shut up, or chained."

"Why?" suddenly asked Somel. "We keep our father cats shut up because we do not want too much fathering; but they are not chained—they have large grounds to run in."

"A valuable dog would be stolen if he was let loose," I said. "We put collars on them, with the owner's name, in case they do stray. Besides, they get into fights—a valuable dog might easily be killed by a bigger one."

"I see," she said. "They fight when they meet—is that common?" We admitted that it was.

"They are kept shut up, or chained." She paused again, and asked, "Is not a dog fond of running? Are they not built for speed?" That we admitted, too, and Jeff, still malicious, enlightened them further.

"I've always thought it was a pathetic sight, both ways—to see a man or a woman taking a dog to walk—at the end of a string."

"Have you bred them to be as neat in their habits as cats are?" was the next question. And when Jeff told them of the effect of dogs on sidewalk merchandise and the streets generally, they found it hard to believe.

You see, their country was as neat as a Dutch kitchen, and as to sanitation—but I might as well start in now with as much as I can remember of the history of this amazing country before further description.

And I'll summarize here a bit as to our opportunities for learning it. I will not try to repeat the careful, detailed account I lost; I'll just say that we were kept in that fortress a good six months all told, and after that, three in a pleasant enough city where—to Terry's infinite disgust—there were only "Colonels" and little children—no young women whatever. Then we were under surveillance for three more—always with a tutor or a guard or both. But those months were pleasant because we were really getting acquainted with the girls. That was a chapter!—or will be—I will try to do justice to it.

We learned their language pretty thoroughly—had to; and they learned ours much more quickly and used it to hasten our own studies.

Jeff, who was never without reading matter of some sort, had two little books with him, a novel and a little anthology of verse; and I had one of those pocket encyclopedias—a fat little thing, bursting with facts. These were used in our education—and theirs. Then as soon as we were up to it, they furnished us with plenty of their own books, and I went in for the history part—I wanted to understand the genesis of this miracle of theirs.

And this is what happened, according to their records.

As to geography—at about the time of the Christian era this land had a free passage to the sea. I'm not saying where, for good reasons. But there was a fairly easy pass through that wall of mountains behind us, and there is no doubt in my mind that these people were of Aryan stock, and were once in contact with the best civilization of the old world. They were "white," but somewhat darker than our northern races because of their constant exposure to sun and air.

The country was far larger then, including much land beyond the pass, and a strip of coast. They had ships, commerce, an army, a king—for at that time they were what they so calmly called us—a bi-sexual race.

What happened to them first was merely a succession of historic misfortunes such as have befallen other nations often enough. They were decimated by war, driven up from their coastline till finally the reduced population, with many of the men killed in battle, occupied this hinterland, and defended it for years, in the mountain passes. Where it was open to any possible attack from below they strengthened the natural defenses so that it became unscalably secure, as we found it.

They were a polygamous people, and a slave-holding people, like all of their time; and during the generation or two of this struggle to defend their mountain home they built the fortresses, such as the one we were held in, and other of their oldest buildings, some still in use. Nothing but earthquakes could destroy such architecture—huge solid blocks, holding by their own weight. They must have had efficient workmen and enough of them in those days.

They made a brave fight for their existence, but no nation can stand up against what the steamship companies call "an act of God." While the whole fighting force was doing its best to defend their mountain pathway, there occurred a volcanic outburst, with some local tremors, and the result was the complete filling up of the pass—their only outlet. Instead of a passage, a new ridge, sheer and high, stood between them and the sea; they were walled in, and beneath that wall lay their whole little army. Very few men were left alive, save the slaves; and these now seized their opportunity, rose in revolt, killed their remaining masters even to the youngest boy, killed the old women too, and the mothers, intending to take possession of the country with the remaining young women and girls.

But this succession of misfortunes was too much for those infuriated virgins. There were many of them, and but few of these would-be masters, so the young women, instead of submitting, rose in sheer desperation and slew their brutal conquerors.

This sounds like Titus Andronicus, I know, but that is their account. I suppose they were about crazy—can you blame them?

There was literally no one left on this beautiful high garden land but a bunch of hysterical girls and some older slave women.

That was about two thousand years ago.

At first there was a period of sheer despair. The mountains towered between them and their old enemies, but also between them and escape. There was no way up or down or out—they simply had to stay there. Some were for suicide, but not the majority. They must have been a plucky lot, as a whole, and they decided to live—as long as they did live. Of course they had hope, as youth must, that something would happen to change their fate.

So they set to work, to bury the dead, to plow and sow, to care for one another.

Speaking of burying the dead, I will set down while I think of it, that they had adopted cremation in about the thirteenth century, for the same reason that they had left off raising cattle—they could not spare the room. They were much surprised to learn that we were still burying—asked our reasons for it, and were much dissatisfied with what we gave. We told them of the belief in the resurrection of the body, and they asked if our

God was not as well able to resurrect from ashes as from long corruption. We told them of how people thought it repugnant to have their loved ones burn, and they asked if it was less repugnant to have them decay. They were inconveniently reasonable, those women.

Well—that original bunch of girls set to work to clean up the place and make their living as best they could. Some of the remaining slave women rendered invaluable service, teaching such trades as they knew. They had such records as were then kept, all the tools and implements of the time, and a most fertile land to work in.

There were a handful of the younger matrons who had escaped slaughter, and a few babies were born after the cataclysm—but only two boys, and they both died.

For five or ten years they worked together, growing stronger and wiser and more and more mutually attached, and then the miracle happened—one of these young women bore a child. Of course they all thought there must be a man somewhere, but none was found. Then they decided it must be a direct gift from the gods, and placed the proud mother in the Temple of Maaia—their Goddess of Motherhood—under strict watch. And there, as years passed, this wonder-woman bore child after child, five of them—all girls.

I did my best, keenly interested as I have always been in sociology and social psychology, to reconstruct in my mind the real position of these ancient women. There were some five or six hundred of them, and they were harem-bred; yet for the few preceding generations they had been reared in the atmosphere of such heroic struggle that the stock must have been toughened somewhat. Left alone in that terrific orphanhood, they had clung together, supporting one another and their little sisters, and developing unknown powers in the stress of new necessity. To this pain-hardened and work-strengthened group, who had lost not only the love and care of parents, but the hope of ever having children of their own, there now dawned the new hope.

Here at last was Motherhood, and though it was not for all of them personally, it might—if the power was inherited—found here a new race.

It may be imagined how those five Daughters of Maaia, Children of the Temple, Mothers of the Future—they had all the titles that love and hope and reverence could give—were reared. The whole little nation of women surrounded them with loving service, and waited, between a boundless hope and an equally boundless despair, to see if they, too, would be mothers.

And they were! As fast as they reached the age of twenty-five they began bearing. Each of them, like her mother, bore five daughters. Presently there were twenty-five New Women, Mothers in their own right, and the whole spirit of the country changed from mourning and mere courageous resignation to proud joy. The older women, those who remembered men, died off; the youngest of all the first lot of course died too, after a while, and by that time there were left one hundred and fifty-five parthenogenetic women, founding a new race.

They inherited all that the devoted care of that declining band of original ones could leave them. Their little country was quite safe. Their farms and gardens were all in full production. Such industries as they had were in careful order. The records of their past were all preserved, and for years the older women had spent their time in the best teaching they were capable of, that they might leave to the little group of sisters and mothers all they possessed of skill and knowledge.

There you have the start of Herland! One family, all descended from one mother! She lived to a hundred years old; lived to see her hundred and twenty-five great-granddaughters born; lived as Queen-Priestess-Mother of them all; and died with a nobler pride and a fuller joy than perhaps any human soul has ever known—she alone had founded a new race!

The first five daughters had grown up in an atmosphere of holy calm, of awed watchful waiting, of breathless prayer. To them the longed-for motherhood was not only a personal joy, but a nation's hope. Their twenty-five daughters in turn, with a stronger hope, a richer, wider outlook, with the devoted love and care of all the surviving population, grew up as a holy sisterhood, their whole ardent youth looking forward to their great office. And at last they were left alone; the white-haired First Mother was gone, and this one family, five sisters, twenty-five first cousins, and a hundred and twenty-five second cousins, began a new race.

Here you have human beings, unquestionably, but what we were slow in understanding was how these ultra-women, inheriting only from women, had eliminated not only certain masculine characteristics, which of course we did not look for, but so much of what we had always thought essentially feminine.

The tradition of men as guardians and protectors had quite died out. These stalwart virgins had no men to fear and therefore no need of protection. As to wild beasts—there were none in their sheltered land.

The power of mother-love, that maternal instinct we so highly laud, was theirs of course, raised to its highest power; and a sister-love which, even while recognizing the actual relationship, we found it hard to credit.

Terry, incredulous, even contemptuous, when we were alone, refused to believe the story. "A lot of traditions as old as Herodotus—and about as trustworthy!" he said. "It's likely women—just a pack of women—would have hung together like that! We all know women can't organize—that they scrap like anything—are frightfully jealous."

"But these New Ladies didn't have anyone to be jealous of, remember," drawled Jeff.

"That's a likely story," Terry sneered.

"Why don't you invent a likelier one?" I asked him. "Here ARE the women—nothing but women, and you yourself admit there's no trace of a man in the country." This was after we had been about a good deal.

"I'll admit that," he growled. "And it's a big miss, too. There's not only no fun without 'em—no real sport—no competition; but these women aren't *womanly*. You know they aren't."

That kind of talk always set Jeff going; and I gradually grew to side with him. "Then you don't call a breed of women whose one concern is motherhood—womanly?" he asked.

"Indeed I don't," snapped Terry. "What does a man care for motherhood —when he hasn't a ghost of a chance at fatherhood? And besides—what's the good of talking sentiment when we are just men together? What a man wants of women is a good deal more than all this 'motherhood'!"

We were as patient as possible with Terry. He had lived about nine months among the "Colonels" when he made that outburst; and with no chance at any more strenuous excitement than our gymnastics gave us— save for our escape fiasco. I don't suppose Terry had ever lived so long with neither Love, Combat, nor Danger to employ his superabundant energies, and he was irritable. Neither Jeff nor I found it so wearing. I was so much interested intellectually that our confinement did not wear on me; and as for Jeff, bless his heart!—he enjoyed the society of that tutor of his almost as much as if she had been a girl—I don't know but more.

As to Terry's criticism, it was true. These women, whose essential distinction of motherhood was the dominant note of their whole culture, were strikingly deficient in what we call "femininity." This led me very promptly to the conviction that those "feminine charms" we are so fond of are not feminine at all, but mere reflected masculinity—developed to please us because they had to please us, and in no way essential to the real fulfillment of their great process. But Terry came to no such conclusion.

"Just you wait till I get out!" he muttered.

Then we both cautioned him. "Look here, Terry, my boy! You be careful! They've been mighty good to us—but do you remember the anesthesia? If you do any mischief in this virgin land, beware of the vengeance of the Maiden Aunts! Come, be a man! It won't be forever."

To return to the history:

They began at once to plan and build for their children, all the strength and intelligence of the whole of them devoted to that one thing. Each girl, of course, was reared in full knowledge of her Crowning Office, and they had, even then, very high ideas of the molding powers of the mother, as well as those of education.

Such high ideals as they had! Beauty, Health, Strength, Intellect, Goodness—for those they prayed and worked.

They had no enemies; they themselves were all sisters and friends. The land was fair before them, and a great future began to form itself in their minds.

The religion they had to begin with was much like that of old Greece—a number of gods and goddesses; but they lost all interest in deities of war and plunder, and gradually centered on their Mother Goddess altogether. Then, as they grew more intelligent, this had turned into a sort of Maternal Pantheism.

Here was Mother Earth, bearing fruit. All that they ate was fruit of motherhood, from seed or egg or their product. By motherhood they were born and by motherhood they lived—life was, to them, just the long cycle of motherhood.

But very early they recognized the need of improvement as well as of mere repetition, and devoted their combined intelligence to that problem—how to make the best kind of people. First this was merely the hope of bearing better ones, and then they recognized that however the children differed at birth, the real growth lay later—through education.

Then things began to hum.

As I learned more and more to appreciate what these women had accomplished, the less proud I was of what we, with all our manhood, had done.

You see, they had had no wars. They had had no kings, and no priests, and no aristocracies. They were sisters, and as they grew, they grew together—not by competition, but by united action.

We tried to put in a good word for competition, and they were keenly interested. Indeed, we soon found from their earnest questions of us that they were prepared to believe our world must be better than theirs. They were not sure; they wanted to know; but there was no such arrogance about them as might have been expected.

We rather spread ourselves, telling of the advantages of competition: how it developed fine qualities; that without it there would be "no stimulus to industry." Terry was very strong on that point.

"No stimulus to industry," they repeated, with that puzzled look we had learned to know so well. "*Stimulus? To Industry?* But don't you *like* to work?"

"No man would work unless he had to," Terry declared.

"Oh, no *man*! You mean that is one of your sex distinctions?"

"No, indeed!" he said hastily. "No one, I mean, man or woman, would work without incentive. Competition is the—the motor power, you see."

"It is not with us," they explained gently, "so it is hard for us to understand. Do you mean, for instance, that with you no mother would work for her children without the stimulus of competition?"

No, he admitted that he did not mean that. Mothers, he supposed, would of course work for their children in the home; but the world's work was different—that had to be done by men, and required the competitive element.

All our teachers were eagerly interested.

"We want so much to know—you have the whole world to tell us of, and we have only our little land! And there are two of you—the two sexes— to love and help one another. It must be a rich and wonderful world. Tell us—what is the work of the world, that men do—which we have not here?"

"Oh, everything," Terry said grandly. "The men do everything, with us." He squared his broad shoulders and lifted his chest. "We do not allow our women to work. Women are loved—idolized—honored—kept in the home to care for the children."

"What is 'the home'?" asked Somel a little wistfully.

But Zava begged: "Tell me first, do *no* women work, really?"

"Why, yes," Terry admitted. "Some have to, of the poorer sort."

"About how many—in your country?"

"About seven or eight million," said Jeff, as mischievous as ever.

[...]

CHAPTER X. *Their Religions and Our Marriages.*

It took me a long time, as a man, a foreigner, and a species of Christian—I was that as much as anything—to get any clear understanding of the religion of Herland.

Its deification of motherhood was obvious enough; but there was far more to it than that; or, at least, than my first interpretation of that.

I think it was only as I grew to love Ellador more than I believed anyone could love anybody, as I grew faintly to appreciate her inner attitude and state of mind, that I began to get some glimpses of this faith of theirs.

When I asked her about it, she tried at first to tell me, and then, seeing me flounder, asked for more information about ours. She soon found that we had many, that they varied widely, but had some points in common. A clear methodical luminous mind had my Ellador, not only reasonable, but swiftly perceptive.

She made a sort of chart, superimposing the different religions as I described them, with a pin run through them all, as it were; their common basis being a Dominant Power or Powers, and some Special Behavior, mostly taboos, to please or placate. There were some common features in certain groups of religions, but the one always present was this Power, and the things which must be done or not done because of it. It was not hard to trace our human imagery of the Divine Force up through successive stages of bloodthirsty, sensual, proud, and cruel gods of early times to the conception of a Common Father with its corollary of a Common Brotherhood.

This pleased her very much, and when I expatiated on the Omniscience, Omnipotence, Omnipresence, and so on, of our God, and of the loving kindness taught by his Son, she was much impressed.

The story of the Virgin birth naturally did not astonish her, but she was greatly puzzled by the Sacrifice, and still more by the Devil, and the theory of Damnation.

When in an inadvertent moment I said that certain sects had believed in infant damnation—and explained it—she sat very still indeed.

"They believed that God was Love—and Wisdom—and Power?"

"Yes—all of that."

Her eyes grew large, her face ghastly pale.

"And yet that such a God could put little new babies to burn—for eternity?" She fell into a sudden shuddering and left me, running swiftly to the nearest temple.

Every smallest village had its temple, and in those gracious retreats sat wise and noble women, quietly busy at some work of their own until they were wanted, always ready to give comfort, light, or help, to any applicant.

Ellador told me afterward how easily this grief of hers was assuaged, and seemed ashamed of not having helped herself out of it.

"You see, we are not accustomed to horrible ideas," she said, coming back to me rather apologetically. "We haven't any. And when we get a thing like that into our minds it's like—oh, like red pepper in your eyes. So I just ran to her, blinded and almost screaming, and she took it out so quickly—so easily!"

"How?" I asked, very curious.

"'Why, you blessed child,' she said, 'you've got the wrong idea altogether. You do not have to think that there ever was such a God—for there wasn't. Or such a happening—for there wasn't. Nor even that this hideous false idea was believed by anybody. But only this—that people who are utterly ignorant will believe anything—which you certainly knew before.'"

"Anyhow," pursued Ellador, "she turned pale for a minute when I first said it."

This was a lesson to me. No wonder this whole nation of women was peaceful and sweet in expression—they had no horrible ideas.

"Surely you had some when you began," I suggested.

"Oh, yes, no doubt. But as soon as our religion grew to any height at all we left them out, of course."

From this, as from many other things, I grew to see what I finally put in words.

"Have you no respect for the past? For what was thought and believed by your foremothers?"

"Why, no," she said. "Why should we? They are all gone. They knew less than we do. If we are not beyond them, we are unworthy of them—and unworthy of the children who must go beyond us."

This set me thinking in good earnest. I had always imagined—simply from hearing it said, I suppose—that women were by nature conservative. Yet these women, quite unassisted by any masculine spirit of enterprise, had ignored their past and built daringly for the future.

Ellador watched me think. She seemed to know pretty much what was going on in my mind.

"It's because we began in a new way, I suppose. All our folks were swept away at once, and then, after that time of despair, came those wonder children—the first. And then the whole breathless hope of us was for *their* children—if they should have them. And they did! Then there was the period of pride and triumph till we grew too numerous; and after that, when it all came down to one child apiece, we began to really work—to make better ones."

"But how does this account for such a radical difference in your religion?" I persisted.

She said she couldn't talk about the difference very intelligently, not being familiar with other religions, but that theirs seemed simple enough. Their great Mother Spirit was to them what their own motherhood was—only magnified beyond human limits. That meant that they felt beneath and behind them an upholding, unfailing, serviceable love—perhaps it was really the accumulated mother-love of the race they felt—but it was a Power.

"Just what is your theory of worship?" I asked her.

"Worship? What is that?"

I found it singularly difficult to explain. This Divine Love which they felt so strongly did not seem to ask anything of them—"any more than our mothers do," she said.

"But surely your mothers expect honor, reverence, obedience, from you. You have to do things for your mothers, surely?"

"Oh, no," she insisted, smiling, shaking her soft brown hair. "We do things *from* our mothers—not *for* them. We don't have to do things *for* them—they don't need it, you know. But we have to live on—splendidly—because of them; and that's the way we feel about God."

I meditated again. I thought of that God of Battles of ours, that Jealous God, that Vengeance-is-mine God. I thought of our world-nightmare—Hell.

"You have no theory of eternal punishment then, I take it?"

Ellador laughed. Her eyes were as bright as stars, and there were tears in them, too. She was so sorry for me.

"How could we?" she asked, fairly enough. "We have no punishments in life, you see, so we don't imagine them after death."

"Have you *no* punishments? Neither for children nor criminals—such mild criminals as you have?" I urged.

"Do you punish a person for a broken leg or a fever? We have preventive measures, and cures; sometimes we have to 'send the patient to bed,' as it were; but that's not a punishment—it's only part of the treatment," she explained.

Then studying my point of view more closely, she added: "You see, we recognize, in our human motherhood, a great tender limitless uplifting force—patience and wisdom and all subtlety of delicate method. We credit God—our idea of God—with all that and more. Our mothers are not angry with us—why should God be?"

"Does God mean a person to you?"

This she thought over a little. "Why—in trying to get close to it in our minds we personify the idea, naturally; but we certainly do not assume a Big Woman somewhere, who is God. What we call God is a Pervading Power, you know, an Indwelling Spirit, something inside of us that we want more of. Is your God a Big Man?" she asked innocently.

"Why—yes, to most of us, I think. Of course we call it an Indwelling Spirit just as you do, but we insist that it is Him, a Person, and a Man—with whiskers."

"Whiskers? Oh yes—because you have them! Or do you wear them because He does?"

"On the contrary, we shave them off—because it seems cleaner and more comfortable."

"Does He wear clothes—in your idea, I mean?"

I was thinking over the pictures of God I had seen—rash advances of the devout mind of man, representing his Omnipotent Deity as an old man in a flowing robe, flowing hair, flowing beard, and in the light of her perfectly frank and innocent questions this concept seemed rather unsatisfying.

I explained that the God of the Christian world was really the ancient Hebrew God, and that we had simply taken over the patriarchal idea—that ancient one which quite inevitably clothed its thought of God with the attributes of the patriarchal ruler, the grandfather.

"I see," she said eagerly, after I had explained the genesis and development of our religious ideals. "They lived in separate groups, with a male head, and he was probably a little—domineering?"

"No doubt of that," I agreed.

"And we live together without any 'head,' in that sense—just our chosen leaders—that *does* make a difference."

"Your difference is deeper than that," I assured her. "It is in your common motherhood. Your children grow up in a world where everybody loves them. They find life made rich and happy for them by the diffused love and wisdom of all mothers. So it is easy for you to think of God in the terms of a similar diffused and competent love. I think you are far nearer right than we are."

"What I cannot understand," she pursued carefully, "is your preservation of such a very ancient state of mind. This patriarchal idea you tell me is thousands of years old?"

"Oh yes—four, five, six thousand—ever so many."

"And you have made wonderful progress in those years—in other things?"

"We certainly have. But religion is different. You see, our religions come from behind us, and are initiated by some great teacher who is dead. He is supposed to have known the whole thing and taught it, finally. All we have to do is believe—and obey."

"Who was the great Hebrew teacher?"

"Oh—there it was different. The Hebrew religion is an accumulation of extremely ancient traditions, some far older than their people, and grew by accretion down the ages. We consider it inspired—'the Word of God.'"

"How do you know it is?"

"Because it says so."

"Does it say so in as many words? Who wrote that in?"

I began to try to recall some text that did say so, and could not bring it to mind.

"Apart from that," she pursued, "what I cannot understand is why you keep these early religious ideas so long. You have changed all your others, haven't you?"

"Pretty generally," I agreed. "But this we call 'revealed religion,' and think it is final. But tell me more about these little temples of yours," I urged. "And these Temple Mothers you run to."

Then she gave me an extended lesson in applied religion, which I will endeavor to concentrate.

They developed their central theory of a Loving Power, and assumed that its relation to them was motherly—that it desired their welfare and especially their development. Their relation to it, similarly, was filial, a loving appreciation and a glad fulfillment of its high purposes. Then, being nothing if not practical, they set their keen and active minds to discover the kind of conduct expected of them. This worked out in a most admirable system of ethics. The principle of Love was universally recognized—and used.

Patience, gentleness, courtesy, all that we call "good breeding," was part of their code of conduct. But where they went far beyond us was in the special application of religious feeling to every field of life. They had no ritual, no little set of performances called "divine service," save those religious pageants I have spoken of, and those were as much educational as religious, and as much social as either. But they had a clear established connection between everything they did—and God. Their cleanliness, their health, their exquisite order, the rich peaceful beauty of the whole land, the happiness of the children, and above all the constant progress they made—all this was their religion.

They applied their minds to the thought of God, and worked out the theory that such an inner power demanded outward expression. They lived as if God was real and at work within them.

As for those little temples everywhere—some of the women were more skilled, more temperamentally inclined, in this direction, than others. These, whatever their work might be, gave certain hours to the Temple Service, which meant being there with all their love and wisdom and trained thought, to smooth out rough places for anyone who needed it. Sometimes it was a real grief, very rarely a quarrel, most often a perplexity; even in Herland the human soul had its hours of darkness. But all through the country their best and wisest were ready to give help.

If the difficulty was unusually profound, the applicant was directed to someone more specially experienced in that line of thought.

Here was a religion which gave to the searching mind a rational basis in life, the concept of an immense Loving Power working steadily out through them, toward good. It gave to the "soul" that sense of contact with the inmost force, of perception of the uttermost purpose, which we always crave. It gave to the "heart" the blessed feeling of being loved, loved and *understood*. It gave clear, simple, rational directions as to how we should live—and why. And for ritual it gave first those triumphant group demonstrations, when with a union of all the arts, the revivifying combination of great multitudes moved rhythmically with march and dance, song and music, among their own noblest products and the open beauty of their groves and hills. Second, it gave these numerous little centers of wisdom where the least wise could go to the most wise and be helped.

"It is beautiful!" I cried enthusiastically. "It is the most practical, comforting, progressive religion I ever heard of. You *do* love one another—you *do* bear one another's burdens—you *do* realize that a little child is a type of the kingdom of heaven. You are more Christian than any people I ever saw. But—how about death? And the life everlasting? What does your religion teach about eternity?"

"Nothing," said Ellador. "What is eternity?"

What indeed? I tried, for the first time in my life, to get a real hold on the idea.

"It is—never stopping."

"Never stopping?" She looked puzzled.

"Yes, life, going on forever."

"Oh—we see that, of course. Life does go on forever, all about us."

"But eternal life goes on *without dying*."

"The same person?"

"Yes, the same person, unending, immortal." I was pleased to think that I had something to teach from our religion, which theirs had never promulgated.

"Here?" asked Ellador. "Never to die—here?" I could see her practical mind heaping up the people, and hurriedly reassured her.

"Oh no, indeed, not here—hereafter. We must die here, of course, but then we 'enter into eternal life.' The soul lives forever."

"How do you know?" she inquired.

"I won't attempt to prove it to you," I hastily continued. "Let us assume it to be so. How does this idea strike you?"

Again she smiled at me, that adorable, dimpling, tender, mischievous, motherly smile of hers. "Shall I be quite, quite honest?"

"You couldn't be anything else," I said, half gladly and half a little sorry. The transparent honesty of these women was a never-ending astonishment to me.

"It seems to me a singularly foolish idea," she said calmly. "And if true, most disagreeable."

Now I had always accepted the doctrine of personal immortality as a thing established. The efforts of inquiring spiritualists, always seeking to woo their beloved ghosts back again, never seemed to me necessary. I don't say I had ever seriously and courageously discussed the subject with myself even; I had simply assumed it to be a fact. And here was the girl I loved, this creature whose character constantly revealed new heights and ranges far beyond my own, this superwoman of a superland, saying she thought immortality foolish! She meant it, too.

"What do you *want* it for?" she asked.

"How can you *not* want it!" I protested. "Do you want to go out like a candle? Don't you want to go on and on—growing and—and—being happy, forever?"

"Why, no," she said. "I don't in the least. I want my child—and my child's child—to go on—and they will. Why should *I* want to?"

"But it means Heaven!" I insisted. "Peace and Beauty and Comfort and Love—with God." I had never been so eloquent on the subject of religion. She could be horrified at Damnation, and question the justice of Salvation, but Immortality—that was surely a noble faith.

"Why, Van," she said, holding out her hands to me. "Why Van—darling! How splendid of you to feel it so keenly. That's what we all want, of course—Peace and Beauty, and Comfort and Love—with God! And Progress too, remember; Growth, always and always. That is what our religion teaches us to want and to work for, and we do!"

"But that is *here*," I said, "only for this life on earth."

"Well? And do not you in your country, with your beautiful religion of love and service have it here, too—for this life—on earth?"

———

None of us were willing to tell the women of Herland about the evils of our own beloved land. It was all very well for us to assume them to be necessary and essential, and to criticize—strictly among ourselves—their all-too-perfect civilization, but when it came to telling them about the failures and wastes of our own, we never could bring ourselves to do it.

Moreover, we sought to avoid too much discussion, and to press the subject of our approaching marriages.

Jeff was the determined one on this score.

"Of course they haven't any marriage ceremony or service, but we can make it a sort of Quaker wedding, and have it in the temple—it is the least we can do for them."

It was. There was so little, after all, that we could do for them. Here we were, penniless guests and strangers, with no chance even to use our strength and courage—nothing to defend them from or protect them against.

"We can at least give them our names," Jeff insisted.

They were very sweet about it, quite willing to do whatever we asked, to please us. As to the names, Alima, frank soul that she was, asked what good it would do.

Terry, always irritating her, said it was a sign of possession. "You are going to be Mrs. Nicholson," he said. "Mrs. T. O. Nicholson. That shows everyone that you are my wife."

"What is a 'wife' exactly?" she demanded, a dangerous gleam in her eye.

"A wife is the woman who belongs to a man," he began.

But Jeff took it up eagerly: "And a husband is the man who belongs to a woman. It is because we are monogamous, you know. And marriage is the ceremony, civil and religious, that joins the two together—'until death do us part,'" he finished, looking at Celis with unutterable devotion.

"What makes us all feel foolish," I told the girls, "is that here we have nothing to give you—except, of course, our names."

"Do your women have no names before they are married?" Celis suddenly demanded.

"Why, yes," Jeff explained. "They have their maiden names—their father's names, that is."

"And what becomes of them?" asked Alima.

"They change them for their husbands', my dear," Terry answered her.

"Change them? Do the husbands then take the wives' 'maiden names'?"

"Oh, no," he laughed. "The man keeps his own and gives it to her, too."

"Then she just loses hers and takes a new one—how unpleasant! We won't do that!" Alima said decidedly.

Terry was good-humored about it. "I don't care what you do or don't do so long as we have that wedding pretty soon," he said, reaching a strong brown hand after Alima's, quite as brown and nearly as strong.

"As to giving us things—of course we can see that you'd like to, but we are glad you can't," Celis continued. "You see, we love you just for yourselves— we wouldn't want you to—to pay anything. Isn't it enough to know that you are loved personally—and just as men?"

Enough or not, that was the way we were married. We had a great triple wedding in the biggest temple of all, and it looked as if most of the na- tion was present. It was very solemn and very beautiful. Someone had written a new song for the occasion, nobly beautiful, about the New Hope for their people—the New Tie with other lands—Brotherhood as well as Sisterhood, and, with evident awe, Fatherhood.

Terry was always restive under their talk of fatherhood. "Anybody'd think we were High Priests of—of Philoprogenitiveness!" he protested. "These women think of *nothing* but children, seems to me! We'll teach 'em!"

He was so certain of what he was going to teach, and Alima so uncer- tain in her moods of reception, that Jeff and I feared the worst. We tried to caution him—much good that did. The big handsome fellow drew himself up to his full height, lifted that great chest of his, and laughed.

"There are three separate marriages," he said. "I won't interfere with yours—nor you with mine."

So the great day came, and the countless crowds of women, and we three bridegrooms without any supporting "best men," or any other men to back us up, felt strangely small as we came forward.

Somel and Zava and Moadine were on hand; we were thankful to have them, too—they seemed almost like relatives.

There was a splendid procession, wreathing dances, the new anthem I spoke of, and the whole great place pulsed with feeling—the deep awe, the sweet hope, the wondering expectation of a new miracle.

"There has been nothing like this in the country since our Motherhood began!" Somel said softly to me, while we watched the symbolic marches. "You see, it is the dawn of a new era. You don't know how much you mean to us. It is not only Fatherhood—that marvelous dual parentage to which we are strangers—the miracle of union in life-giving—but it is Brother-hood. You are the rest of the world. You join us to our kind—to all the strange lands and peoples we have never seen. We hope to know them—to love and help them—and to learn of them. Ah! You cannot know!"

———————

Thousands of voices rose in the soaring climax of that great Hymn of The Coming Life. By the great Altar of Motherhood, with its crown of fruit and flowers, stood a new one, crowned as well. Before the Great Over Mother of the Land and her ring of High Temple Counsellors, before that vast multitude of calm-faced mothers and holy-eyed maidens, came forward our own three chosen ones, and we, three men alone in all that land, joined hands with them and made our marriage vows.

SOURCES

Gilman, Charlotte Perkins. *Herland*. Originally serialized in the *Forerunner*.
     Excerpts from *Forerunner* 6, no. 5 (May 1915): 123–29; no. 10 (October 1915):
     265–70.
———. "The Socialist and the Suffragist," *Forerunner* 1, no. 10 (October 1910): 25.
———. "When I Was a Witch." *Forerunner* 1, no. 7 (May 1910): 1–6.

NOTE

Chapter opening photo: Charlotte Perkins Gilman, ca. 1900. Schlesinger Library, Radcliffe Institute, Harvard University.

Angelina Weld Grimké

1880–1958

ANGELINA WELD GRIMKÉ (not to be confused with her great-aunt and namesake, the abolitionist and suffragist Angelina Grimké Weld) was born in Boston to a biracial family. She was a journalist, teacher, playwright, and poet, with many of her pieces seeing publication in *The Crisis*, the newspaper of the NAACP, edited by W. E. B. Du Bois. Highly educated and well connected, she became one of the prominent literary figures of the Harlem Renaissance, known especially for her poetry. Several of her works, including the play *Rachel* (1920), protest lynching and racial violence. Grimké was a lesbian, and many of her published and unpublished works feature themes of women loving women or the frustrations of unfulfilled love.

El Beso (1923)

Twilight—and you
Quiet—the stars;
Snare of the shine of your teeth,
Your provocative laughter,
The gloom of your hair;
Lure of you, eye and lip;
Yearning, yearning,
Languor, surrender;
Your mouth,
And madness, madness,
Tremulous, breathless, flaming,
The space of a sigh;
Then awakening—remembrance,
Pain, regret—your sobbing;

And again, quiet—the stars,
Twilight—and you.

The Want of You (1923)

A hint of gold where the moon will be;
Through the flocking clouds just a star or two
Leaf sounds, soft and wet and hushed,
And oh! the crying want of you.

The Black Finger (1923)

I have just seen a beautiful thing
Slim and still,
Against a gold, gold sky,
A straight cypress,
Sensitive
Exquisite,
A black finger
Pointing upwards.
Why, beautiful, still finger are you black?
And why are you pointing upwards?

At April (1925)

Toss your gay heads,
Brown girl trees;
Toss your gay lovely heads;
Shake your brown slim bodies;
Stretch your brown slim arms;
Stretch your brown slim toes.
Who knows better than we,
With the dark, dark bodies,
What it means
When April comes a-laughing and a-weeping
Once again
At our hearts?

Trees (1928)

God made them very beautiful, the trees:
He spoke and gnarled of bole or silken sleek
They grew; majestic bowed or very meek;
Huge-bodied, slim; sedate and full of glees.
And He had pleasure deep in all of these.
And to them soft and little tongues to speak
Of Him to us, He gave wherefore they seek
From dawn to dawn to bring unto our knees.

———————

Yet here amid the wistful sounds of leaves,
A black-hued grewsome something swings and swings;
Laughter it knew and joy in little things
Till man's hate ended all.—And so man weaves.
And God, how slow, how very slow weaves He—
Was Christ Himself not nailed to a tree?

SOURCES

Grimké, Angelina Weld. "At April." *Opportunity* 3, no. 3 (March 1925): 83, reproduced with permission from the National Urban League.

———. "El Beso" and "The Want of You." In *Negro Poets and Their Poems*, edited by Robert T. Kerlin, 154. Washington, DC: Associated Publishers, 1923.

———. "The Black Finger." *Opportunity* 1, no. 11 (November 1923): 343.

———. "Trees." *Carolina Magazine* 58, no. 7 (May 1928): 35. https://archive.org /details/carolinamagazine58univ/page/34/mode/2up. Reproduced with permission from University of North Carolina's Dialectic and Philanthropic Societies, former publishers of the *Carolina Magazine*.

Frances E. W. Harper

1825–1911

FRANCES ELLEN WATKINS HARPER was born in Baltimore to two
free Black parents. She began by publishing poetry in abolitionist peri-
odicals, including Frederick Douglass's *North Star*. Her activism began
in 1854, when she was exiled from Maryland because of fugitive slave
laws decreeing that even free Blacks could be arrested and sold into
slavery. The success of her first public speech, "Education and the El-
evation of the Colored Race," led to a two-year speaking tour on behalf
of the Maine Anti-Slavery Society. Her lectures, which incorporated
her poetry and prose, were revolutionary in that they address racism,
feminism, and classism as intersecting issues. Harper formed alliances
with feminist activists such as Susan B. Anthony, spoke at the National
Women's Rights Convention in 1866, and was elected vice president of
the National Association of Colored Women in 1897. Today she is best
known for her novel, *Iola Leroy, or Shadows Uplifted* (1892).

Bible Defense of Slavery (1855)

Take sackcloth of the darkest dye,
 And shroud the pulpits round!
Servants of Him that cannot lie,
 Sit mourning on the ground.

Let holy horror blanch each cheek,
 Pale every brow with fears;
And rocks and stones, if ye could speak,
 Ye well might melt to tears!

Let sorrow breathe in every tone,
 In every strain ye raise;
Insult not God's majestic throne
 With th' mockery of praise.

A "reverend" man, whose light should be
 The guide of age and youth,
Brings to the shrine of Slavery
 The sacrifice of truth!

For the direst wrong by man imposed,
 Since Sodom's fearful cry,
The word of life has been unclos'd,
 To give your God the lie.

Oh! when ye pray for heathen lands,
 And plead for their dark shores,
Remember Slavery's cruel hands
 Make heathens at your doors!

Eliza Harris (1855)

Like a fawn from the arrow, startled and wild,
A woman swept by us, bearing a child;
In her eye was the night of a settled despair,
And her brow was o'ershaded with anguish and care.

She was nearing the river—in reaching the brink,
She heeded no danger, she paused not to think!

For she is a mother—her child is a slave—
And she'll give him his freedom, or find him a grave!

'Twas a vision to haunt us, that innocent face—
So pale in its aspect, so fair in its grace;
As the tramp of the horse and the bay of the hound,
With the fetters that gall, were trailing the ground!

She was nerved by despair, and strengthen'd by woe,
As she leap'd o'er the chasms that yawn'd from below;
Death howl'd in the tempest, and rav'd in the blast,
But she heard not the sound till the danger was past.

Oh! how shall I speak of my proud country's shame?
Of the stains on her glory, how give them their name?
How say that her banner in mockery waves—
Her "star-spangled banner"—o'er millions of slaves?

How say that the lawless may torture and chase
A woman whose crime is the hue of her face?
How the depths of forest may echo around
With the shrieks of despair, and the bay of the hound?

With her step on the ice, and her arm on her child,
The danger was fearful, the pathway was wild;
But, aided by Heaven, she gained a free shore,
Where the friends of humanity open'd their door.

So fragile and lovely, so fearfully pale,
Like a lily that bends to the breath of the gale,
Save the heave of her breast, and the sway of her hair,
You'd have thought her a statue of fear and despair.

In agony close to her bosom she press'd
The life of her heart, the child of her breast:—
Oh! love from its tenderness gathering might,
Had strengthen'd her soul for the dangers of flight.

But she's free!—yes, free from the land where the slave
From the hand of oppression must rest in the grave;
Where bondage and torture, where scourges and chains
Have plac'd on our banner indelible stains.

The bloodhounds have miss'd the scent of her way;
The hunter is rifled and foil'd of his prey;
Fierce jargon and cursing, with clanking of chains,
Make sounds of strange discord on Liberty's plains.

With the rapture of love and fullness of bliss,
She plac'd on his brow a mother's fond kiss:—
Oh! poverty, danger and death she can brave,
For the child of her love is no longer a slave!

Only one night beneath your roof (1859)

[A father was imprisoned in Washington, not long since, for
sheltering his son for a night and giving him food and clothing.[1]]

Only one night beneath your roof
   My father, let me stay,
Break to my hungry lips your bread
   And clothe my limbs I pray.

Only one night: his eager eyes
   Flashed on his father's face.
Only one night with those I love
   Give me a resting place.

The father gazed upon his child,
   His pleading touched his heart,
And love and pity moved his soul;
   He would not say depart.

He would not shut his open doors
   Upon his prayer so wild,
He could not coldly thrust aside
   His wretched, wandering child.

He took him to his heart and home
   And broke to him his bread,
And one short night the father's roof
   Stretched o'er his weary head.

The morning broke, and nature smiled,
  The son was clothed and fed,
And one short night the father's roof
  Stretched o'er his weary head.

'Twas where our country frames her laws
  This deed of shame was done,
A father met a felon's doom
  For sheltering his own son.

Tremble and blush, Oh guilty land,
  Thou smiter of the dumb!
The sighing of the wronged and robbed
  Before our God shall come.

His lightning shall not always sleep
  or slumber in its lair,
His thunderbolts are fused with wrath
  And freighted with despair.

Bury Me in a Free Land (1870)

Make me a grave where'er you will,
In a lowly plain, or a lofty hill
Make it among earth's humblest graves,
But not in a land where men are slaves.

I could not rest if around my grave
I heard the steps of a trembling slave
His shadow above my silent tomb
Would make it a place of fearful gloom.

I could not rest if I heard the tread
Of a coffle gang to the shambles led,
And the mother's shriek of wild despair
Rise like a curse on the trembling air.

I could not sleep if I saw the lash
Drinking her blood at each fearful gash,

And I saw her babes torn from her breast,
Like trembling doves from their parent nest.

I'd shudder and start if I heard the bay
Of bloodhounds seizing their human prey,
And I heard the captive plead in vain
As they bound afresh his galling chain.

If I saw young girls from their mother's arms
Bartered and sold for their youthful charms,
My eye would flash with a mournful flame,
My death-paled cheek grow red with shame.

I would sleep, dear friends, where bloated might
Can rob no man of his dearest right;
My rest shall be calm in any grave
Where none can call his brother a slave.

I ask no monument, proud and high,
To arrest the gaze of the passers-by;
All that my yearning spirit craves,
Is bury me not in a land of slaves.

Learning to Read (1891)

Very soon the Yankee teachers
   Came down and set up school;
But, oh! how the Rebs did hate it,—
   It was agin' their rule.

Our masters always tried to hide
   Book learning from our eyes;
Knowledge did'nt agree with slavery—
   'Twould make us all too wise.

But some of us would try to steal
   A little from the book.
And put the words together,
   And learn by hook or crook.

I remember Uncle Caldwell,
   Who took pot liquor fat
And greased the pages of his book,
   And hid it in his hat.

And had his master ever seen
   The leaves upon his head,
He'd have thought them greasy papers,
   But nothing to be read.

And there was Mr. Turner's Ben,
   Who heard the children spell,
And picked the words right up by heart,
   And learned to read 'em well.

Well, the Northern folks kept sending
   The Yankee teachers down;
And they stood right up and helped us,
   Though Rebs did sneer and frown.

And I longed to read my Bible,
   For precious words it said;
But when I begun to learn it,
   Folks just shook their heads,

And said there is no use trying,
   Oh! Chloe, you're too late;
But as I was rising sixty,
   I had no time to wait.

So I got a pair of glasses,
   And straight to work I went,
And never stopped till I could read
   The hymns and Testament.

Then I got a little cabin
   A place to call my own—
And I felt independent
   As the queen upon her throne.

A Double Standard (1895)

Do you blame me that I loved him?
    If when standing all alone
I cried for bread a careless world
    Pressed to my lips a stone.

Do you blame me that I loved him,
    That my heart beat glad and free,
When he told me in the sweetest tones
    He loved but only me?

Can you blame me that I did not see
    Beneath his burning kiss
The serpent's wiles, nor even hear
    The deadly adder hiss?

Can you blame me that my heart grew cold
    That the tempted, tempter turned;
When he was feted and caressed
    And I was coldly spurned?

Would you blame him, when you draw from me
    Your dainty robes aside,
If he with gilded baits should claim
    Your fairest as his bride?

Would you blame the world if it should press
    On him a civic crown;
And see me struggling in the depth
    Then harshly press me down?

Crime has no sex and yet to-day
    I wear the brand of shame;
Whilst he amid the gay and proud
    Still bears an honored name.

Can you blame me if I've learned to think
    Your hate of vice a sham,
When you so coldly crushed me down
    And then excused the man?

Would you blame me if to-morrow
    The coroner should say,
A wretched girl, outcast, forlorn,
    Has thrown her life away?

Yes, blame me for my downward course,
    But oh! remember well,
Within your homes you press the hand
    That led me down to hell.

I'm glad God's ways are not our ways,
    He does not see as man,
Within His love I know there's room
    For those whom others ban.

I think before His great white throne,
    His throne of spotless light,
That whited sepulchres shall wear
    The hue of endless night.

That I who fell, and he who sinned,
    Shall reap as we have sown;
That each the burden of his loss
    Must bear and bear alone.

No golden weights can turn the scale
    Of justice in His sight;
And what is wrong in woman's life
    In man's cannot be right.

SOURCES

Harper, Frances E. W. "A Double Standard." In *Poems*, 12–14. Philadelphia: published by the author, 1895.

Harper, Frances E. Watkins. "Learning to Read." In *Sketches of Southern Life*, 17–19. Philadelphia: Ferguson Bros., 1891.

Harper, Mrs. F. E. W. "Bury Me in a Free Land." In *Moses: A Story of the Nile*, 3rd ed., 19–20. Philadelphia: Merrihew & Son, 1870.

Watkins, Frances Ellen. "Bible Defense of Slavery." In *Poems on Miscellaneous Subjects*, 8–9. Boston: J. B. Yerrinton & Son, 1855.

———. "Eliza Harris." In *Poems on Miscellaneous Subjects*, 9–11. Boston: J. B. Yerrinton & Son, 1855.

———. "Only one night beneath your roof." *Anti-Slavery Bugle*, May 14, 1859, 4.

NOTES

Chapter opening photo: Frances E. W. Harper, ca. 1860–1870, published 1898. Library of Congress, Prints & Photographs Division, LC-USZ62-118946.

1. [Author's or source editor's note.]

Pauline Hopkins

1859–1930

PAULINE HOPKINS was a successful journalist and author of fiction and drama. Her short story "Talma Gordon" (1900), which we include, is often described as the first African American mystery story. She published three serial novels in the *Colored American Magazine* and became deeply involved in the periodical, joining its board of directors, becoming a shareholder, increasing subscriptions, and writing much of its content. She served as its editor for four years. Although not as well known as some of her Harlem Renaissance contemporaries, Hopkins was the most prolific African American woman writer of the era and one of the most influential literary editors. She was a pioneer in her use of the traditional romantic novel to examine racial and social themes.

Talma Gordon (1900)

The Canterbury Club of Boston was holding its regular monthly meeting at the palatial Beacon-street residence of Dr. William Thornton, expert medical practitioner and specialist. All the members were present, because some rare opinions were to be aired by men of profound thought on a question of vital importance to the life of the Republic, and because the club celebrated its anniversary in a home usually closed to society. The Doctor's winters, since his marriage, were passed at his summer home near his celebrated sanatorium. This winter found him in town with his wife and two boys. We had heard much of the beauty of the former, who was entirely unknown to social life, and about whose life and marriage we felt sure a romantic interest attached. The Doctor himself was too bright a luminary of the professional world to remain long hidden without creating comment. We had accepted the invitation to dine with alacrity, knowing that we should be welcomed to a banquet that would feast both eye and palate; but we had not been favored by even a glimpse of the hostess. The subject for discussion was: "Expansion; Its Effect upon the Future Development of the Anglo-Saxon throughout the World."

Dinner was over, but we still sat about the social board discussing the question of the hour. The Hon. Herbert Clapp, eminent jurist and politician, had painted in glowing colors the advantages to be gained by the increase of wealth and the exalted position which expansion would give the United States in the councils of the great governments of the world. In smoothly flowing sentences marshalled in rhetorical order, with compact ideas, and incisive argument, he drew an effective picture with all the persuasive eloquence of the trained orator.

Joseph Whitman, the theologian of world-wide fame, accepted the arguments of Mr. Clapp, but subordinated all to the great opportunity which expansion would give to the religious enthusiast. None could doubt the sincerity of this man, who looked once into the idealized face on which heaven had set the seal of consecration.

Various opinions were advanced by the twenty-five men present, but the host said nothing; he glanced from one to another with a look of amusement in his shrewd gray-blue eyes. "Wonderful eyes," said his patients who came under their magic spell. "A wonderful man and a wonderful mind," agreed his contemporaries, as they heard in amazement of some great cure of chronic or malignant disease which approached the supernatural.

"What do you think of this question, Doctor?" finally asked the president, turning to the silent host.

"Your arguments are good; they would convince almost anyone."

"But not Doctor Thornton," laughed the theologian.

"I acquiesce which ever way the result turns. Still, I like to view both sides of a question. We have considered but one tonight. Did you ever think that in spite of our prejudices against amalgamation, some of our descendants, indeed many of them, will inevitably intermarry among those far-off tribes of dark-skinned peoples, if they become a part of this great Union?"

"Among the lower classes that may occur, but not to any great extent," remarked a college president.

"My experience teaches me that it will occur among all classes, and to an appalling extent," replied the Doctor.

"You don't believe in intermarriage with other races?"

"Yes, most emphatically, when they possess decent moral development and physical perfection, for then we develop a superior being in the progeny born of the intermarriage. But if we are not ready to receive and assimilate the new material which will be brought to mingle with our pure Anglo-Saxon stream, we should call a halt in our expansion policy."

"I must confess, Doctor, that in the idea of amalgamation you present a new thought to my mind. Will you not favor us with a few of your main points?" asked the president of the club, breaking the silence which followed the Doctor's remarks.

"Yes, Doctor, give us your theories on the subject. We may not agree with you, but we are all open to conviction."

The Doctor removed the half-consumed cigar from his lips, drank what remained in his glass of the choice Burgundy, and leaning back in his chair contemplated the earnest faces before him.

We may make laws, but laws are but straws in the hands of Omnipotence.

"There's a divinity that shapes our ends,
Rough-hew them how we will."[1]

And no man may combat fate. Given a man, propinquity, opportunity fascinating femininity, and there you are. Black, white, green, yellow—nothing will prevent intermarriage. Position, wealth, family, friends—all sink into insignificance before the God-implanted instinct that made Adam, awakening from a deep sleep and finding the woman beside him, accept Eve as bone of his bone; he cared not nor questioned whence she came. So it is with the sons of Adam ever since, through the law of heredity which makes us all one common family. And so it will be with us in our re-formation of this old Republic. Perhaps I can make my meaning clearer by illustration, and with your permission I will tell you a story which came under my observation as a practitioner.

Doubtless all of you heard of the terrible tragedy which occurred at Gordonville, Mass., some years ago, when Capt. Jonathan Gordon, his wife and little son were murdered. I suppose that I am the only man on this side the Atlantic, outside of the police, who can tell you the true story of that crime.

I knew Captain Gordon well; it was through his persuasions that I bought a place in Gordonville and settled down to spending my summers in that charming rural neighborhood. I had rendered the Captain what he was pleased to call valuable medical help, and I became his family physician. Captain Gordon was a retired sea captain, formerly engaged in the East India trade. All his ancestors had been such; but when the bottom fell out of that business he established the Gordonville Mills with his first wife's money, and settled down as a money-making manufacturer of cotton cloth. The Gordons were old New England Puritans who had come over in the "Mayflower"; they had owned Gordon Hall for more than a hundred years. It was a baronial-like pile of granite with towers, standing on a hill which commanded a superb view of Massachusetts Bay and the surrounding country. I imagine the Gordon star was under a cloud about the time Captain Jonathan married his first wife, Miss Isabel Franklin of Boston, who brought to him the money which mended the broken fortunes of the Gordon house, and restored this old Puritan stock to its rightful position. In the person of Captain Gordon the austerity of manner and indomitable will-power that he had inherited were combined with a temper that brooked no contradiction.

The first wife died at the birth of her third child, leaving him two daughters, Jeannette and Talma. Very soon after her death the Captain married again. I have heard it rumored that the Gordon girls did not get on very well with their step-mother. She was a woman with no fortune of her own, and envied the large portion left by the first Mrs. Gordon to her daughters.

Jeannette was tall, dark, and stern like her father; Talma was like her dead mother, and possessed of great talent, so great that her father sent her to the American Academy at Rome, to develop the gift. It was the hottest of July days when her friends were bidden to an afternoon party on the lawn and a dance in the evening, to welcome Talma Gordon among them again. I watched her as she moved about among her guests, a fairy-like blonde in floating white draperies, her face a study in delicate changing tints, like the heart of a flower, sparkling in smiles about the mouth to end in merry laughter in the clear blue eyes. There were all the subtle allurements of birth, wealth and culture about the exquisite creature:

"Smiling, frowning evermore,
Thou art perfect in love-lore,
Ever varying Madeline,"[2]

quoted a celebrated writer as he stood apart with me, gazing upon the scene before us. He sighed as he looked at the girl.

"Doctor, there is genius and passion in her face. Sometime our little friend will do wonderful things. But is it desirable to be singled out for special blessings by the gods? Genius always carries with it intense capacity for suffering: 'Whom the gods love die young.'"

"Ah," I replied, "do not name death and Talma Gordon together. Cease your dismal croakings; such talk is rank heresy."

The dazzling daylight dropped slowly into summer twilight. The merriment continued; more guests arrived; the great dancing pagoda built for the occasion was lighted by myriads of Japanese lanterns. The strains from the band grew sweeter and sweeter, and "all went merry as a marriage bell." It was a rare treat to have this party at Gordon Hall, for Captain Jonathan was not given to hospitality. We broke up shortly before midnight, with expressions of delight from all the guests.

I was a bachelor then, without ties. Captain Gordon insisted upon my having a bed at the Hall. I did not fall asleep readily; there seemed to be something in the air that forbade it. I was still awake when a distant clock struck the second hour of the morning. Suddenly the heavens were lighted by a sheet of ghastly light; a terrific midsummer thunderstorm was breaking over the sleeping town. A lurid flash lit up all the landscape, painting the trees in grotesque shapes against the murky sky, and defining clearly the sullen blackness of the waters of the bay breaking in grandeur against the rocky coast. I had arisen and put back the draperies from the windows, to have an unobstructed view of the grand scene. A low muttering coming nearer and nearer, a terrific roar, and then a tremendous downpour. The storm had burst.

Now the uncanny howling of a dog mingled with the rattling volleys of thunder. I heard the opening and closing of doors; the servants were about looking after things. It was impossible to sleep. The lightning was more vivid. There was a blinding flash of a greenish-white tinge mingled with the crash of falling timbers. Then before my startled gaze arose columns of red flames reflected against the sky. "Heaven help us!" I cried; "it is the left tower; it has been struck and is on fire!"

I hurried on my clothes and stepped into the corridor; the girls were there before me. Jeannette came up to me instantly with anxious face. "Oh, Doctor Thornton, what shall we do? papa and mamma and little Johnny are in the old left tower. It is on fire. I have knocked and knocked, but get no answer."

"Don't be alarmed," said I soothingly. "Jenkins, ring the alarm bell," I continued, turning to the butler who was standing near; "the rest follow me. We will force the entrance to the Captain's room."

Instantly, it seemed to me, the bell boomed out upon the now silent air, for the storm had died down as quickly as it arose; and as our little procession paused before the entrance to the old left tower, we could distinguish the sound of the fire engines already on their way from the village.

The door resisted all our efforts; there seemed to be a barrier against it which nothing could move. The flames were gaining headway. Still the same deathly silence within the rooms.

"Oh, will they never get here?" cried Talma, ringing her hands in terror. Jeannette said nothing, but her face was ashen. The servants were huddled together in a panic-stricken group. I can never tell you what a relief it was when we heard the first sound of the firemen's voices, saw their quick movements, and heard the ringing of the axes with which they cut away every obstacle to our entrance to the rooms. The neighbors who had just enjoyed the hospitality of the house were now gathered around offering all the assistance in their power. In less than fifteen minutes the fire was out, and the men began to bear the unconscious inmates from the ruins. They carried them to the pagoda so lately the scene of mirth and pleasure, and I took up my station there, ready to assume my professional duties. The Captain was nearest me; and as I stooped to make the necessary examination I reeled away from the ghastly sight which confronted me—*gentlemen, across the Captain's throat was a deep gash that severed the jugular vein!*

The Doctor paused, and the hand with which he refilled his glass trembled violently.

"What is it, Doctor?" cried the men, gathering about me.

"Take the women away; this is murder!"

"Murder!" cried Jeannette, as she fell against the side of the pagoda.

"Murder!" screamed Talma, staring at me as if unable to grasp my meaning.

I continued my examination of the bodies, and found that the same thing had happened to Mrs. Gordon and to little Johnny. The police were notified; and when the sun rose over the dripping town he found them in charge of Gordon Hall, the servants standing in excited knots talking over the crime, the friends of the family confounded, and the two girls trying to comfort each other and realize the terrible misfortune that had overtaken them.

Nothing in the rooms of the left tower seemed to have been disturbed. The door of communication between the rooms of the husband and wife was open, as they had arranged it for the night. Little Johnny's crib was placed beside his mother's bed. In it he was found as though never awakened by the storm. It was quite evident that the assassin was no common ruffian. The chief gave strict orders for a watch to be kept on all strangers or suspicious characters who were seen in the neighborhood. He made inquiries among the servants, seeing each one separately, but there was nothing gained from them. No one had heard anything suspicious; all had been awakened by the storm. The chief was puzzled. Here was a triple crime for which no motive could be assigned.

"What do you think of it?" I asked him, as we stood together on the lawn.

"It is my opinion that the deed was committed by one of the higher classes, which makes the mystery more difficult to solve. I tell you, Doctor, there are mysteries that never come to light, and this, I think, is one of them."

While we were talking Jenkins, the butler, an old and trusted servant, came up to the chief and saluted respectfully. "Want to speak with me, Jenkins?" he asked. The man nodded, and they walked away together.

The story of the inquest was short, but appalling. It was shown that Talma had been allowed to go abroad to study because she and Mrs. Gordon did not get on well together. From the testimony of Jenkins it seemed that Talma and her father had quarrelled bitterly about her lover, a young artist whom she had met at Rome, who was unknown to fame, and very poor. There had been terrible things said by each, and threats even had passed, all of which now rose up in judgment against the unhappy girl. The examination of the family solicitor revealed the fact that Captain Gordon intended to leave his daughters only a small annuity, the bulk of the fortune going to his son Jonathan, junior. This was a monstrous injustice, as everyone felt. In vain Talma protested her innocence. Someone must have done it. No one would be benefited so much by these deaths as she and her sister. Moreover, the will, together with other papers, was nowhere to be found. Not the slightest clue bearing upon the disturbing elements in this family, if any there were, was to be found. As the only surviving relatives, Jeannette and Talma became joint heirs to an immense fortune, which only for the bloody tragedy just enacted would, in all probability, have passed them by. Here was the motive. The case was very black against Talma. The foreman stood up. The silence was intense: "We find that Capt. Jonathan Gordon, Mary E. Gordon and Jonathan Gordon, junior, all deceased, came to their deaths by means of a knife or other sharp instrument in the hands of Talma Gordon." The girl was like one stricken with death. The flower-like mouth was drawn and pinched; the great sapphire-blue eyes were black with passionate anguish, terror and despair. She was placed in jail to await her trial at the fall session of the criminal court. The excitement in the hitherto quiet town rose to fever heat. Many points in the evidence seemed incomplete to thinking men. The weapon could not be found, nor could it be divined what had become of it. No reason could be given for the murder except the quarrel between Talma and her father and the ill will which existed between the girl and her stepmother.

When the trial was called Jeannette sat beside Talma in the prisoner's dock; both were arrayed in deepest mourning. Talma was pale and careworn, but seemed uplifted, spiritualized, as it were. Upon Jeannette the full realization of her sister's peril seemed to weigh heavily. She had changed much too: hollow cheeks, tottering steps, eyes blazing with fever, all suggestive of rapid and premature decay. From far-off Italy Edward Turner, growing famous in the art world, came to stand beside his girl-love in this hour of anguish.

The trial was a memorable one. No additional evidence had been collected to strengthen the prosecution; when the attorney-general rose to open the case against Talma he knew, as everyone else did, that he could not convict solely on the evidence adduced. What was given did not always bear upon the case, and brought out strange stories of Captain Jonathan's methods. Tales were told of sailors who had sworn to take his life, in revenge for injuries inflicted upon them by his hand. One or two clues were followed, but without avail. The judge summed up the evidence impartially, giving the prisoner the benefit of the doubt. The points in hand furnished valuable collateral evidence, but were not direct proof. Although the moral presumption was against the prisoner, legal evidence was lacking to actually convict. The jury found the prisoner "Not Guilty," owing to the fact that the evidence was entirely circumstantial. The verdict was received in painful silence; then a murmur of discontent ran through the great crowd.

"She must have done it," said one; "who else has been benefited by the horrible deed?"

"A poor woman would not have fared so well at the hands of the jury, nor a homely one either, for that matter," said another.

The great Gordon trial was ended; innocent or guilty, Talma Gordon could not be tried again. She was free; but her liberty, with blasted prospects and fair fame gone forever, was valueless to her. She seemed to have but one object in her mind: to find the murderer or murderers of her parents and half-brother. By her direction the shrewdest of detectives were employed and money flowed like water, but to no purpose; the Gordon tragedy remained a mystery. I had consented to act as one of the trustees of the immense Gordon estates and business interests, and by my advice the Misses Gordon went abroad. A year later I received a letter from Edward Turner, saying that Jeannette Gordon had died suddenly at Rome, and that Talma, after refusing all his entreaties for an early marriage, had disappeared, leaving no clue as to her whereabouts. I could give the poor fellow no comfort, although I had been duly notified of the death of Jeannette by Talma, in a letter telling me where to forward her remittances, and at the same time requesting me to keep her present residence secret, especially from Edward.

I had established a sanitarium for the cure of chronic diseases at Gordonville, and absorbed in the cares of my profession I gave little thought to the Gordons. I seemed fated to be involved in mysteries.

A man claiming to be an Englishman, and fresh from the California gold fields, engaged board and professional service at my retreat. I found him suffering in the grasp of the tubercle-fiend—the last stages. He called himself Simon Cameron. Seldom have I seen so fascinating and wicked a face. The lines of the mouth were cruel, the eyes cold and sharp, the smile mocking and evil. He had money in plenty but seemed to have no friends, for he had received no letters and had had no visitors in the time he had been with us. He was an enigma to me; and his nationality puzzled me, for of course I did not believe his story of being English. The peaceful influence of the house seemed to sooth him in a measure, and make his last steps to the mysterious valley as easy as possible. For a time he improved, and would sit or walk about the grounds and sing sweet songs for the pleasure of the other inmates. Strange to say, his malady only affected his voice at times. He sang quaint songs in a silvery tenor of great purity and sweetness that was delicious to the listening ear:

"A wet sheet and a flowing sea,
A wind that follows fast,
And fills the white and rustling sail
And bends the gallant mast;
And bends the gallant mast, my boys;
While like the eagle free,
Away the good ship flies, and leaves
Old England on the lea."[3]

There are few singers on the lyric stage who could surpass Simon Cameron.

One night, a few weeks after Cameron's arrival, I sat in my office making up my accounts when the door opened and closed; I glanced up, expecting to see a servant. A lady advanced toward me. She threw back her veil, and then I saw that Talma Gordon, or her ghost, stood before me. After the first excitement of our meeting was over, she told me she had come direct from Paris, to place herself in my care. I had studied her attentively during the first moments of our meeting, and I felt that she was right; unless something unforeseen happened to arouse her from the stupor into which she seemed to have fallen, the last Gordon was doomed to an early death. The next day I told her I had cabled Edward Turner to come to her.

"It will do no good; I cannot marry him," was her only comment.

"Have you no feeling of pity for that faithful fellow?" I asked her sternly, provoked by her seeming indifference. I shall never forget the varied emotions depicted on her speaking face. Fully revealed to my gaze was the sight of a human soul tortured beyond the point of endurance; suffering all things, enduring all things, in the silent agony of despair.

In a few days Edward arrived, and Talma consented to see him and explain her refusal to keep her promise to him. You must be present, Doctor; it is due your long, tried friendship to know that I have not been fickle, but have acted from the best and strongest motives.

I shall never forget that day. It was directly after lunch that we met in the library. I was greatly excited, expecting I knew not what. Edward was agitated, too. Talma was the only calm one. She handed me what seemed to be a letter, with the request that I would read it. Even now I think I can repeat every word of the document, so indelibly are the words engraved upon my mind:

MY DARLING SISTER TALMA: When you read these lines I shall be no more, for I shall not live to see your life blasted by the same knowledge that has blighted mine.

One evening, about a year before your expected return from Rome, I climbed into a hammock in one corner of the veranda outside the breakfast-room windows, intending to spend the twilight hours in lazy comfort, for it was very hot, enervating August weather. I fell asleep. I was awakened by voices. Because of the heat the rooms had been left in semi-darkness. As I lay there, lazily enjoying the beauty of the perfect summer night, my wandering thoughts were arrested by words spoken by our father to Mrs. Gordon, for they were the occupants of the breakfast-room.

"Never fear, Mary; Johnny shall have it all—money, houses, land and business."

"But if you do go first, Jonathan, what will happen if the girls contest the will? People will think that they ought to have the money as it appears to be theirs by law. I never could survive the terrible disgrace of the story."

"Don't borrow trouble; all you would need to do would be to show them papers I have drawn up, and they would be glad to take their annuity and say nothing. After all, I do not think it is so bad. Jeannette can teach; Talma can paint; six hundred dollars a year is quite enough for them."

I had been somewhat mystified by the conversation until now. This last remark solved the riddle. What could he mean? teach, paint, six hundred a year! With my usual impetuosity I sprang from my resting-place, and in a moment stood in the room confronting my father, and asking what he meant. I could see plainly that both were disconcerted by my unexpected appearance.

"Ah, wretched girl! you have been listening. But what could I expect of your mother's daughter?"

At these words I felt the indignant blood rush to my head in a torrent. So it had been all my life. Before you could remember, Talma,

I had felt my little heart swell with anger at the disparaging hints and slurs concerning our mother. Now was my time. I determined that tonight I would know why she was looked upon as an outcast, and her children subjected to every humiliation. So I replied to my father in bitter anger:

"I was not listening; I fell asleep in the hammock. What do you mean by a paltry six hundred a year each to Talma and to me? 'My mother's daughter' demands an explanation from you, sir, of the meaning of the monstrous injustice that you have always practised toward my sister and me."

"Speak more respectfully to your father, Jeannette," broke in Mrs. Gordon.

"How is it, madam, that you look for respect from one whom you have delighted to torment ever since you came into this most unhappy family?"

"Hush, both of you," said Captain Gordon, who seemed to have recovered from the dismay into which my sudden appearance and passionate words had plunged him. "I think I may as well tell you as to wait. Since you know so much, you may as well know the whole miserable story." He motioned me to a seat. I could see that he was deeply agitated. I seated myself in a chair he pointed out, in wonder and expectation,—expectation of I knew not what. I trembled. This was a supreme moment in my life; I felt it. The air was heavy with the intense stillness that had settled over us as the common sounds of day gave place to the early quiet of the rural evening. I could see Mrs. Gordon's face as she sat within the radius of the lighted hallway. There was a smile of triumph upon it. I clinched my hands and bit my lips until the blood came, in the effort to keep from screaming. What was I about to hear? At last he spoke:

"I was disappointed at your birth, and also at the birth of Talma. I wanted a male heir. When I knew that I should again be a father I was torn by hope and fear, but I comforted myself with the thought that luck would be with me in the birth of the third child. When the doctor brought me word that a son was born to the house of Gordon, I was wild with delight, and did not notice his disturbed countenance. In the midst of my joy he said to me:

"Captain Gordon, there is something strange about this birth. I want you to see this child."

Quelling my exultation I followed him to the nursery, and there, lying in the cradle, I saw a child dark as a mulatto, with the characteristic features of the Negro! I was stunned. Gradually it dawned upon me that there was something radically wrong. I turned to the doctor for an explanation.

"There is but one explanation, Captain Gordon; there is Negro blood in this child."

"There is no Negro blood in my veins," I said proudly. Then I paused—the mother!—I glanced at the doctor. He was watching me intently. The same thought was in his mind. I must have lived a thousand years in that cursed five seconds that I stood there confronting the physician and trying to think. "Come," said I to him, "let us end this suspense." Without thinking of consequences, I hurried away to your mother and accused her of infidelity to her marriage vows. I raved like a madman. Your mother fell into convulsions; her life was despaired of. I sent for Mr. and Mrs. Franklin, and then I learned the truth. They were childless. One year while on a Southern tour, they befriended an octoroon girl who had been abandoned by her white lover. Her child was a beautiful girl baby. They, being Northern born, thought little of caste distinction because the child showed no trace of Negro blood. They determined to adopt it. They went abroad, secretly sending back word to their friends at a proper time, of the birth of a little daughter. No one doubted the truth of the statement. They made Isabel their heiress, and all went well until the birth of your brother. Your mother and the unfortunate babe died. This is the story which, if known, would bring dire disgrace upon the Gordon family.

To appease my righteous wrath, Mr. Franklin left a codicil to his will by which all the property is left at my disposal save a small annuity to you and your sister.

I sat there after he had finished his story, stunned by what I had heard. I understood, now, Mrs. Gordon's half contemptuous toleration and lack of consideration for us both. As I rose from my seat to leave the room I said to Captain Gordon:

"Still, in spite of all, sir, I am a Gordon, legally born. I will not tamely give up my birthright."

I left that room a broken-hearted girl, filled with a desire for revenge upon this man, my father, who by his manner disowned us without a regret. Not once in that remarkable interview did he speak of our mother as his wife; he quietly repudiated her and us with all the cold cruelty of relentless caste prejudice. I heard the treatment of your lover's proposal; I knew why Captain Gordon's consent to your marriage was withheld.

The night of the reception and dance was the chance for which I had waited, planned and watched. I crept from my window into the ivy-vines, and so down, down, until I stood upon the window-sill of Captain Gordon's room in the old left tower. How did I do it, you ask? I do not know. The house was silent after the revel; the darkness of the gathering storm favored me, too. The lawyer was there that day. The will was signed and put safely away among my father's papers. I was determined to have the will and the other documents bearing upon the case, and I would have revenge, too, for the cruelties we had suffered. With the old East Indian dagger firmly grasped I entered the room and found—that my revenge had been forestalled! The horror of the discovery I made that night restored me to reason and a realization of the crime I meditated. Scarce knowing what I did, I sought and found the papers, and crept back to my room as I had come. Do you wonder that my disease is past medical aid?"

I looked at Edward as I finished. He sat, his face covered with his hands. Finally he looked up with a glance of haggard despair: "God! Doctor, but this is too much. I could stand the stigma of murder, but add to that the pollution of Negro blood! No man is brave enough to face such a situation."

"It is as I thought it would be," said Talma sadly, while the tears poured over her white face. "I do not blame you, Edward."

He rose from his chair, rung my hand in a convulsive clasp, turned to Talma and bowed profoundly, with his eyes fixed upon the floor, hesitated, turned, paused, bowed again and abruptly left the room. So those two who had been lovers, parted. I turned to Talma, expecting her to give way. She smiled a pitiful smile, and said: "You see, Doctor, I knew best."

From that on she failed rapidly. I was restless. If only I could rouse her to an interest in life, she might live to old age. So rich, so young, so beautiful, so talented, so pure; I grew savage thinking of the injustice of the world. I had not reckoned on the power that never sleeps. Something was about to happen.

On visiting Cameron next morning I found him approaching the end. He had been sinking for a week very rapidly. As I sat by the bedside holding his emaciated hand, he fixed his bright, wicked eyes on me, and asked: "How long have I got to live?"

"Candidly, but a few hours."

"Thank you; well, I want death; I am not afraid to die. Doctor, Cameron is not my name."

"I never supposed it was."

"No? You are sharper than I thought. I heard all your talk yesterday with Talma Gordon. Curse the whole race!"

He clasped his bony fingers around my arm and gasped: *"I murdered the Gordons!"*

Had I the pen of a Dumas I could not paint Cameron as he told his story. It is a question with me whether this wheeling planet, home of the suffering, doubting, dying, may not hold worse agonies on its smiling surface than those of the conventional hell. I sent for Talma and a lawyer. We gave him stimulants, and then with broken intervals of coughing and prostration we got the story of the Gordon murder. I give it to you in a few words:

"I am an East Indian, but my name does not matter, Cameron is as good as any. There is many a soul crying in heaven and hell for vengeance on Jonathan Gordon. Gold was his idol; and many a good man walked the plank, and many a gallant ship was stripped of her treasure, to satisfy his lust for gold. His blackest crime was the murder of my father, who was his friend, and had sailed with him for many a year as mate. One night these two went ashore together to bury their treasure. My father never returned from that expedition. His body was afterward found with a bullet through the heart on the shore where the vessel stopped that night. It was the custom then among pirates for the captain to kill the men who helped bury their treasure. Captain Gordon was no better than a pirate. An East Indian never forgets, and I swore by my mother's deathbed to hunt Captain Gordon down until I had avenged my father's murder. I had the plans of the Gordon estate, and fixed on the night of the reception in honor of Talma as the time for my vengeance. There is a secret entrance from the shore to the chambers where Captain Gordon slept; no one knew of it save the Captain and trusted members of his crew. My mother gave me the plans, and entrance and escape were easy."

"So the great mystery was solved. In a few hours Cameron was no more. We placed the confession in the hands of the police, and there the matter ended."

"But what became of Talma Gordon?" questioned the president. "Did she die?"

"Gentlemen," said the Doctor, rising to his feet and sweeping the faces of the company with his eagle gaze, "gentlemen, if you will follow me to the drawing-room, I shall have much pleasure in introducing you to my wife—*nee* Talma Gordon."

From *Of One Blood; or, The Hidden Self* (1902)

CHAPTER III.

It was Hallow-eve.

The north wind blew a cutting blast over the stately Charles, and broke the waves into a miniature flood; it swept the streets of the University city, and danced on into the outlying suburbs tossing the last leaves about in gay disorder, not even sparing the quiet precincts of Mount Auburn cemetery. A deep, clear, moonless sky stretched overhead, from which hung myriads of sparkling stars.

In Mount Auburn, where the residences of the rich lay far apart, darkness and quietness had early settled down. The main street seemed given over to the duskiness of the evening, and with one exception, there seemed no light on earth or in heaven save the cold gleam of the stars.

The one exception was in the home of Charlie Vance, or "Adonis," as he was called by his familiars. The Vance estate was a spacious house with rambling ells, tortuous chimney-stacks, and corners, eaves and ledges; the grounds were extensive and well kept telling silently of the opulence of its owner. Its windows sent forth a cheering light. Dinner was just over.

Within, on an old-fashioned hearth, blazed a glorious wood fire, which gave a rich coloring to the oak-paneled walls, and fell warmly on a group of young people seated and standing, chatting about the fire. At one side of it, in a chair of the Elizabethan period, sat the hostess, Molly Vance, only daughter of James Vance, Esq., and sister of "Adonis," a beautiful girl of eighteen.

At the opposite side, leaning with folded arms against the high carved mantel, stood Aubrey Livingston; the beauty of his fair hair and blue eyes was never more marked as he stood there in the gleam of the fire and the soft candle light. He was talking vivaciously, his eyes turning from speaker to speaker, as he ran on, but resting chiefly with pride on his beautiful betrothed, Molly Vance.

The group was completed by two or three other men, among them Reuel Briggs, and three pretty girls. Suddenly a clock struck the hour.

"Only nine," exclaimed Molly. "Good people, what shall we do to wile the tedium of waiting for the witching hour? Have any one of you enough wisdom to make a suggestion?"

"Music," said Livingston.

"We don't want anything so commonplace."

"Blind Man's Buff," suggested "Adonis."

"Oh! please not that, the men are so rough!"

"Let us," broke in Cora Scott, "tell ghost stories."

"Good, Cora! yes, yes, yes."

"No, no!" exclaimed a chorus of voices.

"Yes, yes," laughed Molly, gaily, clapping her hands. "It is the very thing. Cora, you are the wise woman of the party. It is the very time, tonight is the new moon, and we can try our projects in the Hyde house."

"The moon should be full to account for such madness," said Livingston.

"Don't be disagreeable, Aubrey," replied Molly. "The 'ayes' have it. You're with me, Mr. Briggs?"

"Of course, Miss Vance," answered Reuel, "to go to the North Pole or Hades—only please tell us where is 'Hyde house.'"

"Have you never heard? Why it's the adjoining estate. It is reputed to be haunted, and a lady in white haunts the avenue in the most approved ghostly style."

"Bosh!" said Livingston.

"Possibly," remarked the laughing Molly, "but it is the 'bosh' of a century."

"Go on, Miss Vance; don't mind Aubrey. Who has seen the lady?"

"She is not easily seen," proceeded Molly, "she only appears on Hallow-eve, when the moon is new, as it will be tonight. I had forgotten that fact when I invited you here. If anyone stands, tonight, in the avenue leading to the house, he will surely see the tall veiled figure gliding among the old hemlock trees."

One or two shivered.

"If, however, the watcher remain, the lady will pause, and utter some sentence of prophecy of his future."

"Has any one done this?" queried Reuel.

"My old nurse says she remembers that the lady was seen once."

"Then, we'll test it again tonight!" exclaimed Reuel, greatly excited over the chance to prove his pet theories.

"Well, Molly, you've started Reuel off on his greatest hobby; I wash my hands of both of you."

"Let us go any way!" chorused the venturesome party.

"But there are conditions," exclaimed Molly. "Only one person must go at a time."

Aubrey laughed as he noticed the consternation in one or two faces.

"So," continued Molly, "as we cannot go together, I propose that each shall stay a quarter of an hour, then whether successful or not, return and let another take his or her place. I will go first."

"No—" it was Charlie who spoke—"I put my veto on that, Molly. If you are mad enough to risk colds in this mad freak, it shall be done fairly. We will draw lots."

"And I add to that, not a girl leave the house; we men will try the charm for the sake of your curiosity, but not a girl goes. You can try the ordinary Hallow-eve projects while we are away."

With many protests, but concealed relief, this plan was reluctantly adopted by the female element. The lots were prepared and placed in a hat, and amid much merriment, drawn.

"You are third, Mr. Briggs," exclaimed Molly who held the hat and watched the checks.

"I'm first," said Livingston, "and Charlie second."

"While we wait for twelve, tell us the story of the house, Molly," cried Cora.

Thus adjured, Molly settled herself comfortably in her chair and began: "Hyde House is nearly opposite the cemetery, and its land joins that of this house; it is indebted for its ill-repute to one of its owners, John Hyde. It has been known for years as a haunted house, and avoided as such by the superstitious. It is low-roofed, rambling, and almost entirely concealed by hemlocks, having an air of desolation and decay in keeping with its ill-repute. In its dozen rooms were enacted the dark deeds which gave the place the name of the 'haunted house.'

"The story is told of an unfaithful husband, a wronged wife and a beautiful governess forming a combination which led to the murder of a guest for his money. The master of the house died from remorse, under peculiar circumstances. These materials give us the plot for a thrilling ghost story."

"Well, where does the lady come in?" interrupted "Adonis."

There was a general laugh.

"This world is all a blank without the ladies for Charlie," remarked Aubrey.

"Molly, go on with your story, my child."

"You may all laugh as much as you please, but what I am telling you is believed in this section by every one. A local magazine speaks of it as follows, as near as I can remember:

"'A most interesting story is told by a woman who occupied the house for a short time. She relates that she had no sooner crossed the threshold than she was met by a beautiful woman in flowing robes of black, who begged permission to speak through her to her friends. The friends were thereupon bidden to be present at a certain time. When all were assembled they were directed by invisible powers to kneel. Then the spirit told the tale of the tragedy through the woman. The spirit was the niece of the murderer, and she was in the house when the crime was committed. She discovered blood stains on the door of the woodshed, and told her uncle that she suspected him of murdering the guest, who had mysteriously disappeared. He secured her promise not to betray him. She had always kept the secret. Although both had been dead for many years, they were chained to the scene of the crime, as was the governess, who was the man's partner in guilt. The final release of the niece from the place was conditional on her making a public confession. This done she would never be heard from again. And she never was, except on Hallow-eve, when the moon is new.'"

"Bring your science and philosophy to bear on this, Reuel. Come, come, man, give us your opinion," exclaimed Aubrey.

"Reuel doesn't believe such stuff; he's too sensible," added Charlie.

"If these are facts, they are only for those who have a mental affinity with them. I believe that if we could but strengthen our mental sight, we could discover the broad highway between this and the other world on which both good and evil travel to earth," replied Reuel.

"And that first highway was beaten out of chaos by Satan, as Milton has it, eh, Briggs?"

"Have it as you like, Smith. No matter. For my own part, I have never believed that the whole mental world is governed by the faculties we understand, and can reduce to reason or definite feeling. But I will keep my ideas to myself; one does not care to be laughed at."

The conversation was kept up for another hour about indifferent subjects, but all felt the excitement underlying the frivolous chatter. At quarter before twelve, Aubrey put on his ulster with the words: "Well, here goes for my lady." The great doors were thrown open, and the company grouped about him to see him depart.

"Mind, honor bright, you go," laughed Charlie.

"Honor bright," he called back.

Then he went on beyond the flood of light into the gloom of the night. Muffled in wraps and ulsters they lingered on the piazzas waiting his return.

"Would he see anything?"

"Of course not!" laughed Charlie and Bert Smith. "Still, we bet he'll be sharp to his time."

They were right. Aubrey returned at five minutes past twelve, a failure.

Charlie ran down the steps briskly, but in ten minutes came hastening back.

"Well," was the chorus, "did you see it?"

"I saw something—a figure in the trees!"

"And you did not wait?" said Molly, scornfully.

"No, I dared not; I own it."

"It's my turn; I'm third," said Reuel.

"Luck to you, old man," they called as he disappeared in the darkness.

Reuel Briggs was a brave man. He knew his own great physical strength and felt no fear as he traversed the patch of woods lying between the two estates. As he reached the avenue of hemlocks he was not thinking of his mission, but of the bright home scene he had just left—of love and home and rest—such a life as was unfolding before Aubrey Livingston and sweet Molly Vance.

"I suppose there are plenty of men in the world as lonely as I am," he mused; "but I suppose it is my own fault. A man though plain and poor can generally manage to marry; and I am both. But I don't regard a wife as one regards bread—better sour bread than starvation; better an uncongenial life-companion than none! What a frightful mistake! No! The woman I marry must be to me a necessity, because I love her; because so loving her, 'all the current of my being flows to her' and I feel she is my supreme need."

Just now he felt strangely happy as he moved in the gloom of the hemlocks, and he wondered many times after that whether the spirit is sometimes mysteriously conscious of the nearness of its kindred spirit; and feels, in anticipation, the "sweet unrest" of the master-passion that rules the world.

The mental restlessness of three weeks before seemed to have possession of him again. Suddenly the "restless, unsatisfied longing," rose again in his heart. He turned his head and saw a female figure just ahead of him in the path, coming toward him. He could not see her features distinctly, only the eyes—large, bright and dark. But their expression! Sorrowful, wistful—almost imploring—gazing straightforward, as if they saw nothing—like the eyes of a person entirely absorbed and not distinguishing one object from another.

She was close to him now, and there was a perceptible pause in her step. Suddenly she covered her face with her clasped hands, as if in uncontrollable grief. Moved by a mighty emotion, Briggs addressed the lonely figure:

"You are in trouble, madam; may I help you?"

Briggs never knew how he survived the next shock. Slowly the hands were removed from the face and the moon gave a distinct view of the lovely features of the jubilee singer—Dianthe Lusk.

She did not seem to look at Briggs, but straight before her, as she said in a low, clear, passionless voice:

"You can help me, but not now; tomorrow."

Reuel's most prominent feeling was one of delight. The way was open to become fully acquainted with the woman who had haunted him sleeping and waking, for weeks past.

"Not now! Yet you are suffering. Shall I see you soon? Forgive me—but oh! tell me—"

He was interrupted. The lady moved or floated away from him, with her face toward him and gazing steadily at him.

He felt that his whole heart was in his eyes, yet hers did not drop, nor did her cheek color.

"The time is not yet," she said in the same, clear, calm, measured tones, in which she had spoken before. Reuel made a quick movement toward her, but she raised her hand, and the gesture forbade him to follow her. He paused involuntarily, and she turned away, and disappeared among the gloomy hemlock trees.

He parried the questions of the merry crowd when he returned to the house, with indifferent replies. How they would have laughed at him— slave of a passion as sudden and romantic as that of Romeo for Juliet; with no more foundation than the "presentments" in books which treat of the "occult." He dropped asleep at last, in the early morning hours, and lived over his experience in his dreams.

CHAPTER IV.

Although not yet a practitioner, Reuel Briggs was a recognized power in the medical profession. In brain diseases he was an authority.

Early the next morning he was aroused from sleep by imperative knocking at his door. It was a messenger from the hospital. There had been a train accident on the Old Colony road, would he come immediately?

Scarcely giving himself time for a cup of coffee, he arrived at the hospital almost as soon as the messenger.

The usual silence of the hospital was broken; all was bustle and movement, without confusion. It was a great call upon the resources of the officials, but they were equal to it. The doctors passed from sufferer to sufferer, dressing their injuries; then they were borne to beds from which some would never rise again.

"Come with me to the women's ward, Doctor Briggs," said a nurse. "There is a woman there who was taken from the wreck. She shows no sign of injury, but the doctors cannot restore her to consciousness. Doctor Livingston pronounces her dead, but it doesn't seem possible. So young, so beautiful. Do something for her, Doctor."

The men about a cot made way for Reuel, as he entered the ward. "It's no use, Briggs," said Livingston to him in reply to his question. "Your science won't save her. The poor girl is already cold and stiff."

He moved aside disclosing to Reuel's gaze the lovely face of Dianthe Lusk!

The most marvellous thing to watch is the death of a person. At that moment the opposite takes place to that which took place when life entered the first unit, after nature had prepared it for the inception of life. How the vigorous life watches the passage of the liberated life out of its earthly environment! What a change is this! How important the knowledge of whither life tends! Here is shown the setting free of a disciplined spirit giving up its mortality for immortality,—the condition necessary to know God. Death! There is no death. Life is everlasting, and from its reality can have no end. Life is real and never changes, but preserves its identity eternally as the angels, and the immortal spirit of man, which are the only realities and continuities in the universe, God being over all, Supreme Ruler and Divine Essence from whom comes all life. Somewhat in this train ran Reuel's thoughts as he stood beside the seeming dead girl, the cynosure of all the medical faculty there assembled.

To the majority of those men, the case was an ordinary death, and that was all there was to it. What did this young upstart expect to make of it? Of his skill and wonderful theories they had heard strange tales, but they viewed him coldly as we are apt to view those who dare to leave the beaten track of conventionality.

Outwardly cool and stolid, showing no sign of recognition, he stood for some seconds gazing down on Dianthe: every nerve quivered, every pulse of his body throbbed. Her face held for him a wonderful charm, an extraordinary fascination. As he gazed he knew that once more he beheld what he had vaguely sought and yearned for all his forlorn life. His whole heart went out to her; destiny, not chance, had brought him to her. He saw, too, that no one knew her, none had a clue to her identity; he determined to remain silent for the present, and immediately he sought to impress Livingston to do likewise.

His keen glance swept the faces of the surrounding physicians. "No, not one," he told himself, "holds the key to unlock this seeming sleep of death." He alone could do it. Advancing far afield in the mysterious regions of science, he had stumbled upon the solution of one of life's problems: *the reanimation of the body after seeming death.*

He had hesitated to tell of his discovery to any one; not even to Livingston had he hinted of the daring possibility, fearing ridicule in case of a miscarriage in his calculations. But for the sake of this girl he would make what he felt to be a premature disclosure of the results of his experiments.

Meantime, Livingston, from his place at the foot of the cot, watched his friend with fascinated eyes. He, too, had resolved, contrary to his first intention, not to speak of his knowledge of the beautiful patient's identity. Curiosity was on tiptoe; expectancy was in the air. All felt that something unusual was about to happen.

Now Reuel, with gentle fingers, touched rapidly the clammy brow, the icy, livid hands, the region of the pulseless heart. No breath came from between the parted lips; the life-giving organ was motionless. As he concluded his examination, he turned to the assembled doctors:

"As I diagnose this case, it is one of suspended animation. This woman has been long and persistently subjected to mesmeric influences, and the nervous shock induced by the excitement of the accident has thrown her into a cataleptic sleep."

"But, man!" broke from the head physician in tones of exasperation, "rigor mortis in unmistakable form is here. The woman is dead!"

At these words there was a perceptible smile on the faces of some of the students—associates who resented his genius as a personal affront, and who considered these words as good as a reprimand for the daring student, and a settler of his pretensions. Malice and envy, from Adam's time until today, have loved a shining mark.

But the reproof was unheeded. Reuel was not listening. Absorbed in thoughts of the combat before him, he was oblivious to all else as he bent over the lifeless figure on the cot. He was full of an earnest purpose. He was strung up to a high tension of force and energy. As he looked down upon the unconscious girl whom none but he could save from the awful fate of a death by post-mortem, and who by some mysterious mesmeric affinity existing between them, had drawn him to her rescue, he felt no fear that he should fail.

Suddenly he bent down and took both cold hands into his left and passed his right hand firmly over her arms from shoulder to wrist. He repeated the movements several times; there was no response to the passes. He straightened up, and again stood silently gazing upon the patient. Then, like a man just aroused from sleep, he looked across the bed at Livingston and said abruptly:

"Dr. Livingston, will you go over to my room and bring me the case of vials in my medicine cabinet? I cannot leave the patient at this point."

Livingston started in surprise as he replied: "Certainly, Briggs, if it will help you any."

"The patient does not respond to any of the ordinary methods of awakening. She would probably lie in this sleep for months, and death ensue from exhaustion, if stronger remedies are not used to restore the vital force to a normal condition."

Livingston left the hospital; he could not return under an hour; Reuel took up his station by the bed whereon was stretched an apparently lifeless body, and the other doctors went the rounds of the wards attending to their regular routine of duty. The nurses gazed at him curiously; the head doctor, upon whom the young student's earnestness and sincerity had evidently made an impression, came a number of times to the bare little room to gaze upon its silent occupants, but there was nothing new. When Livingston returned, the group again gathered about the iron cot where lay the patient.

"Gentlemen," said Reuel, with quiet dignity, when they were once more assembled, "will you individually examine the patient once more and give your verdicts?"

Once more doctors and students carefully examined the inanimate figure in which the characteristics of death were still more pronounced. On the outskirts of the group hovered the house-surgeon's assistants ready to transport the body to the operating room for the post-mortem. Again the head physician spoke, this time impatiently.

"We are wasting our time, Dr. Briggs; I pronounce the woman dead. She was past medical aid when brought here."

"There is no physical damage, apparent or hidden, that you can see, Doctor?" questioned Reuel, respectfully.

"No; it is a perfectly healthful organism, though delicate. I agree entirely with your assertion that death was induced by the shock."

"Not *death*, Doctor," protested Briggs.

"Well, well, call it what you like—call it what you like, it amounts to the same in the end," replied the doctor testily.

"Do you all concur in Doctor Hamilton's diagnosis?" Briggs included all the physicians in his sweeping glance. There was a general assent.

"I am prepared to show you that in some cases of seeming death—or even death in reality—consciousness may be restored or the dead brought back to life. I have numberless times in the past six months restored consciousness to dogs and cats after rigor mortis had set in," he declared calmly.

"Bosh!" broke from a leading surgeon. In this manner the astounding statement, made in all seriousness, was received by the group of scientists mingled with an astonishment that resembled stupidity. But in spite of their scoffs, the young student's confident manner made a decided impression upon his listeners, unwilling as they were to be convinced.

Reuel went on rapidly; his eyes kindled; his whole person took on the majesty of conscious power, and pride in the knowledge he possessed. "I have found by research that life is not dependent upon organic function as a principle. It may be infused into organized bodies even after the organs have ceased to perform their legitimate offices. Where death has been due to causes which have not impaired or injured or destroyed tissue formation or torn down the structure of vital organs, life may be recalled when it has become entirely extinct, which is not so in the present case. This I have discovered by my experiments in animal magnetism."

The medical staff was fairly bewildered. Again Dr. Hamilton spoke:

"You make the assertion that the dead can be brought to life, if I understand your drift, Dr. Briggs, and you expect us to believe such utter nonsense." He added significantly, "My colleagues and I are here to be convinced."

"If you will be patient for a short time longer, Doctor, I will support my assertion by action. The secret of life lies in what we call volatile magnetism—it exists in the free atmosphere. You, Dr. Livingston, understand my meaning; do you see the possibility in my words?" he questioned, appealing to Aubrey for the first time.

"I have a faint conception of your meaning, certainly," replied his friend.

"This subtile magnetic agent is constantly drawn into the body through the lungs, absorbed and held in bounds until chemical combination has occurred through the medium of mineral agents always present in normal animal tissue. When respiration ceases this magnetism cannot be drawn into the lungs. It must be artificially supplied. This, gentlemen, is my discovery. I supply this magnetism. I have it here in the case Dr. Livingston has kindly brought me." He held up to their gaze a small phial wherein reposed a powder. Physicians and students, now eager listeners, gazed spell-bound upon him, straining their ears to catch every tone of the low voice and every change of the luminous eyes; they pressed forward to examine the contents of the bottle. It passed from eager hand to eager hand, then back to the owner.

"This compound, gentlemen, is an exact reproduction of the conditions existing in the human body. It has common salt for its basis. This salt is saturated with oleo resin and then exposed for several hours in an atmosphere of free ammonia. The product becomes a powder, and *that* brings back the seeming dead to life."

"Establish your theory by practical demonstration, Dr. Briggs, and the dreams of many eminent practitioners will be realized," said Dr. Hamilton, greatly agitated by his words.

"Your theory smacks of the supernatural, Dr. Briggs, charlatanism, or dreams of lunacy," said the surgeon. "We leave such assertions to quacks, generally, for the time of miracles is past."

"The supernatural presides over man's formation always," returned Reuel, quietly. "Life is that evidence of supernatural endowment which originally entered nature during the formation of the units for the evolution of man. Perhaps the superstitious masses came nearer to solving the mysteries of creation than the favored elect will ever come. Be that as it may, I will not contend. I will proceed with the demonstration."

There radiated from the speaker the potent presence of a truthful mind, a pure, unselfish nature, and that inborn dignity which repels the shafts of lower minds as ocean's waves absorb the drops of rain. Something like respect mingled with awe hushed the sneers, changing them into admiration as he calmly proceeded to administer the so-called life-giving powder. Each man's watch was in his hand; one minute passed—another—and still another. The body remained inanimate.

A cold smile of triumph began to dawn on the faces of the older members of the profession, but it vanished in its incipiency, for a tremor plainly passed over the rigid form before them. Another second—another convulsive movement of the chest!

"She moves!" cried Aubrey at last, carried out of himself by the strain on his nerves. "Look, gentlemen, she breathes! *She is alive*; Briggs is right! Wonderful! Wonderful!"

"We said there could not be another miracle, and here it is!" exclaimed Dr. Hamilton with strong emotion.

Five minutes more and the startled doctors fell back from the bedside at a motion of Reuel's hand. A wondering nurse, with dilated eyes, unfolded a screen, placed it in position and came and stood beside the bed opposite Reuel. Holding Dianthe's hands, he said in a low voice: "Are you awake?" Her eyes unclosed in a cold, indifferent stare which gradually changed to one of recognition. She looked at him—she smiled, and said in a weak voice, "Oh, it is you; I dreamed of you while I slept."

She was like a child—so trusting that it went straight to the young man's heart, and for an instant a great lump seemed to rise in his throat and choke him. He held her hands and chafed them, but spoke with his eyes only. The nurse said in a low voice: "Dr. Briggs, a few spoonfuls of broth will help her?"

"Yes, thank you, nurse; that will be just right." He drew a chair close beside the bed, bathed her face with water and pushed back the tangle of bright hair. He felt a great relief and quiet joy that his experiment had been successful.

"Have I been ill? Where am I?" she asked after a pause, as her face grew troubled and puzzled.

"No, but you have been asleep a long time; we grew anxious about you. You must not talk until you are stronger."

The muse returned with the broth; Dianthe drank it eagerly and called for water, then with her hand still clasped in Reuel's she sank into a deep sleep, breathing softly like a tired child. It was plain to the man of science that hope for the complete restoration of her faculties would depend upon time, nature and constitution. Her effort to collect her thoughts was unmistakable. In her sleep, presently, from her lips fell incoherent words and phrases; but through it all she clung to Reuel's hand, seeming to recognize in him a friend.

A little later the doctors filed in noiselessly and stood about the bed gazing down upon the sleeper with awe, listening to her breathing, feeling lightly the fluttering pulse. Then they left the quiet house of suffering, marvelling at the miracle just accomplished in their presence. Livingston lingered with Briggs after the other physicians were gone.

"This is a great day for you, Reuel," he said, as he laid a light caressing hand upon the other's shoulder.

Reuel seized the hand in a quick convulsive clasp. "True and tried friend, do not credit me more than I deserve. No praise is due me. I am an instrument—how I know not—a child of circumstances. Do you not perceive: something strange in this case? Can you not deduce conclusions from your own intimate knowledge of this science?"

"What can you mean, Reuel?"

"I mean—it is a *dual* mesmeric trance! The girl is only partly normal now. Binet speaks at length of this possibility in his treatise. We have stumbled upon an extraordinary case. It will take a year to restore her to perfect health."

"In the meantime we ought to search out her friends."

"Is there any hurry, Aubrey?" pleaded Reuel, anxiously.

"Why not wait until her memory returns; it will not be long, I believe, although she may still be liable to the trances."

"We'll put off the evil day to any date you may name, Briggs; for my part, I would preserve her incognito indefinitely."

Reuel made no reply. Livingston was not sure that he heard him.

Converting Fanny (1916)

As told over the telephone by her father, Brother Sam Mingo, to his pastor, Rev. Johnson Brown.

"Reveren' Brown, this is Sam Mingo. Anythin' you want me to do for you, Reveren'?"

"........."

"That's jes' so; I did whop her pow'ful. I'se been convertin' her."

"........."

"What kin' of Christian do I call myse'f? I's a ol'-time Christian, an' I inten's my chillern to meet me in Heaven, an' ef you spare the rod you spile the child."

"........."

"'Salt an' batt'ry! Good Lord, Reveren', *you cayn't make it 'salt an' batt'ry nohow!* Fanny's my child, an' I got the right to whop her ef so fittin' it seem proper to me, sar."

"........."

"*Agin the law!* Lordy, Lordy, what kin' of law is that won't 'low a parient to chestise the onruly child?"

"........."

"I stood gum-stick-um, ox grease, molasses and yaller soap to put white folks' hair on her head; silk dresses an' high-heel boots an' split-up the back skirts, the cakewalk and the tango, but when it comes to—"

"........"

"Don't keer ef it *be* the fashion. No child of mine is gwine to bring my gray hairs in sorrer to the grave because it's the *fashion*. An' you ain't right *yo'self* ef you count'nance sech doin' es that. What's a minister of the Gospel got to do with *fashion* enyhow? Savin' souls an' preachin' is your business. No 'pinion of you, Brother, contra'wise."

"........"

"*College! Hump!* No more of my chillern is goin' to college; this here one's settled that business. *She* don't *eat* eny mo' with her *knife*, says that's *vulgar*, so she *eats with her fork*. Hump!"

"........"

"That's all right, that's all right, Reveren', fer white folks, but I've always eat with a knife, an' too much style ain't good for colored folks nohow."

"........"

"*All right, sar!* Chuch me ef you want to, sar, *Chuch me!* I 'peal to the Trustees an' to the whole Board ef I didn't do my duty as the Lord showed it to me."

"........"

"May be so, Reveren'; but, now, wait a minute, let me tell you jes' how it happened: I asked Fanny to lead us in prayer, an' she say she no more a Methodis', but that now she's a 'Piscopal, an' she got on her knees an' *read that prayer out of a book!* I couldn't stand no mo', sar, no sar! I jes' went out and cut a bunch of switches down in the pastur' an' I shet her up in the barn, an' dog my cats I whop that gal 'til she cry out 'Oh, daddy, daddy! I'm a Methodis' I've got the ol-time religion. Please stop an' I'll never be a 'Piscopal agin'. So you see, by takin' it in season, I converted her right back to the ol'-time religion."

"........"

"Yes, sar; I know it was Communion Sunday, but I was jes' *domned mad*, fit to bust, with that fool gal."

"........"

"'Scuse me, sar, 'scuse me fer cussin'. Nobody respec's the cloth mor'n me, but I'm clean outside myself."

"........"

"*What's that you say: She's swared out a warrant agin me!* Well, well, of all the onregen'rate, honery. . . . Say, Reveren', will you stan' my bail in case this thing goes to co't?"

SOURCES

Hopkins, Pauline E. "Converting Fanny." *New Era Magazine* 1, no. 1 (February 1916): 33–34. Published under the pseudonym "Sarah A. Allen."

———. "Of One Blood; or, The Hidden Self." *Colored American Magazine* 6, no. 1 (November 1902): 36–40, 102–6.

———. "Talma Gordon." *Colored American Magazine* 1, no. 5 (October 1900): 271–90.

NOTES

1. From Shakespeare's *Hamlet* (1609), act 5, scene 2.
2. From "Madeline" by British poet Alfred, Lord Tennyson (1809–1892).
3. "A Wet Sheet and a Flowing Sea" is a sea-song by Scottish dialect poet Allan Cunningham (1784–1842).

Julia Ward Howe

1819–1910

JULIA WARD HOWE was a writer, lecturer, abolitionist, and suffragist born into a well-to-do white family from New York. In her lifetime, she was best known for writing the Civil War anthem "Battle Hymn of the Republic." Much of Howe's work critiqued women's roles as wives and members of society, as well as her own difficult marriage. After the war, she focused her efforts on women's suffrage and pacifism, cofounding (with Lucy Stone) the American Woman Suffrage Association in 1869. She became editor of the suffragist magazine *Woman's Journal* in 1872 and contributed to it for twenty years. Known as the "Dearest Old Lady in America," she lectured widely, and wherever she went, she founded clubs, such as the Association for the Advancement of Women, which advocated for women's educational, professional, and cultural development. In 1908 she was the first woman to be elected to the American

Academy of Arts and Letters. We include excerpts from one of her most
radical works, *The Hermaphrodite*, which was left incomplete in manu-
script but was probably composed between 1846 and 1847. The first page
of the manuscript is missing; the tale begins on page two.

From *The Hermaphrodite* (ca. 1846–47)

[. . .]ration on the part of my parents, it was resolved to invest me with
the dignity and insignia of manhood, which would at least permit me to
choose my own terms in associating with the world, and secure to me an
independence of position most desirable for one who could never hope
to become the half of another. I was baptized therefore by a masculine
name, destined to a masculine profession, and sent to a boarding school
for boys, that I might become robust and manly, and haply learn to seem
that which I could never be.

At school, and afterward at college, my career was more prosperous
than could have been anticipated. I learned quickly, was sensitive to re-
proof, and ambitious of approbation. I became a favorite with my tutors,
and ranked among the first in my class. Even my rough comrades learned
to play more gently with me than with each other—in my intercourse with
them, I instinctively appealed to their generosity, rather than defy their
force. "Laurence is tired, poor fellow, do not hurt him, he is not so strong
as we—" thus they spoke of me, and the most hardy among them agreed
to protect and defend one superior to themselves in grace and agility, but
greatly their inferior in force. I was distinguishable from them chiefly by a
stronger impulse of physical modesty, a greater sensitiveness to kindness,
and a feebler power of reasoning. But a child has, properly speaking, no
sex, and my time of trial came not until childhood had passed—then only
did I learn all that I was, and was not, and this fearful lesson has occupied
my whole life.

I saw my parents only at long intervals during the years I passed at
school. They were cold and reserved towards me, and seemed always to
feel a certain relief at the termination of my short and infrequent vaca-
tions. I learned at last to dread rather than desire the arrival of those peri-
ods so golden in the lives of most children, and was scarcely sorry to learn
that my visits at home were to cease with the beginning of my academic
career. The college for which I was destined was remote from my father's

residence, and on entering it, I saw him for the last time in several years. He came, on this occasion, to announce to me the birth of a younger and only brother, the death of my mother, and his own intention of being absent from the country for the space of a year or more. He seemed to me more cold and repulsive than ever, and I was surprised to find that he had taken pains to inform himself of the minutest details bearing any relation to my character and conduct. His approbation and his counsel were briefly summed up in these words: "Laurence, you have studied well; continue to apply yourself, and to avoid all unnecessary intimacies."

"Yes, Sir."

"Embrace your father, Laurence," cried my old preceptor, who was present at this laconic parting.

"It is quite unnecessary," said the frigid Paternus.

"I am deuced glad of it," rejoined I, with a long breath.

My father fixed his eyes on mine with an expression of some astonishment—he read in my face an indifference and pride which might have seemed the reflection of his own. He coldly bade farewell, and left me—young as I was, I had at least determined that he should never know the pain he had given me.

At this period in my life, I know not how an impartial judge would have decided the doubtful question of my being—my powers of intellect had shot beyond those of my compeers, while yet my form threatened to take a strongly feminine development. My complexion was singularly delicate, and my hair, though continually cropped, would retain its silky softness, and fell in many curls around my neck and brow. At long intervals, my usually robust health was interrupted by fits of indisposition, each of which seemed a sort of crisis, a struggle between death and life. Strange to say, nature had endowed me with rare beauty. I grew tall and slender, my limbs were finely moulded, and my head might have been cited as a perfect model of classic grace. This beauty, under other circumstances, might have been a blessing; as it was, it proved the curse and torment of my life. In vain would I have shrunk into obscurity—I could nowhere show myself without being observed and pointed out of all. Women often gave me proofs of a stronger interest than any inspired by mere benevolence, while the eyes of men so scrutinized me that I was fain to hide myself from them with a perturbation for which I could scarce account to myself. I was anxious to propitiate the good will of all, but any intimacy beyond that of ordinary friendship was incomprehensible to me. For man or woman, as such, I felt an entire indifference—when I wished to trifle, I preferred the latter, when I wished to reason gravely, I chose the former. I sought sympathy from women, advice from men, but love from neither. Like all other young creatures, I was gladly in the company of the gay and of the gentle, but I could not be in it long without learning that a human soul, simply as such, and not invested with the capacity of either entire possession or entire surrender, has but a lame and unsatisfactory part to play in this world.

In the village that surrounded us, my college companions had many female friends, among whom I gradually became known. These pretty moths consumed no small portion of our learned leisure, and our holidays were entirely consecrated to their service. On these occasions, we often arranged parties of pleasure to various caves, ruins, and woods in the romantic neighbourhood, in which every youth was cavalier to some fair maiden, and the time was improved by most of them for the establishment of relations of a more or less intimate nature. Of these, some were passionate, some sentimental, some transitory, some of life long duration, but all partaking of a feeling which was to me utterly incomprehensible. I enjoyed as keenly as any one a gallop on the greensward, or a ramble in the woods—our feasts and frolics, our songs and dances were all delightsome to me then in vivid reality, as now in softened remembrance—my eye was gratified by the grace and loveliness of the young girls, and my heart expanded in the sunshine of their gentle, happy nature, but they were to me even as the flowers, their sisters, and as the birds, their cousins, and as the distant clouds of heaven, and as all things else that were changeful and beautiful like unto them.

It was sufficiently easy for me to vie with my fellow-students in rendering every courtesy to these fair creatures. Like all the rest, I led their gentle feet over rocks and mountain paths, or bent my knee that they might spring from it into the saddle—I twined chaplets for their festivals, and verses for their songs, but no passionate thought or wish was interwoven with either. The enthusiasm expressed in my verses was vague and abstract in its character, and though of warmer blood and more generous nature than most of my fellows, I yet in comparison with them seemed cold and statue-like. The innocence and purity of the young girls did not however lead them to suspect any peculiarity of kind in me. They found me ever gay, affable, and gracefully bold—they often turned from the amorous gabble of a stupid lover, to seek amusement from me, and I can still recall the rage of a sentimental youth whose disdainful sweetheart, wearied, angry, or alarmed at the suit he was pressing, broke from him, and took refuge beside me, saying: I shall go to Laurence, for he never makes love.

[. . .]

CHAPTER 3RD

[. . .] I was ordered to wear my wreath through the evening. Music now sounded in the hall, and couples stood up to dance. I gave my arm to Emma, and led her to the head of the Quadrille. Her momentary sadness had passed away, and as she began to tread her graceful measure, she turned upon me a look of love and delight so radiant, that it sent a strange thrill to the very core of my frozen heart, and again I asked of myself: "what is it to be a woman?"

As we stood together in an interval of repose, I could not avoid over-hearing the conversation of two strangers who occupied a place behind me, and of whom one spoke with a strongly marked Southern accent.

"What a beautiful antique head is this of the young Laureate's," remarked one, "so delicately chiselled, so finely set, one might say an Antinoüs, a Mercury, almost an Apollo."

"None of these," replied the Italian. "His beauty is of a more vague and undecided character—it is a face and form of strange contradictions—the eye and brow command, while the mouth persuades."

"The motions and gestures too are peculiar."

"Do you not see a striking resemblance to the lovely hermaphrodite in the villa Borghese?"

I heard no more—a mist came before my eyes, and a deadly faintness over my heart. With a hurried apology, I resigned Emma to the eager Wilhelm, and staggered to the open air—some minutes passed before I could recover strength to regain my room.

CHAPTER 4TH

Once alone, in my own room, I could breathe more freely, but my whole being had received a shock, an impetus that hurried it to some deed, some resolution, I knew not what. A sort of galvanic agony had taken possession of my body, and forces foreign to itself were playing wildly with it. My vestments seemed to gird in my swelling heart, and I tore them off, half re-solved to wear them no more. I was incapable of thought or of reason, but my brain was in a state of the highest spontaneous action, and a thousand horrible images of disgrace, despair, and utter confusion crowded each other in and out of my mind, like figures in a fever dream. Every thing around me seemed instinct with life—the very walls had eyes to spy out my secret, and tongues to betray it. I hurried hither and thither to escape the scrutiny of mocking spectres, who, all unseen, were yet present to me, and with hideous laughter followed me every where. At length, in very desperation, I threw myself, half undressed, on my bed, and drawing its covering around me, attempted to close my eyes, and compelled myself to lie still. Gradually, the confusion of my thoughts became greater, but less painful—the sounds of music and laughter became fainter in my ears, and soon ceased altogether. I know not how long it was before a light footstep at my bedside, told me that I must have been asleep.

A light footstep? oh how light! a gliding form, a gentle but fervent voice. Could it be? I rubbed my eyes, I was fully awake, and Emma, in all her brilliant beauty, stood before me.

"You were ill, dearest Laurence, and I could not rest until I had seen you—you are to leave tomorrow, and I could not live without one kind farewell from you. Oh Laurence, Laurence, do not look at me thus—you know well, you have long known what I am here to tell you."

I raised my head from the pillow and looked into her eyes. That look must have expressed the horror I felt, for it seemed to destroy the mo-mentary courage which had given firmness to her step, and clearness to her voice. She sank upon her knees beside me, she buried her face in the curtain that hung near us, and was silent for a moment—then, raising it again, she clasped my knees, and spoke with a rapid, unequal, falter-ing intonation, as if she feared that her strength would desert her before she could speak out her meaning. "Listen to me Laurence," she said: "two deaths were before me. If I sought you not, I died of longing, if I came to you, I died of shame. The first I have long endured, it is slowly feeding upon my life—if the second fate must be mine, be merciful, and kill me quick." In stony silence, I sat and listened—she continued: "I do not ask you to marry me, Laurence, I am still young, rich, and perhaps handsome, but I do not pretend to be worthy of you—had I such a hope, I should scarce be at your feet, but look you, I am here alone, in your room, in your power, at dead of night—you cannot misinterpret this, it must convince you that I love you better than life, better than honour, better than my own soul and God. Give me but this one night, but this one hour—do you ask where I shall be tomorrow? I can die tomorrow—I shall have been happy."

I roused myself at length from my stupor—"Emma," said I, laying on hers a hand so cold that she started. "Emma, as you value your soul's peace, fly—fly from me, and think of me only as you think of the dead."

"Never!" cried Emma: "you may smite me, you may kill me, but I will die here at your feet—my last look shall be on you—my last prayer shall bless you."

I pointed to the time piece on the mantel, and said: "Emma, this is madness—to yield to it would be fatal to both of us. One of us must leave this room for the night, I give you five minutes to decide which it shall be."

She sprang to her feet, and stood before me, a beautiful impersonation of scorn and fury. Lightnings flashed from her eyes—a curse rose to her lips and died there—those lips were made for blessings only—tears and convulsive sobs burst forth instead, and brokenly these words: "you cannot cannot—cannot!"

"Listen to me, dearest Emma," I said, and drew her to a seat beside me— "listen to me—can you bear to hear the truth? will you hate me for telling it to you?"

"Tell it gently," she replied, with averted eyes. I continued: "Emma, your love is too beautiful, too glorious a thing to be thrown away upon one who can never make you his. There lies between us a deep, mysterious gulf, seek not to fathom it—with me, your human destiny would be hopelessly imperfect—were I to wed you, I should indeed deserve your curse." She was silent, and I proceeded: "there are between human beings relations independent of sex, relations of pure spirit, of heavenly sympathy, of immaterial and undying affinities—such are the only relations that can exist between us, dearest Emma."

While I spoke, her eyes were suddenly turned upon mine with a look of almost superhuman intelligence. A new and dreadful suspicion seemed to dawn upon her mind. When I had ceased, she came slowly up to me, and uncovering my arm, held it up to the light—it was round and smooth as her own. With the same deliberation, she surveyed me from head to foot, the disordered habiliments revealing to her every outline of the equivocal form before her. She saw the bearded lip and earnest brow, but she saw also the falling shoulders, slender neck, and rounded bosom—then with a look like that of the Medusa, and a hoarse utterance, she murmured: "monster!"

"I am as God made me, Emma."

A shriek, fearful to hear, and thrice fearful to give, followed by another, and another, and a maniac lay foaming and writhing on the floor at my feet.

SOURCE

Howe, Julia Ward. *The Hermaphrodite*, edited by Gary Williams, 3–6, 16–19. Lincoln: University of Nebraska Press, 2004. Reproduced with permission of the University of Nebraska Press.

NOTE

Chapter opening photo: Julia Ward Howe in 1899. From the *National Magazine* (1910), commemorating the author as "the beloved of all America" upon her death.

Georgia Douglas Johnson

1880–1966

GEORGIA DOUGLAS JOHNSON was a poet and one of the earliest African American playwrights. She authored four collections of poetry: *The Heart of a Woman* (1918), *Bronze* (1922), *An Autumn Love Cycle* (1928), and *Share My World* (1962). Her poems were also published in several issues of the NAACP's magazine *The Crisis*, edited by W. E. B. Du Bois. She was the first African American woman poet to gain national attention since Frances E. W. Harper, and her house at 1461 S Street NW in Washington, DC, came to be known as the location of the S Street Salon, an important meeting place for writers of the Harlem Renaissance. Her weekly newspaper column, "Homely Philosophy," ran from 1926–32, and she wrote many plays, including *Blue Blood* (1926) and *Plumes* (1927). Her work explored what it was like to be a woman of color and a mother in the United States at the height of the lynching epidemic.

Smothered Fires (1918)

A woman with a burning flame
   Deep covered through the years
With ashes. Ah! she hid it deep,
   And smothered it with tears.

Sometimes a baleful light would rise
   From out the dusky bed,
And then the woman hushed it quick
   To slumber on, as dead.

At last the weary war was done
   The tapers were alight,
And with a sigh of victory
   She breathed a soft—good-night!

Foredoom (1918)

Her life was dwarfed, and wed to blight,
Her very days were shades of night,
Her every dream was born entombed,
Her soul, a bud,—that never bloomed.

My Little Dreams (1918)

I'm folding up my little dreams
   Within my heart tonight,
And praying I may soon forget
   The torture of their sight.

For time's deft fingers scroll my brow
   With fell relentless art—
I'm folding up my little dreams
   Tonight, within my heart.

Maternity (1922)

Proud?
Perhaps—and yet
I cannot say with surety
That I am happy thus to be
Responsible for this young life's embarking.
Is he not thrall to prevalent conditions?
Does not the day loom dark apace
To weave its cordon of disgrace
Around his lifted throat?
Is not this mezzotint enough and surfeit
For such prescience?

Ah, did I dare
Recall the pulsing life I gave,
And fold him in the kindly grave!

Proud?
Perhaps—could I but ever so faintly scan
The broad horizon of a man
Swept fair for his dominion—
So hesitant and half-afraid
I view this babe of sorrow!

Utopia (1922)

God grant you wider vision, clearer skies, my son,
With morning's rosy kisses on your brow;
May your wild yearnings know repose,
And storm-clouds break to smiles
As you sweep on with spreading wings
Unto a waiting sunset!

Credo (1922)

I believe in the ultimate justice of Fate;
That the races of men front the sun in their turn;
That each soul holds the title to infinite wealth
In fee to the will as it masters itself;
That the heart of humanity sounds the same tone
In impious jungle, or sky-kneeling fane.
I believe that the key to the life-mystery
Lies deeper than reason and further than death.
I believe that the rhythmical conscience within
Is guidance enough for the conduct of men.

Fusion (1922)

How deftly does the gardener blend
This rose and that

To bud a new creation,
More gorgeous and more beautiful
Than any parent portion,
And so,
I trace within my warring blood
The tributary sources,
They potently commingle
And sweep
With new-born forces!

When I Rise Up (1922)

When I rise above the earth,
And look down on the things that fetter me,
I beat my wings upon the air.
Or tranquil lie,
Surge after surge of potent strength
Like incense comes to me
When I rise up above the earth
And look down upon the things that fetter me.

SOURCES

Johnson, Georgia Douglas. "Foredoom," "My Little Dreams," and "Smothered Fires." In *The Heart of a Woman and Other Poems*, 39, 62, 32. Boston: Cornhill, 1918.

———. "Credo," "Fusion," "Maternity," "Utopia," and "When I Rise Up." In *Bronze*, 53, 60, 42, 48, 62. Boston: B. J. Brimmer, 1922.

Amelia E. Johnson

1858–1922

AMELIA E. JOHNSON was a novelist, short fiction writer, poet, and
editor born in Canada to American parents. She wrote under the name
Mrs. A. E. Johnson and was best known for her three novels, including
Clarence and Corinne; or, God's Way (1890). She also wrote children's
literature and Sunday school fiction. Johnson does not explicitly discuss
the racial background of the characters in her novels; instead, she uses
her fiction to comment on domestic violence, alcoholism, and poverty
as societal issues, without tying them to race, and to promote Christian
teachings. Although she achieved marked success during her lifetime,
Johnson's works were out of print for nearly a century before recently
attracting new critical attention. Scholars have commented on her
strategy of indirect representation of feminist and antiracist themes.

From *Clarence and Corinne;*
or, God's Way (1890)

CHAPTER II. A Grim Visitor

By the time the children reached home it was dark. No light, however, shone through the dingy windows of the cottage. The boy pushed open the door, and entered, with his sister close behind him.

They found their mother still seated in the old chair, but she was now rocking herself back and forth, her face hidden in her hands, and crying bitterly, but softly.

"What is it, mother?" asked Clarence, anxiously, coming to her side. "What is the matter?"

For answer, his mother pointed to the miserable bed in the corner, upon which was stretched the form of a man.

The boy understood all now. It was no new thing for him to come home and find his mother sobbing over some fresh ill-treatment inflicted upon her by her drink-maddened husband.

For a moment all was still, save for the heavy breathing of the sleeping man. Then the wretched woman arose, and going noiselessly to the cupboard, took from it two pieces of bread, and putting them into the hands of the two children, motioned them to go to bed. Silently they obeyed, for upon silence depended their chances of a quiet night. Had they been so unfortunate as to waken the figure upon the bed, a torrent of abuse would have been theirs: so they were only too glad to creep off to their beds—Corinne to her pallet on the floor of the room in which they were, and Clarence to his in the bare attic. Then their mother resumed her old position, but she was quiet now.

Poor little Corinne, too wretched to eat, lay quietly in her corner, with the great tears chasing each other down her thin cheeks, until at length she lost sight of her misery in the sound sleep of childhood.

Clarence, in his hard, comfortless bed, was inwardly chafing at his lot; his heart was full of bitter, bitter thoughts against everybody and everything. It was long before he slept.

The night wore away and day dawned. The sunbeams struggled to peep in at the dirty windows of the cottage, with but poor success. They did manage, however, to flit for an instant across the face of sleeping Corinne. Perhaps it was this that awakened her; at any rate, waken she did, and, raising herself on her elbow, looked about for her mother. To her surprise, she saw her sitting in the same position in which she had last seen her the evening before. The father was still sleeping on the bed, across which he had thrown himself, hat, boots, and all.

Corinne arose softly, and crept to her mother's side. She had no dressing to do, for she had laid herself down just as she was. Thinking her mother asleep, she stretched out her hand to touch her.

Why did she start back in alarm? Why, indeed? Those dull eyes that stared at her from that stony face plainly told her, child though she was, that her mother was dead. With a wild, frightened cry, she sprang toward the bed where her father lay, and in her terror losing sight of her fear of him, she frantically shook the sleeping man, crying, "Oh, father, father, wake up; do wake up; mother is dead! Oh, what shall I do?"

With an oath her father rolled over, and raising his clenched hand aimed a blow at his child; but Corinne dodged his upraised fist, at the same time continuing her cry.

At length the fact slowly dawned upon the man's beclouded brain that something out of the common had occurred. He raised himself, and after gazing about him stupidly for a while, arose and walked unsteadily to his wife's side.

Once in front of those wide-open eyes, all apathy disappeared, and he seized her by the shoulder and shook her, calling to her to "Wake up!" But the poor broken-spirited, abused woman was sleeping her last sleep: she would wake no more in this world.

"Oh, father, mother is dead; what made her die?" moaned Corinne.

"I dunno," was the answer. Then hurriedly bidding her call her brother, the hard-hearted father left the house and hastened away, no one knew whither, leaving the two children all alone with the dead.

Just as the door closed, Clarence came down.

"What is the matter, Corrie?" he asked, seeing his sister sobbing so bitterly.

"Oh, Clarence, just look: poor, poor mother is dead."

"Dead? Mother dead?" ejaculated the boy, in a dazed way, slowly advancing toward the motionless figure. He lifted one of the nerveless hands, only to let it drop with a shiver as its cold touch met his. For a moment he was silent; then he murmured, half absently, "Yes, dead. Poor mother!"

"Oh, Clarence!" wailed poor Corrie, pressing close to her brother's side. The boy put his arm around the trembling little figure. Poor child! she was so nervous; such a tender little plant! People used to wonder why she was so different from the rest of the family. The father, rough, uncouth, and almost always under the influence of liquor. The mother, careless and unkempt. Clarence, rugged and impetuous, but thoroughly good-natured. Corinne both looked and was different from these, and had always been so.

"Clarence, why did mother die?" sobbed the child.

"Why did she die?" repeated the boy, vehemently. "How could she live, battered and beaten, and starved as she was, and by our father too; the one who could have made us all comfortable and happy. But instead of that he's made us miserable—no, it wasn't him, either; it was that dreadful, dreadful stuff, whisky. Yes, drink ruined our father, and now it's killed our mother; and nobody cares for us because we're the children of a drunkard. People don't even want to give me work because of it; and they call me 'old drunken Burton's boy.'"

"Oh, don't, don't talk so; you frighten me," cried Corinne, clinging closer to her brother than ever.

The boy, relieved by having given vent to some of the bitterness that had been pent up in his bosom for so long, now burst into tears, and the brother and sister wept together until they were aroused by a rap on the door.

It was one of the neighbors, who said that their father had stopped at her door and told her that there was something the matter with his "old woman," and had asked her to come and see what it was. Not knowing what had happened, Mrs. Greene had not hurried, having stayed to attend to some of her own household affairs.

Great was her astonishment and deep her indignation when she found how matters stood at the cottage; and she was loud in her denunciations of "that heartless Jim Burton." "No wonder he was moving off so fast, he's likely to be took up for murder. If he ain't killed that poor woman outright, he's done it by inches. But come, chicks, cheer up; don't take on so. Run over to my house, while I fix up here a bit, and tell my Tom you're to have your breakfast." And the kind-hearted woman began turning about to see what she should do first. To her surprise, the boy quietly, but firmly said: "Mrs. Greene, I'd rather not go to your house."

"Why not?" she asked.

"I'd rather not go," he repeated. "I don't want any breakfast."

"Oh, well, of course you needn't go if you don't want to, but you ought to have something to eat. But never mind; I'm going up street a minute or so, and I'll bring you something." And away went Mrs. Greene, spreading, as she went, the news that "Jim Burton's wife had died suddent."

The coroner was notified, and of course there was an inquest, and a verdict rendered that "death was caused by heart trouble," which was true enough, in more senses than one.

But to go back to the children: True to her promise, Mrs. Greene brought with her some breakfast, which she pressed Clarence and Corinne to eat. The worthy woman had attributed the boy's reluctance to visit her house to a backwardness on his part, but in reality it was due to the fact that it was the home of Tom Greene. He was poor, wretchedly poor and forlorn, but he was proud. He saw in Tom Greene only the boy who delighted in tormenting him, and calling him and his sister names.

Mrs. Greene had also brought with her a tall, spare, hard-featured personage, whom she addressed as "Miss Rachel Penrose," who it seemed was the owner of the old cottage and the ground upon which it stood. A woman of few words was Miss Rachel; one who was "willing to do her duty," as she expressed it, but it was done much after the manner of the Pharisees: her deeds were done to be seen of men. A woman of another stamp was her companion, simple-hearted Mrs. Greene, who was ever ready, from pure sympathy, to lend a hand wherever it was needed; and it was sadly needed here, in this abode of wretchedness and death. She now urged the children to eat, but neither of them was inclined to do so. The boy "wasn't hungry," and his sister was too full of her trouble, so the food was set away untasted.

The coroner had come and gone, so too had the crowd of curious sightseers; then the task of "cleaning up," which was by no means an easy one, was begun; and Miss Rachel could not forbear remarking in an undertone that it was a mystery to her "how people could be so shiftless," further asserting that to her mind "Mrs. Burton didn't amount to much."

"Ah, Miss Rachel, but you must think of what the poor creature had to put up with! What with Burton's drinkin' and abuse, you wouldn't have much heart to keep things nice if you were starved and knocked about like she was."

Mrs. Greene's defense of the unfortunate woman had but little effect by way of softening her hearer.

"Why didn't she work and keep herself from starving; I'm sure I'd a great sight rather do that and keep myself and children decent, than to give way and just sit down with my hands in my lap and let everything get topsy-turvey."

Miss Rachel's hands were by no means idle while her tongue was busy. Things were getting in pretty good shape under her methodical touch and Mrs. Greene's energetic efforts.

The two forlorn children sat together near the window, in the old rocking chair, too deeply absorbed in their own sorrowful thoughts to heed what was going on around them.

The old bed had been made tidy from good Mrs. Greene's scanty store of bed linen, and the body of the dead woman, neatly arrayed by the same kind hands, was lying peacefully upon it. Nobody knew much about the Burtons, for they talked to no one. All that was known about them was that they had come to the little cottage one day, with their few belongings, but from whence no one knew. Mrs. Burton was neat and respectable looking then; so were her children, who were quite small.

At first, the place was kept as neat as possible, but not long; for as the husband and father grew more and more intemperate, the wife and mother grew disheartened and careless. Then, too, the children had been sent to school, but it had been a long time since they had gone.

Clarence was not an idle boy by nature, and he had tried to get to work, and did work when he could get it to do; but with all his poverty he was very proud, and could not brook the sneers and taunts of those with whom he came in contact; so he was not very fortunate in finding employment. And just as often as not, when he had earned a little money, his father had taken it from him to spend in drink.

Things were in this condition when the grim visitor—"Death"—stepped in and removed the mother.

She had lived a hopeless life, and no one knew otherwise than that she had died a hopeless death. She had gone without a word, and none save God knew aught of her last moments.

SOURCE

Johnson, Amelia E. *Clarence and Corinne; or, God's Way*, 15–25. Philadelphia: American Baptist Publication Society, 1890.

NOTE

Chapter opening photo: Amelia E. Johnson, ca. 1892. From Irvine Garland Penn, "Colored Authors," *Wilkes-Barre Evening Leader*, December 5, 1892.

Maggie Pogue Johnson

1883–1956

MAGGIE POGUE JOHNSON was an African American poet and music composer from Fincastle, Virginia. Not much is known about her life aside from her published work and her two marriages. She published two volumes of poetry in the early twentieth century: *Virginia Dreams: Lyrics for the Idle Hour, Tales of the Time Told in Rhyme* (1910) and *Thoughts for Idle Hours* (1915). Both have been reprinted recently and feature poems written in the dialect of Virginian common folk, as well as in standard English. Later in life, she published *Fallen Blossoms* (1951) and *Childhood Hours: With Songs For Little Tots* (1952). Neither has been reprinted.

I Wish I Was a Grown Up Man (1910)

I wish I was a grown up man,
    And then I'd get a chance,
To wear those great high collars,
    Stiff shirts, and nice long pants.

I wish I was a grown up man,
    Not too big and fat,
But just the size to look nice
    In a beaver hat.

I'd wear the nicest vest and gloves,
    And patent leather shoes,
And all the girls would fall in love,
    And I'd flirt with whom I choose.

I wish I was a grown up man,
   I'd try the girls to please,
I'd wear a long jimswinger coat,
   Just below my knees.

I'd wear eye-glasses, too,
   And wouldn't I look good?
I'd be the swellest dude
   In this neighborhood.

Some day I'll be a man,
   And have everything I say,
And give my heart to some nice girl,
   And then I'd go away.

Old Maid's Soliloquy (1910)

I'se been upon de karpet,
   Fo' lo, dese many days;
De men folks seem to sneer me,
   In der kin' ob way.

But I don't min' der foolin',
   Case I sho' is jis as fine
As any Kershaw pumpkin
   A hangin on de vine.

I looks at dem sometimes,
   But hol's my head up high,
Case I is fer above dem
   As de moon is in de sky.

Dey sho' do t'ink dey's so much,
   But I sho' is jis as fine
As eny sweet potato
   Dat's growd up from de vine.

Dey needn't t'ink I's liken dem,
   Case my match am hard to fin',

En I don't want de watermillion
    Dat's lef' upon de vine.

Case I ain't no spring chicken,
    Dis am solid talk,
En I don't want anything
    Dat's foun' upon de walk.

Case ef I'd wanted anything,
    I'd hitched up years ago,
En had my sher ob trouble.
    But my min' tol' me no.

I'd rader be a single maid,
    A wanderin' bout de town,
Wid skercely way to earn my bread,
    En face all made ob frowns,—

Den hitched up to some numbskull,
    Wid skercely sense to die,
En I know I cud'n kill him,
    Dar'd be no use to try.

So don't let ol' maids boder you,
    I'll fin' a match some day,
Or else I'll sho' 'main single,
    You hear me what I say!

I specs to hol' my head up high
    En always feel as free
As any orange blossom
    A hangin' on de tree.

SOURCE

Johnson, Maggie Pogue. "I Wish I Was a Grown Up Man" and "Old Maid's Solil-
oquy." In *Virginia Dreams: Lyrics for the Idle Hour*, 7–8, 9–11. John M. Leonard,
1910.

Emma Lazarus

1849–1887

EMMA LAZARUS was one of the first renowned Jewish American au-
thors and part of the late nineteenth-century New York literary elite.
She is famous for having written "The New Colossus," a sonnet en-
shrined in the base of the Statue of Liberty. She published two volumes
of poetry, a novel, a play, and often placed individual poems in *Lippin-
cott's Monthly Magazine*. She also received acclaim for her translations
of the German Jewish poet Heinrich Heine. Later in life, she wrote bold
poetry and essays protesting the rise of antisemitism and arguing for
Russian immigrants' rights, including *Songs of a Semite: The Dance to
Death and Other Poems* (1882). She advocated for Jewish refugees and
called on Jews to join together and establish a homeland in Palestine
before the concept of Zionism was in wide circulation. Lazarus was also
likely a queer writer, as evidenced by the poems that follow (published
in her lifetime, with the exception of "Assurance").

Carmela (1875)

See, in this mystic zone of calms,
Like a rich cloud in sunset skies,
From Mexico's warm waters rise
The isle of cocoa and of palms,
The realm where summer never dies.

Ripe golden balls of sumptuous fruit
Hang thick upon the orange trees,
Soft blows the aromatic breeze,
And sweet the wild canaries flute,
And gently roll the purple seas.

Here was thy childhood's dwelling-place,
O love, my love! who lov'st not me:
Here didst thou gain the witchery
Of Southland languor, Spanish grace,
And emerald eyes' arch coquetry.

Thy sisterhood is darkly fair,
With glowing cheek and night-black curls:
Thy pure flesh hath the sheen of pearls;
In waves of light thy loosened hair
Its warm gold to thy feet unfurls.

Thy sisterhood is rich in faith,
Of generous passion, gentle heart:
Whence didst thou glean thy fatal art,
Whose subtle cunning fashioneth
A net no man may rend apart?

If I could deem thee of this earth,
My witch, my siren, my despair!
My curse would blight thee. But, beware!
I know the mystery of thy birth—
The secret of thy life I share.

'Twas on that night, the crown of nights,
All brightest days outshining far;

A separate sun beamed every star;
Soft airs breathed languid from the heights,
Voluptuous as Love's sighings are.

Carmela mine—for mine thou wast
By every promise, pledge and vow,
And by my seal set on thy brow—
Within thy garden all that passed
That night, dost thou remember now?—

How thou, within thy hammock rocked
Beneath the odorous cedar trees—
Rose-white as sprung from foam of seas,
Didst lie with smiling lips unlocked,
And lightly sway with every breeze,

And watch the glimmering fiery flies,
The throbbing stars in heaven's calm,
And point to where a single palm
Stood out against pale seas and skies,
And breathe the night's enchanted balm?

But I saw naught save only thee,
White, lithe, with thy mermaiden's hair,
Thy mild dove's eyes, thy warm throat bare;
And these I never cease to see,
A shadow on the empty air.

I set my seal upon thy brow:
Mine own bears now a deathless flame—
Thy lips remember whence it came:
All men who greet me see and know,
And whisper low thy perjured name.

Once, once! then nevermore again
Within my hair thy wreathed hands met:
Upon my brow the print was set
That fired my blood and seared my brain;
And thou hadst flown. Dost thou forget?

"Follow me not!" I heard thee cry,
And my religion was thy word.
Was it the warble of a bird,
Or a low peal of laughter nigh,
Among the bushes, that I heard?

I pressed my face where thine had pressed,
And sank adown upon my knees
Beneath the odorous cedar trees:
The hanging cradle I caressed
Where thou hadst swayed with every breeze.

I know not if I waked or slept;
A strange, clear vision came to me;
I fancied I had followed thee:
O'er grass and stone and rill we leapt,
Down to the large, smooth tropic sea.

There had I reached thee, but, behold!
With low soft laughter in the wave
Thou springst, and ere I spring to save
Thy sister mermaids' arms enfold,
And draw thee to thy native cave.

There sportest thou the livelong night,
Regretting naught thou leav'st behind:
No trace upon the waves I find,
Save a pale amber-colored light
There where thy hair flew in the wind.

But when the first cool beams of morn
Through the green waters pierce and shine,
Back to these earthly haunts of thine
Thou wilt return, and laugh to scorn
The pledge, the love, the dream divine.

So if I deemed thee of this earth,
My witch, my siren, my despair!
My curse would blight thee. Yet, beware!

I know the mystery of thy birth—
The secret of thy life I share.

Dolores (1876)

A light at her feet and a light at her head,
How fast asleep my Dolores lies!
Awaken, my love, for to-morrow we wed—
Uplift the lids of thy beautiful eyes.

Too soon art thou clad in white, my spouse:
Who placed that garland above thy heart
Which shall wreathe to-morrow thy bridal brows?
How quiet and mute and strange thou art!

And hearest thou not my voice that speaks?
And feelest thou not my hot tears flow
As I kiss thine eyes and thy lips and thy cheeks?
Do they not warm thee, my bride of snow?

Thou knowest no grief, though thy love may weep.
A phantom smile, with a faint, wan beam,
Is fixed on thy features sealed in sleep:
Oh tell me the secret bliss of thy dream.

Does it lead to fair meadows with flowering trees,
Where thy sister-angels hail thee their own?
Was not my love to thee dearer than these?
Thine was my world and my heaven in one.

I dare not call thee aloud, nor cry,
Thou art so solemn, so rapt in rest,
But I will whisper: Dolores, 'tis I:
My heart is breaking within my breast.

Never ere now did I speak thy name,
Itself a caress, but the lovelight leapt
Into thine eyes with a kindling flame,
And a ripple of rose o'er thy soft cheek crept.

But now wilt thou stir not for passion or prayer,
And makest no sign of the lips or the eyes,
With a nun's strait band o'er thy bright black hair—
Blind to mine anguish and deaf to my cries.

I stand no more in the waxen-lit room:
I see thee again as I saw thee that day,
In a world of sunshine and springtide bloom,
'Midst the green and white of the budding May.

Now shadow, now shine, as the branches ope,
Flickereth over my love the while:
From her sunny eyes gleams the May-time hope,
And her pure lips dawn in a wistful smile.

As one who waiteth I see her stand,
Who waits though she knows not what nor whom,
With a lilac spray in her slim soft hand:
All the air is sweet with its spicy bloom.

I knew not her secret, though she held mine:
In that golden hour did we each confess;
And her low voice murmured, Yea, I am thine,
And the large world rang with my happiness.

To-morrow shall be the blessedest day
That ever the all-seeing sun espied:
Though thou sleep till the morning's earliest ray,
Yet then thou must waken to be my bride.

Yea, waken, my love, for to-morrow we wed:
Uplift the lids of thy beautiful eyes.
A light at her feet and a light at her head,
How fast asleep my Dolores lies!

Assurance (ca. 1880)

Last night I slept, and when I woke her kiss
Still floated on my lips. For we had strayed
Together in my dream, through some dim glade,
Where the shy moonbeams scarce dared light our bliss.

The air was dank with dew, between the trees,
The hidden glow-worms kindled and were spent.
Cheek pressed to cheek, the cool, the hot night-breeze
Mingled our hair, our breath, and came and went,
As sporting with our passion. Low and deep
Spake in mine ear her voice: "And didst thou dream,
This could be buried? This could be sleep?
And love be thrall to death! Nay, whatso seem,
Have faith, dear heart; this is the thing that is!"
Thereon I woke, and on my lips her kiss.

SOURCES

Lazarus, Emma. "Assurance." From manuscript notebook of poetry, Emma Lazarus Papers, American Jewish Historical Society, Waltham, MA, and New York, NY, Jewish Women's Archive. https://jwa.org/media/assurance-from-emma-lazarus-copy-book. Reprinted with the permission of the American Jewish Historical Society.

———. "Carmela." *Lippincott's Monthly Magazine* 16 (December 1875): 689–91.

———. "Dolores." *Lippincott's Monthly Magazine* 17 (June 1876): 666–67.

NOTE

Chapter opening photo: Emma Lazarus, ca. 1888. Library of Congress, Prints & Photographs Division, LC-USZ62-53145.

Adah Isaacs Menken

1835–1868

ADAH ISAACS MENKEN was one of the most famous American actresses of the mid-1800s, best known for her performance on horseback (in a nude bodysuit) in *Mazeppa*, a play based on Lord Byron's 1819 poem. She was likely of mixed Creole and African American heritage, but she played into the mystery of her family background, claiming different ethnicities at different times, including the suggestion (after she married Alexander Isaac Menken, a wealthy Jewish businessman) that she was born Jewish. She toured the United States and Europe, developing a Bohemian celebrity persona—smoking cigarettes, wearing her hair short, and having several marriages and public affairs. Her desire, however, was to be known as a writer. Menken published essays and poetry, including a posthumous volume, *Infelicia* (1868), which celebrated Jewish culture and disparaged male control over creative women's lives.

Judith (1868)

"Repent, or I will come unto thee quickly, and will fight
thee with the sword of my mouth."—Revelation ii. 16

I.

Ashkelon is not cut off with the remnant of a valley.
  Baldness dwells not upon Gaza.
  The field of the valley is mine, and it is clothed in verdure.
  The steepness of Baal-perazim is mine;
  And the Philistines spread themselves in the valley of Rephaim.
  They shall yet be delivered into my hands.
  For the God of Battles has gone before me!
  The sword of the mouth shall smite them to dust.
  I have slept in the darkness—
  But the seventh angel woke me, and giving me a sword of flame,
points to the blood-ribbed cloud, that lifts his reeking head above the
mountain.
  Thus am I the prophet.
  I see the dawn that heralds to my waiting soul the advent of power.
        Power that will unseal the thunders!
        Power that will give voice to graves!
        Graves of the living;
        Graves of the dying;
        Graves of the sinning;
        Graves of the loving;
        Graves of the despairing;
  And oh! graves of the deserted!
  These shall speak, each as their voices shall be loosed.
  And the day is dawning.

II.

  Stand back, ye Philistines!
  Practice what ye preach to me;
  I heed ye not, for I know ye all.
  Ye are living burning lies, and profanation to the garments which
with stately steps ye sweep your marble palaces.

Ye places of Sin, around which the damning evidence of guilt hangs like a reeking vapor.

Stand back!

I would pass up the golden road of the world.

A place in the ranks awaits me.

I know that ye are hedged on the borders of my path.

Lie and tremble, for ye well know that I hold with iron grasp the battle axe.

Creep back to your dark tents in the valley.

Slouch back to your haunts of crime.

Ye do not know me, neither do ye see me.

But the sword of the mouth is unsealed, and ye coil yourselves in slime and bitterness at my feet.

I mix your jeweled heads, and your gleaming eyes, and your hissing tongues with the dust.

My garments shall bear no mark of ye.

When I shall return this sword to the angel, your foul blood will not stain its edge.

It will glimmer with the light of truth, and the strong arm shall rest.

III.

Stand back!

I am no Magdalene waiting to kiss the hem of your garment.

It is mid-day.

See ye not what is written on my forehead?

I am Judith!

I wait for the head of my Holofernes!

Ere the last tremble of the conscious death-agony shall have shuddered, I will show it to ye with the long black hair clinging to the glazed eyes, and the great mouth opened in search of voice, and the strong throat all hot and reeking with blood, that will thrill me with wild unspeakable joy as it courses down my bare body and dabbles my cold feet!

My sensuous soul will quake with the burden of so much bliss.

Oh, what wild passionate kisses will I draw up from that bleeding mouth!

I will strangle this pallid throat of mine on the sweet blood!

I will revel in my passion.

At midnight I will feast on it in the darkness.

For it was that which thrilled its crimson tides of reckless passion through the blue veins of my life, and made them leap up in the wild sweetness of Love and agony of Revenge!

I am starving for this feast.

Oh forget not that I am Judith!

And I know where sleeps Holofernes.

Myself (1868)

"La patience est amère; mais le fruit en est doux!"[1]

I.

Away down into the shadowy depths of the Real I once lived.

I thought that to seem was to be.

But the waters of Marah were beautiful, yet they were bitter.

I waited, and hoped, and prayed;

Counting the heart-throbs and the tears that answered them.

Through my earnest pleadings for the True, I learned that the mildest mercy of life was a smiling sneer;

And that the business of the world was to lash with vengeance all who dared to be what their God had made them.

Smother back tears to the red blood of the heart!

Crush out things called souls!

No room for them here!

II.

Now I gloss my pale face with laughter, and sail my voice on with the tide.

Decked in jewels and lace, I laugh beneath the gas-light's glare, and quaff the purple wine.

But the minor-keyed soul is standing naked and hungry upon one of Heaven's high hills of light.

Standing and waiting for the blood of the feast!

Starving for one poor word!

Waiting for God to launch out some beacon on the boundless shores of this Night.

Shivering for the uprising of some soft wing under which it may creep, lizard-like, to warmth and rest.

Waiting! Starving and shivering!

III.

Still I trim my white bosom with crimson roses; for none shall see the thorns.

I bind my aching brow with a jeweled crown, that none shall see the iron one beneath.

My silver-sandaled feet keep impatient time to the music, because I cannot be calm.

I laugh at earth's passion-fever of Love; yet I know that God is near to the soul on the hill, and hears the ceaseless ebb and flow of a hopeless love, through all my laughter.

But if I can cheat my heart with the old comfort, that love can be forgotten, is it not better?

After all, living is but to play a part!

The poorest worm would be a jewel-headed snake if she could!

IV.

All this grandeur of glare and glitter has its night-time.

The pallid eyelids must shut out smiles and daylight.

Then I fold my cold hands, and look down at the restless rivers of a love that rushes through my life.

Unseen and unknown they tide on over black rocks and chasms of Death.

Oh, for one sweet word to bridge their terrible depths!

O jealous soul! why wilt thou crave and yearn for what thou canst not have?

And life is so long—so long.

V.

With the daylight comes the business of living.

The prayers that I sent trembling up the golden thread of hope all come back to me.

I lock them close in my bosom, far under the velvet and roses of the world.

For I know that stronger than these torrents of passion is the soul that hath lifted itself up to the hill.

What care I for his careless laugh?

I do not sigh; but I know that God hears the life-blood dripping as I, too, laugh.

I would not be thought a foolish rose, that flaunts her red heart out to the sun.

Loving is not living!

VI.

Yet through all this I know that night will roll back from the still, gray plain of heaven, and that my triumph shall rise sweet with the dawn!

When these mortal mists shall unclothe the world, then shall I be known as I am!

When I dare be dead and buried behind a wall of wings, then shall he know me!

When this world shall fall, like some old ghost, wrapped in the black skirts of the wind, down into the fathomless eternity of fire, then shall souls uprise!

When God shall lift the frozen seal from struggling voices, then shall we speak!

When the purple-and-gold of our inner natures shall be lighted up in the Eternity of Truth, then will love be mine!

I can wait.

Genius (1868)

"Where'er there's a life to be kindled by love,
    Wherever a soul to inspire,
Strike this key-note of God that trembles above
    Night's silver-tongued voices of fire."[2]

Genius is power.

The power that grasps in the universe, that dives out beyond space, and grapples with the starry worlds of heaven.

If genius achieves nothing, shows us no results, it is so much the less genius.

The man who is constantly fearing a lion in his path is a coward.

The man or woman whom excessive caution holds back from striking the anvil with earnest endeavor, is poor and cowardly of purpose.

The required step must be taken to reach the goal, though a precipice be the result.

Work must be done, and the result left to God.

The soul that is in earnest, will not stop to count the cost.

Circumstances cannot control genius: it will nestle with them: its power will bend and break them to its path.

This very audacity is divine.

Jesus of Nazareth did not ask the consent of the high priests in the temple when he drove out the "money-changers;" but, impelled by inspiration, he knotted the cords and drove them hence.

Genius will find room for itself, or it is none.

Men and women, in all grades of life, do their utmost.

If they do little, it is because they have no capacity to do more.

I hear people speak of "unfortunate genius," of "poets who never penned their inspirations;"[3] that

> "Some mute inglorious Milton here may rest;"[4]

of "unappreciated talent," and "malignant stars," and other contradictory things.

It is all nonsense.

Where power exists, it cannot be suppressed any more than the earthquake can be smothered.

As well attempt to seal up the crater of Vesuvius as to hide God's given power of the soul.

> "You may as well forbid the mountain pines
> To wag their high tops, and to make no noise
> When they are fretten with the gusts of heaven,"[5]

as to hush the voice of genius.

There is no such thing as unfortunate genius.

If a man or woman is fit for work, God appoints the field.

He does more; He points to the earth with her mountains, oceans, and cataracts, and says to man, "Be great!"

He points to the eternal dome of heaven and its blazing worlds, and says: "Bound out thy life with beauty."

He points to the myriads of down-trodden, suffering men and women, and says: "Work with me for the redemption of these, my children."

He lures, and incites, and thrusts greatness upon men, and they will not take the gift.

Genius, on the contrary, loves toil, impediment, and poverty; for from these it gains its strength, throws off the shadows, and lifts its proud head to immortality.

Neglect is but the flat to an undying future.

To be popular is to be endorsed in the To-day and forgotten in the To-morrow.

It is the mess of pottage that alienates the birth-right.

Genius that succumbs to misfortune, that allows itself to be blotted by the slime of slander—and other serpents that infest society—is so much the less genius.

The weak man or woman who stoops to whine over neglect, and poverty, and the snarls of the world, gives the sign of his or her own littleness.

Genius is power.

The eternal power that can silence worlds with its voice, and battle to the death ten thousand arméd Hercules.

Then make way for this God-crowned Spirit of Night, that was born in that Continuing City, but lives in lowly and down-trodden souls!

Fling out the banner!

Its broad folds of sunshine will wave over turret and dome, and over the thunder of oceans on to eternity.

"Fling it out, fling it out o'er the din of the world!
　　Make way for this banner of flame,
That streams from the mast-head of ages unfurled,
　　And inscribed by the deathless in name.
And thus through the years of eternity's flight,
　　This insignia of soul shall prevail,
The centre of glory, the focus of light;
　　O Genius! proud Genius, all hail!"

Drifts That Bar My Door (1868)

I.

O angels! will ye never sweep the drifts from my door?
Will ye never wipe the gathering rust from the hinges?
How long must I plead and cry in vain?
Lift back the iron bars, and lead me hence.
Is there not a land of peace beyond my door?
Oh, lead me to it—give me rest—release me from this unequal strife.
Heaven can attest that I fought bravely when the heavy blows fell fast.
Was it my sin that strength failed?
Was it my sin that the battle was in vain?
Was it my sin that I lost the prize? I do not sorrow for all the bitter
pain and blood it cost me.
Why do ye stand sobbing in the sunshine?
I cannot weep.
There is no sunlight in this dark cell. I am starving for light.
O angels! sweep the drifts away—unbar my door!

II.

Oh, is this all?
Is there nothing more of life?
See how dark and cold my cell.
The pictures on the walls are covered with mould.
The earth-floor is slimy with my wasting blood.
The embers are smouldering in the ashes.
The lamp is dimly flickering, and will soon starve for oil in this horrid
gloom.
My wild eyes paint shadows on the walls.
And I hear the poor ghost of my lost love moaning and sobbing
without.
Shrieks of my unhappiness are borne to me on the wings of the wind.
I sit cowering in fear, with my tattered garments close around my
choking throat.
I move my pale lips to pray; but my soul has lost her wonted power.
Faith is weak.
Hope has laid her whitened corse upon my bosom.

The lamp sinks lower and lower. O angels! sweep the drifts away—unbar my door!

III.

Angels, is this my reward?

Is this the crown ye promised to set down on the foreheads of the loving—the suffering—the deserted?

Where are the sheaves I toiled for?

Where the golden grain ye promised?

These are but withered leaves.

Oh, is this all?

Meekly I have toiled and spun the fleece.

All the work ye assigned, my willing hands have accomplished.

See how thin they are, and how they bleed.

Ah me! what meagre pay, e'en when the task is over!

My fainting child, whose golden head graces e'en this dungeon, looks up to me and pleads for life.

O God! my heart is breaking!

Despair and Death have forced their skeleton forms through the grated window of my cell, and stand clamoring for their prey.

The lamp is almost burnt out.

Angels, sweep the drifts away—unbar my door!

IV.

Life is a lie, and Love a cheat.

There is a graveyard in my poor heart—dark, heaped-up graves, from which no flowers spring.

The walls are so high, that the trembling wings of birds do break ere they reach the summit, and they fall, wounded, and die in my bosom.

I wander 'mid the gray old tombs, and talk with the ghosts of my buried hopes.

They tell me of my Eros, and how they fluttered around him, bearing sweet messages of my love, until one day, with his strong arm, he struck them dead at his feet.

Since then, these poor lonely ghosts have haunted me night and day, for it was I who decked them in my crimson heart-tides, and sent them forth in chariots of fire.

Every breath of wind bears me their shrieks and groans.

I hasten to their graves, and tear back folds and folds of their shrouds, and try to pour into their cold, nerveless veins the quickening tide of life once more.

Too late—too late!

Despair hath driven back Death, and clasps me in his black arms.

And the lamp! See, the lamp is dying out!

O angels! sweep the drifts from my door!—lift up the bars!

v.

Oh, let me sleep.

I close my weary eyes to think—to dream.

Is this what dreams are woven of?

I stand on the brink of a precipice, with my shivering child strained to my bare bosom.

A yawning chasm lies below. My trembling feet are on the brink.

I hear again *his* voice; but he reacheth not out his hand to save me.

Why can I not move my lips to pray?

They are cold.

My soul is dumb, too.

Death hath conquered!

I feel his icy fingers moving slowly along my heart-strings.

How cold and stiff!

The ghosts of my dead hopes are closing around me.

They stifle me.

They whisper that Eros has come back to me.

But I only see a skeleton wrapped in blood-stained cerements.

There are no lips to kiss me back to life.

O ghosts of Love, move back—give me air!

Ye smell of the dusty grave.

Ye have pressed your cold hands upon my eyes until they are eclipsed.

The lamp has burnt out.

O angels! be quick! Sweep the drifts away!—unbar my door!

Oh, light! Light!

Miserimus (1868)

"Sounding through the silent dimness
   Where I faint and weary lay,
Spake a poet: 'I will lead thee
   To the land of song to-day.'"[6]

   I.

O bards! weak heritors of passion and of pain!

Dwellers in the shadowy Palace of Dreams!

With your unmated souls flying insanely at the stars!

Why have you led me lonely and desolate to the Deathless Hill of Song?

You promised that I should ring trancing shivers of rapt melody down to the dumb earth.

You promised that its echoes should vibrate till Time's circles met in old Eternity.

You promised that I should gather the stars like blossoms to my white bosom.

You promised that I should create a new moon of Poesy.

You promised that the wild wings of my soul should shimmer through the dusky locks of the clouds, like burning arrows, down into the deep heart of the dim world.

But, O Bards! sentinels on the Lonely Hill, why breaks there yet no Day to me?

   II.

O lonely watchers for the Light! how long must I grope with my dead eyes in the sand?

Only the red fire of Genius, that narrows up life's chances to the black path that crawls on to the dizzy clouds.

The wailing music that spreads its pinions to the tremble of the wind, has crumbled off to silence.

From the steep ideal the quivering soul falls in its lonely sorrow like an unmated star from the blue heights of Heaven into the dark sea.

O Genius! is this thy promise?

O Bards! is this all?

SOURCE

Menken, Adah Isaacs. "Drifts That Bar My Door," "Genius," "Judith," "Miserimus," and "Myself." In *Infelicia*, 68–72, 64–67, 21–24, 74–75, 48–51. Philadelphia: J. B. Lippincott, 1868.

NOTES

Chapter opening photo: Adah Isaacs Menken in costume, 1866. TCS 19. Houghton Library, Harvard University.

1. "Patience is bitter, but its fruit is sweet" (French). This quotation, commonly attributed to Enlightenment philosopher Jean-Jacques Rousseau, originates in traveler John Chardin's *Voyages en Perse et autres lieux de l'Orient* (1711).
2. The source of this quotation, as well as the quotation that ends this poem, is evidently Menken herself.
3. Other than the indented lines accompanied by notes, the origin of the ostensible quotations in this poem are unknown.
4. From "Elegy Written in a Country Churchyard" (1751) by English poet Thomas Gray (1716–1771).
5. From Shakespeare's *The Merchant of Venice* (1605), act 4, scene 1.
6. The source of this quotation appears to be Menken herself.

Ann Plato

ca. 1824–unknown

ANN PLATO was an African American educator and author born in Hartford, Connecticut. As a teenager, she published her only known work, *Essays: Including Biographies and Miscellaneous Pieces in Prose and Poetry* (1841). The little that is known about her life comes from the book's introduction, written by her pastor, James W. C. Pennington of Hartford's Colored Congregational Church. Her writings promote the New England Puritan values of education, piety, and hard work, and she includes eulogies for four African American women from her community. She seldom alludes to racial issues, except in "The Natives of America" and "To the First of August," included in this section.

Advice to Young Ladies (1841)

Day after day I sit and write,
And thus the moments spend—
The thought that occupies my mind,—
Compose to please my friend.

And then I think I will compose,
And thus myself engage—
To try to please young ladies minds,
Which are about my age.

The greatest word that I can say,—
I think to please, will be,
To try and get your learning young,
And write it back to me.

But this is not the only thing
That I can recommend;
Religion is most needful for
To make in us a friend.

At thirteen years I found a hope,
And did embrace the Lord;
And since, I've found a blessing great,
Within his holy word.

Perchance that we may ne'er fulfill,
The place of aged sires,
But may it with God's holy will,
Be ever our desires.

The Natives of America (1841)

Tell me a story, father please,
And then I sat upon his knees.
Then answer'd he,—"what speech make known,
Or tell the words of native tone,
Of how my Indian fathers dwelt,
And, of sore oppression felt;
And how they mourned a land serene,
It was an ever mournful theme."

Yes, I replied,—I like to hear,
And bring my father's spirit near;
Of every pain they did forego,
Oh, please to tell me all you know.
In history often I do read,
Of pain which none but they did heed.

He thus began. "We were a happy race,
When we no tongue but ours did trace,
We were in ever peace,
We sold, we did release—
Our brethren, far remote, and far unknown,

And spake to them in silent, tender tone.
We all were then as in one band,
We join'd and took each others hand;
Our dress was suited to the clime,
Our food was such as roam'd that time,
Our houses were of sticks compos'd;
No matter,—for they us enclos'd.

But then discover'd was this land indeed
By European men; who then had need
Of this far country. Columbus came afar,
And thus before we could say Ah!
What meaneth this?—we fell in cruel hands.
Though some were kind, yet others then held bands
Of cruel oppression. Then too, foretold our chief,—
Beggars you will become—is my belief.
We sold, then some bought lands,
We altogether moved in foreign hands.

Wars ensued. They knew the handling of fire-arms.
Mothers spoke,—no fear this breast alarms,
They will not cruelly us oppress,
Or thus our lands possess.
Alas! it was a cruel day; we were crush'd:
Into the dark, dark woods we rush'd
To seek a refuge.

My daughter, we are now diminish'd, unknown,
Unfelt! Alas! no tender tone
To cheer us when the hunt is done;
Fathers sleep,—we're silent every one.

Oh! silent the horror, and fierce the fight,
When my brothers were shrouded in night;
Strangers did us invade—strangers destroy'd
The fields, which were by us enjoy'd.

Our country is cultur'd, and looks all sublime,
Our fathers are sleeping who lived in the time

That I tell. Oh! could I tell them my grief
In its flow, that in roaming, we find no relief.

I love my country; and shall, until death
Shall cease my breath.

Now daughter dear I've done,
Seal this upon thy memory; until the morrow's sun
Shall sink, to rise no more;
And if my years should score,
Remember this, though I tell no more."

To the First of August (1841)

Britannia's isles proclaim,
That freedom is their theme;
And we do view those honor'd lands,
With soul-delighting mien.

And unto those they held in gloom,
Gave ev'ry one their right;
They did disdain fell slavery's shade,
And trust in freedom's light.

Then unto ev'ry British blood,
Their noble worth revere,
And think them ever noble men,
And like them, hence appear.

And when on Britain's isles remote,
We're then in freedom's bounds,
And while we stand on British ground,
You're free,—you're free,—resounds.

Lift ye that country's banner high,
And may it nobly wave,
Until beneath the azure sky,
Man shall be no more a slave.

And oh! when youth's extatic hour,
When winds and torrents foam,

And passion's glowing noon are past,
To bless that free born home;

Then let us celebrate the day,
And lay the thought to heart,
And teach the rising race the way,
That they may not depart.

SOURCE

Plato, Ann. "Advice to Young Ladies," "The Natives of America," and "To the First of August." In *Essays: Including Biographies and Miscellaneous Pieces of Prose and Poetry*, 66, 110–12, 114. Hartford, CT: Ann Plato, 1841.

Sarah Forten Purvis

1814–1883

SARAH FORTEN PURVIS was a poet born into one of the most prominent African American families in Philadelphia. She began publishing abolitionist poems in the *Liberator* as a teenager under the pen name "Ada." Like the rest of the Fortens, Sarah was dedicated to the abolitionist cause. Her poems were read widely within the antislavery movement, and "The Grave of the Slave," which follows, was set to music and frequently performed at antislavery events. In 1833, she helped found the Philadelphia Female Anti-Slavery Society—the nation's first biracial women's abolitionist group—with her mother and sisters. In 1834 she published "An Appeal to Woman," also included in this section, which is likely her best-known poem. In it, she implores white women to do their part in the antislavery battle.

The Grave of the Slave (1831)

The cold storms of winter shall chill him no more,
His woes and his sorrows, his pains are all o'er;
The sod of the valley now covers his form,
He is safe in his last home, he feels not the storm.

The poor slave is laid all unheeded and lone,
Where the rich and the poor find a permanent home;
Not his master can rouse him with voice of command;
He knows not, he hears not, his cruel demand.

Not a tear, not a sigh to embalm his cold tomb,
No friend to lament him, no child to bemoan;
Not a stone marks the place, where he peacefully lies,
The earth for his pillow, his curtain the skies.

Poor slave! shall we sorrow that death was thy friend,
The last, and the kindest, that heaven could send?
The grave to the weary is welcomed and blest;
And death, to the captive, is freedom and rest.

An Appeal to Woman (1834)

Oh, woman, woman, in thy brightest hour
Of conscious worth, of pride, of conscious power,
Oh, nobly dare to act a Christian's part,
That well befits a lovely woman's heart!
Dare to be good, as thou canst dare be great;
Despise the taunts of envy, scorn and hate;
Our 'skins may differ,' but from thee we claim
A sister's privilege, in a sister's name.

We are thy sisters,—God has truly said,
That of one blood, the nations he has made.
Oh, christian woman, in a christian land,
Canst thou unblushing read this great command?
Suffer the wrongs which wring our inmost heart
To draw one throb of pity of thy part;
Our 'skins may differ,' but from thee we claim
A sister's privilege, in a sister's name.

Oh, woman!—though upon thy fairer brow
The hues of roses and of lilies glow—
These soon must wither in their kindred earth,
From whence the fair and dark have equal birth.
Let a bright halo o'er thy virtues shed
A lustre, that shall live when thou art dead;
Let coming ages learn to bless thy name
Upon the altar of immortal fame.

SOURCES

Forten, Sarah Louisa. "An Appeal to Woman." *Liberator* 4, no. 5 (February 1, 1834): 20.
———. "The Grave of the Slave." *Liberator* 1, no. 4 (January 22, 1831): 14.

H. Cordelia Ray

1852–1916

HENRIETTA CORDELIA RAY was an African American poet born to an affluent family in New York City. Her father, Charles B. Ray, was a Congregational minister, editor of *Colored American* magazine, and an abolitionist who ran an Underground Railroad station at their home. Ray attended university and became a teacher but soon quit to pursue poetry. Her poetry was often published in the *A.M.E. Church Review*, and her poem "Lincoln" was read at the unveiling ceremony for the Freedman's Monument in Washington, DC, on April 14, 1876. She published *Sonnets* (1893) and *Poems* (1910), as well as a biography of her father.

Niobe (1893)

O mother-heart! when fast the arrows flew,
    Like blinding lightning, smiting as they fell,
    One after one, one after one, what knell
Could fitly voice thy anguish! Sorrow grew
To throes intensest, when thy sad soul knew
    Thy youngest, too, must go. Was it not well,
    Avengers wroth, just one to spare? Ay, tell
The ages of soul-struggle sterner? Through
The flinty stone, O image of despair,
    Sad Niobe, thy maddened grief did flow
In bitt'rest tears, when all thy wailing prayer
    Was so denied. Alas! what weight of woe
Is prisoned in thy melancholy eyes!
What mother-love beneath the Stoic lies!

Lincoln (1893)

To-day, O martyred chief, beneath the sun
We would unveil thy form; to thee who won
Th' applause of nations for thy soul sincere,
A loving tribute we would offer here.
'T was thine not worlds to conquer, but men's hearts;
To change to balm the sting of slavery's darts;
In lowly charity thy joy to find,
And open "gates of mercy on mankind."
And so they come, the freed, with grateful gift,
From whose sad path the shadows thou didst lift.

Eleven years have rolled their seasons round,
Since its most tragic close thy life-work found.
Yet through the vistas of the vanished days
We see thee still, responsive to our gaze,
As ever to thy country's solemn needs.
Not regal coronets, but princely deeds
Were thy chaste diadem; of truer worth
Thy modest virtues than the gems of earth.
Stanch, honest, fervent in the purest cause,
Truth was thy guide; her mandates were thy laws.

Rare heroism, spirit-purity,
The storied Spartan's stern simplicity,
Such moral strength as gleams like burnished gold
Amid the doubt of men of weaker mould,
Were thine. Called in thy country's sorest hour,
When brother knew not brother—mad for power—
To guide the helm through bloody deeps of war,
While distant nations gazed in anxious awe,
Unflinching in the task, thou didst fulfill
Thy mighty mission with a deathless will.

Born to a destiny the most sublime,
Thou wert, O Lincoln! in the march of time,
God bade thee pause and bid the oppressed go free—

Most glorious boon giv'n to humanity.
While slavery ruled the land, what deeds were done!
What tragedies enacted 'neath the sun!
Her page is blurred with records of defeat,
Of lives heroic lived in silence, meet
For the world's praise; of woe, despair and tears,
The speechless agony of weary years.

Thou utteredst the word, and Freedom fair
Rang her sweet bells on the clear winter air;
She waved her magic wand, and lo! from far
A long procession came. With many a scar
Their brows were wrinkled, in the bitter strife,
Full many had said their sad farewell to life.
But on they hastened, free, their shackles gone;
The aged, young,—e'en infancy was borne
To offer unto thee loud paeans of praise,—
Their happy tribute after saddest days.

A race set free! The deed brought joy and light!
It bade calm Justice from her sacred height,
When faith and hope and courage slowly waned,
Unfurl the stars and stripes, at last unstained!
The nations rolled acclaim from sea to sea,
And Heaven's vault rang with Freedom's harmony.
The angels 'mid the amaranths must have hushed
Their chanted cadences, as upward rushed
The hymn sublime: and as the echoes pealed,
God's ceaseless benison the action sealed.

As now we dedicate this shaft to thee,
True champion! in all humility
And solemn earnestness, we would erect
A monument invisible, undecked,
Save by our allied purpose to be true
To Freedom's loftiest precepts, so that through
The fiercest contests we may walk secure,
Fixed on foundations that may still endure,

When granite shall have crumbled to decay,
And generations passed from earth away.

Exalted patriot! illustrious chief!
Thy life's immortal work compels belief.
To-day in radiance thy virtues shine,
And how can we a fitting garland twine?
Thy crown most glorious is a ransomed race!
High on our country's scroll we fondly trace,
In lines of fadeless light that softly blend,
Emancipator, hero, martyr, friend!
While Freedom may her holy sceptre claim,
The world shall echo with Our Lincoln's name.

William Lloyd Garrison (1910)

Some names there are that win the best applause
Of noble souls; then whose shall more than thine
All honored be? Thou heardst the Voice Divine
Tell thee to gird thyself in Freedom's cause,
And cam'st in life's first bloom. No laggard laws
Could quench thy zeal until no slave should pine
In galling chains, caged in the free sunshine.
Till all the shackles fell, thou wouldst not pause.
So to thee who hast climbed heroic heights,
And led the way to where chaste Justice reigns,
An anthem,—tears and gratitude and praise,
Its swelling chords,—uprises and invites
A nation e'en to join the jubilant strains,
Which celebrate thy consecrated days.[1]

Toussaint L'Ouverture (1910)

To those fair isles where crimson sunsets burn,
We send a backward glance to gaze on thee,
Brave Toussaint! thou wast surely born to be
A hero; thy proud spirit could but spurn

Each outrage on thy race. Couldst thou unlearn
The lessons taught by instinct? Nay! and we
Who share the zeal that would make all men free,
Must e'en with pride unto thy life-work turn.
Soul-dignity was thine and purest aim;
And ah! how sad that thou wast left to mourn
In chains 'neath alien skies. On him, shame! shame!
That mighty conqueror who dared to claim
The right to bind thee. Him we heap with scorn,
And noble patriot! guard with love thy name.

SOURCES

Ray, H. Cordelia. *Lincoln; Written for the Occasion of the Unveiling of the Freedmen's Monument in Memory of Abraham Lincoln April 14 1876*. New York: J. J. Little, 1893.

———. "Niobe." In *Sonnets*, 17. New York: J. J. Little, 1893.

———. "Toussaint L'Ouverture" and "William Lloyd Garrison." In *Poems by H. Cordelia Ray*, 88, 86–87. New York: Grafton, 1910. ProQuest Historical Newspapers.

NOTE

1. The poem concludes with the editorial line, "Written for the Occasion of the Garrison Centenary, December 10, 1905."

Harriet Beecher Stowe

1811–1896

HARRIET BEECHER STOWE was a white author and social activist from Litchfield, Connecticut. She is famous for writing the antislavery novel *Uncle Tom's Cabin* (1852), which fueled the abolition debate leading up to the Civil War. In its first year, the book sold three hundred thousand copies, an unprecedented feat; by the end of the nineteenth century, it had become the best-selling book, other than the Bible, in any language. That said, Stowe wrote thirty books altogether, including novels, travel memoirs, and collections of letters and articles. She was known not only for her writing but also for her public opinions on the issues of the day, including the notion that married women's rights should be expanded. We include her antislavery periodical sketch, "Immediate Emancipation," as well as a portion of Stowe's second popular novel, *Dred* (1856). Like *Uncle Tom's Cabin*, they are written for a white audience and deal in harmful and racist stereotypes even as they argue for abolition.

Immediate Emancipation: A Sketch. (1845)

It may be gratifying to those who desire to think well of human nature, to know that the leading incidents of the subjoined sketch are literal matters of fact, occurring in the city of Cincinnati, which have come within the scope of the writer's personal knowledge—the incidents have merely been clothed in a dramatic form, to present them more vividly to the reader.

In one of the hotel parlors of our Queen city, a young gentleman, apparently in no very easy frame of mind, was pacing up and down the room, looking alternately at his watch and out of the window, as if expecting somebody. At last, he rang the bell violently, and a hotel servant soon appeared.

"Has my man, Sam, come in yet," he inquired.

The polished yellow gentleman, to whom this was addressed, answered with a polite, but somewhat sinister smirk, that nothing had been seen of him since early that morning.

"Lazy dog! full three hours since I sent him off to B—— street, and I have seen nothing of him since."

The yellow gentleman remarked, with consolatory politeness, that he "hoped Sam had not *run away*," adding, with an ill-concealed grin, that "them boys was mighty apt to show the clean heel when they come into a free State."

"Oh, no; I'm quite easy as to that," returned the young gentleman; "I'll risk Sam's ever being willing to part from me. I bought him because I was sure of him."

"Don't you be too sure," remarked a gentleman from behind, who had been listening to the conversation. "There are plenty of mischief-making busy-bodies on the train of every Southern gentleman, to interfere with his family matters, and decoy off his servants."

"Didn't I see Sam talking at the corner with Quaker Simmons?" said another servant, who meanwhile had entered.

"Talking with Simmons, was he?" remarked the last speaker, with irritation; "that rascal Simmons does nothing else, I believe, but tote away gentleman's servants. Well, if Simmons has got him, you may as well be quiet; you'll not see your fellow again in a hurry."

"And who the deuce is this Simmons?" said our young gentleman, who, though evidently of a good-natured mould, was now beginning to wax wroth, "and what business has he to interfere with other people's affairs?"

"You had better have asked those questions a few days ago, and then you would have kept a closer eye on your fellow; a meddlesome, canting Quaker rascal, that all the black hounds run to, to be helped into Canada, and nobody knows where all."

The young gentleman jerked out his watch with increasing energy, and then walking fiercely up to the colored waiter, who was setting the dinner table with an air of provoking satisfaction, he thundered at him, "You rascal, you understand this matter; I see it in your eyes."

Our gentleman of color bowed, and with an air of mischievous intelligence, protested that he never interfered with other gentleman's matters, while sundry of his brethren in office, looked unutterable things out of the corners of their eyes.

"There is some cursed plot hatched up among you," said the young man. "You have talked Sam into it; I know he would never thought of leaving me unless he was put up to it. Tell me now," he resumed, "have you heard Sam say any thing about it? Come, be reasonable," he added, in a milder tone, "you shall find your account in it."

Thus adjured, the waiter protested he would be happy to give the gentleman any satisfaction in his power. The fact was, Sam had been pretty full of notions lately, and had been to see Simmons, and, in short, he should not wonder if he never saw any more of him.

And as hour after hour passed, the whole day, the whole night, and no Sam was forthcoming, the truth of the surmise became increasingly evident. Our young hero, Mr. Alfred B——, was a good deal provoked, and strange as the fact may seem, a good deal grieved too, for he really loved the fellow. "Loved him," says some scornful zealot; "a slaveholder *love* his slaves!" Yes, brother; why not? A warmhearted man will love his dog, his horse, even to grieving bitterly for their loss, and why not credit the fact that such a one may *love* the human creature whom accursed custom has placed on the same level. The fact was, Alfred B—— did love this young man; he had been appropriated to him in childhood, and Alfred had always redressed his grievances, fought his battles, got him out of scrapes, and purchased for him with liberal hand, indulgencies to which his comrades were strangers. He had taken pride to dress him smartly, and as for hardship and want, they had never come near him.

"The poor, silly, ungrateful puppy!" soliloquized he, "what can he do with himself?—Confound that Quaker, and all his meddlesome tribe—been at him with their bloody bone stories, I supposed—Sam knows better—the scamp—Halloa, there," he called to one of the waiters, "where does this Simpkins—Simon—Simmons, or what d'ye call him, live?"

"His shop is No. 5, on G street."

"Well, I'll go at him, and see what business he has with my affairs."

The Quaker was sitting at the door of his shop, with a round, rosy, good-humored face, so expressive of placidity and satisfaction, that it was difficult to approach in ireful feeling.

"Is your name Simmons?" demanded Alfred, in a voice whose natural urbanity was somewhat sharpened by vexation.

"Yes, friend; what dost thou wish?"

"I wished to inquire whether you have seen any thing of my colored fellow, Sam; a man of twenty-five or thereabouts, lodging at the Pearl street House?"

"I rather suspect that I have," said the Quaker, in a quiet, meditative tone, as if thinking the matter over with himself.

"And is it true, sir, that you have encouraged and assisted him to get out of my service?"

"Such, truly, is the fact, my friend."

Losing patience at this provoking equanimity, our young friend poured forth his sentiments with no inconsiderable energy, and in terms not the most select or pacific, all which our Quaker received with that placid, full-orbed tranquility of countenance, which seemed to say, "Pray, sir, relieve your mind; don't be particular; scold as hard as you like." The singularity of this expression struck the young man, and as his wrath became gradually spent, he could hardly help laughing at the tranquility of his opponent, and he gradually changed his tone for one of expostulation. "What motive could induce you, sir, thus to incommode a stranger, and one who never injured you at all?"

"I am sorry thou art incommoded," rejoined the Quaker. "Thy servant, as thee calls him, came to me, and I helped him as I would any other poor fellow in distress."

"Poor fellow!" said Alfred angrily; "that's the story of the whole of you. I tell you there is not a free negro in the city so well off as my Sam is, and always has been, and he'll find it out before long."

"But tell me, friend, thou mayest die, as well as another man; thy establishment may fall into debt, as well as another man's; and thy Sam may be sold by the sheriff for debt, or change hands in dividing the estate, and so on, though he was bred easily, and well cared for, he may come to be a field hand, under hard masters, starved, beaten, overworked—such things do happen sometimes, do they not?"

"Sometimes, perhaps, they do," replied the young man.

"Well, look you, by our laws in Ohio, thy Sam is now a free man; as free as I or thou; he hath a strong back, good hands, good courage, can earn his ten or twelve dollars a month—or do better; now taking all things into account, if thee were in his place, what would thee do—would thee go back a slave, or try thy luck as a free man?"

Alfred said nothing in reply to this, only after a while he murmured half to himself, "I thought the fellow had more gratitude, after all my kindness."

"Thee talks of gratitude," said the Quaker, "now how does that account stand? Thou has fed, and clothed, and protected this man; thou hast not starved, beaten, or abused him; it would have been unworthy of thee; thou hast shown him special kindness, and, in return, he has given thee faithful service for fifteen or twenty years; all his time, all his strength, all he could do or be, he has given thee, and ye are about even." The young man looked thoughtful, but made no reply.

"Sir," said he, at last, "I will take no unfair advantage of you; I wish to get my servant once more; can I do so?"

"Certainly. I will bring him to thy lodgings this evening, if thee wish it. I know thee will do what is fair," replied the Quaker.

It were difficult to define the thoughts of the young man, as he returned to his lodgings.—Naturally generous and human, he had never dreamed that he had rendered injustice to the human beings he claimed as his own. Injustice and oppression he had sometimes seen with detestation in other establishments; but it had been his pride that they were excluded from his own. It has been his pride to think that his indulgence and liberality made a situation of dependence on him preferable even to liberty.

The dark picture of possible reverses which the slave system hangs over the lot of the most favored slaves, never occurred to him. Accordingly, at six o'clock that evening, a light tap at the door of Mr. B's. parlor, announced the Quaker, and hanging back behind him, the reluctant Sam, who, with all his newly acquired love of liberty, felt almost as if he were treating his old master rather shabbily, in deserting him.

"So, Sam," said Alfred, "how is this? they say you want to leave me."

"Yes, master."

"Why, what's the matter, Sam? haven't I always been good to you; and has not my father always been good to you?"

"Oh yes, master; very good."

"Have you not always had good food, good clothes, and lived easy?"

"Yes, master."

"And nobody has ever abused you?"

"No, master."

"Well, then, why do you wish to leave me?"

"Oh, massa, I want to be a free man."

"Why, Sam; ain't you well enough off, now?"

"Oh, massa may die; then nobody knows who get me; some dreadful folks, you know, master, might get me, as they did Jim Sanford, and nobody to take my part. No, master. I rather be free man."

Alfred turned to the window, and thought a few moments, and then said, turning about, "Well, Sam, I believe you are right. I think, on the whole, I'd like best to be a free man myself, and I must not wonder that you do.—So, for ought I see, you must go; but then, Sam, there's your wife and child." Sam's countenance fell.

"Never mind, Sam. I will send them up to you."

"Oh, master!"

"I will; but you must remember now, Sam, you have got both yourself and them to take care of, and have no master to look after you; be steady, sober and industrious, and then, if ever you get into distress, send word to me, and I'll help you." Lest any accuse us of overcoloring our story, we will close it by extracting a passage or two from the letter which the generous young man the next day left in the hands of the Quaker, for his emancipated servant. We can assure our readers that we copy from the original document, which now lies before us:

DEAR SAM—I am just on the eve of my departure for Pittsburg: I may not see you again for a long time, possibly never, and I leave this letter with your friends, Messrs. A. & B., for you, and herewith bid you an affectionate farewell. Let me give you some advice, which is, now that you are a free man, in a free State, be obedient as you were when a slave, perform all the duties that are required of you, and do all you can for your own future welfare and respectability. Let me assure you that I have the same good feeling towards you that you know I always had; and let me tell you farther, that if ever you want a friend, call or write to me, and I will be that friend. Should you be sick, and not able to work, and want money to a small amount at different times, write to me, and I will always let you have it. I have not with me at present much money, though I will leave with my agents here, the Messrs. W., $5 for you; you must give them your receipt for it. On my return from

Pittsburg, I will call and see you if I have time; fail not to write to my father, for he made you a good master, and you should always treat him with respect, and cherish his memory so long as you live. Be good, industrious and honorable, and if unfortunate in your undertakings, never forget that you have a friend in me—farewell, and believe me your affectionate young master and friend,

ALFRED B——.

That dispositions as ingenuous and noble as that of this young man, are commonly to be found either in slave States or in free, is more than we dare assert. But when we see such found even among those who are born and bred slaveholders, we cannot but feel that there is encouragement for a fair, and mild, and brotherly presentation of truth, and every reason to lament hasty and wholesale denunciations.—The great error of controversy is, that it is ever ready to assail *persons* rather than *principles*. The slave *system* as a system, perhaps, concentrates more wrong than any other now existing, and yet those who live under and in it may be, as we see, enlightened, generous, and amenable to reason. If the *system* alone is attacked, such minds will be the first to perceive its evils and to turn against it; but if the system be attacked through individuals, self-love, wounded pride, and a thousand natural feelings will be at once enlisted for its preservation. We therefore subjoin it as the moral of our story, that a man who has had the misfortune to be born and bred a slaveholder, may be enlightened, generous, humane, and capable of the most disinterested regard to the welfare of his slave.

From *Dred; A Tale of the Great Dismal Swamp* (1856)

CHAPTER IV. The Gordon Family

A week or two had passed over the head of Nina Gordon since she was first introduced to our readers, and during this time she had become familiar with the details of her home life. Nominally, she stood at the head of her plantation, as mistress and queen in her own right of all, both in doors and out; but, really, she found herself, by her own youth and inexperience, her ignorance of practical details, very much in the hands of those she professed to govern.

The duties of a southern housekeeper, on a plantation, are onerous beyond any amount of northern conception. Every article wanted for daily consumption must be kept under lock and key, and doled out as need arises. For the most part, the servants are only grown-up children, without consideration, forethought, or self-control, quarrelling with each other, and divided into parties and factions, hopeless of any reasonable control. Every article of wear, for some hundreds of people, must be thought of, purchased, cut and made, under the direction of the mistress; and add to this the care of young children, whose childish mothers are totally unfit to govern or care for them, and we have some slight idea of what devolves on southern housekeepers.

Our reader has seen what Nina was on her return from New York, and can easily imagine that she had no idea of embracing, in good earnest, the hard duties of such a life.

In fact, since the death of Nina's mother, the situation of the mistress of the family had been only nominally filled by her aunt, Mrs. Nesbit. The real housekeeper, in fact, was an old mulatto woman, named Katy, who had been trained by Nina's mother. Notwithstanding the general inefficiency and childishness of negro servants, there often are to be found among them those of great practical ability. Whenever owners, through necessity or from tact, select such servants, and subject them to the kind of training and responsibility which belongs to a state of freedom, the same qualities are developed which exist in free society. Nina's mother, being always in delicate health, had, from necessity, been obliged to commit much responsibility to "Aunt Katy," as she was called; and she had grown up under the discipline into a very efficient housekeeper. With her tall red turban, her jingling bunch of keys, and an abundant sense of the importance of her office, she was a dignitary not lightly to be disregarded.

It is true that she professed the utmost deference for her young mistress, and very generally passed the compliment of inquiring what she would have done; but it was pretty generally understood that her assent to Aunt Katy's propositions was considered as much a matter of course as the queen's to a ministerial recommendation. Indeed, had Nina chosen to demur, her prime minister had the power, without departing in the slightest degree from a respectful bearing, to involve her in labyrinths of perplexity without end. And, as Nina hated trouble, and wanted, above all things, to have her time to herself for her own amusement, she wisely

concluded not to interfere with Aunt Katy's reign, and to get by persua-
sion and coaxing, what the old body would have been far too consequen-
tial and opinionated to give to authority.

In like manner, at the head of all out-door affairs was the young qua-
droon, Harry, whom we introduced in the first chapter. In order to come
fully at the relation in which he stood to the estate, we must, after the
fashion of historians generally, go back a hundred years or so, in order
to give our readers a fair start. Behold us, therefore, assuming historic
dignity, as follows.

Among the first emigrants to Virginia, in its colonial days, was one
Thomas Gordon, Knight, a distant offshoot of the noble Gordon family,
renowned in Scottish history. Being a gentleman of some considerable en-
ergy, and impatient of the narrow limits of the Old World, where he found
little opportunity to obtain that wealth which was necessary to meet
the demands of his family pride, he struck off for himself into Virginia.
Naturally of an adventurous turn, he was one of the first to propose the
enterprise which afterwards resulted in a settlement on the banks of the
Chowan River, in North Carolina. Here he took up for himself a large tract
of the finest alluvial land, and set himself to the business of planting, with
the energy and skill characteristic of his nation; and, as the soil was new
and fertile, he soon received a very munificent return for his enterprise.
Inspired with remembrances of old ancestral renown, the Gordon family
transmitted in their descent all the traditions, feelings, and habits, which
were the growth of the aristocratic caste from which they sprung. The
name of Canema, given to the estate, came from an Indian guide and in-
terpreter, who accompanied the first Col. Gordon as confidential servant.

The estate, being entailed, passed down through the colonial times un-
broken in the family, whose wealth, for some years, seemed to increase
with every generation.

The family mansion was one of those fond reproductions of the archi-
tectural style of the landed gentry in England, in which, as far as their
means could compass it, the planters were fond of indulging.

Carpenters and carvers had been brought over, at great expense, from
the old country, to give the fruits of their skill in its erection; and it was a
fancy of the ancestor who built it, to display, in its wood-work, that exu-
berance of new and rare woods with which the American continent was
supposed to abound. He had made an adventurous voyage into South

America, and brought from thence specimens of those materials more brilliant than rose-wood, and hard as ebony, which grow so profusely on the banks of the Amazon that the natives use them for timber. The floor of the central hall of the house was a curiously-inlaid parquet of these brilliant materials, arranged in fine block-work, highly polished.

The outside of the house was built in the old Virginian fashion, with two tiers of balconies running completely round, as being much better suited to the American climate than any of European mode. The inside, however, was decorated with sculpture and carvings, copied, many of them, from ancestral residences in Scotland, giving to the mansion an air of premature antiquity.

Here, for two or three generations, the Gordon family had lived in opulence. During the time, however, of Nina's father, and still more after his death, there appeared evidently on the place signs of that gradual decay which has conducted many an old Virginian family to poverty and ruin. Slave labor, of all others the most worthless and profitless, had exhausted the first vigor of the soil, and the proprietors gradually degenerated from those habits of energy which were called forth by the necessities of the first settlers, and everything proceeded with that free-and-easy *abandon*, in which both master and slave appeared to have one common object,— that of proving who should waste with most freedom.

At Colonel Gordon's death, he had bequeathed, as we have already shown, the whole family estate to his daughter, under the care of a servant, of whose uncommon intelligence and thorough devotion of heart he had the most ample proof. When it is reflected that the overseers are generally taken from a class of whites who are often lower in ignorance and barbarism than even the slaves, and that their wastefulness and rapacity are a by-word among the planters, it is no wonder that Colonel Gordon thought that, in leaving his plantation under the care of one so energetic, competent, and faithful, as Harry, he had made the best possible provision for his daughter.

Harry was the son of his master, and inherited much of the temper and constitution of his father, tempered by the soft and genial temperament of the beautiful Eboe mulattress who was his mother. From this circumstance Harry had received advantages of education very superior to what commonly fell to the lot of his class. He had also accompanied his master as valet during the tour of Europe, and thus his opportunities of general observation had been still further enlarged, and that tact by which those of the mixed blood seem so peculiarly fitted to appreciate all the finer aspects of conventional life, had been called out and exercised; so that it would be difficult in any circle to meet with a more agreeable and gentlemanly person. In leaving a man of this character, and his own son, still in the bonds of slavery, Colonel Gordon was influenced by that passionate devotion to his daughter which with him overpowered every consideration. A man so cultivated, he argued to himself, might find many avenues opened to him in freedom; might be tempted to leave the estate to other hands, and seek his own fortune. He therefore resolved to leave him bound by an indissoluble tie for a term of years, trusting to his attachment to Nina to make this service tolerable.

Possessed of very uncommon judgment, firmness, and knowledge of human nature, Harry had found means to acquire great ascendency over the hands of the plantation; and, either through fear or through friendship, there was a universal subordination to him. The executors of the estate scarcely made even a feint of overseeing him; and he proceeded, to all intents and purposes, with the perfect ease of a free man. Everybody, for miles around, knew and respected him; and, had he not been possessed of a good share of the thoughtful, forecasting temperament derived from his Scottish parentage, he might have been completely happy, and forgotten even the existence of the chains whose weight he never felt.

It was only in the presence of Tom Gordon—Colonel Gordon's lawful son—that he ever realized that he was a slave. From childhood, there had been a rooted enmity between the brothers, which deepened as years passed on; and, as he found himself, on every return of the young man to the place, subjected to taunts and ill-usage, to which his defenceless position left him no power to reply, he had resolved never to marry, and lay the foundation for a family, until such time as he should be able to have the command of his own destiny, and that of his household. But the charms of a pretty French quadroon overcame the dictates of prudence.

[...]

A young person could scarce stand more entirely alone, as to sympathetic intercourse with relations, than Nina. It is true that the presence of her mother's sister in the family caused it to be said that she was residing under the care of an aunt.

Mrs. Nesbit, however, was simply one of those well-bred, well-dressed lay-figures, whose only office in life seems to be to occupy a certain room in a house, to sit in certain chairs at proper hours, to make certain remarks at suitable intervals of conversation. In her youth this lady had run quite a career as a belle and beauty. Nature had endowed her with a handsome face and figure, and youth and the pleasure of admiration for some years supplied a sufficient flow of animal spirits to make the beauty effective. Early married, she became the mother of several children, who were one by one swept into the grave. The death of her husband, last of all, left her with a very small fortune alone in the world; and, like many in similar circumstances, she was content to sink into an appendage to another's family.

Mrs. Nesbit considered herself very religious; and, as there is a great deal that passes for religion, ordinarily, of which she may be fairly considered a representative, we will present our readers with a philosophical analysis of the article. When young, she had thought only of self in the form of admiration, and the indulgence of her animal spirits. When married, she had thought of self only in her husband and children, whom she loved because they were *hers*, and for no other reason.

When death swept away her domestic circle, and time stole the beauty and freshness of animal spirits, her self-love took another form; and, perceiving that this world was becoming to her somewhat passé, she determined to make the best of her chance for another.

Religion she looked upon in the light of a ticket, which, being once purchased, and snugly laid away in a pocket-book, is to be produced at the celestial gate, and thus secure admission to heaven.

At a certain period of her life, while she deemed this ticket unpurchased, she was extremely low-spirited and gloomy, and went through a quantity of theological reading enough to have astonished herself, had she foreseen it in the days of her belle-ship. As the result of all, she at last presented herself as a candidate for admission to a Presbyterian church in the vicinity, there professing her determination to run the Christian race. By the Christian race, she understood going at certain stated times to religious meetings, reading the Bible and hymn-book at certain hours in the day, giving at regular intervals stipulated sums to religious charities, and preserving a general state of leaden indifference to everybody and everything in the world.

She thus fondly imagined that she had renounced the world, because she looked back with disgust on gayeties for which she had no longer strength or spirits. Nor did she dream that the intensity with which her mind travelled the narrow world of self, dwelling on the plaits of her caps, the cut of her stone-colored satin gowns, the making of her tea and her bed, and the saving of her narrow income, was exactly the same in kind, though far less agreeable in development, as that which once expended itself in dressing and dancing. Like many other apparently negative characters, she had a pertinacious intensity of an extremely narrow and aimless self-will. Her plans of life, small as they were, had a thousand crimps and plaits, to every one of which she adhered with invincible pertinacity. The poor lady little imagined, when she sat, with such punctilious satisfaction, while the Rev. Mr. Orthodoxy demonstrated that selfishness is the essence of all moral evil, that the sentiment had the slightest application to her; nor dreamed that the little, quiet, muddy current of self-will, which ran without noise or indecorum under the whole structure of her being, might be found, in a future day, to have undermined all her hopes of heaven. Of course, Mrs. Nesbit regarded Nina, and all other lively young people, with a kind of melancholy endurance—as shocking spectacles of worldliness. There was but little sympathy, to be sure, between the dashing, and out-spoken, and almost defiant little Nina, and the sombre silver-gray apparition which glided quietly about the wide halls of her paternal mansion. In fact, it seemed to afford the latter a mischievous pleasure to shock her respectable relative on all convenient occasions. Mrs. Nesbit felt it occasionally her duty, as she remarked, to call her lively niece into her apartment, and endeavor to persuade her to read some such volume as Law's Serious Call, or Owen on the One Hundred and Nineteenth Psalm; and to give her a general and solemn warning against all the vanities of the world, in which were generally included dressing in any color but black and drab, dancing, flirting, writing love-letters, and all other enormities, down to the eating of pea-nut candy. One of these scenes is just now enacting in this good lady's apartment, upon which we will raise the curtain.

Mrs. Nesbit, a diminutive, blue-eyed, fair-complexioned little woman, of some five feet high, sat gently swaying in that respectable asylum for American old age, commonly called a rocking-chair. Every rustle of her silvery silk gown, every fold of the snowy kerchief on her neck, every plait of her immaculate cap, spoke a soul long retired from this world and its cares. The bed, arranged with extremest precision, however, was covered with a melange of French finery, flounces, laces, among which Nina kept up a continual agitation like that produced by a breeze in a flowerbed, as she unfolded, turned, and fluttered them, before the eyes of her relative.

"I have been through all this, Nina," said the latter, with a melancholy shake of her head, "and I know the vanity of it."

"Well, aunty, I *have n't* been through it, so *I* don't know."

"Yes, my dear, when I was of your age, I used to go to balls and parties, and could think of nothing but of dress and admiration. I have been through it all, and seen the vanity of it."

"Well, aunt, I want to go through it, and see the vanity of it, too. That's just what I'm after. I'm on the way to be as sombre and solemn as you are, but I'm bound to have a good time first. Now, look at this pink brocade!"

Had the brocade been a pall, it could scarcely have been regarded with a more lugubrious aspect.

"Ah, child! such a dying world as this! To spend so much time and thought on dress!"

"Why, Aunt Nesbit, yesterday you spent just two whole hours in thinking whether you should turn the breadths of your black silk dress upside down, or down side up; and this was a dying world all the time. Now, I don't see that it is any better to think of black silk than it is of pink."

This was a view of the subject which seemed never to have occurred to the good lady.

"But, now, aunt, do cheer up, and look at this box of artificial flowers. You know I thought I'd bring a stock on from New York. Now, are n't these perfectly lovely? I like flowers that *mean* something. Now, these are all imitations of natural flowers, so perfect that you'd scarcely know them from the real. See—there, that's a moss-rose; and now look at these sweet peas, you'd think they had just been picked; and, there—that heliotrope, and these jessamines, and those orange-blossoms, and that wax camelia—"

"Turn off my eyes from beholding vanity!" said Mrs. Nesbit, shutting her eyes, and shaking her head:

"'What if we wear the richest vest,—
Peacocks and flies are better drest;
This flesh, with all its glorious forms,
Must drop to earth, and feed the worms.'"[1]

"Aunt, I do think you have the most horrid, disgusting set of hymns, all about worms, and dust, and such things!"

"It 's my duty, child, when I see you so much taken up with such sinful finery."

"Why, aunt, do you think artificial flowers are sinful?"

"Yes, dear; they are a sinful waste of time and money, and take off our mind from more important things."

"Well, aunt, then what did the Lord make sweet peas, and roses, and orange-blossoms for? I 'm sure it 's only doing as he does, to make flowers. He don't make everything gray, or stone-color. Now, if you only would come out in the garden, this morning, and see the oleanders, and the crape myrtle, and the pinks, the roses, and the tulips, and the hyacinths, I 'm sure it would do you good."

"O, I should certainly catch cold, child, if I went out doors. Milly left a crack opened in the window, last night, and I 've sneezed three or four times since. It will never do for me to go out in the garden; the feeling of the ground striking up through my shoes is very unhealthy."

"Well, at any rate, aunt, I should think, if the Lord did n't wish us to wear roses and jessamines, he would not have made them. And it is the most natural thing in the world to want to wear flowers."

"It only feeds vanity and a love of display, my dear."

"I don't think it 's vanity, or a love of display. I should want to dress prettily, if I were the only person in the world. I love pretty things because they *are* pretty. I like to wear them because they make me look pretty."

"There it is, child; you want to dress up your poor perishing body to look pretty—that 's the thing!"

"To be sure I do. Why should n't I? I mean to look as pretty as I can, as long as I live."

"You seem to have quite a conceit of your beauty!" said Aunt Nesbit.

"Well, I know I am pretty. I 'm not going to pretend I don't. I like my own looks, now, that's a fact. I 'm not like one of your Greek statues, I know. I'm not wonderfully handsome, nor likely to set the world on fire with my beauty. I 'm just a pretty little thing; and I like flowers and laces, and all of those things; and I mean to like them, and I don't think there 'll be a bit of religion in my not liking them; and as for all that disagreeable stuff about the worms, that you are always telling me, I don't think it does me a particle of good. And, if religion is going to make me so *poky*, I shall put it off as long as I can."

"I used to feel just as you do, dear, but I 've seen the folly of it!"

"If I 've got to lose my love for everything that is bright, everything that is lively, and everything that is pretty, and like to read such horrid stupid books, why, I 'd rather be buried, and done with it!"

"That 's the opposition of the natural heart, my dear."

The conversation was here interrupted by the entrance of a bright, curly-headed mulatto boy, bearing Mrs. Nesbit's daily luncheon.

"O, here comes Tomtit," said Nina; "now for a scene! Let 's see what he has forgotten, now."

Tomtit was, in his way, a great character in the mansion. He and his grandmother were the property of Mrs. Nesbit. His true name was no less respectable and methodical than that of Thomas; but, as he was one of those restless and effervescent sprites, who seem to be born for the confusion of quiet people, Nina had rechristened him Tomtit, which sobriquet was immediately recognized by the whole household as being eminently descriptive and appropriate. A constant ripple and eddy of drollery seemed to pervade his whole being; his large, saucy black eyes had always a laughing fire in them, that it was impossible to meet without a smile in return. Slave and property though he was, yet the first sentiment of reverence for any created thing seemed yet wholly unawakened in his curly pate. Breezy, idle, careless, flighty, as his woodland namesake, life to him seemed only a repressed and pent-up ebullition of animal enjoyment; and almost the only excitement of Mrs. Nesbit's quiet life was her chronic controversy with Tomtit. Forty or fifty times a day did the old body assure him "that she was astonished at his conduct;" and as many times would he reply by showing the whole set of his handsome teeth, on the broad grin, wholly inconsiderate of the state of despair into which he thus reduced her.

On the present occasion, as he entered the room, his eye was caught by the great display of finery on the bed; and, hastily dumping the waiter on the first chair that occurred, with a flirt and a spring as lithe as that of a squirrel, he was seated in a moment astride the foot-board, indulging in a burst of merriment.

"Good law, Miss Nina, whar on earth dese yer come from? Good law, some on 'em for me, is n't 'er?"

"You see that child!" now said Mrs. Nesbit, rocking back in her chair with the air of a martyr. "After all my talkings to him! Nina, you ought not to allow that; it just encourages him!"

"Tom, get down, you naughty creature you, and get the stand and put the waiter on it. Mind yourself, now!" said Nina, laughing.

Tomtit cut a somerset from the foot-board to the floor, and, striking up, on a very high key, "I 'll bet my money on a bob-tail nag,"[2] he danced out a small table, as if it had been a partner, and deposited it, with a jerk, at the side of Mrs. Nesbit, who aimed a cuff at his ears; but, as he adroitly ducked his head, the intended blow came down upon the table with more force than was comfortable to the inflictor.

"I believe that child is made of air!—I never can hit him!" said the good lady, waxing red in the face. "He is enough to provoke a saint!"

"So he is, aunt; enough to provoke two saints like you and me. Tomtit, you rogue," said she, giving a gentle pull to a handful of his curly hair, "be good, now, and I 'll show you the pretty things, by and by. Come, put the waiter on the table, now; see if you can't walk, for once!"

Casting down his eyes with an irresistible look of mock solemnity, Tomtit marched with the waiter, and placed it by his mistress.

The good lady, after drawing off her gloves and making sundry little decorous preparations, said a short grace over her meal, during which time Tomtit seemed to be holding his sides with repressed merriment; then, gravely laying hold of the handle of the teapot she stopped short, gave an exclamation, and flirted her fingers, as she felt it almost scalding hot.

"Tomtit, I do believe you intend to burn me to death, some day!"

"Laws, missus, dat are hot? O, sure I was tickler to set the nose round to the fire."

"No, you did n't! you stuck the handle right into the fire, as you 're always doing!"

"Laws, now, wonder if I did," said Tomtit, assuming an abstracted appearance. "'Pears as if never can 'member which dem dare is nose, and which handle. Now, I 's a studdin on dat dare most all de morning—was so," said he, gathering confidence, as he saw, by Nina's dancing eyes, how greatly she was amused.

"You need a sound whipping, sir—that 's what you need!" said Mrs. Nesbit, kindling up in sudden wrath.

"O, I knows it," said Tomtit. "We 's unprofitable servants, all on us. Lord's marcy that we an't 'sumed, all on us!"

Nina was so completely overcome by this novel application of the text which she had heard her aunt laboriously drumming into Tomtit, the Sabbath before, that she laughed aloud, with rather uproarious merriment.

"O, aunt, there 's no use! He don't know anything! He 's nothing but an incarnate joke, a walking hoax!"

"No, I does n't know nothing, Miss Nina," said Tomtit, at the same time looking out from under his long eyelashes. "Don't know nothing at all— never can."

"Well, now, Tomtit," said Mrs. Nesbit, drawing out a little blue cowhide from under her chair, and looking at him resolutely, "you see, if this teapot handle is hot again, I 'll give it to you! Do you hear?"

"Yes, missis," said Tomtit, with that indescribable sing-song of indifference, which is so common and so provoking in his class.

"And, now, Tomtit, you go down stairs and clean the knives for dinner."

"Yes, missis," said he, pirouetting towards the door. And once in the passage, he struck up a vigorous "O, I 'm going to glory, won't you go along with me;"[3] accompanying himself, by slapping his own sides, as he went down two stairs at a time.

"Going to glory!" said Mrs. Nesbit, rather shortly; "he looks like it, I think! It 's the third or fourth time that that child has blistered my fingers with this teapot, and I know he does it on purpose! So ungrateful, when I spend my time, teaching him, hour after hour, laboring with him so! I declare, I don't believe these children have got any souls!"

"Well, aunt, I declare, I should think you 'd get out of all patience with him; yet he 's so funny, I cannot, for the life of me, help laughing."

Here a distant whoop on the staircase, and a tempestuous chorus to a methodist hymn, with the words, "O come, my loving brethren," announced that Tomtit was on the return; and very soon, throwing open the door, he marched in, with an air of the greatest importance.

"Tomtit, did n't I tell you to go and clean the knives?"

"Law, missis, come up here to bring Miss Nina's love-letters," said he, producing two or three letters. "Good law, though," said he, checking himself, "forgot to put them on a waity!" and, before a word could be said, he was out of the room and down stairs, and at the height of furious contest with the girl who was cleaning the silver, for a waiter to put Miss Nina's letters on.

"Dar, Miss Nina," appealing to her when she appeared, "Rosa won't let me have no waity!"

"I could pull your hair for you, you little image!" said Nina, seizing the letters from his hands, and laughing while she cuffed his ears.

"Well," said Tomtit, looking after her with great solemnity, "missis in de right on 't. An't no kind of order in this here house, 'pite of all I can do. One says put letters on waity. Another one won't let you have waity to put letters on. And, finally, Miss Nina, she pull them all away. Just the way things going on in dis yer house, all the time! I can't help it; done all I can. Just the way missus says!"

There was one member of Nina's establishment of a character so marked that we cannot refrain from giving her a separate place in our picture of her surroundings,—and this was Milly, the waiting-woman of Aunt Nesbit.

Aunt Milly, as she was commonly called, was a tall, broad-shouldered, deep-chested African woman, with a fulness of figure approaching to corpulence. Her habit of standing and of motion was peculiar and majestic, reminding one of the Scripture expression "upright as the palm-tree." Her skin was of a peculiar blackness and softness, not unlike black velvet. Her eyes were large, full, and dark, and had about them that expression of wishfulness and longing which one may sometimes have remarked in dark eyes. Her mouth was large, and the lips, though partaking of the African fulness, had, nevertheless, something decided and energetic in their outline, which was still further seconded by the heavy moulding of the chin. A frank smile, which was common with her, disclosed a row of most splendid and perfect teeth. Her hair, without approaching to the character of the Anglo-Saxon, was still different from the ordinary woolly coat of the negro, and seemed more like an infinite number of close-knotted curls, of brilliant, glossy blackness.

The parents of Milly were prisoners taken in African wars; and she was a fine specimen of one of those warlike and splendid races, of whom, as they have seldom been reduced to slavery, there are but few and rare specimens among the slaves of the south.

Her usual head-dress was a high turban, of those brilliant colored Madras handkerchiefs in which the instinctive taste of the dark races leads them to delight. Milly's was always put on and worn with a regal air, as if it were the coronet of the queen. For the rest, her dress consisted of a well-fitted gown of dark stuff, of a quality somewhat finer than the usual household apparel. A neatly-starched white muslin handkerchief folded across her bosom, and a clean white apron, completed her usual costume.

No one could regard her, as a whole, and not feel their prejudice in favor of the exclusive comeliness of white races somewhat shaken. Placed among the gorgeous surroundings of African landscape and scenery, it might be doubted whether any one's taste could have desired, as a completion to her appearance, to have blanched the glossy skin whose depth of coloring harmonizes so well with the intense and fiery glories of a tropical landscape.

In character, Milly was worthy of her remarkable external appearance. Heaven had endowed her with a soul as broad and generous as her ample frame. Her passions rolled and burned in her bosom with a tropical fervor; a shrewd and abundant mother wit, united with a vein of occasional drollery, gave to her habits of speech a quaint vivacity.

A native adroitness gave an unwonted command over all the functions of her fine body; so that she was endowed with that much-coveted property which the New Englander denominates "faculty," which means the intuitive ability to seize at once on the right and best way of doing everything which is to be done. At the same time, she was possessed of that high degree of self-respect which led her to be incorruptibly faithful and thorough in all she undertook; less, as it often seemed, from any fealty or deference to those whom she served, than from a kind of native pride in well-doing, which led her to deem it beneath herself to slight or pass over the least thing which she had undertaken. Her promises were inviolable. Her owners always knew that what she once said would be done, if it were within the bounds of possibility.

The value of an individual thus endowed in person and character may be easily conceived by those who understand how rare, either among slaves or freemen, is such a combination. Milly was, therefore, always considered in the family as a most valuable piece of property, and treated with more than common consideration.

As a mind, even when uncultivated, will ever find its level, it often happened that Milly's amount of being and force of character gave her ascendency even over those who were nominally her superiors. As her ways were commonly found to be the best ways, she was left, in most cases, to pursue them without opposition or control. But, favorite as she was, her life had been one of deep sorrows. She had been suffered, it is true, to contract a marriage with a very finely-endowed mulatto man, on a plantation adjoining her owner's, by whom she had a numerous family of children, who inherited all her fine physical and mental endowments. With more than usual sensibility and power of reflection, the idea that the children so dear to her were from their birth not her own,—that they were, from the first hour of their existence, merchantable articles, having a fixed market value in proportion to every excellence, and liable to all the reverses of merchantable goods,—sank with deep weight into her mind. Unfortunately, the family to which she belonged being reduced to poverty, there remained, often, no other means of making up the deficiency of income than the annual sale of one or two negroes. Milly's children, from their fine developments, were much-coveted articles. Their owner was often tempted by extravagant offers for them; and therefore, to meet one crisis or another of family difficulties, they had been successively sold from her. At first, she had met this doom with almost the ferocity of a lioness; but the blow, oftentimes repeated, had brought with it a dull endurance, and Christianity had entered, as it often does with the slave, through the rents and fissures of a broken heart. Those instances of piety which are sometimes, though rarely, found among slaves, and which transcend the ordinary development of the best-instructed, are generally the results of calamities and afflictions so utterly desolating as to force the soul to depend on God alone. But, where one soul is thus raised to higher piety, thousands are crushed in hopeless imbecility.

SOURCES

Stowe, Harriet Beecher. *Dred; A Tale of the Great Dismal Swamp*, 1:41–61. Boston: Phillips, Sampson.
———. "Immediate Emancipation: A Sketch." *New York Evangelist*, January 2, 1845, 1.

NOTES

1. From "Gravity and Decency," a hymn by English minister and hymnist Isaac Watts (1674–1748).
2. From "Camptown Races" (1850, alternately titled "Gwine to Run All Night, or De Camptown Races"), a minstrel song by American songwriter Stephen Foster (1826–1864).
3. From the spiritual "Bound for the Promised Land," which Stowe also quotes in *Uncle Tom's Cabin* (1852).

.

Eloise Bibb Thompson

1878–1928

ELOISE BIBB THOMPSON was an African American writer, teacher, and religious activist from New Orleans, primarily known for her works of drama, journalism, and short fiction. She directed the Social Settlement program at Howard University, and contributed to such outlets as the *Los Angeles Tribune* and the *Morning Sun*. Thompson wrote four plays, three of which were produced in Los Angeles with Black casts for Black audiences. She and her husband, journalist Noah Thompson, were devout Catholics who worked together to try to help Black Americans advance socially. Her short fictions, including the following selection, often examined the issue of "passing" among Creoles.

Masks, A Story (1927)

Paupet, an octoroon and born free, was a man of considerable insight. That was because, having brains, he used them. The cause of Julie's, his wife's, trouble was no secret to him. Although it never dawned upon him fully until after she died. Then he dictated the words to be placed upon her tombstone. The inscription proved to be unique, but not more than the cemeteries themselves of old New Orleans. The motto written in 1832 read as follows: "Because she saw with the eyes of her grandfather, she died at the sight of her babe's face."

This grandfather, Aristile Blanchard, had been an enigma to the whole Quadroon Quarter of New Orleans. But he was no enigma to Paupet although he had never lain eyes upon him. Seeing him had not been necessary for Paupet had heard his whole life's history from Paul, Julie's brother, whom he met in Mobile before he had known Julie. Paul, although a ne'er do well who had left the home-fires early, admired his grandfather immensely. Hence he had found delight even as a youth in securing from the old man those facts of his life which had proved so interesting to Paupet.

Now Paupet, among other things, was a natural psychologist albeit an unconscious one. He was accustomed to ponder the motives of men, their peculiar mental traits and their similarity to those of their parents whom he happened to know. No one was more interesting to Paupet than Julie, his wife. So of course he gave much thought to her. But the occasion is always necessary for the knowledge of a soul, and the opportunity for really knowing Julie came only when she was expecting her offspring. But even then Paupet would not have known where to place the blame for her peculiarity had he not known, as we have said, all there was to know about old Aristile Blanchard.

That Aristile was a man to be pitied Paupet felt there was no question. For what man does not deserve pity who sees his fondest dream fall with the swiftness of a rocket from a starlit sky to the darkness of midnight? No wonder that hallucination then seized him. With such a nature as his that was to be expected. But that the influence of such a delusion should have blighted Julie's young life was the thing of which Paupet most bitterly complained.

Aristile, Paul told Paupet, had been a native of Hayti. Coming to New Orleans in 1795 when the slave insurrection was hottest, he had set up an atmosphere of revolt as forceful as the one he had left behind him. Of course when Julie entered the world, the revolution had long been over; Toussaint L'Ouverture had demonstrated his fitness to rule, had eventually been thrown in an ignominious dungeon and been mouldering in the grave some five years or more. But the fact that distressed Paupet was that Aristile lived on to throw his baneful influence over the granddaughter entrusted by a dying mother to his care.

Of all the free men of color in Hayti at the time none were more favored than Aristile. A quadroon of prepossessing appearance with some capital at hand, he had been sent to Bordeaux, France, by a doting mother to study the arts for which he was thought to show marked predilection. In reality he was but a dabbler in the arts, returning at length to his native land with some acquaintance with most of them, as for instance sculpture, painting, woodcarving and the like but with no very comprehensive knowledge of any one of them. There was one thing, however, that did not escape him—being there at the time when France was a hotbed of that revolt which finally stormed the Bastile—and that was the spirit of liberty. "Liberty, Fraternity, Equality" was in the very air he breathed. He returned from France with revolutionary tendencies far in advance of any free man in the island, tendencies that awaited but the opportunity to blossom into the strongest sort of heroism.

Although he burned to be of service to his race on returning to his native land he forced himself to resume his usual tenor of life. He sought apprenticeship to an Oriental mask-maker, a rare genius in his line where the rich French planters were wont to go in preparation for their masquerades and feast-day festivities. Masks had always had a strange fascination for Aristile. He would often sit lost in thought beside their maker, his mind full of conflicting emotions. But when the French slave-owners assembled at Cape Haitien to formulate measures against the free men of color to whom the National Assembly in France had decreed full citizenship, he forgot everything and throwing down his tools immediately headed the revolt that followed.

With Rigaud, the mulatto captain of the slaves, he gave himself to the cause of France, offering at the risk of his life to spy upon the English when they came to the support of the native French planters bent upon re-establishing slavery upon the island.

Making up as a white man as best he could, he boldly entered the port of Jeremie where the English had but recently landed. His ruse would have succeeded had it not been for a native white planter all too familiar with his African earmarks, who standing by at the time readily spotted him out. Without warning, Aristile was seized, flogged unmercifully and thrown into a dungeon to die. But he was rescued after a time by a good angel in the form of an octoroon planter identified with whites all his life because of a face that defied detection; not only rescued but shipped with his daughter in safety to New Orleans. Then the octoroon rescuer took up the work of spy upon the English which Aristile had been forced to relinquish. That he was successful is manifested in the subsequent work of Toussaint L'Ouverture who because of him was able before very long to drive in all the troops of the English, to invest their strongholds, to assault their forts, and ultimately to destroy them totally.

This incident had a lifelong effect upon Aristile. Full of despondency, disappointment over his failure in the work he had set himself to do with the enthusiasm and glow of a martyr, his mind dwelt wholly upon the facial lineaments that had brought about his defeat. "Cheated!" he would exclaim bitterly. "Cheated out of the opportunity of doing the highest service because of a face four degrees from the pattern prescribed for success. Fate has been against me.—Nature has been against me. It was never meant that I should do the thing I burned to do.—O, why did not Nature give me the face of my father?—Then all things would have been possible to me. Other quadroons have been so blessed. Hundreds of them—thousands of them! Save for a slight sallowness of the skin there was absolutely nothing to show their African lineage. But Nature in projecting my lips and expanding my nose has set me apart for the contumely of the world.—The ancients lied when they said the gods made man's face from the nose upwards, leaving their lower portion for him to make himself. Try as I may I will never be able to change the mask that Nature has imposed upon me."

Day and night these thoughts were with him. Paul described this state to Paupet declaring that his mother had feared for Aristile's mind. At length this mood suddenly changed to one of exultation and he rose from his bed a new man.

"I have found the formula for greatness!" he told those about him, "It reads, Thou shalt be seen wearing a while man's face.—But only a fraction being able to carry out this prescription it is left for me to create a symbol so perfect in its imitation of Nature that the remainder of mankind may likewise receive a place in the sun. My brothers and I shall no longer be marked for defeat. I shall make a mask that will defy Nature herself. There shall be no more distinct and unmistakable signs that will determine whether a man shall be master or slave. All men in future shall have the privilege of being what they will."

With this end in view he repaired to the Quadroon Quarter of New Orleans and set up a workshop that soon became the talk of the district because of the strange-looking objects it contained. Paupet could vouch for their strangeness for they were still in existence when he came to the place. Upon the walls of this room hung many attempts of the thing Aristile had set himself to do. There were masks of paper patiently glued in small bits together in a brave effort to imitate Nature in the making of a white man's face. Likewise masks of wood, of papier mache and of some soft, clinging, leaf-like material which it is very likely he discovered in Louisiana's wonderous woods. Interesting-looking objects they were, everyone of them, most of them, however, were far from the goal; but a few in their skin-like possibility of stretching over a man's face might have been made perfect—who knows—greater marvels have been seen—had their completion not been suddenly broken off. There was about the whole of this room an unmistakable depression, an atmosphere of shattered hope as if the maker of these objects had set out with high purpose toward their completion then suddenly been chilled by some unforeseen happening that filled him with despair. And so it really had been. While Negro supremacy existed in his beloved country Aristile worked with ever-increasing enthusiasm toward his cherished dream. He had been unable, he told himself, to assist his brothers as a soldier because of the lineaments that Nature had imposed. But he would present them with a talisman like unto Aladdin's lamp that would work wonders for them in a world where to be blessed was to be white. But when the news reached him that Toussaint, the savior of his race had been tricked and thrown into a French prison to die, he was plunged into the deepest sorrow and turned from his purpose in despair. Laying aside his implements, for a long time he could not be induced to take interest in anything. At length when his funds began to dwindle, it was bourne in upon him that men must work if they would live. Then he turned to the making of those limp figures in sweeping gowns that when Paupet saw them were no doubt of his own distorted mind, designed for standing in the farthest corner of the room—grotesque figures wearing hideous masks, the reflection, clowns and actors of the comic stage.

It was not very long before the place began to be frequented by patrons of the Quadroon Masques and of those open-air African dances and debaucheries known as "Voodoo Carousals" held in the Congo Square. Later actors from the French Opera looked in upon him. Then he conceived the idea of having Clotile, his daughter, already an expert with the needle, prepare for his patrons of the masque and stage to be rented at a nominal fee, those gowns and wraps that were now fading behind the glass doors of yonder cabinets. But though he worked continuously it had no power, apparently, to change his usual course of thought. His mind ever dwelt upon the disaster that had blighted his life.

And then came Julie in this atmosphere of depression to take up in time the work which fate decreed Clotile should lay down. As apt with the needle as her dead mother had been she was able, when her grandfather through age and ill-health became enfeebled, to maintain them both. And those were formative years for the young Julie, obliged to listen to her grandfather's half-crazed tirade against Nature's way of fixing a man to his clan through the color of his skin. Unaccustomed to thinking independently she, however, could see something of the disastrousness of it all because of the stringent laws confronting her in New Orleans. As much as she longed to do so, for instance, she dared not wear any of the head-gear of the times, although much of it was made by her own fingers, because of the law forbidding it; a bandana handkerchief being decreed to all free women of color so that they might easily be distinguished from white ladies. And that was only one of the minor laws. There were others graver and more disastrous by far. So these conditions forced her to realize early that her grandfather had good reason for his lament. She too deplored the failure of his design—the making of a mask that would open the barred and bolted doors of privilege for those who knocked thereon. Without anything like bitterness for these conditions, she began to reason that color and not mental endowment or loftiness of character determined the caliber of a man. For did not color determine his destiny? He was rich or poor, happy or unhappy according to his complexion and not according to his efforts at all. And so the words superior and inferior were invariably dependent upon the color of his skin. She, a brunette-like quadroon, the counterpart of her grandfather, was far superior to the black slave-peddlers who sometimes came into the Quadroon Quarter begging a place to rest. And that was why the Quarter guarded the section so jealously from all black dwellers, however free they might be because they wanted only superior people in their midst.

One morning some months after her grandfather's death she awoke trembling with a great discovery, for years she reflected in wonderment her revered relative had tried to make a mask that when fitted to a man's face would change his entire future and had failed. And lo! the secret had just been whispered to her. "To me," she whispered to herself ecstatically, "to po' lil' me. An' I know it ees tr-rue, yes. It got to be tr-rue. 'Cause madda Nature, she will help in de work, an' w'at else you want?" For the life-mate she would choose for herself would be an octoroon, as fair as a lily. With her complexion and his she knew that she would be able to give to her children the mask which her grandfather had yearned. She saw now why he had failed. No doubt it was never meant for men to know anything about it at all. It must be in the keepings of mothers alone. "Now we will see," she told herself exultantly. "Ef my daughter got to wear a head hand-gcher lak me. Fo' me it ees notting. I cannot help. But jes' de same a son of mine goin' be king of some Carnival yet. You watch out fo' me."

And so when Paupet, the whitest octoroon that she had ever seen, came to the Quarter, she showed her preference for him at once. When, after their marriage, in the course of time their first born was expected she was like an experimentalist in the mating of cross-breeds, painfully nervous and full of the greatest anxiety over the outcome of a situation that she had been planning so long. What preparations she made! She fitted up a room especially for the event. She was extravagance itself in the selection of the garments, buying enough material to clothe half a dozen infants. She literally covered the fly leaves of the Bible with male and female names in preparation for the Christening: and made so many trips to town for all sorts of purchases that Paupet became full of anxiety for the outcome of it all.

To him she talked very freely now of her readiness in marrying him—it was really for the good of the child that was about to come to them. Her trials would not be her infant's. She had seen to that. He would look like Paupet, and could therefore choose his own way in life unhampered by custom or law.

To the midwife too she communicated her hopes and expectations, dwelling at great length upon the future of the child the whiteness of whose face would be a charm against every prevailing ill. Such optimism augured ill to the midwife who rarely vouchsafed her a word. When at length the child was born, the midwife tarried a long time before placing it into Julie's arms. It was sympathy upon her part that caused the delay. But Julie could not understand it. In the midst of her great sufferings she marvelled at it, until at length she caught a glimpse of her child's face. Then she screamed. With horror she saw that it was identical with the one in the locket about her neck. It was the image of her chocolate-colored mother.

SOURCE

Thompson, Eloise Bibb. "Masks, A Story." *Opportunity* 5, no. 10 (October 1927): 300–302. Reprinted with the permission of the National Urban League.

Katherine Davis Chapman Tillman

1870–?

KATHERINE DAVIS CHAPMAN TILLMAN was an African American writer born in Mound City, Illinois. She started writing poetry and corresponding with newspapers at a young age, publishing her first poem in the *Christian Recorder* in 1888. Her poetry and essays frequently appeared in religious publications, such as the *A.M.E. Church Review*,[1] and, along with two historical plays, she authored two novellas, *Beryl Weston's Ambition: The Story of an Afro-American Girl's Life* (1893) and *Clancy Street* (serialized 1898–99). In 1902, she published her book of poetry, *Recitations*. Tillman's avowed mission was to uplift African American women and girls with her writing, encouraging them to believe in their own abilities and their equality with men.

Lines to Ida B. Wells (1894)

Charlotte Corday for the English,
　Joan of Arc for the French,
And Ida B. Wells for the Negro,
　His life from the lynchers to wrench.

Thank God, there are hearts in old England
　That feel for the Negro's distress,
And gladly give of their substance
　To obtain for his wrongs a redress.

Speed on the day when the lynchers
　No more shall reign in our land,
When even the poorest of Negroes
　Protected by Justice shall stand.

When no more shall cries of terror
  Break on the midnight air;
While poor and defenseless Negroes
  Surrender their lives in despair.

When the spirits of Phillips and Lincoln,
  Of Sumner and Garrison brave,
Shall hurl the murderous lynch-law
  Down to its dishonored grave.

When loyal hearts in the Southland,
  And those of the North that are true
Shall give to the struggling Negro
  That which is by nature his due.

And the cloud that threatens our land
  Shall pale beneath Liberty's Sun,
And in the prosperous future
  Shall vanish the wrongs to us done.

Go on, thou brave woman leader,
  Spread our wrongs from shore unto shore;
Until clothed with his rights is the Negro,
  And lynchings are heard of no more.

And centuries hence little children,
  Sprung up from the Hamitic race,
On History's glowing pages
  Thy loving deeds shall trace.

And the wise Afro-American mother,
  Who her children of heroines tells,
Shall speak in tones of gratitude,
  The name of Ida B. Wells!

Clotelle—A Tale of Florida (1902)

Clotelle! Orange-blossoms, "A lover and a grave."
"Sweets to the sweet," and laurels for the brave!
Can I tell the story as it was told to me
Down in Florida by the deep murmuring sea?

Gentle muse, I now invoke thee,
Lend thy power while I shall tell
Men the story of a slave-maid
Of the bright-eyed slave Clotelle!

Light and tripping were her footsteps,
Beauteous both her face and form,
Yet no power could protect her
From the trader's golden charm.

Lived Clotelle on a plantation
Near the Gulf Stream's turbid wave
Lived through childhood's years unheeding;
She was but a helpless slave.

Sixteen years had lightly o'er her,
Tenderly o'er the maid had sped,
When the time came to Clotelle
That love's dreams her fancies led.

Cupid threw at her an arrow
Aimed at fair Clotelle his dart,
And love entered the recesses
Of her innocent young heart.

Dark her lover was and stately
As a prince of olden days,
And among slaves both old and young
Naught was heard of Pierre but praise.

Fate smiled on the poor slave lovers,
Oft they met in woodland bowers,
Oft exchanged love-vows in rapture
In those happy stolen hours.

Planned the two a little cabin,
Orange blossoms overhead,
Mocking-birds to lend their music;
Ah, those days too quickly sped!

But one day to the maiden
Sorrow, agony and shame,

For with words of subtile meaning
To her side her master came.

Said the planter to the maiden,
"Thou art by far too fair to toil;
Hands like thine, so small and shapely,
Were not meant to till the soil."

"Come and be my loved companion,
Robed in silks and jewels rare;
'Tis no miser who entreats thee,
Come and all my riches share."

Shrank poor Clotelle from her master
With a countenance of shame,
While in low and tender accents
She sobbed forth her lover's name.

"I love Pierre, O worthy master,
And death with him beneath the sea
Would suit better far thy maiden
Than a life of shame with thee!"

Then the planter's brow grew clouded
And his voice both harsh and stern.
"If you thus my will defy, girl,
That I am your master you shall learn.

You love Pierre, you say—my servant;
You prefer my slave to me,
Your love will but prove his ruin;
Never thou his bride wilt be."

Sank Clotelle's young heart with boding,
All her joy was turned to pain,
All the fond hopes she had cherished,
Vanished, ne'er to come again.

From that hour Pierre was doomed
By the planter's wish to die;
For he swore to see him hanging
Lifeless 'neath the southern sky.

At last accused of awful crime
Too hideous to breathe aloud,
Poor Pierre was hanged one fatal day,
Surrounded by a pitying crowd.

Clotelle gazed on him in anguish.
"Farewell, Pierre, my love," she cried.
"Farewell, sweet," to her he whispered,
Ere the fatal noose was tied.

When 'twas o'er, Clotelle stood silent,
Till her eyes the planter's met,
Then she ran like one demented,
Shrieking, "Pierre, thine am I yet."

Rushing to the water's edge,
Plunged she in its maddening foam,
And returned the planter, baffled,
To his princely, slave-bought home.

Rest in peace, Clotelle, sweet maiden;
Near the Gulf Stream's turbid wave,
Thou who for the love of virtue,
All untimely filled thy grave!

Bashy (1902)

"A Negro girl killed in a house of shame."
In cities oft you may hear the same.
How the poor girls go down in the struggle of life,
And yield to dishonor, both maid and wife.

But Bashy, I'll swear, never had a chance;
A black face never does enhance
A woman's value in our land.
Black faces are, well—not just in demand.

Not only in proud Anglo-Saxon race,
But Negroes there are who hate a black face!
We have men who will pass a black girl by
Because she is black—that's the reason why.

You see, we look up to the Saxon race,
And prize above all a white man's face!
And our Bashy was black and ignorant, too,
And what was a poor black outcast to do?

She tried hard to work, but a green farm hand,
Is it strange she never could understand
How to please Miladi on the avenue,
Who could not teach her what to do.

Bashy loved, and she gave her all.
The man who caused her awful fall
Thought her too black to make a wife,
So she drifted on to a dreadful life.

Till one day, while filled with a maddening drink,
Bashy was thrust o'er eternity's brink
Without a chance for a whispered prayer
That God would have mercy on her despair.

Her murderer was hung, but every day
Some poor girl goes down in the self-same way,
Some Bashy of our struggling race
Is made an outcast by her face!

Some black mother crooning her baby to sleep
Prays now that the Father of all may keep
Her girl away in the city to toil,
Pure from the deeds and thoughts that soil.

When she hears the news of her girl's dark shame,
And the strain she has brought on her soul and her name,
The house will be dark and the mother's heart
Ache till the life-threads break apart.

Oh, women and men of the Negro Race,
Can we not rise above color of face?
Teach our girls that the worst disgrace
Is blackness of life, not blackness of face!
That women are needed pure-souled and high,

Who sooner than fall will prefer to die!
That a black girl needing a helping hand
Will be helped by the blackmen of the land.
Lift the women up and the race ascends;
Let the women go down, and our progress ends.

SOURCES

Tillman, Katherine Davis Chapman. "Bashy" and "Clotelle—A Tale of Florida."
In *Recitations*, 38–40, 10–13. Philadelphia: A. M. E. Book Concern, 1902. https://
babel.hathitrust.org/cgi/pt?id=emu.010002588420&view=2up&seq=16.
———. "Lines to Ida B. Wells." *Christian Recorder*, July 5, 1894, 1. Nineteenth Cen-
tury Collections Online.

NOTE

1. See, for example, "The Negro among Anglo-Saxon Poets" in volume 2.

Harriet E. Wilson

1825–1900

HARRIET E. WILSON was born in New Hampshire to a white mother and a Black father. Her mother, after being widowed, abandoned Wilson, resulting in the court's binding the young girl into indentured servitude to an abusive family until the age of eighteen. These experiences inspired Wilson's novel, *Our Nig; or, Sketches from the Life of a Free Black*, which was anonymously published in 1859 and quickly forgotten, until scholar Henry Louis Gates Jr. rediscovered it in 1981. Long thought to have been by a white author, it may have been the first novel published by an African American in the United States. In the preface, Wilson states that she wrote *Our Nig* to raise funds to reclaim her child, left in foster care. The child died, however, while Wilson was away trying to make a living. Wilson later gave lectures about her life, labor reform, and children's education, as well as performing as a Spiritualist medium and psychic healer.

From *Our Nig; or, Sketches from the Life of a Free Black* (1859)

CHAPTER II. My Father's Death.

> Misery! we have known each other,
> Like a sister and a brother,
> Living in the same lone home
> Many years—we must live some
> Hours or ages yet to come.[1]
> —SHELLEY.

Jim, proud of his treasure,—a white wife,—tried hard to fulfil his promises; and furnished her with a more comfortable dwelling, diet, and apparel. It was comparatively a comfortable winter she passed after her marriage. When Jim could work, all went on well. Industrious, and fond of Mag, he was determined she should not regret her union to him. Time levied an additional charge upon him, in the form of two pretty mulattos, whose infantile pranks amply repaid the additional toil. A few years, and a severe cough and pain in his side compelled him to be an idler for weeks together, and Mag had thus a reminder of by-gones. She cared for him only as a means to subserve her own comfort; yet she nursed him faithfully and true to marriage vows till death released her. He became the victim of consumption. He loved Mag to the last. So long as life continued, he stifled his sensibility to pain, and toiled for her sustenance long after he was able to do so.

A few expressive wishes for her welfare; a hope of better days for her; an anxiety lest they should not all go to the "good place;" brief advice about their children; a hope expressed that Mag would not be neglected as she used to be; the manifestation of Christian patience; these were *all* the legacy of miserable Mag. A feeling of cold desolation came over her, as she turned from the grave of one who had been truly faithful to her.

She was now expelled from companionship with white people; this last step—her union with a black—was the climax of repulsion.

Seth Shipley, a partner in Jim's business, wished her to remain in her present home; but she declined, and returned to her hovel again, with obstacles threefold more insurmountable than before. Seth accompanied her, giving her a weekly allowance which furnished most of the food necessary for the four inmates. After a time, work failed; their means were reduced.

How Mag toiled and suffered, yielding to fits of desperation, bursts of anger, and uttering curses too fearful to repeat. When both were supplied with work, they prospered; if idle, they were hungry together. In this way their interests became united; they planned for the future together. Mag had lived an outcast for years. She had ceased to feel the gushings of penitence; she had crushed the sharp agonies of an awakened conscience. She had no longings for a purer heart, a better life. Far easier to descend lower. She entered the darkness of perpetual infamy. She asked not the rite of civilization or Christianity. Her will made her the wife of Seth. Soon followed scenes familiar and trying.

"It's no use," said Seth one day; "we must give the children away, and try to get work in some other place."

"Who 'll take the black devils?" snarled Mag.

"They 're none of mine," said Seth; "what you growling about?"

"Nobody will want anything of mine, or yours either," she replied.

"We'll make 'em, p'r'aps," he said. "There's Frado 's six years old, and pretty, if she is yours, and white folks 'll say so. She 'd be a prize somewhere," he continued, tipping his chair back against the wall, and placing his feet upon the rounds, as if he had much more to say when in the right position.

Frado, as they called one of Mag's children, was a beautiful mulatto, with long, curly black hair, and handsome, roguish eyes, sparkling with an exuberance of spirit almost beyond restraint.

Hearing her name mentioned, she looked up from her play, to see what Seth had to say of her.

"Would n't the Bellmonts take her?" asked Seth.

"Bellmonts?" shouted Mag. "His wife is a right she-devil! and if—"

"Had n't they better be all together?" interrupted Seth, reminding her of a like epithet used in reference to her little ones.

Without seeming to notice him, she continued, "She can't keep a girl in the house over a week; and Mr. Bellmont wants to hire a boy to work for him, but he can't find one that will live in the house with her; she's so ugly, they can't."

"Well, we 've got to make a move soon," answered Seth; "if you go with me, we shall go right off. Had you rather spare the other one?" asked Seth, after a short pause.

"One 's as bad as t' other," replied Mag. "Frado is such a wild, frolicky thing, and means to do jest as she 's a mind to; she wo n't go if she don't want to. I do n't want to tell her she is to be given away."

"I will," said Seth. "Come here, Frado?"

The child seemed to have some dim foreshadowing of evil, and declined.

"Come here," he continued; "I want to tell you something."

She came reluctantly. He took her hand and said: "We 're going to move, by-'m-bye; will you go?"

"No!" screamed she; and giving a sudden jerk which destroyed Seth's equilibrium, left him sprawling on the floor, while she escaped through the open door.

"She's a hard one," said Seth, brushing his patched coat sleeve. "I'd risk her at Bellmont's."

They discussed the expediency of a speedy departure. Seth would first seek employment, and then return for Mag. They would take with them what they could carry, and leave the rest with Pete Greene, and come for them when they were wanted. They were long in arranging affairs satisfactorily, and were not a little startled at the close of their conference to find Frado missing. They thought approaching night would bring her. Twilight passed into darkness, and she did not come. They thought she had understood their plans, and had, perhaps, permanently withdrawn. They could not rest without making some effort to ascertain her retreat. Seth went in pursuit, and returned without her. They rallied others when they discovered that another little colored girl was missing, a favorite playmate of Frado's. All effort proved unavailing. Mag felt sure her fears were realized, and that she might never see her again. Before her anxieties became realities, both were safely returned, and from them and their attendant they learned that they went to walk, and not minding the direction soon found themselves lost. They had climbed fences and walls, passed through thickets and marshes, and when night approached selected a thick cluster of shrubbery as a covert for the night. They were discovered by the person who now restored them, chatting of their prospects, Frado attempting to banish the childish fears of her companion. As they were some miles from home, they were kindly cared for until morning. Mag was relieved to know her child was not driven to desperation by their intentions to relieve themselves of her, and she was inclined to think severe restraint would be healthful.

The removal was all arranged; the few days necessary for such migrations passed quickly, and one bright summer morning they bade farewell to their Singleton hovel, and with budgets and bundles commenced their weary march. As they neared the village, they heard the merry shouts of children gathered around the schoolroom, awaiting the coming of their teacher.

"Halloo!" screamed one, "Black, white and yeller!" "Black, white and yeller," echoed a dozen voices.

It did not grate so harshly on poor Mag as once it would. She did not even turn her head to look at them. She had passed into an insensibility no childish taunt could penetrate, else she would have reproached herself as she passed familiar scenes, for extending the separation once so easily annihilated by steadfast integrity. Two miles beyond lived the Bellmonts, in a large, old fashioned, two-story white house, environed by fruitful acres, and embellished by shrubbery and shade trees. Years ago a youthful couple consecrated it as home; and after many little feet had worn paths to favorite fruit trees, and over its green hills, and mingled at last with brother man in the race which belongs neither to the swift or strong, the sire became grey-haired and decrepit, and went to his last repose. His aged consort soon followed him. The old homestead thus passed into the hands of a son, to whose wife Mag had applied the epithet "she-devil," as may be remembered. John, the son, had not in his family arrangements departed from the example of the father. The pastimes of his boyhood were ever freshly revived by witnessing the games of his own sons as they rallied about the same goal his youthful feet had often won; as well as by the amusements of his daughters in their imitations of maternal duties.

At the time we introduce them, however, John is wearing the badge of age. Most of his children were from home; some seeking employment; some were already settled in homes of their own. A maiden sister shared with him the estate on which he resided, and occupied a portion of the house.

Within sight of the house, Seth seated himself with his bundles and the child he had been leading, while Mag walked onward to the house leading Frado. A knock at the door brought Mrs. Bellmont, and Mag asked if she would be willing to let that child stop there while she went to the Reed's house to wash, and when she came back she would call and get her. It seemed a novel request, but she consented. Why the impetuous child entered the house, we cannot tell; the door closed, and Mag hastily departed. Frado waited for the close of day, which was to bring back her mother. Alas! it never came. It was the last time she ever saw or heard of her mother.

SOURCE

Wilson, Harriet E. *Our Nig; or, Sketches from the Life of a Free Black*, 14–23. Boston: G. C. Rand & Avery, 1859.

NOTE

1. From Percy Bysshe Shelley's "Misery—A Fragment," probably written 1819, first published 1832.

Constance Fenimore Woolson

1840–1894

CONSTANCE FENIMORE WOOLSON was a white author from Cleveland, Ohio. She traveled a great deal in the eastern and southern United States when she was young, and published travel sketches and local color stories in the leading magazines of the day, such as *Harper's*, *Putnam's*, *Lippincott's*, and *Atlantic Monthly*. In 1879 she moved to Europe, spending the majority of her time in England and Italy. All told, she wrote four novels, a novella, and four collections of short stories, in addition to her early poetry, travel pieces, and literary criticism. Although she is best known today for her close friendship with Henry James and her possible death by suicide in Venice, Woolson was seen by her contemporaries as one of the greatest female authors of the English language—a popular and a critical success. Recently, an effort has been made to return focus to her work, with its detailed representation of place and its psychological nuance.

Miss Grief. (1880)

"A conceited fool" is a not uncommon expression. Now, I know that I am not a fool, but I also know that I am conceited. But, candidly, can it be helped if one happens to be young, well and strong, passably good-looking, with some money that one has inherited and more that one has earned—in all, enough to make life comfortable—and if upon this foundation rests also the pleasant superstructure of a literary success? The success is deserved, I think: certainly it was not lightly gained. Yet even with this I fully appreciate its rarity. Thus, I find myself very well entertained in life: I have all I wish in the way of society, and a deep, though of course carefully concealed, satisfaction in my own little fame; which fame

I foster by a gentle system of non-interference. I know that I am spoken of as "that quiet young fellow who writes those delightful little studies of society, you know"; and I live up to that definition.

A year ago I was in Rome, and enjoying life particularly. I had a large number of my acquaintances there, both American and English, and no day passed without its invitation. Of course I understood it: it is seldom that you find a literary man who is good-tempered, well-dressed, sufficiently provided with money, and amiably obedient to all the rules and requirements of "society." "When found, make a note of it"; and the note was generally an invitation.

One evening, upon returning to my lodgings, my man Simpson informed me that a person had called in the afternoon, and upon learning that I was absent had left not a card, but her name—"Miss Grief." The title lingered—Miss Grief! "Grief has not so far visited me here," I said to myself, dismissing Simpson and seeking my little balcony for a final smoke, "and she shall not now. I shall take care to be 'not at home' to her if she continues to call." And then I fell to thinking of Isabel Abercrombie, in whose society I had spent that and many evenings: they were golden thoughts.

The next day there was an excursion; it was late when I reached my rooms, and again Simpson informed me that Miss Grief had called.

"Is she coming continuously?" I said, half to myself.

"Yes, sir: she mentioned that she should call again."

"How does she look?"

"Well, sir, a lady, but not so prosperous as she was, I should say," answered Simpson, discreetly.

"Young?"

"No, sir."

"Alone?"

"A maid with her, sir."

But once outside in my little high-up balcony with my cigar, I again forgot Miss Grief and whatever she might represent. Who would not forget in that moonlight, with Isabel Abercrombie's face to remember?

The stranger came a third time, and I was absent; then she let two days pass, and began again. It grew to be a regular dialogue between Simpson and myself when I came in at night: "Grief to-day?"

"Yes, sir."

"What time?"

"Four, sir."

"Happy the man," I thought, "who can keep her confined to a particular hour!"

But I should not have treated my visitor so cavalierly if I had not felt sure that she was eccentric and unconventional—qualities extremely tiresome in a woman no longer young or attractive. If she were not eccentric she would not have persisted in coming to my door day after day in this silent way, without stating her errand, leaving a note, or presenting her credentials in any shape. I made up my mind that she had something to sell—a bit of carving or some intaglio supposed to be antique. It was known that I had a fancy for oddities. I said to myself, "She has read or heard of my 'Old Gold' story, or else 'The Buried God,' and she thinks me an idealizing ignoramus upon whom she can impose. Her sepulchral name is at least not Italian; probably she is a sharp country-woman of mine, turning, by means of the present æsthetic craze, an honest penny when she can."

She had called seven times during a period of two weeks without seeing me, when one day I happened to be at home in the afternoon, owing to a pouring rain and a fit of doubt concerning Miss Abercrombie. For I had constructed a careful theory of that young lady's characteristics in my own mind, and she had lived up to it delightfully until the previous evening, when with one word she had blown it to atoms and taken flight, leaving me standing, as it were, on a desolate shore, with nothing but a handful of mistaken inductions wherewith to console myself. I do not know a more exasperating frame of mind, at least for a constructor of theories. I could not write, and so I took up a French novel (I model myself a little on Balzac). I had been turning over its pages but a few moments when Simpson knocked, and, entering softly, said, with just a shadow of a smile on his well-trained face, "Miss Grief." I briefly consigned Miss Grief to all the Furies, and then, as he still lingered—perhaps not knowing where they resided—I asked where the visitor was.

"Outside, sir—in the hall. I told her I would see if you were at home."

"She must be unpleasantly wet if she had no carriage."

"No carriage, sir: they always come on foot. I think she *is* a little damp, sir."

"Well, let her in; but I don't want the maid. I may as well see her now, I suppose, and end the affair."

"Yes, sir."

I did not put down my book. My visitor should have a hearing, but not much more: she had sacrificed her womanly claims by her persistent attacks upon my door. Presently Simpson ushered her in. "Miss Grief," he said, and then went out, closing the curtain behind him.

A woman—yes, a lady—but shabby, unattractive, and more than middle-aged.

I rose, bowed slightly, and then dropped into my chair again, still keeping the book in my hand. "Miss Grief?" I said interrogatively as I indicated a seat with my eyebrows.

"Not Grief," she answered—"Crief: my name is Crief."

She sat down, and I saw that she held a small flat box.

"Not carving, then," I thought—"probably old lace, something that belonged to Tullia or Lucrezia Borgia." But as she did not speak I found myself obliged to begin: "You have been here, I think, once or twice before?"

"Seven times; this is the eighth."

A silence.

"I am often out; indeed, I may say that I am never in," I remarked carelessly.

"Yes; you have many friends."

"—Who will perhaps buy old lace," I mentally added. But this time I too remained silent; why should I trouble myself to draw her out? She had sought me; let her advance her idea, whatever it was, now that entrance was gained.

But Miss Grief (I preferred to call her so) did not look as though she could advance anything; her black gown, damp with rain, seemed to retreat fearfully to her thin self, while her thin self retreated as far as possible from me, from the chair, from everything. Her eyes were cast down; an old-fashioned lace veil with a heavy border shaded her face. She looked at the floor, and I looked at her.

I grew a little impatient, but I made up my mind that I would continue silent and see how long a time she would consider necessary to give due effect to her little pantomime. Comedy? Or was it tragedy? I suppose full five minutes passed thus in our double silence; and that is a long time when two persons are sitting opposite each other alone in a small still room.

At last my visitor, without raising her eyes, said slowly, "You are very happy, are you not, with youth, health, friends, riches, fame?"

It was a singular beginning. Her voice was clear, low, and very sweet as she thus enumerated my advantages one by one in a list. I was attracted by it, but repelled by her words, which seemed to me flattery both dull and bold.

"Thanks," I said, "for your kindness, but I fear it is undeserved. I seldom discuss myself even when with my friends."

"I am your friend," replied Miss Grief. Then, after a moment, she added slowly, "I have read every word you have written."

I curled the edges of my book indifferently; I am not a fop, I hope, but— others have said the same.

"What is more, I know much of it by heart," continued my visitor. "Wait: I will show you"; and then, without pause, she began to repeat something of mine word for word, just as I had written it. On she went, and I— listened. I intended interrupting her after a moment, but I did not, be- cause she was reciting so well, and also because I felt a desire gaining upon me to see what she would make of a certain conversation which I knew was coming—a conversation between two of my characters which was, to say the least, sphinx-like, and somewhat incandescent as well. What won me a little, too, was the fact that the scene she was reciting (it was hardly more than that, though called a story) was secretly my favorite among all the sketches from my pen which a gracious public has received with favor. I never said so, but it was; and I had always felt a wondering annoyance that the aforesaid public, while kindly praising beyond their worth other attempts of mine, had never noticed the higher purpose of this little shaft, aimed not at the balconies and lighted windows of society, but straight up toward the distant stars. So she went on, and presently reached the conversation: my two people began to talk. She had raised her eyes now, and was looking at me soberly as she gave the words of the woman, quiet, gentle, cold, and the replies of the man, bitter, hot, and scathing. Her very voice changed, and took, though always sweetly, the different tones required, while no point of meaning, however small, no breath of delicate emphasis which I had meant, but which the dull types could not give, escaped an appreciative and full, almost overfull, recog- nition which startled me. For she had understood me—understood me almost better than I had understood myself. It seemed to me that while I had labored to interpret, partially, a psychological riddle, she, coming after, had comprehended its bearings better than I had, though confining herself strictly to my own words and emphasis. The scene ended (and it ended rather suddenly), she dropped her eyes, and moved her hand nervously to and fro over the box she held; her gloves were old and shabby, her hands small.

I was secretly much surprised by what I had heard, but my ill-humor was deep-seated that day, and I still felt sure, besides, that the box contained something which I was expected to buy.

"You recite remarkably well," I said carelessly, "and I am much flattered also by your appreciation of my attempt. But it is not, I presume, to that alone that I owe the pleasure of this visit?"

"Yes," she answered, still looking down, "it is, for if you had not written that scene I should not have sought you. Your other sketches are interiors—exquisitely painted and delicately finished, but of small scope. *This* is a sketch in a few bold, masterly lines—work of entirely different spirit and purpose."

I was nettled by her insight. "You have bestowed so much of your kind attention upon me that I feel your debtor," I said, conventionally. "It may be that there is something I can do for you—connected, possibly, with that little box?"

It was impertinent, but it was true; for she answered, "Yes."

I smiled, but her eyes were cast down and she did not see the smile.

"What I have to show you is a manuscript," she said after a pause which I did not break; "it is a drama. I thought that perhaps you would read it."

"An authoress! This is worse than old lace," I said to myself in dismay.—Then, aloud, "My opinion would be worth nothing, Miss Crief."

"Not in a business way, I know. But it might be—an assistance personally." Her voice had sunk to a whisper; outside, the rain was pouring steadily down. She was a very depressing object to me as she sat there with her box.

"I hardly think I have the time at present—" I began.

She had raised her eyes and was looking at me; then, when I paused, she rose and came suddenly toward my chair. "Yes, you will read it," she said with her hand on my arm—"you will read it. Look at this room; look at yourself; look at all you have. Then look at me, and have pity."

I had risen, for she held my arm, and her damp skirt was brushing my knees.

Her large dark eyes looked intently into mine as she went on; "I have no shame in asking. Why should I have? It is my last endeavor; but a calm and well-considered one. If you refuse I shall go away, knowing that Fate has willed it so. And I shall be content."

"She is mad," I thought. But she did not look so, and she had spoken quietly, even gently.—"Sit down," I said, moving away from her. I felt as if I had been magnetized; but it was only the nearness of her eyes to mine, and their intensity. I drew forward a chair, but she remained standing.

"I cannot," she said in the same sweet, gentle tone, "unless you promise."

"Very well, I promise; only sit down."

As I took her arm to lead her to the chair I perceived that she was trembling, but her face continued unmoved.

"You do not, of course, wish me to look at your manuscript now?" I said, temporizing; "it would be much better to leave it. Give me your address, and I will return it to you with my written opinion; though, I repeat, the latter will be of no use to you. It is the opinion of an editor or publisher that you want."

"It shall be as you please. And I will go in a moment," said Miss Grief, pressing her palms together, as if trying to control the tremor that had seized her slight frame.

She looked so pallid that I thought of offering her a glass of wine; then I remembered that if I did it might be a bait to bring her there again, and this I was desirous to prevent. She rose while the thought was passing through my mind. Her pasteboard box lay on the chair she had first occupied; she took it, wrote an address on the cover, laid it down, and then, bowing with a little air of formality, drew her black shawl round her shoulders and turned toward the door.

I followed, after touching the bell. "You will hear from me by letter," I said.

Simpson opened the door, and I caught a glimpse of the maid, who was waiting in the anteroom. She was an old woman, shorter than her mistress, equally thin, and dressed like her in rusty black. As the door opened she turned toward it a pair of small, dim blue eyes with a look of furtive suspense. Simpson dropped the curtain, shutting me into the inner room; he had no intention of allowing me to accompany my visitor further. But

I had the curiosity to go to a bay-window in an angle from whence I could command the street-door, and presently I saw them issue forth in the rain and walk away side by side, the mistress, being the taller, holding the umbrella: probably there was not much difference in rank between persons so poor and forlorn as these.

It grew dark. I was invited out for the evening, and I knew that if I should go I should meet Miss Abercrombie. I said to myself that I would not go. I got out my paper for writing, I made my preparations for a quiet evening at home with myself; but it was of no use. It all ended slavishly in my going. At the last allowable moment I presented myself, and—as a punishment for my vacillation, I suppose—I never passed a more disagreeable evening. I drove homeward in a murky temper; it was foggy without, and very foggy within. What Isabel really was, now that she had broken through my elaborately-built theories, I was not able to decide. There was, to tell the truth, a certain young Englishman—But that is apart from this story.

I reached home, went up to my rooms, and had a supper. It was to console myself; I am obliged to console myself scientifically once in a while. I was walking up and down afterward, smoking and feeling somewhat better, when my eye fell upon the pasteboard box. I took it up; on the cover was written an address which showed that my visitor must have walked a long distance in order to see me: "A. Crief."—"A Grief," I thought; "and so she is. I positively believe she has brought all this trouble upon me: she has the evil eye." I took out the manuscript and looked at it. It was in the form of a little volume, and clearly written; on the cover was the word "Armor" in German text, and, underneath, a pen-and-ink sketch of a helmet, breastplate, and shield.

"Grief certainly needs armor," I said to myself, sitting down by the table and turning over the pages. "I may as well look over the thing now; I could not be in a worse mood." And then I began to read.

Early the next morning Simpson took a note from me to the given address, returning with the following reply: "No; I prefer to come to you; at four; A. CRIEF." These words, with their three semicolons, were written in pencil upon a piece of coarse printing-paper, but the handwriting was as clear and delicate as that of the manuscript in ink.

"What sort of a place was it, Simpson?"

"Very poor, sir, but I did not go all the way up. The elder person came down, sir, took the note, and requested me to wait where I was."

"You had no chance, then, to make inquiries?" I said, knowing full well that he had emptied the entire neighborhood of any information it might possess concerning these two lodgers.

"Well, sir, you know how these foreigners will talk, whether one wants to hear or not. But it seems that these two persons have been there but a few weeks; they live alone, and are uncommonly silent and reserved. The people round there call them something that signifies 'the Madames American, thin and dumb.'"

At four the "Madames American" arrived; it was raining again, and they came on foot under their old umbrella. The maid waited in the anteroom, and Miss Grief was ushered into my bachelor's parlor. I had thought that I should meet her with great deference; but she looked so forlorn that my deference changed to pity. It was the woman that impressed me then, more than the writer—the fragile, nerveless body more than the inspired mind. For it was inspired: I had sat up half the night over her drama, and had felt thrilled through and through more than once by its earnestness, passion, and power.

No one could have been more surprised than I was to find myself thus enthusiastic. I thought I had outgrown that sort of thing. And one would have supposed, too (I myself should have supposed so the day before), that the faults of the drama, which were many and prominent, would have chilled any liking I might have felt, I being a writer myself, and therefore critical; for writers are as apt to make much of the "how," rather than the "what," as painters, who, it is well known, prefer an exquisitely rendered representation of a commonplace theme to an imperfectly executed picture of even the most striking subject. But in this case, on the contrary, the scattered rays of splendor in Miss Grief's drama had made me forget the dark spots, which were numerous and disfiguring; or, rather, the splendor had made me anxious to have the spots removed. And this also was a philanthropic state very unusual with me. Regarding unsuccessful writers, my motto had been "Væ victis!"

My visitor took a seat and folded her hands; I could see, in spite of her quiet manner, that she was in breathless suspense. It seemed so pitiful that she should be trembling there before me—a woman so much older than I was, a woman who possessed the divine spark of genius, which I was by no means sure (in spite of my success) had been granted to me— that I felt as if I ought to go down on my knees before her, and entreat her to take her proper place of supremacy at once. But there! one does not go down on one's knees, combustively, as it were, before a woman over fifty, plain in feature, thin, dejected, and ill-dressed. I contented myself with taking her hands (in their miserable old gloves) in mine, while I said cordially, "Miss Crief, your drama seems to me full of original power. It has roused my enthusiasm: I sat up half the night reading it."

The hands I held shook, but something (perhaps a shame for having evaded the knees business) made me tighten my hold and bestow upon her also a reassuring smile. She looked at me for a moment, and then, suddenly and noiselessly, tears rose and rolled down her cheeks. I dropped her hands and retreated. I had not thought her tearful: on the contrary, her voice and face had seemed rigidly controlled. But now here she was bending herself over the side of the chair with her head resting on her arms, not sobbing aloud, but her whole frame shaken by the strength of her emotion. I rushed for a glass of wine; I pressed her to take it. I did not quite know what to do, but, putting myself in her place, I decided to praise the drama; and praise it I did. I do not know when I have used so many adjectives. She raised her head and began to wipe her eyes.

"Do take the wine," I said, interrupting myself in my cataract of language.

"I dare not," she answered; then added humbly, "that is, unless you have a biscuit here or a bit of bread."

I found some biscuit; she ate two, and then slowly drank the wine, while I resumed my verbal Niagara. Under its influence—and that of the wine too, perhaps—she began to show new life. It was not that she looked radiant—she could not—but simply that she looked warm. I now perceived what had been the principal discomfort of her appearance heretofore: it was that she had looked all the time as if suffering from cold.

At last I could think of nothing more to say, and stopped. I really admired the drama, but I thought I had exerted myself sufficiently as an anti-hysteric, and that adjectives enough, for the present at least, had been administered. She had put down her empty wine-glass, and was resting her hands on the broad cushioned arms of her chair with, for a thin person, a sort of expanded content.

"You must pardon my tears," she said, smiling; "it was the revulsion of feeling. My life was at a low ebb: if your sentence had been against me it would have been my end."

"Your end?"

"Yes, the end of my life; I should have destroyed myself."

"Then you would have been a weak as well as wicked woman," I said in a tone of disgust. I do hate sensationalism.

"Oh no, you know nothing about it. I should have destroyed only this poor worn tenement of clay. But I can well understand how you would look upon it. Regarding the desirableness of life the prince and the beggar may have different opinions.—We will say no more of it, but talk of the drama instead." As she spoke the word "drama" a triumphant brightness came into her eyes.

I took the manuscript from a drawer and sat down beside her. "I suppose you know that there are faults," I said, expecting ready acquiescence.

"I was not aware that there were any," was her gentle reply.

Here was a beginning! After all my interest in her—and, I may say under the circumstances, my kindness—she received me in this way! However, my belief in her genius was too sincere to be altered by her whimsies; so I persevered. "Let us go over it together," I said. "Shall I read it to you, or will you read it to me?"

"I will not read it, but recite it."

"That will never do; you will recite it so well that we shall see only the good points, and what we have to concern ourselves with now is the bad ones."

"I will recite it," she repeated.

"Now, Miss Crief," I said bluntly, "for what purpose did you come to me? Certainly not merely to recite: I am no stage-manager. In plain English, was it not your idea that I might help you in obtaining a publisher?"

"Yes, yes," she answered, looking at me apprehensively, all her old manner returning.

I followed up my advantage, opened the little paper volume and began. I first took the drama line by line, and spoke of the faults of expression and structure; then I turned back and touched upon two or three glaring impossibilities in the plot. "Your absorbed interest in the motive of the whole no doubt made you forget these blemishes," I said apologetically.

But, to my surprise, I found that she did not see the blemishes—that she appreciated nothing I had said, comprehended nothing. Such unaccountable obtuseness puzzled me. I began again, going over the whole with even greater minuteness and care. I worked hard: the perspiration stood in beads upon my forehead as I struggled with her—what shall I call it—obstinacy? But it was not exactly obstinacy. She simply could not see the faults of her own work, any more than a blind man can see the smoke that dims a patch of blue sky. When I had finished my task the second time she still remained as gently impassive as before. I leaned back in my chair exhausted, and looked at her.

Even then she did not seem to comprehend (whether she agreed with it or not) what I must be thinking. "It is such a heaven to me that you like it!" she murmured dreamily, breaking the silence. Then, with more animation, "And now you will let me recite it?"

I was too weary to oppose her; she threw aside her shawl and bonnet, and, standing in the centre of the room, began.

And she carried me along with her: all the strong passages were doubly strong when spoken, and the faults, which seemed nothing to her, were made by her earnestness to seem nothing to me, at least for that moment. When it was ended she stood looking at me with a triumphant smile.

"Yes," I said, "I like it, and you see that I do. But I like it because my taste is peculiar. To me originality and force are everything—perhaps because I have them not to any marked degree myself—but the world at large will not overlook as I do your absolutely barbarous shortcomings on account of them. Will you trust me to go over the drama and correct it at my pleasure?" This was a vast deal for me to offer; I was surprised at myself.

"No," she answered softly, still smiling. "There shall not be so much as a comma altered." Then she sat down and fell into a reverie as though she were alone.

"Have you written anything else?" I said after a while, when I had become tired of the silence.

"Yes."

"Can I see it? Or is it *them*?"

"It is *them*. Yes, you can see all."

"I will call upon you for the purpose."

"No, you must not," she said, coming back to the present nervously. "I prefer to come to you."

At this moment Simpson entered to light the room, and busied himself rather longer than was necessary over the task. When he finally went out I saw that my visitor's manner had sunk into its former depression: the presence of the servant seemed to have chilled her.

"When did you say I might come?" I repeated, ignoring her refusal.

"I did not say it. It would be impossible."

"Well, then, when will you come here?" There was, I fear, a trace of fatigue in my tone.

"At your good pleasure, sir," she answered humbly.

My chivalry was touched by this: after all, she was a woman. "Come to-morrow," I said. "By the way, come and dine with me then; why not?" I was curious to see what she would reply.

"Why not, indeed? Yes, I will come. I am forty-three: I might have been your mother."

This was not quite true, as I am over thirty: but I look young, while she—Well, I had thought her over fifty. "I can hardly call you 'mother,' but we might compromise upon 'aunt,'" I said, laughing. "Aunt what?"

"My name is Aaronna," she gravely answered. "My father was much disappointed that I was not a boy, and gave me as nearly as possible the name he had prepared—Aaron."

"Then come and dine with me to-morrow, and bring with you the other manuscripts, Aaronna," I said, amused at the quaint sound of the name. On the whole, I did not like "aunt."

"I will come," she answered.

It was twilight and still raining, but she refused all offers of escort or carriage, departing with her maid, as she had come, under the brown umbrella. The next day we had the dinner. Simpson was astonished—and more than astonished, grieved—when I told him that he was to dine with the maid; but he could not complain in words, since my own guest, the mistress, was hardly more attractive. When our preparations were complete I could not help laughing: the two prim little tables, one in the parlor and one in the anteroom, and Simpson disapprovingly going back and forth between them, were irresistible.

I greeted my guest hilariously when she arrived, and, fortunately, her manner was not quite so depressed as usual: I could never have accorded myself with a tearful mood. I had thought that perhaps she would make, for the occasion, some change in her attire; I have never known a woman who had not some scrap of finery, however small, in reserve for that unexpected occasion of which she is ever dreaming. But no: Miss Grief wore the same black gown, unadorned and unaltered. I was glad that there was no rain that day, so that the skirt did not at least look so damp and rheumatic.

She ate quietly, almost furtively, yet with a good appetite, and she did not refuse the wine. Then, when the meal was over and Simpson had removed the dishes, I asked for the new manuscripts. She gave me an old green copybook filled with short poems, and a prose sketch by itself; I lit a cigar and sat down at my desk to look them over.

"Perhaps you will try a cigarette?" I suggested, more for amusement than anything else, for there was not a shade of Bohemianism about her; her whole appearance was puritanical.

"I have not yet succeeded in learning to smoke."

"You have tried?" I said, turning round.

"Yes: Serena and I tried, but we did not succeed."

"Serena is your maid?"

"She lives with me."

I was seized with inward laughter, and began hastily to look over her manuscripts with my back toward her, so that she might not see it. A vision had risen before me of those two forlorn women, alone in their room with locked doors, patiently trying to acquire the smoker's art.

But my attention was soon absorbed by the papers before me. Such a fantastic collection of words, lines, and epithets I had never before seen, or even in dreams imagined. In truth, they were like the work of dreams: they were *Kubla Khan*, only more so. Here and there was radiance like the flash of a diamond, but each poem, almost each verse and line, was marred by some fault or lack which seemed wilful perversity, like the work of an evil sprite. It was like a case of jeweller's wares set before you, with each ring unfinished, each bracelet too large or too small for its purpose, each breastpin without its fastening, each necklace purposely broken. I turned the pages, marvelling. When about half an hour had passed, and I was leaning back for a moment to light another cigar, I glanced toward my visitor. She was behind me, in an easy-chair before my small fire, and she was—fast asleep! In the relaxation of her unconsciousness I was struck anew by the poverty her appearance expressed; her feet were visible, and I saw the miserable worn old shoes which hitherto she had kept concealed.

After looking at her for a moment I returned to my task and took up the prose story; in prose she must be more reasonable. She was less fantastic perhaps, but hardly more reasonable. The story was that of a profligate and commonplace man forced by two of his friends, in order not to break the heart of a dying girl who loves him, to live up to a high imaginary ideal of himself which her pure but mistaken mind has formed. He has a handsome face and sweet voice, and repeats what they tell him. Her long, slow decline and happy death, and his own inward ennui and profound weariness of the rôle he has to play, made the vivid points of the story. So far, well enough, but here was the trouble: through the whole narrative moved another character, a physician of tender heart and exquisite mercy, who practised murder as a fine art, and was regarded (by the author) as a second Messiah! This was monstrous. I read it through twice, and threw it down; then, fatigued, I turned round and leaned back, waiting for her to wake. I could see her profile against the dark hue of the easy-chair.

Presently she seemed to feel my gaze, for she stirred, then opened her eyes. "I have been asleep," she said, rising hurriedly.

"No harm in that, Aaronna."

But she was deeply embarrassed and troubled, much more so than the occasion required; so much so, indeed, that I turned the conversation back upon the manuscripts as a diversion. "I cannot stand that doctor of yours," I said, indicating the prose story; "no one would. You must cut him out."

Her self-possession returned as if by magic. "Certainly not," she answered haughtily.

"Oh, if you do not care—I had labored under the impression that you were anxious these things should find a purchaser."

"I am, I am," she said, her manner changing to deep humility with wonderful rapidity. With such alternations of feeling as this sweeping over her like great waves, no wonder she was old before her time.

"Then you must take out that doctor."

"I am willing, but do not know how," she answered, pressing her hands together helplessly. "In my mind he belongs to the story so closely that he cannot be separated from it."

Here Simpson entered, bringing a note for me: it was a line from Mrs. Abercrombie inviting me for that evening—an unexpected gathering, and therefore likely to be all the more agreeable. My heart bounded in spite of me; I forgot Miss Grief and her manuscripts for the moment as completely as though they had never existed. But, bodily, being still in the same room with her, her speech brought me back to the present.

"You have had good news?" she said.

"Oh no, nothing especial—merely an invitation."

"But good news also," she repeated. "And now, as for me, I must go."

Not supposing that she would stay much later in any case, I had that morning ordered a carriage to come for her at about that hour. I told her this. She made no reply beyond putting on her bonnet and shawl.

"You will hear from me soon," I said; "I shall do all I can for you."

She had reached the door, but before opening it she stopped, turned and extended her hand. "You are good," she said: "I give you thanks. Do not think me ungrateful or envious. It is only that you are young, and I am so—so old." Then she opened the door and passed through the anteroom without pause, her maid accompanying her and Simpson with gladness lighting the way. They were gone. I dressed hastily and went out—to continue my studies in psychology.

Time passed; I was busy, amused and perhaps a little excited (sometimes psychology is exciting). But, though much occupied with my own affairs, I did not altogether neglect my self-imposed task regarding Miss Grief. I began by sending her prose story to a friend, the editor of a monthly magazine, with a letter making a strong plea for its admittance. It should have a chance first on its own merits. Then I forwarded the drama to a publisher, also an acquaintance, a man with a taste for phantasms and a soul above mere common popularity, as his own coffers knew to their cost. This done, I waited with conscience clear.

Four weeks passed. During this waiting period I heard nothing from Miss Grief. At last one morning came a letter from my editor. "The story has force, but I cannot stand that doctor," he wrote. "Let her cut him out, and I might print it." Just what I myself had said. The package lay there on my table, travel-worn and grimed; a returned manuscript is, I think, the most melancholy object on earth. I decided to wait, before writing to Aaronna, until the second letter was received. A week later it came. "Armor" was declined. The publisher had been "impressed" by the power displayed in certain passages, but the "impossibilities of the plot" rendered it "unavailable for publication"—in fact, would "bury it in ridicule" if brought before the public, a public "lamentably" fond of amusement, "seeking it, undaunted, even in the cannon's mouth." I doubt if he knew himself what he meant. But one thing, at any rate, was clear: "Armor" was declined.

Now, I am, as I have remarked before, a little obstinate. I was determined that Miss Grief's work should be received. I would alter and improve it myself, without letting her know: the end justified the means. Surely the sieve of my own good taste, whose mesh had been pronounced so fine and delicate, would serve for two. I began; and utterly failed.

I set to work first upon "Armor." I amended, altered, left out, put in, pieced, condensed, lengthened; I did my best, and all to no avail. I could not succeed in completing anything that satisfied me, or that approached, in truth, Miss Grief's own work just as it stood. I suppose I went over that manuscript twenty times: I covered sheets of paper with my copies. But the obstinate drama refused to be corrected; as it was it must stand or fall.

Wearied and annoyed, I threw it aside and took up the prose story: that would be easier. But, to my surprise, I found that that apparently gentle "doctor" would not out: he was so closely interwoven with every part of the tale that to take him out was like taking out one especial figure in a carpet: that is, impossible, unless you unravel the whole. At last I did unravel the whole, and then the story was no longer good, or Aaronna's: it was weak, and mine. All this took time, for of course I had much to do in connection with my own life and tasks. But, though slowly and at my leisure, I really did try my best as regarded Miss Grief, and without success. I was forced at last to make up my mind that either my own powers were not equal to the task, or else that her perversities were as essential a part of her work as her inspirations, and not to be separated from it. Once during this period I showed two of the short poems to Isabel, withholding of course the writer's name. "They were written by a woman," I explained.

"Her mind must have been disordered, poor thing!" Isabel said in her gentle way when she returned them—"at least, judging by these. They are hopelessly mixed and vague."

Now, they were not vague so much as vast. But I knew that I could not make Isabel comprehend it, and (so complex a creature is man) I do not know that I wanted her to comprehend it. These were the only ones in the whole collection that I would have shown her, and I was rather glad that she did not like even these. Not that poor Aaronna's poems were evil: they were simply unrestrained, large, vast, like the skies or the wind. Isabel was bounded on all sides, like a violet in a garden-bed. And I liked her so.

One afternoon, about the time when I was beginning to see that I could not "improve" Miss Grief, I came upon the maid. I was driving, and she had stopped on the crossing to let the carriage pass. I recognized her at a glance (by her general forlornness), and called to the driver to stop: "How is Miss Grief?" I said. "I have been intending to write to her for some time."

"And your note, when it comes," answered the old woman on the crosswalk fiercely, "she shall not see."

"What?"

"I say she shall not see it. Your patronizing face shows that you have no good news, and you shall not rack and stab her any more on *this* earth, please God, while I have authority."

"Who has racked or stabbed her, Serena?"

"Serena, indeed! Rubbish! I'm no Serena: I'm her aunt. And as to who has racked and stabbed her, I say you, you—*you* literary men!" She had put her old head inside my carriage, and flung out these words at me in a shrill, menacing tone. "But she shall die in peace in spite of you," she continued. "Vampires! you take her ideas and fatten on them, and leave her to starve. You know you do—*you* who have had her poor manuscripts these months and months!"

"Is she ill?" I asked in real concern, gathering that much at least from the incoherent tirade.

"She is dying," answered the desolate old creature, her voice softening and her dim eyes filling with tears.

"Oh, I trust not. Perhaps something can be done. Can I help you in any way?"

"In all ways if you would," she said, breaking down and beginning to sob weakly, with her head resting on the sill of the carriage-window. "Oh, what have we not been through together, we two! Piece by piece I have sold all."

I am good-hearted enough, but I do not like to have old women weeping across my carriage-door. I suggested, therefore, that she should come inside and let me take her home. Her shabby old skirt was soon beside me, and, following her directions, the driver turned toward one of the most wretched quarters of the city, the abode of poverty, crowded and unclean. Here, in a large bare chamber up many flights of stairs, I found Miss Grief.

As I entered I was startled: I thought she was dead. There seemed no life present until she opened her eyes, and even then they rested upon us vaguely, as though she did not know who we were. But as I approached a light came into them: she recognized me, and this sudden revivification, this return of the soul to the almost deserted body, was the most wonderful thing I ever saw. "You have good news of the drama?" she whispered as I bent over her: "Tell me. I *know* you have good news."

What was I to answer? Pray, what would you have answered, puritan?

"Yes, I have good news, Aaronna," I said. "The drama will appear." (And who knows? Perhaps it will in some other world.)

She smiled, and her now brilliant eyes did not leave my face.

"He knows I'm your aunt: I told him," said the old woman, coming to the bedside.

"Did you?" whispered Miss Grief, still gazing at me with a smile. "Then please, dear Aunt Martha, give me something to eat."

Aunt Martha hurried across the room, and I followed her. "It's the first time she's asked for food in weeks," she said in a husky tone.

She opened a cupboard-door vaguely, but I could see nothing within. "What have you for her?" I asked with some impatience, though in a low voice.

"Please God, nothing!" answered the poor old woman, hiding her reply and her tears behind the broad cupboard-door. "I was going out to get a little something when I met you."

"Good Heavens! is it money you need? Here, take this and send; or go yourself in the carriage waiting below."

She hurried out breathless, and I went back to the bedside, much disturbed by what I had seen and heard. But Miss Grief's eyes were full of life, and as I sat down beside her she whispered earnestly, "Tell me."

And I did tell her—a romance invented for the occasion. I venture to say that none of my published sketches could compare with it. As for the lie involved, it will stand among my few good deeds, I know, at the judgment-bar.

And she was satisfied. "I have never known what it was," she whispered, "to be fully happy until now." She closed her eyes, and when the lids fell I again thought that she had passed away. But no, there was still pulsation in her small, thin wrist. As she perceived my touch she smiled. "Yes, I am happy," she said again, though without audible sound.

The old aunt returned; food was prepared, and she took some. I myself went out after wine that should be rich and pure. She rallied a little, but I did not leave her: her eyes dwelt upon me and compelled me to stay, or rather my conscience compelled me. It was a damp night, and I had a little fire made. The wine, fruit, flowers, and candles I had ordered made the bare place for the time being bright and fragrant. Aunt Martha dozed in her chair from sheer fatigue—she had watched many nights—but Miss Grief was awake, and I sat beside her.

"I make you my executor," she murmured, "as to the drama. But my other manuscripts place, when I am gone, under my head, and let them be buried with me. They are not many—those you have and these. See!"

I followed her gesture, and saw under her pillows the edges of two more copybooks like the one I had. "Do not look at them—my poor dead children!" she said tenderly. "Let them depart with me—unread, as I have been."

Later she whispered, "Did you wonder why I came to you? It was the contrast. You were young—strong—rich—praised—loved—successful: all that I was not. I wanted to look at you—and imagine how it would feel. You had success—but I had the greater power. Tell me, did I not have it?"

"Yes, Aaronna."

"It is all in the past now. But I am satisfied."

After another pause she said with a faint smile, "Do you remember when I fell asleep in your parlor? It was the good and rich food. It was so long since I had had food like that!"

I took her hand and held it, conscience-stricken, but now she hardly seemed to perceive my touch. "And the smoking?" she whispered. "Do you remember how you laughed? I saw it. But I had heard that smoking soothed—that one was no longer tired and hungry—with a cigar."

In little whispers of this sort, separated by long rests and pauses, the night passed. Once she asked if her aunt was asleep, and when I answered in the affirmative she said, "Help her to return home—to America: the drama will pay for it. I ought never to have brought her away."

I promised, and she resumed her bright-eyed silence.

I think she did not speak again. Toward morning the change came, and soon after sunrise, with her old aunt kneeling by her side, she passed away.

All was arranged as she had wished. Her manuscripts, covered with violets, formed her pillow. No one followed her to the grave save her aunt and myself; I thought she would prefer it so. Her name was not "Crief," after all, but "Moncrief;" I saw it written out by Aunt Martha for the coffin-plate, as follows: "Aaronna Moncrief, aged forty-three years, two months, and eight days."

I never knew more of her history than is written here. If there was more that I might have learned, it remained unlearned, for I did not ask.

And the drama? I keep it here in this locked case. I could have had it published at my own expense; but I think that now she knows its faults herself, perhaps, and would not like it.

I keep it; and, once in a while, I read it over—not as a *memento mori* exactly, but rather as a memento of my own good fortune, for which I should continually give thanks. The want of one grain made all her work void, and that one grain was given to me. She, with the greater power, failed—I, with the less, succeeded. But no praise is due to me for that. When I die "Armor" is to be destroyed unread: not even Isabel is to see it. For women will misunderstand each other; and, dear and precious to me as my sweet wife is, I could not bear that she or any one should cast so much as a thought of scorn upon the memory of the writer, upon my poor dead, "unavailable," unaccepted "Miss Grief."

SOURCE

Woolson, Constance Fenimore. "Miss Grief." *Lippincott's Magazine* 25, no. 5 (May 1880): 574–85.

Zitkala-Sa

1876–1938

ZITKALA-SA (Lakota: Red Bird) was a Yankton Dakota Sioux writer and reformer born on the Yankton Indian Reservation in South Dakota. She was also known by her missionary-given name, Gertrude Simmons Bonnin. When she was eight years old, she was taken by Quaker missionaries to a boarding school. As an adult, she wrote several works on the oppression of Native Americans at the hands of the church and the state and her struggles with cultural identity because of forced assimilation.[1] She also published many of the traditional oral stories she had heard growing up, making them available to an English-speaking audience for the first time, and wrote the first Native American opera, *Sun Dance Opera* (1913). She was cofounder and president of the National Council of American Indians, which lobbied for Native Americans' right to citizenship and other civil rights that they had long been denied. She was one of the foremost Native American activists of the twentieth century.

The Soft-Hearted Sioux (1901)

I.

Beside the open fire I sat within our tepee. With my red blanket wrapped tightly about my crossed legs, I was thinking of the coming season, my sixteenth winter. On either side of the wigwam were my parents. My father was whistling a tune between his teeth while polishing with his bare hand a red stone pipe he had recently carved. Almost in front of me, beyond the centre fire, my old grandmother sat near the entranceway.

She turned her face toward her right and addressed most of her words to my mother. Now and then she spoke to me, but never did she allow her eyes to rest upon her daughter's husband, my father. It was only upon rare occasions that my grandmother said anything to him. Thus his ears were open and ready to catch the smallest wish she might express. Sometimes when my grandmother had been saying things which pleased him, my father used to comment upon them. At other times, when he could not approve of what was spoken, he used to work or smoke silently.

On this night my old grandmother began her talk about me. Filling the bowl of her red stone pipe with dry willow bark, she looked across at me. "My grandchild, you are tall and are no longer a little boy." Narrowing her old eyes, she asked, "My grandchild, when are you going to bring here a handsome young woman?" I stared into the fire rather than meet her gaze. Waiting for my answer, she stooped forward and through the long stem drew a flame into the red stone pipe.

I smiled while my eyes were still fixed upon the bright fire, but I said nothing in reply. Turning to my mother, she offered her the pipe. I glanced at my grandmother. The loose buckskin sleeve fell off at her elbow and showed a wrist covered with silver bracelets. Holding up the fingers of her left hand, she named off the desirable young women of our village.

"Which one, my grandchild, which one?" she questioned.

"Hoh!" I said, pulling at my blanket in confusion. "Not yet!" Here my mother passed the pipe over the fire to my father. Then she too began speaking of what I should do.

"My son, be always active. Do not dislike a long hunt. Learn to provide much buffalo meat and many buckskins before you bring home a wife." Presently my father gave the pipe to my grandmother, and he took his turn in the exhortations.

"Ho, my son, I have been counting in my heart the bravest warriors of our people. There is not one of them who won his title in his sixteenth winter. My son, it is a great thing for some brave of sixteen winters to do."

Not a word had I to give in answer. I knew well the fame of my warrior father. He had earned the right of speaking such words, though even he himself was a brave only at my age. Refusing to smoke my grandmother's pipe because my heart was too much stirred by their words, and sorely troubled with a fear lest I should disappoint them, I arose to go. Drawing my blanket over my shoulders, I said, as I stepped toward the entrance-way: "I go to hobble my pony. It is now late in the night."

II.

Nine winters' snows had buried deep that night when my old grand-mother, together with my father and mother, designed my future with the glow of a camp fire upon it.

Yet I did not grow up the warrior, huntsman, and husband I was to have been. At the mission school I learned it was wrong to kill. Nine winters I hunted for the soft heart of Christ, and prayed for the huntsmen who chased the buffalo on the plains.

In the autumn of the tenth year I was sent back to my tribe to preach Christianity to them. With the white man's Bible in my hand, and the white man's tender heart in my breast, I returned to my own people.

Wearing a foreigner's dress, I walked, a stranger, into my father's village.

Asking my way, for I had not forgotten my native tongue, an old man led me toward the tepee where my father lay. From my old companion I learned that my father had been sick many moons. As we drew near the tepee, I heard the chanting of a medicine-man within it. At once I wished to enter in and drive from my home the sorcerer of the plains, but the old warrior checked me. "Ho, wait outside until the medicine-man leaves your father," he said. While talking he scanned me from head to feet. Then he retraced his steps toward the heart of the camping-ground.

My father's dwelling was on the outer limits of the round-faced village. With every heart-throb I grew more impatient to enter the wigwam.

While I turned the leaves of my Bible with nervous fingers, the medicine-man came forth from the dwelling and walked hurriedly away. His head and face were closely covered with the loose robe which draped his entire figure.

He was tall and large. His long strides I have never forgot. They seemed to me then the uncanny gait of eternal death. Quickly pocketing my Bible, I went into the tepee.

Upon a mat lay my father, with furrowed face and gray hair. His eyes and cheeks were sunken far into his head. His sallow skin lay thin upon his pinched nose and high cheek-bones. Stooping over him, I took his fevered hand. "How, Ate?" I greeted him. A light flashed from his listless eyes and his dried lips parted. "My son!" he murmured, in a feeble voice. Then again the wave of joy and recognition receded. He closed his eyes, and his hand dropped from my open palm to the ground.

Looking about, I saw an old woman sitting with bowed head. Shaking hands with her, I recognized my mother. I sat down between my father and mother as I used to do, but I did not feel at home. The place where my old grandmother used to sit was now unoccupied. With my mother I bowed my head. Alike our throats were choked and tears were streaming from our eyes; but far apart in spirit our ideas and faiths separated us. My grief was for the soul unsaved; and I thought my mother wept to see a brave man's body broken by sickness.

Useless was my attempt to change the faith in the medicine-man to that abstract power named God. Then one day I became righteously mad with anger that the medicine-man should thus ensnare my father's soul. And when he came to chant his sacred songs I pointed toward the door and bade him go! The man's eyes glared upon me for an instant. Slowly gathering his robe about him, he turned his back upon the sick man and stepped out of our wigwam. "Hā, hā, hā! my son, I cannot live without the medicine-man!" I heard my father cry when the sacred man was gone.

III.

On a bright day, when the winged seeds of the prairie-grass were flying hither and thither, I walked solemnly toward the centre of the camping-ground. My heart beat hard and irregularly at my side. Tighter I grasped the sacred book I carried under my arm. Now was the beginning of life's work.

Though I knew it would be hard, I did not once feel that failure was to be my reward. As I stepped unevenly on the rolling ground, I thought of the warriors soon to wash off their war-paints and follow me.

At length I reached the place where the people had assembled to hear me preach. In a large circle men and women sat upon the dry red grass. Within the ring I stood, with the white man's Bible in my hand. I tried to tell them of the soft heart of Christ.

In silence the vast circle of bareheaded warriors sat under an afternoon sun. At last, wiping the wet from my brow, I took my place in the ring. The hush of the assembly filled me with great hope.

I was turning my thoughts upward to the sky in gratitude, when a stir called me to earth again.

A tall, strong man arose. His loose robe hung in folds over his right shoulder. A pair of snapping black eyes fastened themselves like the poisonous fangs of a serpent upon me. He was the medicine-man. A tremor played about my heart and a chill cooled the fire in my veins.

Scornfully he pointed a long forefinger in my direction and asked,

"What loyal son is he who, returning to his father's people, wears a foreigner's dress?" He paused a moment, and then continued: "The dress of that foreigner of whom a story says he bound a native of our land, and heaping dry sticks around him, kindled a fire at his feet!" Waving his hand toward me, he exclaimed, "Here is the traitor to his people!"

I was helpless. Before the eyes of the crowd the cunning magician turned my honest heart into a vile nest of treachery. Alas! the people frowned as they looked upon me.

"Listen!" he went on. "Which one of you who have eyed the young man can see through his bosom and warn the people of the nest of young snakes hatching there? Whose ear was so acute that he caught the hissing of snakes whenever the young man opened his mouth? This one has not only proven false to you, but even to the Great Spirit who made him. He is a fool! Why do you sit here giving ear to a foolish man who could not defend his people because he fears to kill, who could not bring venison to renew the life of his sick father? With his prayers, let him drive away the enemy! With his soft heart, let him keep off starvation! We shall go elsewhere to dwell upon an untainted ground."

With this he disbanded the people. When the sun lowered in the west and the winds were quiet, the village of cone-shaped tepees was gone. The medicine-man had won the hearts of the people.

Only my father's dwelling was left to mark the fighting-ground.

IV.

From a long night at my father's bedside I came out to look upon the morning. The yellow sun hung equally between the snow-covered land and the cloudless blue sky. The light of the new day was cold. The strong breath of winter crusted the snow and fitted crystal shells over the rivers and lakes. As I stood in front of the tepee, thinking of the vast prairies which separated us from our tribe, and wondering if the high sky likewise separated the soft-hearted Son of God from us, the icy blast from the North blew through my hair and skull. My neglected hair had grown long and fell upon my neck.

My father had not risen from his bed since the day the medicine-man led the people away. Though I read from the Bible and prayed beside him upon my knees, my father would not listen. Yet I believed my prayers were not unheeded in heaven.

"Hā, hā, hā! my son," my father groaned upon the first snowfall. "My son, our food is gone. There is no one to bring me meat! My son, your soft heart has unfitted you for everything!" Then covering his face with the buffalo-robe, he said no more. Now while I stood out in that cold winter morning, I was starving. For two days I had not seen any food. But my own cold and hunger did not harass my soul as did the whining cry of the sick old man.

Stepping again into the tepee, I untied my snow-shoes, which were fastened to the tent-poles.

My poor mother, watching by the sick one, and faithfully heaping wood upon the centre fire, spoke to me:

"My son, do not fail again to bring your father meat, or he will starve to death."

"How, Ina," I answered, sorrowfully. From the tepee I started forth again to hunt food for my aged parents. All day I tracked the white level lands in vain. Nowhere, nowhere were there any other footprints but my own! In the evening of this third fast-day I came back without meat. Only a bundle of sticks for the fire I brought on my back. Dropping the wood outside, I lifted the door-flap and set one foot within the tepee.

There I grew dizzy and numb. My eyes swam in tears. Before me lay my old gray-haired father sobbing like a child. In his horny hands he clutched the buffalo-robe, and with his teeth he was gnawing off the edges. Chewing the dry stiff hair and buffalo-skin, my father's eyes sought my hands. Upon seeing them empty, he cried out:

"My son, your soft heart will let me starve before you bring me meat! Two hills eastward stand a herd of cattle. Yet you will see me die before you bring me food!"

Leaving my mother lying with covered head upon her mat, I rushed out into the night.

With a strange warmth in my heart and swiftness in my feet, I climbed over the first hill, and soon the second one. The moonlight upon the white country showed me a clear path to the white man's cattle. With my hand upon the knife in my belt, I leaned heavily against the fence while counting the herd.

Twenty in all I numbered. From among them I chose the best-fattened creature. Leaping over the fence, I plunged my knife into it.

My long knife was sharp, and my hands, no more fearful and slow, slashed off choice chunks of warm flesh. Bending under the meat I had taken for my starving father, I hurried across the prairie.

Toward home I fairly ran with the life-giving food I carried upon my back. Hardly had I climbed the second hill when I heard sounds coming after me. Faster and faster I ran with my load for my father, but the sounds were gaining upon me. I heard the clicking of snowshoes and the squeaking of the leather straps at my heels; yet I did not turn to see what pursued me, for I was intent upon reaching my father. Suddenly like thunder an angry voice shouted curses and threats into my ear! A rough hand wrenched my shoulder and took the meat from me! I stopped struggling to run. A deafening whir filled my head. The moon and stars began to move. Now the white prairie was sky, and the stars lay under my feet. Now again they were turning. At last the starry blue rose up into place. The noise in my ears was still. A great quiet filled the air. In my hand I found my long knife dripping with blood. At my feet a man's figure lay prone in blood-red snow. The horrible scene about me seemed a trick of my senses, for I could not understand it was real. Looking long upon the blood-stained snow, the load of meat for my starving father reached my recognition at last. Quickly I tossed it over my shoulder and started again homeward.

Tired and haunted I reached the door of the wigwam. Carrying the food before me, I entered with it into the tepee.

"Father, here is food!" I cried, as I dropped the meat near my mother. No answer came. Turning about, I beheld my gray-haired father dead! I saw by the unsteady firelight an old gray-haired skeleton lying rigid and stiff.

Out into the open I started, but the snow at my feet became bloody.

V.

On the day after my father's death, having led my mother to the camp of the medicine-man, I gave myself up to those who were searching for the murderer of the paleface.

They bound me hand and foot. Here in this cell I was placed four days ago.

The shrieking winter winds have followed me hither. Rattling the bars, they howl unceasingly: "Your soft heart! your soft heart will see me die before you bring me food!" Hark! something is clanking the chain on the door. It is being opened. From the dark night without a black figure crosses the threshold. . . . It is the guard. He comes to warn me of my fate. He tells me that tomorrow I must die. In his stern face I laugh aloud. I do not fear death.

Yet I wonder who shall come to welcome me in the realm of strange sight. Will the loving Jesus grant me pardon and give my soul a soothing sleep? or will my warrior father greet me and receive me as his son? Will my spirit fly upward to a happy heaven? or shall I sink into the bottomless pit, an outcast from a God of infinite love?

Soon, soon I shall know, for now I see the east is growing red. My heart is strong. My face is calm. My eyes are dry and eager for new scenes. My hands hang quietly at my side. Serene and brave, my soul awaits the men to perch me on the gallows for another flight. I go.

SOURCE

Zitkala-Sa. "The Soft-Hearted Sioux." *Harper's Monthly Magazine* 102, no. 610 (March 1901): 505–8.

NOTES

Chapter opening photo: Zitkala-Sa, ca. 1898. Gertrude Kasebier Collection, Division of Work and Industry, National Museum of American History, Smithsonian Institution.

1. See the selections in volume 2.

Acknowledgments

We would like to acknowledge the following people and institutions for permitting us to reprint texts or images found among their holdings: Diana Birchall; Emily Dickinson Collection, Amherst College, Archives and Special Collections; Harvard University Press; John O'Connor and Jack Watson of the Dialectic and Philanthropic Societies of the University of North Carolina; National Museum of American History, Smithsonian Institution; the National Urban League; University of Massachusetts Press; and University of Nebraska Press. Our own institutions, the Universities of Idaho and Iowa, deserve thanks as well for supporting our work over the past year, particularly the University of Idaho's Center for Digital Inquiry and Learning, whose resources, staff, and Digital Scholarship Fellowship helped make this anthology possible.

We would also like to offer our deepest gratitude to Roxane Gay and Katha Pollitt, for their words and their wisdom—it has been the opportunity of a lifetime to work with you and benefit from your insights and expertise. We are grateful for all of the work that you share with the world and your fearless advocacy on behalf of women; you are the modern-day counterparts to the women we celebrate in *Radicals*.

Thanks, too, are owed to professor emerita Ellen DuBois, for pointing us to Elizabeth Cady Stanton, Susan B. Anthony, and Matilda Joslyn Gage's landmark introduction to *History of Woman Suffrage, Volume 1*; as well as to Linda Chamberlin, Alan Chamberlin, and David Chamberlin, great-grandchildren of Charlotte Perkins Gilman, for generously granting us permission to reprint "The Right to Die" and a passage from *The Living of Charlotte Perkins Gilman*. The work of their great-grandmother is indeed a blessing to humanity; we are glad to be able to help continue her legacy.

We also wish to express our gratitude and appreciation to everyone at the University of Iowa Press who made this project possible, especially James McCoy, Jacob Roosa, Susan Hill Newton, Karen Copp, Allison Means, Sara Hales-Brittain, Suzanne Glémot, and Angela Dickey, as well as copyeditor extraordinaire Carolyn Brown. You're not only the crafters of important books but also great souls and good friends.

Finally, in a time when we are reminded daily and hourly of the debts we owe to activists, journalists, and truth-tellers of the past and present, debts we will never be able to repay—thank you to the women whose words make up these volumes.